JOHNNY RANDOLPH HUNT

Asking THE *Moon* TO *Leave*

outskirts
press

Outskirts Press, Inc.
http://www.outskirtspress.com

ISBN: 978-1-9772-0689-3

PRINTED IN THE UNITED STATES OF AMERICA

For

My mother Jane, Jeffrey, and the family and friends
who continue to be 'lanterns' in my life including:

Daniel W. Fulmer
Darla J. Juhl
Dorothy Stacy
James E. Pinkerton
Jeffrey D. Miller
Jannette S. Hunt
Marino Posadas de Martin
Motanna Hunt Cason
Patricia Nelson Horelick
Rocky J. Hunt

FOREWORD

One day, years ago, I was walking on a trail with my brother. It was a beautiful autumn day and we were in the woods enjoying each other's company – just talking about anything. He stopped suddenly; and sat down on a stump. I looked over at him wondering if he was tired; and asked if anything was wrong. He looked a bit sad: and said one of the most unexpectedly prophetic things.

"I was just thinking about the difference between our generation, and my kids' generation. We go for a walk just to enjoy it. But my kids only walk for one reason – to get somewhere."

Similarly, I was driving in a car with my dear Jeffrey. He asked about some blooming plant we passed on a drive through the mountains. I identified it for him and then casually made a remark about 'most people considering it to be a weed'. He continued to drive for awhile; and then said to me,

"I think it's arrogant for man to call something a weed..."

For years, I worked for someone who was one of the finest men I've ever had the pleasure of meeting. Jim's favorite thing to say was:

"Only dead fish swim with the stream..."

A woman named Daisy, whom I met through a low-income housing program, was one of the most solid and beautiful people who – quite unintentionally – showed me how chance could be turned into something good. But that is a fine story to be told at another time.

And how lucky I was to have an education to allow me to read two wonderful books,

'Walden', [1] by Henry David Thoreau – writing:

"I have great faith in a seed."

And; "Black Elk Speaks"[2]- which is a powerful book from another time.

There are people, events, and influences in life that are 'golden'. They often come from unexpected places. They help us focus on something outside of ourselves – and question ourselves. Otherwise - maybe we become too invested in 'our time' and our life.

---

1   *"Walden" or "Life in the Woods", Henry David Thoreau, Published 1845, Boston, Ticknor & Fields*
2   *Black Elk Speaks, 1932, John G. Neihart (Flaming Rainbow), William Morrow & Company*

Much of what is written here reflects things I heard as dialect and conversation. If outlandish, so be it. If it is funny or interesting, better! If it provokes thought, well then, maybe it's been worth 'the read'. Of course, this is not an empirical story of scientific proportions in any sense of those words - it's not meant to be.

Human limitations fascinate; and a thought provoking quote that humorously summed it up for this writer was from a film featuring the late 'Shirley Temple'. In a movie trailer for one of the child star's films,[3] she says to a woman, named Mrs. Higgins

"I have a duck and she can lay an egg!"

To which the woman responds crisply,

"And what is so wonderful about that?!"

The child star replies,

"Well...can YOU lay an egg?"

Who can deny such incomparably straightforward logic?

If one wants to probe more deeply there is existential philosophy related to the human condition; or the metaphysics behind all 'material things'. This story is a small work about the human gamble with science; the oddity of chance; dream and 'reality'; and perhaps, disappearing magic in the world. It's just a story. Meanwhile, birds flock together in flight as if in some cosmic consciousness? Insects build, defend, and dance together. Plants communicate. We can explain it away as 'chemistry', but perhaps that doesn't allow for the chemistry behind our own decisions – or the 'magic' behind things. The world is sad without secrets.

We produce music. Debussy's 'Clair de Lune' evokes a sensation in us – but why does it evoke anything? We can envision the moon on the water as easily as if were looking at it. But the music has no words; and there is no picture before us – except what we create in our minds. Is that not real enough?

When we walk in the moon's presence, it might seem to 'speak'. It certainly did for someone I know, who once saw a lunar eclipse that changed his life. So simple and yet so complex - that the phenomena of the light might do this.

Are the 'myths' of ages any less real than 'facts of today' – and who decides that? The moon continues to spill down and we feel it. There seems to be no clear reason for that feeling. But, how beautiful it is that the 'feeling' has not been extinguished? In the end, perhaps we should simply enjoy a journey bestowed upon us; and, as my brother once observed, have no particular destination in mind.

---

3   "Curly Top" (1935)

PART I

NEW MOON

TWO LIGHTS

They say...we were all part of many places; and the light of billions of years falls upon and within each of us. Born in the light and carrying it with us, our first home was a miracle which made us...and in which we lived. Like some young Frankenstein, we were 'sewn' together and given life in a great storm; and - like the monster – wobble endlessly between merit and iniquity. With vestiges of both, we continue to fall into the great gift that we think of as 'present'.

Our world is both beautiful and perilous. Some parts of it are like a wild mustang that whets its hooves upon the stone ridge, until sparks fly. His mane is glorious and whipping about in the wind. His breath pushes through dilated nostrils and collects like dew upon his whiskers which shine in the moonlight. His characteristic cry bounds down the valley; and about the wild grasslands – as he announces his powerful animus; and entreats a Great Spirit for that love for which we all search. The land, in response, sends echo back across the nation of grasses and sagebrush; and the 'Great Bear' twinkles in the heavens as if to seek the same. Farther away, the sand swirls about, continuing to build pink-banded spires of rock in the lost places that artists long to paint. A sunset eddy of colorful confection dances across the sky like a lively fandango; and the goose sails down and pulls froth across the water. Those parts are like the hand of God which casts a warm shadow across the land and holds all souls in the music of the night.

But other parts are not so lovely, like the rubbish that blows along the road or the predator that waits; sails; and sinks curved talons into flesh – and then eviscerates. Lightning strikes unpredictably like a hot razor and splits decades-old trees. Mighty water rushes across land and snuffs out life. Pious wars pile up human cords of wood; and the fruit falls rotten to the ground. Mosquitoes siphon blood; and time marches across the face of everything. The viper waits in a corner, never wiping its mouth. There are horrified screams as bigotry cuts through the fair fight and greets a fallen angel.

Before all of this, the world was primal. Stars collapsed, exploded, and sent their remnants hurtling through time and space to collide with other stars. Part of a great 'celestial neighborhood', we drifted in from far away and many places...immigrants from other galaxies. Waiting to collide with something else and start again, we do not really know from where we came. That we might dream; write lofty thoughts; and strive to be excellent - did not occur to us. The world, as we know it, did not seem to start with 'our' studied thoughts and ethics. All we can say is that 'it happened'.

Born anew into this world we might know that the pilgrimage each spirit makes has no beginning or end. Part of a circle or 'great sacred hoop', and fresh from the spirit world - we might connect only briefly to time and place; and our 'home' might simply be part of a journey.

The newborn knows that it was once only particles of light pulled away from darkness; and part of 'many'. They say the hand of God gently sealed the lips of each child thing to ensure that His most sacred secrets would never be revealed. And from us, the Creator pulled away the memories of other lives so that we might live in the 'present' he gave to us...and perhaps, learn from it.

We do not remember that we were part of the land that others once walked upon; part of the trees that others sat under; or part of the great boulders they rested against. The mark of the Creator, they say, may be witnessed in the indentation above our lips which sealed away secrets. He brought us into our world ignorant of the languages of all other things of which we had once been a part. The bird, tree, rock, and light spirits became mysterious things about which to marvel. And the memory that we were part of other things – is a fortune soon lost. And are these thoughts really so fantastic? To know what we don't know might be the biggest admonition of our place in a world we often view as 'less than'.

Laughing and screaming into journey; reveling in profanity more often than not; and surrounded by the sacred ...there is more space to us, than substance. Once particles of light, now held together by will, we might not realize that we are the proof of something much greater. And we may not believe that we will someday become part of all light once again.

This is where it began for him. He didn't know what truth was. Perhaps it was love that led him to where he now found himself. He simply remembered a dream - as much as anyone can know what is 'real' and what is 'dream'. And when he could no longer stand his own thoughts and had become crazy - he went to a place by the sea to find himself again. But the dream haunted him. 'RC' remembered now.

...Long ago, there were two small points of light racing side-by-side through the universe – each had a will and soul given to it. One spoke. Really, it didn't speak - it was more like a thought that was communicated to the other traveling by its side.

"What a beautiful blue and green planet! Why don't we stop there for awhile?"

But the one did not feel like he belonged on that blue and green planet; and wasn't sure what 'being there' really meant.

So the point of light that had exclaimed about the beauty of the planet - sliced through the air for hundreds of miles. It was filled with joy and trust. And like a child, it jumped – as if from a swing – not really caring where it landed, fully in love with life.

And it did land - upon the golden funnel of daffodil which had been planted by a missionary. It was pleased that it had found a 'home'; and was next to a river. More light joined it. It listened to the jangle of the tangled wood as the wind came through; and smelled the warm land, just below. It watched men going to and from rice paddies – or sometimes collecting shoots to eat. It stayed within the plant, watching it burnish in cooler weather and helping sustain it. It listened to the ancient instruments of farming people, playing in celebration in the evening – their panpipes made from nearby plants. It watched the children running; and saw the floods wash loam over the feet of the great trees. It saw women working with hoes and tanning under the tropical sun; and listened to their chattering and jokes. It smelled perspiration and heard planes passing overhead. It listened to other light, newly fallen. They 'talked' of their journeys – knowing that few 'men' could hear or understand them.

But quietly, it thought of the light that it had been traveling with and wondered where it was. And it patiently waited, believing that it would again become part of something else – and hoping the other light would join it in its journey.

The other light had swerved at the moon. It was filled with uncertainty. It rested there - waiting for time to pass; feeling lifeless and feeding nothing. In the visual purple it existed; wondering why it had left the light that had headed for the blue and green planet. The wine-colored landscape of the moon slowly filled with more light. They collected like tiny grains...waiting to continue their journeys.

The moon held the light that had swerved from the other – very close to it. It did not speak to it; but held it in a small pocket. For the soul of the moon was old. It knew the light was not ready for its freedom – but one day, would know when it was time for it to leave. And the light stayed rooted within the moon until one day - it was drawn to a river thousands of miles away on a blue and green planet. There, a bed of daffodils grew. And within it, the joyous light that it had traveled with - now dwelled.

This is where their story begins. It is a story of two lights – one who came to be called 'Anna' and the other who became 'RC'. It is a story about the complicated poetry of 'love and chance' ...which would seem to define all of us.

THE TWO WINDS

Eighty six-light years away, the constellation, Leo, was roaring in the spring and the start of a new year. It had no regard for the calendar of man – its story had been written on a more ancient calendar.

As the Native American saw it, it was the month of the Crow Moon and - like a crow sentry - seemed to foretell 'a coming' of significance. The wind on earth was ready – ready to see what mankind had become, ready to play with whatever was on the surface of the earth. It knew there was a man somewhere looking up at the sky – who did not believe in the 'milk of human kindnesses'. He felt discouraged and afraid. But something had finally touched him as he sat precipitously close to the edge of nothing, staring at moonlight that he had at once left and yet, felt a part of. He believed his story had begun – if one can believe in beginnings - much earlier and in the company of a kindred spirit, both traveling through space and time together.

The wind had started in the West - the black direction according to Lakota beliefs. They were actually two winds that combined and separated at will. Collectively they had started somewhere; and most thought they had their beginning near a town which had seen so much wind that it barely noticed.

But the indigenous people knew that the two winds had started in the Wind Cave of the Dakotas. There, deep inside Mother Earth, they had been created. They had mixed together for many years. The ugly (cold) wind – or 'sica' as some called it - had chased the beautiful (warm) wind – or 'waste' – through the dark cave for centuries until at last they had come together inharmoniously, and been jettisoned from the earth. Twin winds, they seemed to share nothing other than the moment of their birth.

The two winds headed west where they twisted together again and gathered their individual strengths. Then, combining as one again, slipped somewhere through the cutting teeth of the Rocky Mountains and fell upon the land like spittle from a baby's mouth. They headed northward briefly leaving scars across some of the western states like broad scratches upon a smooth table. They sped into North Dakota where they sent structures sprawling and twisting. They unearthed the flimsy structures of man; and lifted up parts of the pavement, perhaps scoffing at the impermanence of both.

They let stand a North Dakota road signs that showed the silhouette of Red Tomahawk - who was said to have been in the gunfight where Sitting Bull and 12 others had died. Nobody understood why the signs had been spared. They tore southward like competing hounds turning and wrestling with each other; and picking up an invisible scent.

In the western part of Nebraska, they toppled the once-welcomed sight of so many pioneers - the 325-foot spire named, Chimney Rock. The rock came crashing to the ground with a sound that would have been heard for many miles, had there been anyone near enough to hear it over the howling. The fact that animals heard it – or that the sound had bounced off nearby mountains did not seem to be of consequence. The clattering boom pushed into the evening sky; and then disappeared quietly like a ripple in a large black pond that we think of as the night sky.

The winds quickly made their way across the land together. They seemed as one – but were like an old parchment. That is to say, it is like they were made of two things: an empty skin...and the words written upon it - that gave it meaning.

One wind brushed the golden flowing hair of wheat fields in the moonlit night. It raised tiny spiders that clung to their strands – in flight. It carried the breath of wild buffalo across frosted plains. It carried the sweet scent of warm rain. It gently blew sand from the banded shell of an ancient beach. It watched quietly on tree limbs – just out of reach. It melted into the visual purple of the sunset land. It welcomed the rose-colored light on the hoodoo. It hoisted the hawk upwards and entreated it to sail. It gently untangled cares and emotions; and restored music to souls. It was enough for the warm wind that it simply tried to make something better.

While the other wind puffed off languishing dewdrops on flower petals. It knocked the leaves from trees causing them to fall and finally settle. Its icy fingers convinced the waiting bud not to unfold. It leapt and plunged in a frenzied dance with a blizzard - unaware of its cold. It forced the red into some captive trees. It helped naked, contorted spirits sail on the evening breeze. It tossed away the daisies at graves. It chased away the faithful pet who forgave. And it climbed into some people – freezing into their hearts.

Like large snails – unemotional, slow, oblivious to anything other than sensory signals, radar giants scanned the skies. We, as humans, could not decipher information that their antennae collected or tell whether it was important. The snail giants transmitted the information magically to a local weather station.

There, a sleepy-eyed forecaster, who was concentrating more on keeping himself awake than titillating his audience, pulled up the information in time for a 4 a.m. forecast on a local Midwest station. The story would be played over and over again; and early into the next morning while we watched, poured our coffee or juice; and tried to awaken and prepare for our own audiences. The forecaster referred to it as "an air mass."

"And watch out for this one! It is moving rapidly across the state of Nebraska. It's going to roll across Iowa and Kentucky and make its way to the Alleghenies by mid-week. We don't foresee any problems here in the local areas - but you folks back east may want to watch the future activities of this extremely strong air current. It seems unpredictable at this point, ladies and gentlemen – but please stay with us for any updates!"

The camera panned over to "Sports". The forecaster, now safely out of view, pulled at his hair and breathed a sigh of relief. He grumbled and cursed to himself quietly.

"I paid a thousand bucks for this hair piece and it still doesn't fit right. People don't give a damn about the weather unless they have some young stud with super hair delivering it directly to their bedroom."

He pulled at his "rug" again and winced.

Five hours by car and to the northwest of the station in a remote corner of the prairie, they already knew about the 'disturbance'. The native man, Bob, had seen the sacred corn move; and it worried him. He looked about the dwelling – there was no visible intrusion.

The corn had been grown from old seed and had –much like his own skin - burnt orange and red in the sun. It had survived on its own – without care, prayer, or poison.

He knew it was holy; and when it was finally ready - prayed not to it, but for it. Then he gently removed the corn from its cob; strung the corn seeds together; and placed this, his relative, in a quiet corner of the house, where it had floated like a spirit sentinel.

Glancing away from a book he was reading, he looked again at the corn; and saw it move ever so slightly. Bob put down his copy of "In Cold Blood" – reasoning that even a Renaissance man could dwell for awhile with murder and suspense. Then quietly, he dropped the book in a tote bag. He was an odd man. Long ago, a restaurateur had stopped Bob at the front door of a local diner – and pushed a red tie in his face. Then, and in a churlish way, the man had said,

"No tie – no service!"

Bob looked at him impishly; simply smiled...and tied it around his head in order to hold back his long dark hair – looking more 'Indian' than ever before. Then, he walked away forever from the man and his restaurant; knowing that every experience could be made into a gift. He still had the tie; and today, would use it to keep back his hair - and prepare for something that could not be predicted.

The corn had moved once more. Bob recognized it as a message of 'woni-ya sinoko' – (the sacred monster wind). He felt the strong presence of a force that would not commit itself to anything other than the freedom of its own will.

"Louise," he shouted out to his partner, "Close the windows - or open them up all the way. The wind doesn't like compromise." Louise was a heavy woman with a calm, abundant nature. Somewhat out of character for her, she closed all of the windows, and braced the door.

Bob secretly doted over her, but they had no photos of each other for they believed that photos were 'soul-catchers'- and would deprive the waiting owls. He had met Louise years ago while attending a meaningless conference at a hotel. A maid there, she had 'caught his eye'- but paid him not one 'iota' of attention. He reasoned that the only way to meet her was to strategically disconnect the 'spaghetti' of wires in her car – and coincidentally appear at the sound of engine trouble. They exchanged notes for a year before she consented to move in with him. After their first night together, she snuck out and disconnected the same wires in his car. They laughed about it; and had been together ever since.

Now she said to him, "Bad storm's blowin' up Bob."

Bob nodded; and said in prairie monotone, "It moved the corn, Louise."

She looked back at him and her eyes widened, "The prayer corn?"

He only nodded.

"Where do you think it will split up?"

"I dunno. It's not lookin' too promising. Looks like mainly a dark wind. I hope it don't find the wrong ones. Enough dogs, birds and invisible ones walkin' around this evening."

"Remember...don't talk about it Bob." Louise was giving him a serious look. "Might be bad luck - ya' think the house will stand?"

The 'soddie', a sod house was only 15-by-20 feet. It had been long-abandoned by 'settlers'. When Bob and Louise found it, they had made some small repairs and ushered a few uninvited 'guests' from its premises – but essentially the sod hut was unchanged.

He looked about.

"I figure we've got about 70 tons around us…yeah, I think it'll hold."

Suddenly, the wind churned across the sparse rolling hills of the flatlands near the reservation. It kicked at the dirt; and tossed the sagebrush into the air. Then it rumbled low and rolled along the ground. When it came to the large cottonwood tree that grew near the water - it blasted into it and scattered the cottonwood down like a coyote sprinting into a garden of hens. It moved rapidly across the ground as if it were running away from the sun and into the vast open arms of night.

Then it stopped at the 'soddie' and seemed to sniff and growl. Barely more than a risen mound of dirt dug into an ample hill, the house had withstood the ferocity of many winter winds. The 'woniya sinoko' moved stealthily around. It wanted inside. A powerful blast sent the bolted door sprawling; and then - as if evil had found entry – it blew a lantern out.

Louise was the first to move. Recognizing the wind's power, she pushed open every window with all her might – feeling the licking of the wind about her. If the wind wanted in that badly - she would not try to hold it back. The slender, powerful fingers of the wind pushed through the windows - pulling and caressing. It hissed. Sometimes its grip was strong and willful – other times soft as the caress of a child. Would it kiss or kill? It seemed vacuous, wanting of decision, and thinking....

They were still. They waited for its judgment. They could hear it growling; and see it clawing at the strung corn. Then, they heard it suck itself together – and felt a draft streaming around them and through the open door. The wind had left.

Louise calmly lifted the door off of the floor; propped it against the nearby wall; tried to light the lantern; and found a hammer and nails. She nailed a blanket over the opening; and ushered out a small scorpion that had wandered into the dwelling.

Bob came to her side. He gently pulled back a few strands of hair from her face and she felt his warm breath on her shoulder. His arm around her waist, the two of them stood together at the 'soddie' entrance. Pulling the blanket aside slightly, they watched the wind from afar and looked at the carnage before them. A basket had been picked up; and thrown outside. Its contents had been scattered and stomped it into the dirt.

She sighed to herself. The basket had been used to gather every part of Typha Latifolia as Bob called it. She had planned on using the roots, shoots, and early head of the cattails as a stew - but now it was gone. She gazed quietly at the basket which looked like a broken toy. Made from the same cattails – it had held up rather well and would only take a little effort to repair. She could have gone to a local mall and replaced it – but Louise preferred to stay close to as many of the old ways as possible.

They watched as the wind sped across the prairie. It kicked up dust and trampled through the corn. Louise thought about dinner again; and wondered what it would be – now that the basket's contents had been taken away. Maybe Bob would find the muskrat unharmed at the edge of the water. Surely the old man of the marsh would be fat after feeding on the cattails in the pothole.

Then she strolled outside to examine an old coat she had left on a fallen log – it had been spared. She was chilly. But when she opened the coat, found a small nest of naked baby field mice that had just been born. She gently rolled it back over the mice and left the coat where it was. She would wait until the mice decided to move on and then reclaim the coat. It was meant to be.

Inside, Bob had started a fire and 'turned up' the lantern. The sky was dark and the house looked inviting – its small pins of light seemed like stars on a warm night. Louise walked back to the house. There, she found Bob sitting; and calmly eating a slice of buttered bread. He seemed reflective. She knew he was trying to understand what he had just seen. Soon he would dream – it would be a quest to discover the meaning of what had just happened. Dreaming was a soft and comfortable passage for him - a door that he passed in and out of as easily as if it was the door of their sod hut. Meanwhile, she would wait for the warm wind that followed.

BOB'S DREAM

After he was finished eating, Bob lay back on a cot that he did not share. It was next to an open window. He could hear the crickets chirping; and a breeze making its way through the high grass surrounding the house. He imagined the 'homesteaders' – large grasshoppers of the Sandhills – chewing outside and catching the last warmth of the earth while the sky became darker. Then, he closed his eyes; and felt the light breeze enter the open window and gently lift him up. To him, the mind had always been just a series of pictures – only some of which we saw with our eyes open.

There seemed no reason to distinguish between images simply because of the opening and closing of eyelids. All images were significant.

Within minutes he had started REM sleep. Like all who dream, he didn't care whether it was necessary to process the previous day's events in dreams – or whether it was simply needed to provide much-needed oxygen to the aqueous substance of the cornea of the eye. He simply dreamt. And, in his dream, he sailed above the prairie like a quiet and bashful ghost. A powerful wind had gripped him. It rapidly carried him across the countryside.

The wind sped into Missouri, the "Show Me" State. According to legend, the State's motto had come from a Congressman, who once declared in a Philadelphia meeting,

"I come from a state that raises corn and cotton and cockleburs and Democrats, and frothy eloquence neither convinces nor satisfies me. I am from Missouri. You have got to show me."

The wind ravaged the state with such ferocity that it prompted some to say the State's new motto should be changed to: "Missouri doesn't like company!"

Just as rapidly as the wind had appeared, it left Missouri; and headed for Kentucky. In Kentucky, it did nothing more than play in the grasses - as if it were a child who had found the quintessential beach and built a waving blue sea from nothing but the grasses and an abundant imagination.

Such was the schizophrenia of the wind.

Upon reaching the eastern coast, there was another surprise. What the young mountains of the West had failed to do, the older Alleghenies did with relative ease. They caused the wind to pause. The gentle mountains split the wind up. The two winds seemed to diverge. Like running dogs that had found separate scents; at first, they mangled the foot lands as they ran together. Upon reaching the mountain precipice, they split, going in separate directions. A meteorologist on one of the local weather stations reported the odd behavior of the system and revealed his western roots by referring to the old mountains as the 'Appelation Mountains'. He called them a series of 'hills'.

The 'waste' – or pretty wind - gently followed the Appalachian Trail northward scooping up leaves and playing with the wild Hepatica, Bluets, and Vipers Bugloss. It wiped the sweaty brows of hikers; and rippled quiet waters. In the northernmost section of the Appalachian range, it seemed to stall and sit idly - as if not quite sure of its direction or whether it wanted to travel. It seemed content to linger. Then it skipped about - sampling the mountain tops; playfully rolled down their sides; and leapt from mountain to mountain, like a child playing hopscotch. Though the 'waste' seemed to lack purpose, it reveled in whimsy. It wandered from earth to sky as if finding joy everywhere. It tickled the undersides of clouds. It gave the keen-eyed eagle a lift – causing it to forget the intent of its sailing flight; and to delight instead in curling heavenward surf.

But the other part of the wind tore southward through the mountains. It pushed over tents and old trees like an investigator looking for clues. It gathered up in a massive gray, billowy cloak; and flashed its amber lightning. It flooded the valleys with torrents of silvery steel. It blew an unsuspecting rappeller earthward; before continuing through the sweltering southern lands. There it fanned flames that looked like crackling golden hair against the dry mountains. It dispensed enough heat to curl plants into smoky brocade; and beat the remaining plants into a tarnished fringe. It etched new lines in the ancient and weary face of the earth. It scattered the poor and loosely built nests of the mourning doves. Then, tearing through the woods, it seemed to sift through the remnants of old hillbilly rubble. When it could find nothing more to blow down or turn over, it shredded the remains of daffodils - as if eager to erase any sign of hope. But the flowers dug into the earth and rock and hung tight to the weight of their foundation – as hope is apt to do.

Media finally reported the air mass had 'run out of steam'; and been buffeted back by a pressure system fed by the azure sea.

Louise prayed again and thanked the sacred mountain ancestors (tunka shila). At the end of the prayer – she simply said, "Mitakuye oyasin" - Lakotah for "all my relatives". It was gratitude and respect to all relatives – from the great buffalo to stone ancestors – and was the way all prayers ended.

Bob continued to dream. The breeze that had 'lifted him' now carried him as quietly as a balloon. It carried him deep into the pretty evenings of the past. He floated around mountains with snowcaps and evergreen feet. He floated into time under the sliver of a reddened moon. Sometimes, he would wave at the earth below; and sometimes he would look up at the vast sprinkle of stars, wondering where the dream was taking him. But he did not fret. He knew that to fully understand a journey – it must enter the heart. Worry would not let it pass

And finally, he floated into a morning that was so wedded to spring, that dew twinkled in the barely perceptible morning light. Pieces of sun, small flowers called 'buttercups', caught more of the soft light and held it there – unwilling to give it up again. The rosy sky announced the gift of light to birds who sung back their appreciation, while honey colored bees went about their business - dusty with pollen. Earthworms wearing the same rose color as the sky emerged glistening from warm holes as if they had been awakened by the berry blossom perfume in the air. The grass – which held a bit of the lapis sky - had been shot through by the golden rays of sun. It beckoned in its fusion of the two colors; and bragged in green'ness.

This was where the dream had taken him. And in the middle of that dream, lying in the wondrous grass and fully awake for hours, a boy watched the darkish and dappled sky change. He could see its black stoniness had begun to show an edge of polish. The dawn was beginning to come. The boy, Rowan - thought it brilliant as a fire opal.

But the dream can visit at any time, in sleep, inebriation, inspired speech – or even while sitting quietly and eating a piece of toast. Some have said there is very little separation between what we see and what we think we see. The dream bounces back and forth through time. And as he lie thinking about what was real and what was not, a jolting vision came to Bob – one that seemed as prescient and certain as his next heartbeat.

The bad wind had stirred the hunger of a great cat; and as it sat waiting on a flat rock by a trail...a jogger came within its sight. It hunched down, making quiet mewing sounds. Its large maw trembled; it salivated; and dug its claws into the rock. Its tail twitched slightly as it calculated its leap – it would be over in seconds, and the woman would barely have enough time to scream.

'RC' AND JOE

Volpecula, the little fox constellation that the boy had been staring at, began to fade. The boy, who Bob had seen in his dream, slipped out of the sleeping bag; and then began to roll it up. It was larger than he had remembered – heavy and damp from dew.

Rowan Chamberlain hated his name. It sounded abysmally 'stuffy'. There were the typical petty arguments and tantrums with parents that every child has when forging their identity. But one day the boy's anger whipped into intensity and exploded. It was at this point that his mother sat him down and calmly told him about the significance of his names. 'Rowan', she explained, was a 'protector tree' that used to be planted outside of houses. 'Chamberlain' was an English family name indicating the family had emptied the ashes from the fireplaces of royalty. Both were names to be proud of - and he had been born under the sign of a lion. It made him feel better temporarily. But children, in the farming community where they found themselves - and being the way children frequently are – mercilessly teased him. Finally, an intervening gym teacher shortened his name to 'RC' - partly to accommodate the brevity required in team sports. Thus 'Rowan Chamberlain' became 'RC'. The boy was curiously comfortable with the anonymity it provided while in the midst of establishing a toe-hold in adolescence. But something told him he was older than his age; and that part of him was missing.

'RC' finished rolling up the sleeping bag; tied it together; and stuffed it into its soiled duffel. The last bit of evening seemed cooler immediately before the full appearance of the sun. He could smell the faint scent of bacon; and knew his mother was already in the kitchen, cooking. He would stop by quickly for the requisite morning hug; take a bite or two of food – and then run out the door to find his best friend, Joe.

Joe Jefferson was an older black man whose father had been a driver for a wealthy landowner. At the time, the term 'driver' had meant 'a class of skilled men who flushed (or 'drove') game from the bushes' so landowners could continue the hunt. Joe was the patriarch of the Jefferson family. He was worldly, keenly practical, and abundantly knowledgeable of 'natural' things.

He had a lilting laugh, good will, and humor.

His wife, 'Trudence', – or 'True' as she was called – was outspoken, friendly, and forthcoming. No one ever asked for True's opinion. They knew she would give it readily and without invitation. Her laugh was loud and seemed to roll through the air like tumbleweeds in the wind.

A daughter named 'Earnestine' was self-absorbed, clinical, and made lists in their dirt basement. She kept times, dates and notes of every day, and what occurred in her adolescent world.

Then, there was a son, 'Angus', who frequently 'had his head in a book' and often ignored his parent's pleas for any sort of assistance with chores. He was much too busy reading to take any notice of 'RC'; and had a remarkable autonomy – living inside of his head. He seemed to eat the past from the ground up; and appeared to be stretching for something, perhaps a more favorable sun.

Unlike the Chamberlains - who were recent emigrants from the city - the Jefferson's family had roots in the area and had lived there for generations. They were kind, gracious people who were fully aware of the new family's country naiveté.

Joe, the patriarch, was 'RC's best friend. His absence made any day lamentable. 'RC' enjoyed tagging along as Joe did chores. While Angus was never present – 'RC' was always willing to help; willing to talk; and never ran out of questions. The older man enjoyed the boy's company; and secretly wished his own son had the curiosity which made days more real. Indeed, he would not admit that he liked 'RC' better.

Bob, the native man, reflected on what he saw – and continued his dream journey....

Philosophers had concluded that people do not usually know when they are dreaming; and had asked the question, 'Could one actually be dreaming constantly, instead of being in waking reality?' The indigenous community had accepted such 'fuzziness' long before; and Bob was quite comfortable with it. He was only sure that he could not be certain, at any given point in time that he was not dreaming...and that he really didn't care! He jokingly referred to all of it - as 'dreality'.

Now the breeze seemed to rock him gently; and then set him down in a comfortable part of what seemed past.

It was evening at the Jefferson's farm. 'RC' was sitting with his best friend. Joe was lightly playing a harmonica when he stopped and said in a low, soft tone,

"Coons are out."

'RC' glanced briefly at his friend to confirm that he wanted conversation; and then looked over to where he was pointing. Then he parroted,

"Yeah, the coons are out."

In the near distance and down by the fence line near the pig sty, Joe had left two buckets. Raccoons now busied themselves, looking into the buckets, sniffing and examining their contents. One bucket was 'slop' and the other was water. They made for the slop, turning it over and raucously spilling out the contents. In the distance a dog howled - seemingly aware of debauchery. An Orthoptera scurried away from the bottom of one bucket where it had landed earlier, hoping to stay out of sight. It suddenly rose, and exposed its folded hind wings – then hurried off in flight.

'RC' stood up, but Joe grabbed him firmly by the arm.

"Jus give a minit, 'RC'."

"But that's the pigs' food!"

"Pigs 'll be okay, 'RC'. Been a rough yeah fo' the coons. Let'm have a little fun."

The coons played in the table scraps - sniffing and chewing at everything, rolling it over in their delicate hands and then snipping and snarling at each other over various morsels. They stuffed themselves. Some pulled at apple scraps like children fighting over toys. When they were just about done, one of the animals went over to the bucket of water and poked his nose down into it. He reached down into the bucket as if he were trying to fish something out - finally coming up wet and sneezing, he shook himself heartily. There was obviously no prize at the bottom of the water bucket. Joe and 'RC' watched the nutty behavior with much amusement.

"He's a lookin' fo watah food. No clams or shells in theah, though. He may even be lookin' for a frog. Ya know bullfrogs holds they note a litta longa when planes go ovahead. Sometimes the coon he wait fo' a plane to go ova-head – jus so he kin locate a big bullfrog. Animals smahta then we thenk."

Then, as if the animal had heard, it puttered around until it found a small rock; picked it up with both hands; and tossed it into the bucket. It picked up another and repeated the action. Bending back into the bucket it fished the stones out and examined them; and let them drop back in again. A large rather matronly raccoon watched quietly. She was like a mother who did not like her neighbors; and had decided to inflict the terrorism of uncontrolled children as retribution – allowing them to make as much noise and bedlam as possible.

"What's he doin', Joe?"

"He's playin'. Coons loves tah play - even when theys grown. Bucks more'na does. They learn summa thet from they folks but learn sumofit fum watchin' they cousins." South'n coons like to play mo'n those inna mountain. They's too busy lookin' fo food innah mountains.. Don' have as much time."

"Cousins?"

"Yeah, boy,...dawgs ..'n skunks...n' beahs.... Dawgs always playin'. Coons won' come neah them but they watches 'em play. Jus' like they lern about egg-eatin' from da skunks. Skunks and coons don' like each othah - tho. You won' nevah see'em togetha. Bof'n likin the same thing – eggs! But da' skunk ain't know nuthin' bout turtle eggs. 'En the coon - he keep thet to hisself."

"Is that all skunks eat, Joe, is eggs?"

"Naww, ony when they gits 'em. Usually they eats insects and berries and fruit. Sometime a mouse o' two.

Friend a mine said he once saw a coon pull a conch shell outta the water - tho I don't know as he's rightin about thet."

"Do they talk to each other, Joe?"

"Shoah! Animals talk ta each other'ns. Meby not likin' we do - but they reads each othah purty well."

"How?"

"Don' know how xackly. Jus' knows they do. Not evahthin' done thru talkin', 'RC'. Animals can' say more' n we can wifout speakin'. They has a sense 'bout things."

"Everybody needs to speak somehow. I don't think you're right."

"Jus' knows what I know', 'RC'. They speaks in othah langijez, othah ways. Don' know how they does it - jus' knows they do. Not evahthing needs words. Maybe we peepah jus' be the only ones."

"That's because were smart enough to talk. Animals aren't that smart."

Joe pulled out his harmonica. He raised it to his lips and blew some notes that flowed together and seemed to travel along the vaporous air of the summer night. The coons looked startled and then stopped to sniff the air. They watched.

He played some more - making short bursts. Then he pulled an old jacket over his shoulders like a poncho.

"Joe, you're gonna scare them."

"They's fine. They may beat back to the bushes - but they aint' really scared. They's mo' curious. You jus' lis'en to me play, okay?"

So 'RC' listened, lying comfortably on the porch's weather-beaten floor. A nearly non-existent breeze seemed intent on restoring balance in an otherwise insufferably humid night. It blew across his face.

"Whatchu thinkin' bout, 'RC'?"

"It's too weird I'm not gonna say."

"Shoot, boy, you cain't suprise me."

"Okay, I'm thinking about water runnin' in Shiloh Creek."

"Why you thinkin' bout thet?"

"I dunno. The music just reminds me of how it runs over the rocks."

"What else you thinkin' bout?"

"Nuthin'"

"Come on now. You cain't hold nothin' back from Joe. Dun saw a smile come across yo' face."

"I'm thinkin' about some girl I met the other day. She's stupid."

"But you kinda likes her."

"I don't like her. I just think she's stupid."

"Ah thinks you like her. Cuz you ain't thinkin' bout stupid stuff by thet look on yo' face."

"Well....she does have pretty hair. But she's still stupid."

"Music done reminded you of thet haih?" He blew some more notes.

"Yeah it's long ...and pretty ....in the wind."

'RC' looked back at the raccoons. One was cleaning the other's face.

"Thet's the womin'. She's mo clean then the man. She's sayin' good job to him and cleanin him."

"You don't know that. You could only know that if they could talk to you."

Joe just rolled his eyes away from 'RC' and stared out into the moonlight. "Um-huhn...my music dun' spoke to you...an' I ain't hardly said a word."

LITTLE GIRL LOST

Bob continued to drift in the state of being that he referred to as 'dreality'. He was now high above the land, its people, and the great Wind Cave. He floated comfortably in a blackness that seemed like a fluid of octopus ether – not certain whether he faced up or down until he saw the thousands of stars reflecting like pearls in water. To his left, he saw the constellation that he knew as 'Pegasus', the winged horse. It seemed to paw restlessly - and snort out a warning.

Almost immediately the writhing dark forms of animals galloping quickly through the evening sky appeared. They thundered as they approached. He could discern their burning eyes and flaming nostrils. Their hooves kicked up random sparks, like flint hitting steel. He recognized them as 'night mares' - and was certain they were a sign of ill fortune.

He had twisted and bound his hair together in a diagonal band that looked like a whip cord; and tethered it with hide from a golden-antlered deer. Such deer were said to be sacred to Diana, Goddess of Hunt and Moon. Now, reaching behind him, he quickly grabbed the long braid of hair - and with a single motion - cut it off with a bone knife that he carried. Then, brandishing the braid before him, he snapped it back and forth loudly like a whip in front of the smoldering equine faces. Though fighting the urge to retreat, the 'night mares' turned; and galloped back into the dark corner of the sky from where they had come.

Then, Bob floated earthward until the breeze that had first borne him out of the 'soddie' across the prairie - embraced him; and allowed him to drift with it again. They were over a very dry land.

Below, he could see veteran men who had experience war's atrocity. They were playing baseball in a park. The breeze lingered only long enough to allow him to know the nature of a few who – far from being dutiful – had enjoyed that atrocity. Then - and as if in spite - the wind picked up a 'high-flying' ball which had been hit by one of the men; carried it past the boundary of the park; and threw it down at the feet of a young man who appeared to be running from something.

Before Bob could fully understand...the breeze had lifted him again; and sped away with his thoughts into time – as only the wind could do. What did these dreams mean?

...Meanwhile, Louise stood at the bedroom door; watching the wind playing with the curtains; and listening to the crickets chirp outside their earthen hut. She watched Bob's chest rise and fall as he breathed; and wondered if she should wake him. Finally, she walked back to the corner of the 'soddie' where a pot was boiling. It was filled with greens she had clipped. The greens were cooking well with dough balls in salted water. When Bob 'returned'...supper would be waiting.

But, for now, he continued to drift with the breeze. Like a blip on radar, the breeze seemed to announce to him that a change had occurred. He had traveled decades back and to a tropical environment; and was now looking at a very young girl who sat with an ancient woman – a grandmother. They were sitting on the ground looking up at the sky. Neither saw him.

The old woman's face had been worn for thousands of days. Her hair was silver and supple. She held her granddaughter in her lap; and both seemed to be dreaming – one, perhaps of trips taken and the other, of voyages to be. The old woman wore a light dress, while the child wore a dark frock that barely covered her legs. The child had become restless; and she twisted about in the arms of her grandmother. Together they looked like yin-yang. The little girl had just finished eating a shoot from the great bamboo that grew by the river. Unexpectedly she felt as if she was filled with light. She had been practicing her words, trying to learn how to respectfully converse with an older person.

Nearby they could smell the grain that had been recently threshed; it's fragrance like the perfume of an earthen flower. Puppies in a small shed yipped and played with each other, rolling around and snarling - notifying the night that they were awake; and falling around their mother who waited patiently for them to tire. The slender shadow of a village man could be seen carrying home a string of caught fish that he had slung loosely over his shoulder. The fish would be cooked with ginger root. The reflection of light in nearby water revealed the full moon that would kindle the activities of night animals. Warmth lingered from the day and mingled with the scents of wild flowers. A night blooming cereus beckoned to a large moth shining like pearl and silver in the muted light. The moth fluttered about the flower, trying to discover the best approach. A high breeze seemed to carry dreaming men. It gently rustled bamboo chimes, knocking them into each other and causing the reeds to make hollow popping sounds. It tinkled tiny bells over some doorways. Small frogs sang in the nearby thrush, responding to the caress of the tingling breeze; and knowing it would carry their voices like calling cards to prospective mates. Meanwhile, somewhere in a nearby tree, the ripening fruit of a wild vine invited a netherworld of life that did not concern itself with the comings and goings of man.

"Ba Noi, do you ever want anything real bad?"

"I have a terrible greed, child."

"You, Ba Noi...?"

"Yes, me..."

"But, what do you want? I will get it for you."

"No, child, you cannot get this for me. I would have the past."

"I don't understand."

The old woman continued, "The moon – it will rise about 50 minutes later every night – than the night before. Everyone once knew that – hardly anyone remembers anymore." Then she pointed to the single bulbs that lit up the myriad of shack houses.

"We try to be the stars with our pretend light. And by doing so, we can hardly make out the Fish Moon anymore."

Her granddaughter's face was suddenly frowning. The old woman looked concerned. Thinking that her comment might have had an unintended impact, she asked,

"What can we do to exorcise your grief, my dear? You are too young to look so sad."

The child responded, "I'm sorry, Ba Noi. I was thinking of my mother. I don't want to ever forget her."

"Hush, child." The old woman put her finger gently over the crease above the child's lips.

"We must first forget something – in order to remember it. That's what makes memory sweet."

Her granddaughter responded almost impetuously,

"I want to travel, 'Ba Noi'. I want to get out of here!"

"Walk toward the east, my dear. 25,000 miles from now, do you know what you will find? "

"What?"

"...yourself." And then the old woman looked up at the sky as if she was aware that someone was floating above them; and said,

"Give me your hand, my dear. I must hold onto the living...that, I may convince my soul not to fly..." and then, "Oh ...a light has been left on. I cannot seem to turn it off...is it the Fish Moon?"

Within a breath, she was gone - and the little girl could not stop screaming.

Somewhere on the other side of the world it was day and a mountain lion continued to tear at the carcass of a jogger it had just killed. Bob mused, thinking that is the way of the world. Like the wind he had seen both misfortunes. And from the vantage point of his 'floating dream', he could see the girl's small village in its entirety. The village seemed content in its harness to the slope of the mountain just above the sea. ....But on the other side of the mountain, he saw a forest that was disturbed and rustling - and the feet of many men.

The wind then, took him further...into the next day, a day of horrific catastrophe, lament...and miracles that sometimes come from mud. The child might want from despair, but would soon realize her wish – to leave where she was.

On the horizon and above the village, the man who had many feet behind him would soon cast a long shadow over the tranquil village below. Gregor had enlisted. He wanted to fight. Having neither ideal nor principle, he peered at the humanity below him and thought only of gain. Though cunning and adept with language, he had never really felt the meaning behind words. 'Atrocity' had no more significance to him than 'second' does to a century. He surveyed the village below, biding his time; and wondering what might be there for the taking. A dark wind swept over him; murmured murderous things; and had plans for how he might twist the light.

While, a few mountains away from him, a tall capable woman played with a rosary; and prayed in the slim light of the early morning. She had come there with her church. Sister Frances watched the sunlight pushing its way through a mangling of trees that seemed moribund. The darkness of the jungle bothered her – it was an odd complement to the sunrise. However, she was comfortable enough knowing that shadow could not exist without light.

SOPHIA

Bob, the native man, had seen the mountain lion with its 'kill', the young boy in the grass, the black man called 'Old Joe', the little girl who ate from the bamboo; the man with many feet behind him; and the nun who was comfortable in light and darkness. But now, the wind carried him to another. He was restless. He moved about in his state of sleep journey through thought, time, and space – wondering if such distinctions really meant anything. But the wind would not say...

From where she was at the stove, Louise thought she heard him moaning. She quietly stirred the pot of greens and dough balls that had now become dumplings in a pot of thickened soup. Then she put the large spoon down and went into the room to check on him. Perhaps he needed to be awakened. She stopped at the bedroom entrance and looked at her 'old man'. He had put on some 'winter weight' and the 'tummy' made him look like a pleasant Buddha. She wanted to kiss him on his forehead; and awaken him for supper. She was tired of waiting - and long past 'hungry'. But, knowing how little he sometimes slept - and that he sought answers to things that might not be explained in conventional ways - she decided it was best not to disturb him.

The window was still open; and a breeze had come through. It seemed to play about in the curtains; and then made its way to the corner of the room where Bob was sleeping. It suddenly puffed up the clutch of eagle feathers that Bob had found long ago and attached to the 'journey stick' that he kept by the bed. To Louise, the breeze's actions were a message. Though some might think it coincident and silly, she did not discount what she saw. Neither did she see it as magic or witchcraft. She simply believed that we were all part of life and part of all life; that we were connected to everything in some way – even the great stone ancestors. She did not expect others to believe as she did. Faith was a personal journey that all traveled alone.

Like Bob, she believed that she could see the yearning for such a connection in all people; and in the various 'flights of fantasy' that had become common. Forays into parks and wilderness areas certainly had to be about that connection – the need for solitude its catalyst. Such things did not in any way diminish the presence of a higher power. Nor did it presume the deification of single parts of nature. Rather it increased the mystery; and was far more interesting. It seemed a profound pronouncement of an architect who was much greater...and she felt humbled.

After one more glance at Bob, she was certain that she was not needed. She turned and went back to the stove where she knew that – less supper be burned – another vessel required her attention.

Meanwhile, Bob - as if being carried through principles by a teacher - continued to drift with the wind and in a dream state. He sampled the specialties that it chose to reveal; and which seemed part of a larger corpus. In that 'dream', the wind had carried him to an island that pulsated with music, lively people, and what some call - 'legends'.

To him, it was easy to see how things which had been long ago discounted by science – could be classified as 'legend' or 'myth'. He thought of it as a basic human need to want to label things; and a discomfort with mystery. Though well-educated in curricula that were based in science - his culture allowed for beliefs that might be outside of the bounds of scientific principle. To him, eliminating the possibility of any free thought was like closing a door. Just as Biblical teachings required belief, other parts of life might require the same. Any set of principles could be victim of an inherent flaw. Thus, he dismissed very little.

Humans had once believed that the earth was flat. Though it had long since been disproved - understanding was always evolving. Research by cognitive scientists had revealed that the brain decides what one perceives; that it processes information in order to determine what the best interpretation is for 'what's out there'. This finding did not mean that Bob believed the earth was flat – only that interpretation of anything might be subjective. And he was comfortable with that.

Now, he floated over an island that was close to Turkey; and whose people were certain that their celebrated past was more than just the 'stuff' of legends. Theirs was the land of the god, Apollo. It was where the infant, Asklepios, had been snatched away from the womb of his mother - as she lay on a burning pyre. The jealous Apollo had demanded the sacrifice of Corinus because of her infidelity; for she had slept with a young man even after she carried his child. Apollo had taken his infant son from Corinus; and sent him to be raised by Chiron, a centaur. There, and somewhat ironically, Chiron had schooled the boy in the art of healing.

Hippocrates, the father of modern medicine had also been born on the island over which Bob currently floated. The magnificent plane tree that he had once planted - and under which Hippocrates had taught - reputedly still existed. The island's tiny bright-eyed birds had visceral-red patches of color on their crowns, wings, bills, and throats as if they had once soaked in the crimson remains of Hippocrates' medical instruction. They twisted about playfully in the air forming bright ribbons that sometimes resembled a barber's pole.

But, for now, there were no legends to prove or to disprove; to believe or to discount. Instead, he floated silently along with the wind and looked below upon a young woman who seemed to be pondering something much more familiar – a situation which had its roots in days before...

Sophia was thinking of her father. The big generous man with aquiline nose and broken-toothed smile had been torn from her life; and she vowed never to forget him. She was standing outside of her parents' home; and could smell warm pretzels being made in her mother's kitchen. The hanging baskets of deep blue lobelia, which framed the door to the house, were practically invisible in the darkness - even under the street lamp.

Night was good to Sophia. She thought of herself as an average look-ing girl whom light did not favor. She preferred to focus on the light itself, not what it illuminated. And she liked the night sky. The moon and stars were steady, and lacked contrivance. They shined without and throughout difficulty. Their radiant and oblivious independence was proof to her that her father was still there. This night, she quietly hummed 'Santa Lucia'; felt the power of the night sky; and wondered how something might heal – even without touching.

Many days earlier, she had argued with her mother. The mother had scolded her, saying,

"You have no soul, Sophia!"

"But I don't want to do it!" the girl had responded angrily.

"Your father may have his problems - but he is one of God's children."

"Yes, well, he's old and his breath smells like a dogs butt!"

"That is very rude – and is no excuse!! How can you say such things?"

"Have you ever smelled a dog's butt?!"

"Don't be smart with me, Sophia!"

"THAT would be counter-productive..." Sophia responded; and then ran up to her room and slammed the door.

She hadn't meant to be so curt - but the reply had escaped her mouth before she could stop it. Now she regretted her impertinence; and realized the anger had missed its mark. Minutes later she returned to apologize.

Her father was the village hack who had a 'drinking problem' – and she was embarrassed by him. Old, toothless, and with ruddy skin - he reminded her more of a jack-o-lantern than a father. Her parents no longer lived together; and the man was destitute. Most days he could be found wandering the streets or sitting with his hat out, waiting for someone to drop something in it. If he didn't smell badly – the liquor made him smell as if he had been embalmed.

By the time she returned and issued an apology, her mother had put together the small package of food. She asked her daughter to deliver it. Sophia had once again complained loudly. She couldn't help herself – she was hot with anger.

"All he does is sit on somebody's doorstep - full of wine and wishes! I don't know why you care!"

She continued to complain until tears put out the small fire she felt inside of her head. And when she had finished, her mother said,

"All of life is a choice, Sophia. This will cost you nothing. Your father has no friends; and has nothing good going for him. Why not try for once in your life to restore some balance to the world?"

"He was never around!"

"That's true...and that's past. But he is a generous man. He gives things to others when he cannot even provide for himself. And he has a good sense of humor - if you coax it out of him. Remember...none of us is without flaw."

After pausing to consider her mother's statements, Sophia put on her shoes; pulled on a light coat; and - with protest fastened about her - dumped the package of food in an old soiled sack. She hated having to do this 'gifting', but had resigned herself to find the old man with the worn coat and torn pants. She would sit and watch disgustedly as he mixed the carefully prepared meal together with milk, in a large can. Then, when it was slurry, he would drink what his teeth could no longer chew. It was disgusting.

It was the latter part of the day and she had taken her time – enjoying the warm Mediterranean air; and delaying the inevitable. She found him sitting on a bench, near the road in the center of town. Begrudgingly she approached him. He had a gray demeanor; and sat like an ugly, sharp rock in the middle of a foot path.

She came forth and addressed him - but he ignored her. He smelled as badly as she had remembered. She addressed him again. He ignored her once more; and she was now certain that her mother's request had been a mistake. Perhaps he had gone deaf. Getting closer to him than she could tolerate, she addressed him one more time very loudly. But he registered no apparent concern, continuing instead to look ahead as if he was watching the theater of life on the busy road. It was obvious that he had drunk himself into another stupor.

She slammed the package down on the bench, hoping she had mashed its contents. Then, and in a fit of rage, she gave him a shove. As he toppled forward and face first, she realized that she had been addressing a corpse – her father had been dead for hours.

She ran down the street screaming....

Days later - after her father had been buried - she had calmed down enough to reflect. She looked at old photos of him that seemed to have appeared from nowhere. Like layers of sediment unearthed, albums and musty old boxes of photos had appeared.

And, suddenly, there her father was – pretty as a round rock at the bottom of a river. In the photos, he was tall and slim. His skin was supple and smooth. Dark waves of hair seemed to curl determinedly about his forehead. Dressed in a tuxedo, he celebrated in matrimonial splendor; holding a glass high – as if in a toast. He was metropolitan in appearance, debonair and worldly. That time had been born in front of her – the time when we are all golden - a time that we only rent. There he was, the man she had only known after life had been squeezed out of him.

Like a woman fishing through her satchel for something important, she had finally found a tattered and torn treasure. Somewhere, a watch had stopped; and it revealed the handsome, friendly man he once was - a man who loved to laugh.

It was then that she realized she had missed an opportunity. She did not know that much later, she would find someone who might restore it. Instead she felt a warm wind on her forehead. It seemed to whisper, saying ...'nothing really dies'.

TROUT LILY

Bob awakened suddenly. He was certain that he was awake because he could smell the pot liquor with dough balls, boiling on the stove. Louise stirred the stew gently. Looking at him casually, she said,

"Almost time for bed, Bob." And then, she smiled as if she had told a good joke.

He barely heard her. Instead he was focused on a verse that he had 'carried back' from his dream journey. Like some sort of ritualistic memorization, the verse had remained inside of his head – and he did not know from where it had come.

> 'I love the sound of the horn, the night, in the land of trees
> It seems to sing the sadness of the deer of the forest.
> Or the hunter's goodbye - the echo of a foiled capture
> That the North wind carries from leaf to leaf.'

The verse confused him - as did other visions from his dream journey. Letting go of the verse for awhile, he thought of other unresolved clues; and wondered what they might mean. For, though he was certain that he had understood the language of the wind - like any wind creature; it sometimes spoke in riddles. And these were the puzzle pieces with which it had left him.

A young man named, Sincero was in his thoughts. Bob had been there when the breeze had thrown a baseball at the feet of the young man. And the breeze had whispered something strange to the native man - something about 'a secret – and two flights'.

And then, there was an image – that of a small girl who had been plucked from mud and massacre - clutching a yellow flower given to her by a grandmother. In Bob's vision, the girl had floated to a new land.

Neither had Bob determined what the image of the young man on a beach, might mean. But he believed that somehow, they were destined to share many conversations and campfires. The breeze had whispered to him again ...something about a great cat holding a mystery within its maw.

And what of a fleeting vision of the young boy who spoke in a tongue that he could barely understand? There, the breeze had whispered nothing – it only revealed a great light shone about the boy.

However - and above all - it was a competing memory that held his attention more than the verse of which he could not rid himself. A confounding clue that the breeze had whispered to him in their travel together made him wonder about the dream's whimsy – and his own credential. The breeze had murmured that,

"An answer might be revealed where the fish, the snake, and the dog came together".

Hardly awake, he thought of the clues that had been thrown at his feet by the wind; and realized that he must try to interpret them before their meaning dissolved. The dream had ended more abruptly than he wished; and the wind had left him. The only vestige of it was the soliloquy of lonely howls which it made - as it wiped the brows of the great Sandhills and continued its journey under the silent might of a new moon.

Louise noticed his discomfort; and she said,

"You was sleepin' so soundly, I thought you was dead, Bob - but you didn't have to put a flower on your chest!"

And then, she laughed good-naturedly at her own joke, pointing at him.

He was still lying on the bed. As he strained his neck forward to look down to where she pointed, he saw a small flower lying just above his heart; and realized the joke. Evidently the wind had picked it up and pushed it in through the open window. The flower was different from anything he had seen in the Sandhill region.

"Louise," he cried out. "Get me the 'flower book' – I wanna see where this little flower fits in the scheme of things..."

She looked over at him with a deadpan expression. "Somethin' wrong with your legs...?" And she continued her attention to the pot that she was stirring.

Bob rose carefully. Cupping the spotted, lemon-colored flower in his left hand, he stretched out to a nearby shelf; and removed the taxonomy book that he sought.

"Too bad you're just wakin' up, Bob. Saw the neatest thing while you was sleeping. Two shooting stars come in together and then disappeared over the horizon -I made two wishes!"

"They're not really stars, Louise. It's the visible path of a 'meteoroid', which is to say, a small rocky or metallic object traveling through space. As it enters our atmosphere it becomes a 'meteor'. If it survives impact with the

Earth's surface - then it becomes a 'meteorite'. You probably saw a 'meteor' breaking up into two pieces."

"That right!? Well, call 'em watcha want professor, I call 'em 'shooting stars'...." She was not at all humbled by his erudite explanation.

Bob continued to page through the 'flower book'. It was organized into colors and shapes for ease of identification. After a minute or two, he had found what he wanted.

"Here it is! Louise, this is a Trout Lily – a woodland plant! They call it 'Erythronium americanum'.... He read on, "...North American native wild-flower that produces clusters of golden flowers reversed in purplish brown on leafless stems sprouting from mottled foliage... grows 10 inches tall. What the heck is she doin' in the Sandhills?"

"Oh, there you go again, Bob....maybe 'woniya sinoko' sent you a mes-sage. Can't everything be explained with science...dontcha think? Well I guess that monster wind coulda' picked it up from the mountains somewhere. They say this system has been travellin' quite the distance – and done a lotta dam-age in some places...."

He wasn't listening to her. Instead he was fascinated by what he read in the taxonomy. .

"Hmmmm...trout lily'...also called the 'dog-toothed violet'...and the 'ad-der's tongue'.

He went over to the open window and bent out to view the night sky – listening. The stars looked like bright seed that had been shaken roughly from the wild grass and scattered by the wind - and which now, rested within the dark hair of a boy who had fallen asleep in a meadow. Smoke, from a fire that Louise had started in the stove, was curling about lazily in the air. It seemed to be begging for direction wanting to return to something greater than itself. He could just see the shadows of a few night swallows borrowing the breeze to catch their supper. Their curved, twisted soaring seemed sensual. The tension between day and night was over. Light had craved attention long enough. Darkness had pushed it out and was now displaying dusky dressage as it pranced across the sky. It was a clear night.

In the distance, antelope that had been startled by something, leapt about in the lightly illuminated landscape; and finally stopped at the top of a hill as if to gaze at the night's currency. The golden stars were out of their reach. That realization reconciled, they put their heads down and milled about look-ing for the choice grasses - as they had done for centuries. Pulling at and sheering the grass with their incisors; they moved the food back to chewing molars. They were built by the prairie. Their enviable speed and adaptability were currency enough. They felt a freedom that could not be purchased. Bob leaned out the window as far as he could; genuinely rapt by the beauty before him. The light from the lanterns inside shone through the sparse windows; and highlighted the grass nearby. It seemed prettier than any park.

Then, and turning abruptly, he snatched the walking stick from its cubby and said to Louise,

"Wind says it's too quiet here, Louise. Going on a journey soon to find what the noise is all about."

Louise, meanwhile, was quite content to stay where she was and watch the riot of life that she knew existed just past the kitchen window outside of the 'soddie'. She looked for two bowls to serve up the stew that she had been stirring. Standing tall and erect as an old cottonwood, she was bothered by very little about her.

PART II

QUARTER MOON

THE DETECTIVE AND THE BOY WHO SPOKE A TONGUE

It is early spring. In another corner of the world, an obsidian sky holds the clear light of distant stars. Detective, Conley Tweeter, is sitting at his desk thinking about a recent domestic case. He looks at a drawing given to him. It would hardly be of any use in his police work. Still, he trims it as neatly as he can - so that it will fit – and then, carefully puts the drawing in his wallet.

The domestic case started when he had received a public complaint; causing him to bring a mother and her child to the police station. The mother was artificially hyperactive. The child was dirty – and slimmer than an excuse. The detective had called 'Social Services' who would determine what must be done. The mother seemed incredibly preoccupied and distracted as if she was waiting for the surreality of her next 'fix'. She was oblivious to any need that her child might have.

Pulling the boy aside, the detective carried him down to the restroom – he could not walk. His mother hardly noticed the boy's absence. Entering the restroom, the detective turned on the water and waited for it to get warm. Then - using a paper towel – he cleaned a weeks worth of grime from the boy's face and hands; combed his beastly mop of hair; and tried to brush off some of the filth from his clothing. The boy looked like he had been rolling in enough dirt to fill a truck.

Once clean, the child looked strangely angelic. He smiled broadly at the detective who then, took him back to his office. Tweeter gave the boy a lollipop; and tried not to feel any attachment while he waited for 'Social Services'. Not knowing what else to do; and bothered by the child's attentive adoration, he gave him a scrap of paper and a pencil – and asked him to draw something. Then, he picked the child up from a nearby bench; sat him down next to his desk; and watched him doodle with as much control as he could muster. The boy seemed happy - beaming as if there was a great light within him. He seemed unconcerned with the day's earlier events; grateful for the sparse attention; and preoccupied with scribbling. When he finished, the boy gave the drawing to the detective; and tried to speak. But his speech was so garbled that the well-intentioned Detective Tweeter could only smile and pat him on the head.

The drawing was an awkward sketch of a daffodil. This was what Tweeter had folded so carefully; and put in his wallet. It would remind him that in the midst of the world's ugliness, some beauty and hope could always be found. He would think of it – even when the child eventually caused him to question his own beliefs.

...Far up in the heavens, a drama was occurring which involved a different mother and child. The violence and journey of an ancient Greek tale was being replayed in the sky - as it was every night of the year.

The constellation Andromeda had appeared. She could be seen south of her mother, Queen Cassiopeia. Beautiful Andromeda was chained to a rock and next to a frothing sea. She struggled in fearful desperation, aware that she was to be sacrificed.

Queen Cassiopeia looked on with tears streaming down her face; her mouth twisted in agony; her hands alternately clutching her husband, King Cepheus, and then pounding her chest in anguish. She would tear out her own heart to save her daughter. The king's face was dark and worried.

The sea nymphs had released the beast from its deep watery dungeon. Delphinus delphus - for whom Apollo's oracle at Delphi was named - had ceased to play. The dolphin had righted himself from his upside down courtship position. He was aware of a great disturbance in the waters. He and his mate swam away hastily. The water was turbulent and seemed to tremble from the powerful strokes of Cetus who had been released from the giant cage that kept him imprisoned. Cetus, the great beast, was angry and ravenous. Free from his cage, he strode along the ocean bottom looking for anything that might satisfy his appetite. But the dolphins were well out of reach.

This is a play that has been rehearsed over and over again. The beast stumbles through his lines as he stumbles through time. Through the subtle direction of instinct and the profundity of myth - the careless, brutish steps have become choreography. Cetus will burst above the icy sea reaching for food and heaven – and seeking the sustenance of both.

Andromeda is there to sate his hunger; and to avenge a goddess who has been offended by Queen Cassiopeia. The Queen bleats like a frightened sheep. She is unaware of the great winged horse that carries the hero across the seas. She again regrets the vanity of her earlier offense. How could she have known that the gods believed that vengeance was best when served more than once?

Perseus, carrying the head of Medusa, will confront Cetus. Once the beast has gazed upon Medusa's head, Cetus will turn to stone; and fall apart. Splitting into great rocky shards, the beast will return to the ocean; and Perseus will drop the head of Medusa into the sea. The waters will roil like a spreading pox.

The winged horse will then, alight quietly on the cliff - as if in socked feet - and Perseus will free Andromeda. On the shore there will be a joyous outcry - as Andromeda is returned to her parents. The hero's moxie will be celebrated by many guests pounding tables for the great feast.

But down on earth, the daily heroics of the constellations, the myths, go unnoticed. 'Social Services' had picked up the child and the mother was also gone. Detective Tweeter was alone and thinking about the boy who had given him the drawing.

When he found the child, the boy had been dirty and shivering – not from cold or fever - but from the anguish of a daily drama that had occurred frequently. The benefit (if one could call it that) of Tweeter's experience had made it easy for him to fill in the gaps of the child's life. The boy's existence and survival both perplexed and yet, gave hope – no less than a miracle that was in cadence with the constellations.

Tweeter had come upon him in a dark room that smelled badly. The boy was grinding his teeth - the noise audible because he was in a room alone. The dark flat, in which the boy lay barely conscious, glowed faintly from moonlight coming through an open window. Shadows which might have held daisies instead - hid monsters. The boy was frightened. Rats could be heard gnawing in the walls; and squeaking like an audience beyond an orchestra pit, waiting for the finale of a tragedy.

The boy was dreaming and huddled against a wall next to the door. The room was filthy. Scared, unable to go to the bathroom because his hands were tied to the doorknob, he had banged his puny fists against the door until they were bruised and bleeding. When he could no longer 'hold it', he had urinated all over himself. Having relieved himself, he was finally able to go to sleep. But the ghosts of old dreams had been plucked like sour fruit from a twisted tree; and he fed on them. He was dreaming about the past – not wanting to remember, but unable to forget. His mother frequently left him to go out at night. It had been months before an observant and gutsy neighbor intervened.

Tweeter reflected. He was certain he already knew the rest of the story. The case would go to court. A social worker with a giant caseload would argue that the boy was in an untenable situation – living with a mother who was a drug addict and prostitute. The social worker would strive to get the attention of a sleepy judge who had seen too much inhumanity.

A defense attorney would counter the argument. He would not be motivated by a desire to maintain a family, but to ensure that his client would not be charged with neglect and would be able to continue her 'employment'. His interest would only be to fulfill a legal obligation for which the court paid him. He would indicate that his client was an unfortunate single mother in treatment who was doing the best for her handicapped son; and would ask the court for understanding. The mother would wear something dark and conservative and would look mournful, scared - or germanically serious. .

The ruling would show the court's sympathy but the judge would argue that the child's development was incompatible with drinking, drugging, and prostitution – or locking him to a bedroom door, without benefit of a bathroom, food, or water. The mother would lose the child to a social service facility, but would maintain visitation rights. She would be required to seek treatment before her record might be expunged; and before being eligible to receive the review required for custody of the child again.

The boy, Zeke, would be turned over to a state-approved facility because of his need for specialized care. There he would receive good food, the attention he required, and could 'go potty' when he needed. The rope scars around his slender wrists would gradually disappear. The facility would then have the difficult task of sustaining him while trying to suture an invisible wound which had long spilled away happiness. The mother would not come for him. He would probably become a 'court-puppy' - waiting for adoption. That was the way Detective Tweeter envisioned the boy's life and it left him in a dark mood...hoping that he was wrong.

But the detective wasn't wrong.

The mother did not put up a fight. Her buzzing brain hardly let her know that her son was gone. The boy had been a mistake. His 'condition' required more work than she could muster amidst her tragic and spiraling dysfunction. She had made mistakes that seemed uncorrectable. She did the only thing that – and through the ether of her illness – she could think to do. She blew the boy a kiss; told him to 'be good' and that she loved him.

Minutes later, and after a crying, screaming and forced departure from her side, the boy was trying to understand the pain. The mother meanwhile was scrolling through a field of printed "Personals". She was trying to understand things as well; and dreaming of a change that would not come. Within days, she was heading for a destination that she hoped would allow a 'fresh start'. She would try to pick up the pieces of a life that had been poorly planned; and hope that – for the first time in her life - she might truly soar.

The detective continued to brood. He wondered why such scenes were daily replayed. The wind had come in through an open window. It blew about the papers on his desk creating mayhem. He did not move. He was busy thinking about careless, brutish steps that had become the choreography of a judicial system that seemed to stumble through lines and time - like a monstrous Cetus.

Just as there were chained Andromedas in the sky, there were children with rope burns around their wrists, on earth. And all were waiting for their Perseus; and for someone to speak a tongue they could understand.

'RC'S RECOVERY

It is years later. Like two elderly noblewomen, borne of the manor, Time and History are sharing a room uncomfortably. Time does not appear to recognize History, anymore than History recognizes Time. But in Time's eyes – if Time might have them – it is no more than the flutter of an eyelash. From History's perspective, the actions that have occurred within the space of Time's drawing room - are as inconsequential as the crumbs of a scone left on good china.

But time had passed; and 'Old Joe' was gone. The curious boy who Bob had seen in a dream - lying in the grass...no longer held 'Harvard' at the knees of the old black man. The boy, now grown, scarcely remembered the night of the raccoons. Nor could he remember the harmonica tune that 'Old Joe' had played, or the practical wisdom the old man had imparted. But, though he could not remember the facts, he could remember the feelings of a happier time.

'RC' was now, sitting on a beach; and getting more uncomfortable by the moment. He had come there to relax; think about the past; and contemplate how to resurrect his life. He had discovered that the surest way to make God laugh was to tell Him that you had a 'fool-proof' plan. God would find a fool to dismantle it. And that's exactly what 'RC' had done – exceeding even heavenly expectations. As the victim of yet another 'love affair gone bad' and so many other disappointments in life, he could only envision his next enterprise might involve opening up a shop and selling 'misfortune cookies'.

A well-intentioned and worried college roommate had coincidentally called. He had persuaded 'RC' to seek assistance at a retreat that bordered a beach. The roommate's concern was out of character; and had convinced 'RC' that he probably needed some type of help. But now, 'RC' was certain he had a pound of sand in his shorts. And the sun was so damned hot that he was sure the innermost part of his swimsuit was fusing glass together. He vowed to find the college roommate; and exact physical pain. But first - there would be therapy.

He stared out at the ocean. If this was the primordial soup from which we had all come, it surely must be 'Junky Beef Vegetable'. There was so much flotsam that Jesus didn't need to show off anymore. 'RC' believed that he too, could probably walk across the water without any trouble.

Late spring, a month of heavy storms had created a rugged dirty beach that looked like a soiled strip of carpet in a foyer. Off-coast storms combined with a ripened moon to cause a strong tide and a severe undertow. Many culinary delights had been put forth for the Herring Gulls' beach buffet. Their querulous keeyow, kyow-kyow-kyow was overpowering and contributed to his throbbing headache. The birds had tired of what the nearby dump had to offer; and traveled to the beach for some fresh seafood.

But much more damage had been done by something the East Coast rarely saw – a tsunami. Twenty-foot waves had crashed into many of the Southern and mid-Atlantic coastal towns - buckling tin roofs like aluminum foil, and causing vintage rivers to dig channels. Weather patrols had at first blamed the destruction on a freak 'Category 4' hurricane that had been a spin-off of a fierce wind that had swept across the prairie. No one could explain 'where' the wind had originated – or where it had disappeared. The natives said it came from the 'Wind Cave'.

Now, experts were reasonably certain that the event had been caused by the shifting and slippage of huge fault lines which had dislocated a sizeable portion of a land mass from the 'Canaries'. The resulting wave had traveled across ocean with deadly speed – carving away great swathes of the shoreline on the East coast. It had slashed and trampled everything in its path. Bodies had floated for weeks – looking like bloated hominy from the air. Geologists pointed to similar evidence of a tsunami that had occurred nearly 18,000 years ago in a nearby bay.

The media devoted weeks of reporting that focused on human-interest stories, lives lost, and properties being swept out to sea. They had proved that the best way to ensure that people forget tragedy and cataclysm was to make it available to them 24 hours a day. Legend had been starved to death through too much attention.

Still one image endured in 'RC's mind. In the town where he now found himself, a single sign had survived the crashing waves that had swept away the land around it. The sign was now offshore. At high tide, it was immersed in water and just barely visible above the pummeling indifference of the surf. It read simply:

"BEACHFRONT PROPERTY AVAILABLE!"

The irony momentarily took his mind off of a failed relationship that had been the source of great angst. Then, and through the deviousness of memory, he found himself thinking of a woman he had met in college. Suddenly he felt common and stupid and wondered why he had allowed a college roommate to exercise 'pop psychology' to convince him to seek help. What was he doing on this brutally hot beach?

He brushed the hair out of his face; and examined the mashed profusion of seashells at his feet. He didn't come to the beach often, being more sylvan by nature. The wind lifted a heavy odor to his nose. It smelled of salt and something that had died recently. His keen eyes panned the immediate horizon until he spotted a small brown lump. An active cloud of flies provided a target for his suspicions. Getting up from where he was sitting he walked about 50 yards along the shore break. There, a black-hooded laughing gull was curious and circling. Its loud ha-ha-ha-ha-haah-haah-haah sounds could be heard above the ocean din.

The seal was small - a juvenile. Its decomposing body smelled intensely. The bottom half of it had been ripped away from the top half – probably long since devoured by a predator. The insides hung out from the body and looked like Christmas confetti in the sand. Its eyes were now cloudy, but still had a pretty puppy dog look. Its mouth was open. Had it been suckling on the 50 percent milk fat that came from its mother? A flipper was barely attached and dangling. The monster fish hadn't finished. The spotted coat convinced 'RC' that he was looking at a Harbor Seal. Perhaps it had been used as bait. It was a nefarious practice that some fishermen occasionally used to catch shark.

He focused on the sand around the seal. Nature wasted nothing. The body of the seal pup had already been visited. There was the curving oxtail pattern of periwinkles with their sharply pointed spiral shells, checkered outer lip; and chocolate brown interior. Then there were eight parallel broken lines of numerous ghost crabs that walked sideways – constantly observant. 'RC' looked closer at the sand and could just determine the wide print of a horseshoe crab with its characteristic center line – evidence of a spiked tail that had been dragged along. He momentarily thought about an ocean biology course he had taken. A professor had indicated that the horseshoe crab was considered a 'living fossil' - having existed for 450 million years – and that it could detect ultraviolet light.

All had come to pay homage to the seal pup. And like well groomed friends at a funeral, they expected a meal after the brief service. 'RC' marveled at the miracles of animals; and wondered why his abilities seemed so puny by comparison.

The tracks in the sand revealed a predictable history. The nearby detergent froth of shore break charged forward as if to erase any story, but the tide was not quite high enough. The breaking action of the waves at the shoreline seemed to encompass everything, even thought. Their pounding 'whooosshhhhsssssss' - as they threw themselves against the beach and then receded with a rattle of broken shells and sand -seemed a therapeutic and universal life force. He hated to admit that it was having a positive effect on him. He looked up and out at the ocean again. The open sky was turning bright colors; and seemed to announce the end of the day. Puffy angel hair clouds captured the light; and removed the choking thoughts that had accompanied him. A nearby sailboat seemed to turn direction suddenly – looking like an impetuous dancer flashing a petticoat. It would soon be twilight - the time when one naturally looked up expecting a lunar show or constellations that made the evening sky seem like an elaborate punched tin lampshade. The lantern of a full moon might entice fish from gray-green waters, looking for a nighttime snack. Fisherman of years past (or less means) sometimes dangled a lantern over the edge of a boat to attract such bait fish and their predators.

The sun was going down rapidly. Increasing wind seemed to create a floating checkered pattern in the water, as white caps emerged and then suddenly disappeared. The fresh smell of salt air removed the odor of the seal carcass; and 'RC' could see a gamut of ghost crabs making their way along the beach, but keeping a respectful distance, like cautious partygoers.

He began to think of the urban life he had just left. There were tracks in the sand of human behavior as well, but they were sometimes harder to read. The degree of morbidity that was creeping back into his thoughts was suddenly driven away by a large wave that stomped at the shoreline, grabbing sand and spinning it around like loose laundry.

'RC' had unconsciously strolled away from the seal carcass. He looked back at it one more time. Small crustaceans called sand bubblers were already galloping away with part of it. A banquet would be had at the local sand castle tonight. The high-pitched 'kip'-'kit' of Sanderlings chasing after the marauding mollusks was suddenly apparent and he saw the little sandpipers running like plump bakers with thin legs. It caused him to laugh. The gulls circling above; and the squirming sand revealed an army of organisms that would efficiently work at the carcass until there would be practically nothing left.

Suddenly his attention was drawn outwardly. He could discern an object being lifted out to the gray-green oblivion of an active sea.

"More trash on the beach," he thought disgustedly.

He stared at the gleaming tip of the wandering junk. It had been pulled under by the strong tide and then miraculously appeared again on top of the water about 20 feet away from shoreline. A determined swell had formed in the distance behind. It pushed over the flotsam, submerging it. He surmised that it was gone forever to an inky green death.

Then, dismissing the bottle, he continued to pick through the cornucopia of shells that were remnants of small lives; and that had surfaced like unexpected bones at a graveyard. There was another productive crash of waves on the beach. He turned to observe a foaming degeneration of waves that seemed to miraculously cleanse his thoughts. As the glistening waves receded, there on the sand and wedged between the crevice of two large rocks and some old fishing line - was the green bottle he had seen a few minutes before.

Determined not to let the garbage distract him, he turned away. Still it bothered him that the purity of such a moment would be interrupted by something as crass as trash that had probably been jettisoned by a lazy 'redneck' who thought the ocean was his personal dumpster.

He had spent two weeks in this beach retreat - most of it in a melancholy mood; and had spent much time thinking; making probing personal assessments; and trying to plan for a future that no longer seemed to be in front of him. The time had not been entirely 'unproductive'. He hated that word. But then he hated everything today. He felt like he had simply wallowed for hours. Then he realized he felt very much like the bottle that had been buoyed up by the magic of the sea – and found land.

He stood up; walked over to the bottle; untangled it from the fishing line; and brushed as much sand away as possible. It surprised 'RC' that the worn bottle still had a very tight cork in it. It had been sanded relentlessly; and must have been floating for some time. More surprising - there appeared to be a paper in the bottle.

That realization only fomented his curiosity. With every bit of reserved masculinity he possessed, he struggle to uncork the bottle and see its contents. Pushing the cork back and forth; he prodded and twisted it with a firm delicacy, much like someone trying to pull off a tight ring. The cork was being dislodged, but would only give itself up by millimeters. He continued to work at it wondering if the effort he was expending would reveal anything that was a 'tittle' of interest, or whether it would be one more in a long list of daily afflictions that bore no reward. Finally, and with a mastery he did not think he possessed he was able to pull the cork out.

The inside of the bottle had remained remarkably dry. He shook it like a ketchup bottle until the paper was just within reach of the lip and then gently fished the curled note from the inside of its sanctum. The paper had yellowed but was dryer than Jonah had been in the belly of a whale. He opened it gingerly. Though the print was smeared and faded in places, he was able to make out something that quite startled him. It was a verse that read as follows:

> J'aime le son du cor, le soir, au fond des bois,
> Soit qu'il chante les pleurs de la bich aux bois,
> Ou l'adieu du chasseur que l'echo faible accueille,
> Et que le vent du nord porte de feuille en feuille.

It was a verse written by Alfred de Comte Vigny. He knew what it meant immediately. Someone he had loved and let go was still searching for him. 'RC' marveled at the serendipity of life. What he had found was worth more than a month of therapy; for it had given him a hope that he had heretofore lacked.

A LOVE AND A MENTOR

The wind had swept into the drawing room that Time and History shared. It piqued History's attention and perhaps, caused her to reconsider the crumbs she had left on Time's good china. It had only been a second in their world; and caused History to comment idly,

"Dear me, I seem to have left a morsel or two. I hope you don't mind if I use a finger to sweep them up. The scone is simply too good to waste any of it."

But Time ignored History; and continued her stony stare out the drawing room window – a window that Light and Darkness shared. Being a mentor for History – who was a noblewoman of lesser birth – she merely arched one eyebrow slightly as if she was tired of their sitting conversation. It was enough to allow History to know that her comment had registered; and to realize that Time was quite dominant when she was in her own drawing room.

'RC' was not particularly aware of either of the ancient women – anymore than he was of the constellations. He had just 'fished' a note from the safety of a salt-encrusted and barnacled vessel that the ocean had steered to the beach. The green bottle did not interest him any longer, though it had been made from sand that could just as easily have poured through an hourglass in the drawing room of Time. But really - Time had no need for an hourglass and would barely have noticed an hour. It was the note inside of the bottle that had meaning for 'RC'; and it caused him to dream an extended dream that was only a millisecond in the world of two ancient noblewomen.

He was remembering the 'past'. Though a distant and extended period to him, it was less than the beginning of a breath to Time or History; for none but the greatest trees and mountains had ever heard an entire breath of either great women – and they never spoke of it to men.

In his distant day dream, 'RC' was in a French class at the private school where his parents had sent him. He was bored with the class and failing it. An instructor had given him the lecture of a lifetime but - realizing his salary was being paid by parents of means - had given 'RC' a way to make up the failing marks. It required the memorization, class recitation, and explanation of verse penned by one of the 'old masters' of French literature, Alfred de Comte Vigny.

'RC' had been a lazy, distracted, hot headed student – resentful of parents who he believed had shipped him off so they could have some 'quality time'. After the professorial tongue-lashing, he had securely fastened the 'required reading' to his chest using straps that he tied under his arms; and hoping to prevent the 'tome' from bouncing about as he moved. Then, pulling on a warm sweatshirt and sweat pants, he headed out of the dormitory to find a place where he hoped 'The Comte' might have some life breathed into him. There, he would try to commit himself to a task that had no meaning; but that might secure a passing mark.

It was chilly, with an early spring flurry of light snow which did not stick - winter's viaticum. His pace quickened and he felt as if he could run across the broad plains, keeping up with the antelope. He longed for the freedom that such animals possessed and felt the strength of young blood. He had run past a dormitory that was being constructed. He continued past a ring of sorority girls, who seemed to cluck and honk like a gaggle of geese; a small planetarium that had just been built; and a brutish fellow who appeared to be headed for rugby practice. Within minutes he was just past the outward ring of the campus. That ring was gilded by a church which sat like a gold and white stone; and rested near a silver-banded stream that seemed to meander in a Celtic pattern. It was a day made of crystal - one that most of us remember and whose luster lasts well into our twilight.

He had never noticed the small notch in the silver stream which flowed past the church. But today, he stopped. The book by 'the Comte' was beginning to annoy him. It had slipped from his meticulous binding and was now bouncing up and down on his diaphragm. The freedom that he had felt when he first started running had vanished; and the book now felt like a stone around his neck. It bounced up and down inside of his sweatshirt; and was far from the gracefully anonymous appearance that he had hoped for. Instead, he felt clumsy and awkward.

Stopping at the notch in the stream, he pulled the book from under his sweatshirt. It amused him slightly that the sweat from his body had smeared and wrinkled the book jacket; and seemed a fitting 'tribute' to something for which he had no interest. This was the proverbial 'final straw'. He would be done with 'the Comte' and his education once and for all. He had just raised the book over his head and prepared to pitch it into the water when he noticed the slender form of a young woman, casually watching. It startled him; and he immediately wondered if she had noticed his impetuousness and his awkwardly juvenile body. He blushed slightly.

Anna was dressed in a green plaid dress; and wore a white blouse that contrasted well with hair that cascaded comfortably across her shoulders and had a slight waviness that made her more than just a little intriguing. She wore a light jacket that had a subtle silvery sheen. It caught the light of the day and faintly reflected it like a vintage mirror. It gave her the appearance of something that did not seem real – a fetch floating in a bed of daffodils.

Noticing his discomfort and more than slightly amused, she sat up from a willow tree that she had been leaning against. Then she gently folded the remains of a light lunch in a napkin; and put down a book that she had been reading. She was pretty; and seemed keenly perceptive. Pulling out some 'ear buds' she looked up, and said, teasingly,

"Ah...Alfred De Comte Vigny...I'd throw him in the ocean. I'm afraid the stream isn't 'deep' enough for him. On the other hand, he did write a tremendous account of 'the hunt' – have you read it?"

He was stunned that she new of 'the Comte'. More than a bit self-conscious from his behavior and the glimpse of a naked tummy - that he was sure she had seen – he hesitated. But after a few minutes of good-natured and unguarded conversation which she delivered with the apparent ease of someone who was quite comfortable with herself, he was struck by his good fortune. Her intimate nature drew him in; and he was able to relax long enough to recognize two things about her – she was much prettier than he had first realized...and seemed the most incredibly interesting person he had ever met.

But now, RC focused back on the penned note he had fished from a green bottle bouncing in the surf. The hours in the company of that interesting young woman had been reduced to only minutes of memories which now seemed impossibly distant. It made him wretchedly sad. They had read, joked, recited verse, and flirted with an intensity that seemed as if it had been conjured. He could remember the color of her hair as the light rested upon it; and her soulful eyes. Those eyes seemed to have no beginning or end in depth; and had led him to places that he had not imagined. The curve of her lips and form rivaled the serpentine nature of the stream by which they sat. The light from her jacket competed openly with the sheen from the stream. All came together to make a liquid memory - for which he still thirsted.

As if to counterattack this hypnosis from his past, 'RC' shook his head; drew a long breath – and then released the memory again. Now, he concentrated on the chunk of junk that had previously seemed inconsequential. The ocean had offered up something that had sent him hurtling back to what seemed like ancient thoughts. And – as crazy as it seemed - he had momentarily been in a joyful delirium; soaring like a large bird; and remembering the stanza of a poem from a French author who had long since been buried.

Yes, Alfred de Comte de Vigny had resurfaced as so much flotsam. But this time he no longer wrestled with the writing. Instead the old verse had resurrected something. Its author did not block a way forward any longer. In his mind, 'RC' strolled and recited with the author – as if they were old friends. 'The Comte' had brought him back where he had started; and insinuated that 'RC' needed to revisit the path – that he had missed something that he needed in his life. He could not escape the memory so easily; and was now remembering a verse that had been nearly lost.

> J'aime le son du cor, le soir, au fond des bois,
> Soit qu'il chante les pleurs de la bich aux bois,
> Ou l'adieu du chasseur que l'echo faible accueille,
> Et que le vent du nord porte de feuille en feuille.

He was thinking of Anna again. Long ago, she had chased away a wan winter day. She had loosely translated the verse for him; and held it out. It resonated like a bell in her presence. He had felt full in life - for he had never understood the power of poetry when it is spoken under the influence of love. She had helped him translate it and the memory had been running silently beside him - it just needed refreshing.

> 'I love the sound of the horn, the night, in the land of trees
> It seems to sing the sadness of the deer of the forest.
> Or the hunter's goodbye - the echo of a foiled capture
> That the North wind carries from leaf to leaf.'

The verse seemed to capture the complicated simplicity of primal human feeling related to the woods; and to convey the ancient march from the protection of trees to open savannah. That fearful migration had been crowned in the triumph of something that - once prey - was now also predator. The woods had become strange and beautiful. With her help, he had befriended 'The Comte'; and could feel the poem's passion, as he thought the author had intended.

But now 'RC' felt certain sadness from the verse. It had been written over a century before the age of high-powered rifles and bows, fast-food, feed lots, sonar fishing, four-wheel drive vehicles, and geocentering technology.

The magic that had kept hominids frightened – yet captivated – by their surroundings, seemed to be ending.

But it was the gravity of another stanza that Anna had translated for him all those years before that now crawled inside of him. It made him doubtful and despairing.

"C'est le serpent, dit-elle, je l'ai ecoute, et il m'a trompee."

Translated,

"It was the serpent, said she. I listened to it and it deceived me."

It was not the advance of apes into the grasslands from the forest that concerned him, nor the fact that some magic had been scraped away. He realized that he feared the woods obscurity and what might be hiding in the grass much less than the dark distractions he had seen in hominids. He wished that he had the mysterious girl at the notch of the stream by his side again. She could untangle the prolific vines that now grew throughout him. Of course, the death of anything precious is a crystal hole that time must soften. He gazed at a crusted shell that moved slowly as some animal made its way up the beach looking for something.

"Barnacle'd little bastard," he thought. "I wonder if he knows the next bone-crunching wave is going to suck him back out to sea...that he'll spend most of his existence trying to claw his way back to happiness."

It seemed a similar 'story' to him; caused him to focus on his self-centered angst. Where was he going? And like a kind of sonar, there were more images that bounced around inside of his head. And they had targeted another distant memory....

Now, he was back at the boyhood farm. And then - sloughing that memory off like skin -was on the front porch of Old Joe's house listening to the playful rising and falling melody of the old man's harmonica. That melody easily competed with the ebb and flow of the waves on the beach where he currently sat; and it seemed equally rich and profound.

In his dream, 'RC' was a boy again. The music of the harmonica had relaxed him enough to allow him to daydream. In semi-conscious thought the integer of one dream had become fraction of another.

A young 'RC' was distractedly examining his fingernails in the sun. He looked at the bone structure of his stubby fingers and the fat folds of flesh that led up to the smooth surface of the nails. Then he looked more closely.

Holding his hand out in the sun, he could just see a structure – as if the nails had been made from compressed vertical hairs. Joe had been watching him; and pulled back from his harmonica. He let the soulful music evaporate.

"'RC', how you like to go up to the 'stoah' with me and get a cone?"

Then he smiled widely. The boy was still not quite with him, so he continued,

"Well, maybe a 'jelly roll', then..."

The boy suddenly looked away from his fingers, his thoughts dispelled by two treats.

"Nuts on the top - and you got a deal!"

The old man just laughed and said, pointing to 'RC's bare feet.

"You the 'boss', 'RC'...best 'putcha' shoes on though - we goin' cross some rough road."

Joe was what some might call 'old school'. A calm, sturdy quietude belied the internal electricity that spread light to whomever he befriended. He gave power to anyone he felt needed it – or for whom he cared.

And he knew things. Once, when they were walking along the bank of a low river, the old man had stopped and picked up a large round stone. He rolled it over and over again in his hands - it was ordinary in appearance. Suddenly and with great strength Joe had smashed it against another rock – revealing the shimmering crystals inside. And now – many years later - 'RC' realized the geode was much like the man who had found it.

Old Joe was a solid spiritual man who 'believed' – but never pushed. Though he meandered more than he approached things directly, he was neat in his work and thorough. Folks were relaxed in his presence – much like they were relaxed in a pair of old shoes. He spoke simply; and had a 'gift' for expressing lofty thoughts in an earthly way. His laugh bounced off ceilings. What had been denied to him in life, had only served to make him fluid, strong, and oddly eloquent.

Now, in 'RC's dream, it was a warmish day that had made him shed his shirt and tie it around his waist. He felt comfortable enough to ask Old Joe anything, knowing that the hue of any question would not be objectionable.

"Joe", the boy said, "I don't understand fingernails."

Joe let out a roar of laughter; and teased,

"'Whatchu' don' unnahstand about them, 'RC'? You uses them to scratch yo'self."

"Well, yes. But why don't we use a stick? ...And we can't fight with them - they're too puny."

He never expected what came next.

"Well, 'RC', I think they's our last links to our heritage."

"What do you mean 'our heritage'?"

"Why, the sea, a course! They's what's lef' of our shells. Evahthin' done started out in the sea."

He was suddenly upset.

"But that's not right, Joe. God created man. That's what they tell us in church."

Joe just beamed a big smile at him and said,

"Why shoah, 'RC'! But who you done think created the sea?"

'RC' persisted.

"But God created us in his own image. That's what they say. And I believe them. Mr. Green wouldn't lie."

"Rever'n Green crazy if he think God only got one image. Evahthing on this beautiful earth got God in it. And God done created it foah reason. It's all part a' his big plan. We part a' that plan – tho we cain't nevah know it all."

'RC' continued.

"But I don't understand, Joe. Mr. Green can't be crazy he's a preacher."

"Mah, mah, mah. Sho' is a lotta big questions come outta little man. But'cha know, son. Sometimes havin' a pedigree make a good man a little blind or crazy. It ain't always that way, but it sho' nuff is fo' lotsa animals."

"Well, Mr. Green says that it's silly for anyone to claim that we're descended from any animal that's lower than us – and that it's not Christian to think that way."

"Rever'nt Green a nice man, son. But he only see God's work in some things. I think God in evahthing – even the flowers and trees. Thinkin anything less might jus' take you further away from God. And sayin' you know God's plan...um, um, ummmmh....Well, that' a mighty big claim - and one I ain't soon likely to say. Asides, why God pick a few a' us to share his plan with? Naww...I ain't too keen on claimin to know God's plan. I think he show it to me soon enuf."

"But I can't believe we would be kin to animals."

"Now 'RC', I tells you the truth. I'd sooner be kin to a good horse 'then a bad man anyday – now wooden-chu?!"

"I dunno. Animals can be pretty scary...pretty bad, Joe."

"Shoot. You an animal, RC." Joe was pointing at the boy's bare feet.

"I'm not an animal!"

'Well 'en' whatchu call at, boy!?" He pointed to the ground on which 'RC' had recently stood. In the dust were the slight indentations of the 'RC's feet.

"A footprint."

"Zackly! You gotta feetprints, tracks, an' you strides jus' like an animal. So what make you think you ain't one?"

"My footprint doesn't look like an animal's foot print!"

"You ain't thet' diffunt, 'RC'. Skunk footprint don' look like deer footprint eithah. Single wide trough with toes pointing' inwahd - mos' likely otter, skunk or porkpine. Two narrow troughs in snow with foot pointing' straight and sharp mos' likely deer o' moose – if it a big print."

"I don't wanna be an animal, Joe. They're mean!"

"Men much mo' meaner, 'RC'."

'RC' was looking at his fingers one more time.

"Joe...what are these little half moons on my fingernails?"

"Oh now, thet ain't no half-moon. Thet there's a risin' sun."

He looked skeptical.

"But I don't understand - why would we have a rising sun on our fingernails?"

"It's a remindah, boy! If'n you believe as I does, then you know that God lettin' us know that no mattah how bad a day we havin'...he givin' us another one so as we's can try again!"

"That's silly – he's not giving us a day!!"

"Say watchu wan't. We don't have to take it...but He the only one who kin make it!"

'RC' snapped back to the present. Was it really as silly as he had once thought? He looked down self-consciously at his fingernails and then up at the sky. The small lights of a few stars had come out. He gazed at them the way he had once looked at the abundance of shiny life under a microscope. It caused him to reflect on the relativity of size. Was the distance between things he had seen on a slide really that much different than the relative distance between planets. Maybe it depended on the observer.

He panned back to the dead seal pup that was near him. Galloping crustaceans danced madly around shore break – searching for food that must be vacuum-packed in waves. It was a strange tango as they dance backward, and then forward again toward the receding waves. They darted 'to and from' any movement or shadow - searching for food yet, trying not to become it. Everywhere he looked - the question of relative size and the purpose of an invisible web that seemed to connect things seemed pervasive. Were his thoughts simply a diversion from a 'soul-searching' retreat?

He gazed back at the islands of stars that seemed to float in twilight and wondered about the mythology of constellations. He was mystified by the human mind and some of the creatures that were invented for the sake of prose - harpies, Minotaur, two headed dogs, dragons, centaurs. Why were myths so frightening and violent? Were they the spawn of dreams? He had read that 'dreams were either unresolved past conflicts or harbingers of things to come'. But maybe the ancient Greeks and Romans drank too much; and suffered from poor hygiene. Abstinence, soap, and a piece of baked chicken could banish much madness.

Now, there was no one to ask. Old Joe Jefferson was gone. Time had not proved a good erasure. 'RC' had been unable to abort the memory of that day, the discussion of the fingernails – and what had occurred later.

They had stopped by the stable so Joe could complete one more of the countless chores he had forgotten. He had been talking to 'RC' – when he suddenly stopped and shivered. A cold wind had come through the open door. Indeed, the wind had pushed the door open as if it sought capitulation. It blew dust around the barn roughly and then, set upon the loosely stacked hay, rushing about and throwing it against the wall. Joe had looked up momentarily; shivered again; and went to close the stable door. 'RC' heard him say,

"Unusual cool fo' dis time uh yeaah. The hawk's comin'. Colder than a 'dammit' at a church picnic. You best look fo' a wahm spot, son."

With some effort, Joe had forced the door shut. After doing so, he looked upwards momentarily; and stared in the air as if something had startled him. Then, suddenly – like a window whose weights snap - he collapsed to the floor.

'RC' had bent down and shook the old man by the shoulder. But there was no movement. He jumped up and tried to budge the heavy door - but could not move it. Then he started screaming for help. Inside the stable, the horses whinnied, kicked and cowered in a corner. They seemed aware of something that the boy could not see.

Then 'RC' had heard it. The wind moved more forcefully through the stable. It was as if robbing the breath from something that had been living, had made it stronger. Nearby and on a rafter, a barn owl hunched and straightened its back, rocking back and forth. It seemed to dance to a quiet dirge; and made hissing sounds as if to commemorate the passing of a soul.

'RC' looked down again at the still form of Joe Jefferson. Then pressing his face to the glass – 'RC' began to scream and cry uncontrollably. He pounded the stable window until the small glass broke. Through the cracked glass, he saw a 'cross fox' running away. It looked back only once before it disappeared into a thicket of mist. The stable had become as cold as a refrigerator.

In the darkest corner, he could hear the wind moving its large bulk around. Scratching out a space for itself, it seemed to growl quietly – as if trifling with prey; and deciding whether or not to move on in its hunt.

It was many hours later before Trudence Jefferson and her son 'Angus' had broken through the door. It was supper time and they had come looking for 'Old Joe'. They discovered the body on the floor. After much screaming and crying, they had heard a muffled sound; and found 'RC' burrowed deep in the hay in a far corner of the stable. He was shivering, overcome with despair; and drenched in weariness. Trudence Jefferson had directed her son to take the traumatized 'RC' out of the stable.

Far from grateful, the frantic boy had bit hard into the hand that was trying to help him. Thirteen stitches and numerous apologies later, things were finally better. But Trudence Jefferson had lost the love of her life - and her son, Angus, had a lifetime scar. 'RC' became known locally as "the wild boy".

'RC' shook his head. His selfish stomach would not allow him to focus on the loss and lament of a close friend. Darkness had adeptly maneuvered into place; and he felt hungry. The smoky fires of Indians were in the starlit sky. The burnished moon glowed like a giant ember ascending from the water.

He had left the country, his home, and its people long ago...but shame and memories had traveled with him. He still remembered the discussion with 'Old Joe' about fingernails. And he remembered a girl who had once held his thoughts so deeply.

He regretted having lost contact with the family. Trudence Jefferson, her son, Angus, and daughter, Earnestine clung like fruit that would never ripen. They were memories clinging to some nameless tree that he had walked past in his own journey from forest to savannah.

He turned away from the ocean and walked down the beach toward a nearby dune that he knew would lead him to shelter and food - and hoped he would find sustenance in both. And as he did so, he looked back at the moon ascending over the water; and thought of a lost love and mentor. Despair and doubt fell on him like age. He had let one go and another had been 'taken' from him. Shouting as loudly as he could - he asked the moon to leave.

PART III

HALF MOON

ANNA

She sat on the porch swing admiring the night sky and looking at an unfinished moon. Was it a part of the 'Fish Moon' her grandmother had once spoken of? The memory of being with 'Ba Noi' under a similar moon and watching men come back to the village with their catch over their shoulders – made her heart content, much like the dance of a slow waltz. She had forgotten much of her past, but a set of bamboo chimes 'tinkling' invisibly in a dark corner of the porch had entreated old memories this evening.

And she dreamed of a passionate, awkward boy whom she had once met in school. She could remember only a little of the poetry they had once spent hours reciting. She wondered if he too might be looking at the moon.

'Beaumont', her cat, had curled up beside her on the swing and was purring. Occasionally he would let out a soft 'meow'. Anna thought his calls sounded curiously egocentric. The large cat had the voice of a kitten; and he always seemed to be saying "Me! Me! Me!" Beaumont basked in her attention; and she willingly obliged. The cat only wanted to eat, and have his stomach rubbed.

'Why couldn't people be that easy?' she mused; as she stroked him distractedly.

It was one of those rare nights that mended life - pleasantly temperate with a faint breeze that blew - just enough to keep the gnats and early mosquitoes away. The fireflies were holding a light show. The trees of a nearby ridge lit up with their erratic explosions and resembled 'heat lightning'. She could imagine Tchaikovsky composing his music to their energy. Anna turned away from the sky for a moment and stared out at the garden. She could just see the heads of some late-blooming yellow spring flowers whose bulbs she had planted two seasons ago. They glowed faintly under the moonlight like a quorum of light-haired fairies who were deliberating about the various plants they might wear to conceal themselves. Just then, a beautifully intense star caught her attention. She wondered what it was - and was pulled to identify it.

Her eyes were brown, but seemed to hold the twilight like an ember - as if the light had found a home. She was slender. Her long dark hair undulated in the soft breeze and seemed to become part of the night sky. It framed her face – a face that was just barely visible under the light of the moon. Sitting on the swing with the advancing night, Anna seemed to be a mirror to the sky as if the sky's reflection had somehow been caught over water. She had a warm temperament that belied an ability to slice through most arrogance or absurdity; and her perception was venerably keen. But she was also fun-loving; and had a laugh that would manifest itself most unexpectedly - much like the tapping of some wild bird in quiet woods. Many might walk past her...never noticing her simple resplendency.

But Anna was not fully happy. She felt incomplete, for she did not possess that ancient tool that could untangle a knotted life. Love had managed to evade her watchful eye. Frustrated by the boy whom she had 'lost', for a time she considered a life with the church. It was hardly a derivative thought - rather it had been sown by the woman who had adopted her. She had tried that life briefly; but the light streaming through church windows did not pull her into solitude. Instead it had reinvigorated her intensity to experience a more corporeal existence. The light seemed to seek her shelter and ardent disposition. Indeed, Anna seemed to be able to bend any light or situation like a prism – revealing the intensity of colors. The light sought her as a complement – others sought her company...but just her company.

Now a big cat named Beaumont lavished in her attention. She stroked his back until he rolled over. Then she rubbed his tummy. He did not deny or conceal his mass but seemed immensely proud of it. However, something seemed to distract him tonight. Anna followed his line of vision. It seemed to rest on the same bright star that she had noticed earlier. Though she knew that she would have to endure the cat's resentful stare she felt compelled to find a star chart.

She had been able to identify and make basic associations in the stellar neighborhood - but she was really quite a novice; and wished to learn more. For example, she knew that the two outermost stars of the bowl of the 'Big Dipper' pointed to Polaris, the 'North Star'. She could identify Arcturus of the constellation Bootes, the brightest star in the northern celestial hemisphere. And Orion's Belt was always an 'easy find' with its three stars; Alnitak, Alnilam and Mintaka that made up the 'belt'. And, of course, there were the brightest visible stars known in astronomy - the Pleiades or Seven Sisters. But, this small star had caught her attention. Like any child – it needed a name; and she was bent on finding one for it. She scooted away gently from Beaumont and his 'largesse'; and tip-toed toward the screen door that led to the inside of the house.

To her, the bright star she and Beaumont had noticed seemed like an orphan. She felt compelled to identify it before an errant cloud moving through the sky concealed the little star forever. She entered the house, making her way through darkness to the bedroom. Opening a drawer, she searched through the collection of objects that had been thrown into a 'junk drawer' until she felt a thin disk shaped object. She recognized the glowing object immediately as the star chart she had been seeking. Savvy vendors had painted it with a photo luminescent pigment. Marketing had made them aware that not everyone was a millennialist with a phone 'app' - some still liked to hold something more physical in their hands.

As she headed back toward the front porch, she briefly caught sight of the moon through the nearby window. The silhouette of a large bird seemed to float over the face of it. No doubt, a late-feeding heron was heading for its rookery.

She continued to stumble through the house. Turning on a light would have been easy, but she liked the faint light of the night sky; and did not want her eyes to have to readjust when she reached the outside. After nearly toppling over a photograph on a nearby desk and stubbing her toe on a bag of garbage that had made its way a little closer to the outdoor can, she found the screen door to the porch. She opened and closed the door gently so as not to disturb the sleeping Beaumont. But the cat opened one eye ever so lazily; and watched Anna walk into the open yard. He seemed to know what she was doing; and nonchalantly agreed with her quest.

Competition for brilliance was stiff. She knew that she must find just the right spot on the lawn to afford her the best view. For, though the plethora of modern lighting had not diminished the beauty of the night sky; it had brushed it to the side, like a theater understudy. After a few moments of futility, she realized that the glare of the streetlights was too intense. There was only one thing to do - she must ascend the hill next to her neighbors, the Gregors. At the top of the hill she might gain a more unobstructed view of the dark sacred night.

Hesitating slightly, she walked over to the hill to begin her ascent. She gazed skyward noticing how – as she climbed the hill - the black dome above her seemed to illuminate ever so slightly. It was as if bands of rice lights had been gathering power all day and were now becoming dimly apparent. The stars seemed to instigate festivity and interrupt the dark silence with exclamation. She stopped midway up the hill just to glance homeward. Beaumont was still curled up in the swing. She could just make out his comfortable bulk, courtesy of a nearby street lamp.

The hill was a soft, loamy relief to her bare feet. She gazed at the gallery of hills, coves, and structures below; and realized that she had never thought about how incredible the view might be from her neighbors' property. Just below were a few small tree stumps – remnants of a clearing. The stumps had rounded out from weather. Their curious pointy tops gave them the appearance of gnomes in hats – gnomes who had come out of hiding and were also admiring the view. She thought once more of a young man that she had known in school; and the poem that they had once practiced together.

J'aime le son du cor, le soir, au fond des bois,
Soit qu'il chante les pleurs de la bich aux bois,
Ou l'adieu du chasseur que l'echo faible accueille,
Et que le vent du nord porte de feuille en feuille.

She marveled that she remembered any of Alfred de Comte Vigny's poem; and found it curious that she remembered it at that moment - or that she had any memory of the young man. The breeze roamed playfully about her. It induced her to relax in the midst of her benevolent trespass; and she wished that the young man she once knew - was with her now. They might practice poetry again from ancient tomes; and share in each others intimacy one more time. How she missed that tender time; and wondered what had brought her to where she now found herself.

At the top of the hill, she stopped. The climb had been a pleasant exertion. She sat in the lush grass and looked up at the sky. Almost immediately she was able to see the bright asterism known as 'the Teapot'. 'Scorpius' was to its west and 'Capricornus' to its east. The constellation, Sagittarius, was pointing his bow as if to secure the beauty of the night. Meanwhile the constellation Leo rested comfortably in repose and close to the constellation Virgo. She followed the arc of Arcturus and found the 'orphan star' in the constellation Virgo. Pleased that it rested brightly in her zodiacal constellation, she quickly managed to identify it as Spica. Momentarily she gazed at it – comfortable that it now felt less like an orphan; and that its name made it familiar.

But, really - her thoughts were about a boy who had captured her attention a few nights before. His name was Ezekiel – a name that meant 'shooting star'. She wondered how he was; and hoped to see him soon. He would help her forget the emptiness that she felt. And she would forget the prosaic thoughts of a young man that she once knew as 'RC'; and with whom she had once spent hours reciting poetry. And she thought of her mother – the woman who had adopted her – and the long journey she had made from the foot of the great bamboo. ...Then she wondered if the moon held a love in its light.

GREGORS

Though she admired the view; and had identified the small star that caught her attention, Anna was disappointed that there was no breeze at the top of the hill. It was as if the wind had chosen not to follow – and seemed peculiar to her.

She stood in the darkness near an imposing house on which she had never really focused. Artificial light oozed from one of the rooms of the Gregors' house - a room that she rapidly realized must be her neighbor's bedroom. She immediately felt awkward and out of place. How could she have put herself in such a position at this time of night?

Though drawn to the light, conflicting emotions now left her in a state of paralysis. After sensible thoughts had forged consensus, she believed the most prudent action was to sit on a nearby clump of grass; pull out the star chart; and quietly continue her star-gazing activities. She would wait for the light to go out and then pick her way back down the hill as quietly as she could – praying that there might be no unforeseen 'sentinel' to alert the Gregors of the mistaken intrusion.

She shifted uncomfortably on the soft lawn and waited. After a few minutes and various small rotations of the star chart she could no longer remain motionless. She lay back on the grass staring up at the quarter moon – tired and wishing she could disappear.

Quiet voices inside had escalated slightly; and there was a faint scent that poured from the open window. It wafted about on the breeze – at first, seeming a familiar wildflower. But the scent gained in intensity like that of an overly vigorous potpourri that had been introduced to suppress any hint of unseemliness. After a few minutes of assault on her senses, she found the scent overly sweet and disagreeable.

The voices inside the house became louder. Her desire to star gaze had unwittingly left her in a state of transgression; and she dared not move.

"I like your new perfume, darlin'.... Smells awful purty......"

She unwillingly leaned into the conversation, wishing she was not there – and now realized from where the overpowering fragrance came. The light from the Gregor's bedroom was hard and dim; and the voices were becoming mean. Anna burrowed further down into the grass. The conversation from the Gregor's bedroom continued.

"I told you not to do it! But, no – you had to be greedy! And don't try changing the subject by talkin' about my perfume!"

"Is that perfume you got on what they call that 'Morning Glory' stuff?"

"Shut-up, 'Rog'!"

"You smell a little like a 'sweet tater' - you know morning glories and 'sweet taters' are in the same family, darlin'."

"I don't care," was the repetitive and unrehearsed reply.

"Now, calm down, darlin'…just tryin' to tell you that you smell good."

Anna cowered in the grass – realizing why she tried to avoid becoming familiar with her neighbors. What could have possibly drawn the two of them together? The husband was a brutishly large man who needed a better razor. Reasoning and friendship seemed vaporous concepts to him; and ambition was always just a 'swallow' away. Gregor seemed to relish in the frustration he caused others. Displeasure seemed to be a condiment that he sprinkled on things to make them more palatable. Ms. Gregor was clean and more educated – a small, sturdy, tough-looking woman who had a drawn prettiness which did not seem authentic. She now projected her voice to a shout - as was her convention when the couple was together.

"The perfume I'm wearin' is called 'Lilac Serenity'!"

Then, as if she was aware that her tone was in contravention to the product name, she lowered her voice.

"What the hell are these damn flowers you brought home to me?"

"Just a few daffodils, my love…"

"Yeah, well they look 'picked'; and unless they jump in a vase and water themselves, they ain't gonna be around much longer!"

He caressed the corner of her ear. It usually 'drove her crazy'. But she was already crazy; and so he withdrew his hand quickly – in no mood for a short trip.

"I ain't no green queen, Rog. And don't bring me anymore of these things unless they're tied up in dollar bills."

Anna felt the wind pick up. She could see clouds 'milling about' as if they were bent on concealing all starlight. She wondered how much longer she could endure being on the hill; and listening to their conversation.

Gregor guffawed. "LORD, HONEY! Take off your Birkenstocks - you scarin' me! And while you' at it - you can remove anything else…"

"Very funny, Rog'! Christ! Shut the window- will you? The wind is kickin'up."

Roger Gregor liked the cold breeze. Instead, he put his finger in his nose. The flickering light of the bedroom made him look like a child who was mining for something.

"You're a fake, Rog?" and she hardened her eyes.

He pulled his finger out of his nose and replied calmly, "Not a fake, darlin', just an 'entremanure'...."

"Listen, Rog - I don't mind fake, and if you want to call yourself an 'entrepreneur', that's fine with me. But just out of curiosity what's the difference between what you call an 'entrepreneur' and what I call a 'fake'?"?

The light flickered – the wind was in a state of agitation. It seemed to be tossing about nearby electric lines.

"Money, honey..." He grinned in honesty that was rare and usually highlighted by his yellow dentifrice.

Ms. Gregor straightened suddenly; and appeared to perk up. She was beginning to feel slightly amorous at the mention of currency.

"I still don't understand why you have to kill those animals, Rog – they say some of them are rare. Police are gonna be all over you? I don't mind the greed as much as I mind the stupidity." She slammed shut the book that she had been reading.

Roger Gregor hated revisiting old arguments. "Ain't nothin' but a stupid animal! Hell, there's probably tons more out there just like it." It was now he who had become excitable.

"Anyway...I ain't gonna lose any sleep over a bit of spilled blood. You gotta take - to get." He abruptly rose from the bed; and made his way over to the window, as if he was considering smashing it.

"It's illegal, for Christ sake! You know that!" She turned away from him and roughly tugged her dressing gown over her shoulders. She felt cold again.

"Shhhhhh! Nawww - now it ain't illegal, honey. It's all in how you define it. We just change the name of the species...make it a bit more 'specialized'. Done named one of them things after a Congressman's wife," he beamed.

"I heard about what you did for that woman! And what about the Congressman... is he 'on sabbatical'...thought he was representin' us?"

"You're jumpin' to conclusions again, honey. We didn't do nothin' wrong by killin' one a' them animals. Sides – made her feel like she owned the damn thing. It's all about ownership. The science ain't that exact. You know they's splittin' hairs on species identification these days. Got one bunch of wolves that's exactly like the other bunch 'cept it's in a different location. That don't make it different. They's also namin' fish as different species even thought they start out in the same waters and one is a slightly different color than the other. Look at the salmon. Damn thing looks totally different depending on the time of its life!"

"You knew it was wrong, Roger! And you coulda' got me in trouble!"

Suddenly she reached over to the nightstand for a black and red afghan that she had been knitting. Her brightly painted nails nimbly moved through the yarn like she was building a web.

"You fool - I got to think about how I look. You could have caused me a lot of trouble at work!"

"So I did it for money...ain't ever bothered you before. A congressman wants to shoot somethin' different is all. Ain't that much different than golf... just a game. Maybe we name a species a slightly new name so they can cross if off a list. Bit a heaven in findin' somethin' new and havin' it named after 'yerself'. Tree huggers defining things so narrowly - your toenail could be endangered! Why should they 'play God'?! It ain't religion – just commerce."

"Did you ever stop to think that God doesn't have to 'play' anything', 'Rog'? Maybe you're trying too hard to be something you don't need to be. Besides, the news says that - just a few strands of DNA - we all could be something else." Then, she extended her leg suggestively; and worked the cream into her calves. "Maybe we're all just part of a big puzzle that fits together - and falls apart – if we mess with it."

"Commerce is commerce, darlin'. Green ain't ever bothered you before."

"I like a crisp salad – if that's what you're saying."

"Now, honey, I believe you know what I'm sayin'. I'm just providin' a service...and makin' a little cash on the side."

"Do you believe in anything, 'Rog'?!"

"Just trolls under bridges..."

"Oh, shut up! You must have been a lawyer in a former life."

"Well, if you're askin' me all serious, darlin'...I guess I believe we weren't put on this planet with a thinkin' brain just to accept everything the way it is. Maybe this is purgatory and He put us here to figure a way around it. The scriptures say he done made us in his own image. Maybe he wants us to figure out how to change things. Maybe this is just our final test before becomin' gods ourselves. Maybe he done made riddles on this earth for us to figure out so we become more like him. We'll be second in command in the kingdom - know what I mean?"

"That doesn't sound like God talking. You're sounding like those 'tree huggers' you don't like... or somethin' else!"

The wind had pushed clouds across the moon. Gregor's wife felt the chill and ordered her husband to close the window. Meanwhile she continued to apply cream to herself. Roger Gregor begrudgingly strolled over to the window hoping it would buy her favor. He briefly looked out the window and down the long hill to the town below; and wondered what else might be there for the taking. Then he thought of the hundreds of feet that he once had behind him under his command. The wind crept in. It seemed to pander about him.

Anna could see the shadow of the large man framed by the window in the hard light. She sank down further into the landscape trying not to breathe – hoping that he had not seen her and that she could soon descend the hill safely. The baying of a distant hound momentarily arrested Gregor's attention and he panned the nearby horizon. Anna trembled like a rabbit in the grass.

Gregor slowly closed the window. Content that nothing outside was amiss - he left it open just a crack. He turned and sauntered to the side of the bed, quietly plotting the next step in what he hoped would be conquest. Did you know that you can get a 'mean' $2000 bucks for a bontebok? Looks real good mounted on the wall!"

"I don't give a crap," his wife responded. He knew she was lying.

"Two thousand bucks can buy a good-lookin' stone for that cute little hand a' yours."

He reached over to the nightstand on his side of the bed; opened a drawer; and pulled out a list. There were smudges up and down the list – some from dirt and some from blood. He put on a pair of reading glasses and began to study it, trying to appear erudite and coyly acting disinterested in her.

"This here's put out by Safari United. Look at all these animals. I shot about half of them. Hell, I shoot 'em for those rich 'wannabe-hunter' Congressmen that still want to show their wives they 'got something'. On paper, I let them say they 'took it'; and we gets it mounted somewhere. I show 'em which port to bring it in and do everything except show them how to wipe their butts. It's all about commerce, darlin'.

Got a couple different goats on this list – mountain goats, of course...got a bontebok, some impalas, couple different types of gazelles.... You name it we got it. We'd like to put a lion, an elephant an' a rhino on it eventually – but we gotta figure a way to make it lucrative enough to keep the money coming. You know – folks gotta be willing to take the risk and plunk down the bucks. Gotta be willing to hear animal rights groups screamin' all that psycho-babble crap about animals havin' souls. We just conservationists is all. Local folks just as soon kill them animals as look at 'em. Ya' only care about animals havin' souls...if you got a full belly. I got plans to put a lot more 'types' of animals on this here list."

"Yeah...well I'm looking into my crystal ball – and I see you doin' 'The Jailhouse Rock'. She squirted some more cream and rubbed it into her hands. "These 'animal welfare' types, as you call 'em, are going to catch you one day – and I don't think I can stand it."

"You worry too much, darlin' - I say feed em to the sharks! Let's see whose 'welfare' they believe in then."

Cynthia Gregor dropped the afghan she had been working on; and nonchalantly rubbed more cream into one of her legs. Gregor reached out and flicked off the light.

"I hope you die and come back as a cockroach!" She smirked and then turned the light back on.

Gregor turned the light off again.

"Besides...my list ain't that much different than them 'bird-watchin' lists. I mean...what's the point in that?! Think anybody's gonna care if someone saw 200 different birds? I know I sure wouldn't!"

She turned to him in disbelief.

"What are you talking about?! There's a world of difference between your list and bird watching lists! You ain't killin' the birds! You're just markin down the ones you've seen. People come from all over the world to do that. That's commerce too! Some think that...whadda you call it...'Ivory-Bill Woodpecker', is still around. I saw them discussing it on t.v.!"

"Shoot, honey! That's just porch-sittin biology. They sure as hell won't find any a' them things...unless we create it again."

"How do you know that, Rog? You been all over the Southern swamps!? Besides I think it'd be kind of neat if they did find one."

"Cynthia, they won't find one – and that's that. But I wouldn't mind 'finding' something that's been a little rare lately." His fingers were dabbling around the covers and had made their way over to her.

She smacked his hand and angrily switched on the light again, grabbing one of the books that she kept on the nightstand. They were kept there as a defense against such unwanted advances. She opened the book randomly and pretended to read.

Roger Gregor sighed loudly – a fortress of books was something he hadn't counted on. Frustrated, he started a slow rant,

"This whole endangered species stuff is over-rated. I don't care about some stupid woodpecker. Species been dyin' all the time. We don't care when an asteroid knocks 'em out. We don't care when they kill off each other. Man woulda' been endangered too - if we hadn't used our brains. We even listin' flies these days."

"Rog - why don't you just stop your travelin'...stay home...and shoot a turkey? At least you wouldn't get in trouble - and we could eat it!" She was tired of his rambling complaint.

Gregor was almost contrite in his tone. "Now, Cynthia, you just don't understand. Some of these area's are loaded with history and got some damn excitin' wildlife for the takin'. That's why I travel. I done hunted almost ever'thing on the Safaris Unlimited list - they almost run out of species for me to kill. I'm in top standing. The big fellas jus' wanna have the same opportunity as a real hunter. So I travel; grease some palms; and then make me some extra money. Big whigs got lots a' money to give up – and I'm just here for them."

"Regular 'Robin Hood' – aren't you? Can't you guys just 'press flowers'? It'd be a lot less risky and expensive."

"I gotta zoology degree – just name somethin slightly different; show 'em you got a long list a' qualifications to do it – and let the money flow! Does it really matter?"

"What is it with you men - and hunting?"

Cynthia Gregor had blurted it out before she knew it. The polarity of the sexes related to hunting seemed striking - she wondered if 'pursuit' and 'conquest' were written into a man's DNA. Trying to vanquish any such difference between the sexes, Roger Gregor responded.

"Au contraire...women hunters are beginning to increase in number and some of 'em can shoot as well as any man. We're an equal opportunity sport - know what I mean?"

Outside the wind had pushed in a watery paste of clouds. As if by design, they lightly smeared the face of the starry sky. Anna had heard enough; and decided to begin her descent.

Cynthia Gregor decided to change the subject. "If it gets any cooler out there, you're gonna have to scrape ice off the car for me, tomorrow."

Gregor brushed her leg longingly with his hairy fingers. She jerked it away. "I'm tired of your grabbing - let's go to sleep."

"Yep, next stop - probably be Turkey. See if I can organize a hunt over in the Ottoman Empire....'"

She looked at him disinterestedly. "You want Chinese carry-out tomorrow night?"

He rose up from the bed. He was suddenly hungry and considering a trip to the kitchen.

"Where are you going'?"

He didn't respond to her question.

Outside Anna had begun to climb quietly down the hill. Halfway down, the wind greeted her like a cool disciple. She glanced up at the sky to see if a storm was coming; and then, hunched over - hanging close to the ground and wishing she had dressed more warmly.

Inside the Gregor house, Cynthia was remembering how sweet manipulation could be -and that she was out of practice. She retrieved a Bible from under the pile of books that she kept on the nightstand. Then, blowing briefly on her nails, said,

"I need to read a verse or two before I go to sleep, Rog. You don't mind do you?"

"Not at all, darlin'...virtue can be excitin' in a woman."

She suddenly slammed the Bible down hard on the ground, killing a moth that had made its way into the room. Then - picking the book back up again - flicked off the moth's remains with her hard nails. She looked at Roger Gregor and said sweetly,

"I read somewhere that the incidents of giving birth in water are going up, Roger..."

She knew exactly where to hit him.

"I thought I told you not to bring that up," he snarled.

"Roger, your mother couldn't help it. God rest her soul, maybe she'd like some of those daffodils you brought me. You could lay em' on her stone. She was just tryin' to get baptized. You know as well as I do that's the way they used to do it in those days. Take you down to the river and dunk you. She couldn't help the fact that you needed to come slidin' out at that time. Besides she's gone now."

This was her wild card. She could control him so easily. She knew the memories were always fresh; and that the pain could be reincarnated at any time. Gregor had shared the story in an intimate moment – but preferred it to be entombed in his past. Now, the story distinguished itself whenever Cynthia Gregor chose.

His mother's pains had come earlier than expected. It had secretly been her intention to dispose of the baby after birthing it - but her father had insisted that she be baptized that weekend. When immersed in the cold river, the contractions had come early. The baby floated to the surface before the young mother. A horrified minister had pulled the screaming child out of the water. But before he could attend to the young woman, the father had rushed in and pushed his daughter deep into the water – until there was no more breath.

A strong current had carried Gregor's mother downstream. When finally found, the body had become white as an alabaster statue – with vitreous eyes that seemed to look through a man she had once loved. The father of the baby – and the father of the mother - had been one and the same. Roger Gregor had grown up tough and mean – and the 'baby' within him had long-since died.

Suddenly, he shot up from the bed and left angrily. When he returned from the bathroom, she could see that she had him where she wanted him. She loosened a couple of the buttons of her nightgown; and he began to blubber. Then she said,

"A few more 'nips and tucks'; and I'll be perfect, darling." And she extended one of her long legs. Gregor was obsequious in his appreciation. But the quiet of the night was suddenly punctuated by the rapid burst of a little dog who had been disturbed.

"Roger! Go see what's got 'Buster' so upset…it was the perfect ploy – her fortress had been rebuilt…and she didn't even need a book.

"Awww HELL, Cynthia!"

Anna was home on her front porch now; and aware of the dog's yapping. Her stomach was upset. The Gregor's conversation had left her unhappy and scared. Beaumont, the cat, was still on the porch swing. He lazily extended his paw as if to comfort, but the meanness she had had heard on the hill had seeped into her. And - though she understood the foundation of its hard shine - its luster was sickeningly superficial. She decided to focus instead on the boy whom she would see the next day. His embrace would be panacea.

Anna gazed up at the little star that had prompted her ascent. The dog was still barking and seemed to be making enough noise for two or three. She ignored the noise and continued to look at the heavens. The small star, Spica, seemed to gaze at her lovingly. She had named the orphan. A blue-white 1st-magnitude star about 230 light years away, it floated comfortably near Virgo's belly - signaling the birth of a late spring.

Somewhere on a high and warm sunny ridge the buds of tree were beginning to swell. The resinous foliage of the trees would be shaped by the wind. But now, the wind blew snow dust away that seemed to sparkle in the half-mooned light; and it whispered to awaken animals that were in their comfortable lairs.

Far below, Anna stared deep into the funnel of a bright daffodil that she had plucked by the house. Its light made her happy and seemed to swirl about like a cosmic vortex. She fell asleep - dreaming about the light in the face of a boy she once knew…and not fully understanding that she had heard a gluttonous secret.

PART IV

THREE QUARTER
MOON

DIFFERENT TRACKS

Bob, the Indian, sat on the ground looking up at the trees and listening to the whispering wind. He was grateful to the trees for it was only with their help that anyone could occasionally know the wind's complicated language. But the trees spoke in a cadence that most men could not understand; because, for the trees, time moved much more slowly.

Long ago and through centuries of discussions, the wind had forged an agreement with the old souls of the earth. The trees had agreed that they would interpret the wind as it moved through them. But the trees were cautious beings. The wind's secrets could only be known by those who respected and were willing to listen to the voices of others. It was the only agreement they would have with the wind; and that agreement had lasted for millennia.

So today, Bob listened to the voice of the wind - as interpreted by the trees. The trees spoke of him. They had heard that he had floated on the wind in a dream state; and had seen many things. They laughed among themselves about his 'dream' - and a journey he had once said he would soon take. Though Bob had spoken of the journey years ago in the Sandhills, the trees had good memories and strong, invisible lines of communication. In 'tree time', it seemed his conversation with Louise had just occurred.

In the space of that time, the boy whom Bob had seen in his dream – the boy in the sleeping bag – had grown older. He had become a young man. And the time the boy had spent on the beach – when he discovered the bottle with the verse rolled up inside of it – had passed as quickly to the trees...as smoke might seem to vanish in front of us.

The wind discussed all of this and the trees translated it. The trees spoke of how quickly men seemed to age; and how men did nothing to assist time in its passing. It amused them greatly; and was an ancient joke. For a long time, Bob smiled at their humor knowing that the trees would scarcely notice.

Finally, he looked away from them; and over to Rowan Chamberlain, who people called, 'RC' – and who he recognized immediately from his 'dream'. Years ago, and in that dream, the wind had introduced him to the young boy in the sleeping bag; and the wind had allowed that they would share many conversations and fires...and something about a great cat holding a mystery within its maw. Then, the trees silently chuckled at Bob's recollection, his sense of time – and indeed, wondered why men think that there are separate things called 'dream' and 'reality'.

'RC's time at the beach had long since passed.

His 'sabbatical' had ended and he had returned to employment. Those he worked with had decided he was ready for an assignment; and had partnered him with a native man who appeared to be eccentric – though knowledgeable. It didn't matter to 'RC' that Bob was native; and he didn't care what tribe he claimed. 'RC' was emotionally numb. But he could not ignore Bob's penetrating stare. Both had taken the job for money; but 'RC' observed that Bob's fixed gaze did not seem 'legal' or 'tender'. And he wondered if the native might not be somewhat 'calculating'.

Bob suddenly looked away from 'RC' and up to the sky. He thought of Louise; how he missed the taste of her homemade pot liquor. He thought of their discussion related to his dream and the journey he would take. He missed her; and wondered what she might be doing. And he reflected once more about the powerful wind that had blown open the door to their 'soddie' all those years ago. He felt old; and knew that the trees would find such a thought - comical.

'RC', in turn, decided to ignore Bob. The main office had put them together. In his cynicism, he wondered if the office did not expect failure. Perhaps, the temporary inconvenience of the pairing was advantageous to management - a way to remove two teetering personalities during a probationary period.

The job involved tracking and hunting. Though his rural background had initiated him to both jobs, neither had commended themselves to him. They were seeking a great cat – 'felis concolor', more commonly know as a mountain lion. This one had killed a jogger.

His father had encouraged 'RC' to hunt; and he had never learned to fully appreciate the activity. By 'RC's standards, it ruined an otherwise good day in the woods. But the participation had made him strong and 'outdoorsy'; and had given him the advantage he needed to procure his current employment. More importantly the modicum of 'bonding' that had occurred during such father-son outings were sparse memories he leaned upon.

But now, he was on a tracking/hunting assignment with a man whom he was not sure that he fully trusted. Their assignment was to track and capture the great mountain lion that had killed a jogger - a mother of two. As if some sort of drawbridge had been let down, his thoughts seemed like weary soldiers marching in darkness over murky water to confront a faceless specter. He wondered if the performance of ordinary men and women facing their destinies might be the only meaning in an otherwise unexplainable and meaningless human calendar that we called 'life'.

Then – in a rare self-examination of his egocentricity - he questioned whether animals might have the same feelings. Were they any less? There was something haunting in the cry of an owl. Where did life flee? And who had the right to take it? Did purpose make killing just? Did survival? Did prayer? Did might? Could anything survive without red being spattered across its mouth? ....Some said that owls carried the souls of the dead.

After a few minutes of mental genuflecting, the questions seemed unanswerable and their origins indecipherable. He dismissed the thoughts as silly; and they were replaced with early memories.

The thought of his first deer hunt seemed distant. The animal had separated from the woods quietly as light moves across land. Then it was before them – grass in motion, large eyes and ears ever wary. It sniffed for 'fingerprints' in the wind - its antlers like winter branches. Its fur caught the morning light and looked like the color of fallen leaves. The rock-shard hooves made less noise than a canoe in water. He had marveled at the grace and brawn of the deer. Who had 'authorized' this beautiful beastly shape? Was it a consciously constructed bauble meant to decorate some dull place? This son of the woods, this faun of myth…Artiodactyla cervidae… had thrown down its gauntlet as if to say,

"Hunt me!" And I will haunt you. And when you are at last gone – I will vault over you. Ours hooves will be the last thunder that you hear."

It shook 'RC'; and caused him to marvel whether such thoughts were his – or spawned by something greater. Were they his manifestations? Or were they filtered for him? And, once more, he remembered the verse he had found in the bottle and wondered about the girl who had once helped him see the beauty and poetry of things.

Now, the memories of that first hunt began to seep in to him. His father and he were dressed in 'camouflage'. He saw his father raise the gun slowly. He sighted the animal and aimed carefully. It was as if the buck – like many things – knew that death was about. It raised its head for an instant, knowing that it was too late. Its energy would be transferred elsewhere. There was the thunder of the gun and a god's decision to take the animal away. The deer slumped back and then fell over. A bullet had passed through; and grabbed life as quickly as a pickpocket. His father looked victorious – but only for a moment. He had seen 'RC's face. The boy was frowning. He was angry and told his father that 'he'd rather be stalking a wild 'Twinkie'.

His father had explained that hunting made the species strong. 'RC' could not reconcile the explanation. Wolves chased and culled the weak. His father and he - on the other hand - had not sought the animals out of such a sixth sense. The deer had wondered into their sight; and the killing seemed random. It seemed an opportunistic killing; and the choreography of its death, too ordinary when juxtaposed to its majesty. He immediately threw down his gun. Though he could be won over easily by a bucket of fried chicken – he would not be 'shammed' by such an easy explanation or the lie behind it.

"Hey man! What the hell?! You eat some stale beans? You're dreamin' too much!"

It was the native 'guide'. 'RC' had heard that the man's last assignment had been to participate in a 'bird count'. It caused him to speculate about the native's qualifications. His words dribbled out like waste,

"Huhn?! What?"

"I said not too much, dude – too much dreamin'...you know...bad for sex!" And then he winked.

"But it's only our first date..." 'RC' retorted.

Bob guffawed.

"You're dreaming too much. Save that for the evening when the 'wakan oyohe' [4] are roamin' about..."

"...Yeah, whatever..."

'RC' thought about their assignment. A mountain lion had killed a thirty-five year old mother of two. The woman had gone for a twilight jog in the remote hill country. He knew the cat had stuffed itself, starting first with the stomach, intestines and internal organs. The body they found had been a bloody mess – and the face unrecognizable. The lion had probably buried the remainder of its prey somewhere nearby its lair – covering it with brush and leaves. It must have kits to feed.

'RC' stared at a blob of camp food trying to decide if he could eat it; and felt resentful that his familiarity with hunting – had led him to a job that he could barely stomach. Then he reflected how easy it was to play a philosopher when he had not experienced the terror of an eviscerating death at the hand of another animal.

He pulled his coat up around his neck; and wondered at the unpredictable beauty and chaotic horror of nature.

---

4   Lakotah – 'evil spirits'

IF YOU LISTEN

Day had smashed into evening. Before 'RC' could dwell on any more morose thoughts, the stars had popped out; and distracted him into happiness. It was the first day and night together on the trail with the native guide. 'Bob' seemed almost bumbling in his approach to things; and that did not fit within 'RC's stereotype. He had assured 'RC' that they were closing in on the great cat ...but lost the tracks in the middle of the bush. The man seemed confused; and suddenly announced that it was time to stop and set up camp. He would build a fire.

'RC' watched as Bob unpacked; disappeared – and then, miraculously appeared with a bundle of wood in his arms. Within seconds he had built an explosive fire. Then, he lit some fragrant rolled up leaves and walked the perimeter of the camp swinging the burning bundle around him and making low chants. When the sagebrush had burned down practically to the nubs of his fingers, he threw it into the fire and watched sparks shoot about wildly. He said,

"Time to read..."

'RC' had barely finished unrolling his camp bedding. He yanked his head sideways to stare at the Indian. It had been a long day of disappointments and he was very tired. He countered,

"Read? What do you mean 'read'?!"

Bob cocked his head slightly to listen to the baying of distant coyotes; and then simply said.

"The fire..."

The wind – as if in agreement – blew across the embers. It caused a crackling combustion; and the resulting firelight threw long shadows about the camp.

'RC' shook his head, visibly upset at having been placed with someone who was inept. Then, he struggled to let the words escape from him.

"I suppose this has something to do with the cat and its victim."

Without missing a beat, Bob responded.

"Absolutely nothing..." and he vigorously prodded the fire with a stick.

He found the response to be frustrating and yet, strangely literal and amusing. There was a cacophony of evening sounds. The wind pushed through the trees. It sounded a bit like waves; and caused 'RC' to reminisce briefly about his time on the beach. The sudden 'cawing' sound of a night bird caused his heart to skip.

He watched the fire burn down. The native man had put a can of opened beef stew at the edge of the coals. Within seconds it was bubbling; and the scent had overtaken them.

The light reflected off some fishing lures that Bob had tacked to one side of a knapsack. They shimmered like they were swimming through air. Then he opened up a bottle of fizzy "Root Beer"; and offered some to 'RC'. When 'RC' declined, Bob said sarcastically,

"Go ahead, man. It's free – a good will gesture... I don't have any wampum."

"RC' ignored him – he was tiring of the man's stoic cynicism.

For a long period of time, there wasn't much conversation. They ate in silence. Bob didn't seem to be a 'continuer'. His usual response was "Unnhhh". In 'RC's opinion, he'd held more interesting conversations with pets.

In the distance, the hair-raising call of a loon on a nearby pond could be heard. It was a perfected 'spookiness' that seemed to reinforce the bird's 65 million year old past. He glanced over casually at Bob who was reading a book that had serpentine gold lettering on its cover – and swigging from the bottle of root beer.

"Whatcha doing'?"

'RC' really wasn't that interested, but decided it might be a way to get to know the man. They needed to establish some sense of partnership. Besides, something had pushed the question out of his mouth before he could stop himself.

"You'd call it mythology. Probably boring for ya' – but I'm fresh out of 'National Enquirers'."

"Yeah...well I'm interested in all types of mythology: dragons, creatures from the black lagoon...the sincerity of politicians?" And then he smirked.

"It's a translation from relatives...book about snakes." .

"You mean like - identification of snakes...?"

The fire crackled. It spit sparks around the perimeter. They glowed momentarily; and then, blackened – like seeds of light waiting to grow in the dirt.

"No, I mean like the Snake Kingdom. Some of my 'folkses' happen to believe that we came from snakes; and someone wrote a story about it – whatcha

think about that? Bet you think it's just some more native mumbo-jumbo..."
And then he stuck his tongue in and out like he was 'mugging' a serpent.

'RC' ignored his cynicism.

"Oh – you mean like kingdom, phylum, genus, species…that's not my-thology, its classification."

Bob's response seemed calculated,

"Uh…listen. I'm not that much of a 'tracker'. The agency paired us up for a reason. I already know a lot about you – so you wanna skip the formality of us getting to know each other?"

It threw 'RC' off balance. How much did the native know- and what could have prompted the pithy response? Perhaps he had been presumptu-ous regarding his earliest observation of the man's skills. It bothered him that Bob might not like him – they needed to work together. He reasoned that the Indian must have perceived his judging nature and earlier suspicion – traits that were his 'default'. Had he been unfair? After all, he was basking in the warmth of a fire that Bob had made; and had refused his offer to share a drink. Though he thought the response was unnecessarily harsh – the rare self-reflection allowed him to understand how he might have offended the native. Oddly, he could only perceive the slightest irritation in the man's countenance – one that hardly matched the rebuke, or his apparent opinion.

The sudden beating of wings through the woods could be heard nearby as if an animal had spooked a bird that was in hiding.

"Words should be used with care," Bob said. He glanced over at 'RC' to see if his ego had been terminally squelched. Then, and slowly…he recounted the following.

"It's said that the Snake Kingdom was once very powerful, but the Humans overcame it. The ghosts of that kingdom still walk sometimes be-cause nothing is ever lost – Einstein knew that."

'RC's cynicism was predatory. Before he could stop the instinct, he had said,

"Sounds a little bit like the 'Golden Bough' – you know, monsters with two heads, that sorta thing."

"Call it what you want," Bob responded nonchalantly.

A wind-gust blew something over and it made a dinging sound as it fell. The noise prompted 'RC' to immediately realize the error in his remark. He would fish for a more favorable reception. He stuttered,

"Well, I mean, I read some of that stuff when I was a kid. I found it fas-cinating how ancient beliefs affect modern thought."

He immediately thought about how awkward and insensitive his second comment sounded; and his embarrassment cascaded. The laughing sound of the loon could be heard across the lake water.

Bob replied. "...there are many Human stories of origins and gods."

"Well...yeah, I guess you could say that....Uh, I'm sorry..." He had done it again.

Bob apparently understood that 'RC's intentions were neither mean nor base. He continued his story,

"The Snake Kingdom was a powerful kingdom in the ancient World. The ancestors say they were handsome people – brave, wily. Humans were envious of their power and wealth. They implored the powerful Earth God to weaken the Kingdom, but the Earth God would not do it.

So the Humans told the Earth God about the Cloud Tower. The Earth God, of course, knew about this tower but thought it to be a temple by which to worship him. He knew that the Beetle People – the largest tribe – had helped the Snake Kingdom build it. They had many workers.

But the Humans were jealous and fearful. They told the Earth God that the Cloud Tower was being built to reach the sky. Once there, the Snake warriors would use their powerful legs to chase down and capture the Rain Goddess. When they seized her, she would allow no rain to fall – and the great color-wheel in the rain sky would be theirs."

Fascinated, 'RC' listened as Bob continued,

"The Earth God became furious. He shook and shook and destroyed the Cloud Tower. It rumbled down to the ground taking the people of the Snake Kingdom with it. And when they hit the ground, their legs broke off. The brown dust of the tower coated the people in scales – and they were condemned to be without legs; and to crawl on their stomachs forever.

The Snake people realized what the humans had done. They hissed until they got the Earth God's attention. They told him that the Humans had lied. Though it was true that they had ambitions to capture the Rain Goddess, it was only in order to steal the color wheel that they might use some of its brilliant color. They wished to paint their bodies in glorious hues; and ready themselves for war with other kingdoms. They had borrowed the yellow from the daffodil and the red from the wild rose – but neither was equal in quality to the colors that the Rain Goddess possessed. Their colors lacked light.

The Earth God listened carefully. He observed that the Humans had become powerful and strode across the land mashing the once proud people of the Snake Kingdom. He decided to make them pay for their lie. But the Earth God was also wary of the Snake people's ambition.

They say the light of the sky is made up of souls. They shone brightly for the Earth God so that he might see the magnificent color wheel in all its beauty. Without speaking, they told the Earth God that he must protect the color wheel...that the Snake Kingdom had schemes to own the heavens.

The Rain Goddess told him that she had seen the misery that Humans could cause, for she had been made from tears. The Earth God asked to borrow pigment from the great color wheel. He then gave the Snake Kingdom coats of many bright colors. And he gave the people of the Snake Kingdom teeth and poison. The Humans learned that they could no longer stride arrogantly across the Earth – for the Snake Kingdom could hunt and defend itself.

To this day, the earth shakes and the skies rumble to show the displeasure the Earth God has with the Humans; and to reveal the contrivance of the Snake Kingdom....that was how order was restored."

'RC's mouth was open. "Awesome!" Bob looked away. He knew that 'RC' did not understand.

"Uhnnn...young folks on the 'res' – they call it 'old people's crap'."

He looked back to the fire; and poked at the embers. Then – glancing up at the sky – concentrated on a small star, separate and beaming like a child who had learned its name.

"Uhnnn..." he said; and looked back at the fire. "Ready to read...."

Not wishing to embellish his previous insensitivity, 'RC' said nothing.

Bob peered into the fire. "Things talk to those who are willing to listen." And then, "You're gonna be in big trouble."

"What?" 'RC's face reddened like baked clay. The wind stopped; and fire had receded.

"Big trouble comin' your way..."

The confederation of an arched eyebrow and slack jaw registered 'RC's befuddled discontent. He would not disguise his unhappiness with the path of Bob's discourse.

"...followed by big love...painful too...could be an interesting ride."

"Should I just 'call it quits' now?" 'RC' rolled his eyes.

"No, wait awhile..."

The response was painfully matter-of-fact; and 'RC' resented the doctrine that impelled it.

"Only way out is to know the key."

"Well...what is the key?

"Don't know. The fire just says it is forwards and backwards...." Bob's face revealed no emotion.

"That's it?!" 'RC' responded, obviously annoyed.

"Yep…love and pain are forwards and backwards." Then, Bob looked to the sky and – motioning in the four directions – said,

"Mitakuye Oyasin."[5]

"You can't tell me anymore than that!? I could get better information from a fortune cookie."

"What…you think I know everything because I'm a Native?" Bob retorted. Then he unrolled his knapsack by the light of the remaining embers. He slipped inside of the bedding; rolled over; and turned his back to the fire.

'RC' stared at the fire for a few minutes wondering how anyone could read anything from it. And he wondered again how Bob – this man who believed he was related to snakes – knew so much about him. He nervously jingled a bit of currency in his pocket; and swallowed the remainder of some over-heated coffee that tasted medicinal. Then he unrolled his sleeping bag, slipped in; and zipped it up – looking like a cocoon. But he couldn't sleep. He stared at the three quarter moon. Its curve resembled the arch of a viaduct; and he imagined it carrying starlight across the sky. The clinical nature of his mind would not allow him to forget Bob's last utterance. He was certain the Indian was awake; and so turned to him and blurted out,

"What was that last thing you said?!"

With his back to him, Bob replied.

"Reading over…fortune teller has bad case of droopy-eye. Could it be from lack of sleep – or is customer's destiny just plain boring?"

"You said something like "Minnie Coodie Oleo Resin" – I don't get it."

Bob shook his head, "Naww…I sure as hell didn't say that crap. Anyway – means 'all my relatives'. You wouldn't understand it, 'city britches'. It's an Indian thing."

"Oh really….You think I'm some sort of sissy? Is that it?"

Bob turned and looked at him wearily. "If you mean a 'Two-Spirits'[6], naawww…you ain't smart enough…I have a cousin who's a 'Two-Spirit'. Make you look like the 'missing link'." He continued, "It's the way we end all of our prayers. It means that all things are related. "And here I thought the age of dinosaurs had ended 70 million years ago…" He muttered under his breath and then rolled back over on his side; and adjusted his bedding. Then said,

"You believe in reincarnation?"

The question emanated from darkness – like the cry of a night animal. It startled 'RC', but he regained his composure and replied coolly, "When you're dead, you're dead." Then he reached for his cup again. If there was

---

5   Lakota for 'all my relatives' – a traditional way of ending a prayer.
6   'Gay'

going to be conversation, he might as well make more coffee.

Bob turned around to face the fire. He watched his breath mingle in the air with the smoke; and then disappear – the night would be cold. Then he said, "Gee...guess I didn't get the notice. Apparently neither did 'all my relatives'..."

He studied 'RC's face for any trace of emotion. "I shot a lion once. Folks used to call 'em 'mountain hags' – cause a' the way they scream. It's a good way to scare 'brats' into bein' nice. I know...hard to believe – ain't it? Bet you think all native kids are polite...play house...throw tea parties."

Even though they were tracking a 'mountain hag', Bob's prosaic statement bothered 'RC'. After a moment he responded,

"You killed a mountain lion? That doesn't seem very... umm...Indian."

"Why not...you think we just eat roots and berries? Some of the Ute's did that. They were a sorry bunch too. Every time they turned around – some other tribe was kickin' their butt. Sorry man. I'm a carnivore – got five toes on my front feet."

Well...uh...how did it taste?" He didn't know why he asked.

"Don't know. I'm sure it's watchin' me now – maybe you should ask it."

"What do you mean you don't know?! Didn't you kill it to eat?"

"Not me – I'd rather have a burger."

"Well then why did you kill it?"

"For Roxanne – that woman could make the best peas amandine!"

"You killed it for a woman?!"

"Yep, couldn't afford a Porsche."

Another pause...Bob licked his lips and then continued.

"She said it was the only way I could have her. Prove I had a strong heart. Spent the better part of two days tracking the cat...saw the claw marks on the logs, and fresh prints in the mud. You know – the retracted claw prints in a straight line, walking on its toes. It was such an obvious digitigrade – built for speed. Then I found the remains of a raccoon. Well at least I'm purty sure it was a coon. There wasn't much left of it – just a whole 'lotta' blood. Had all the tell-tale signs of a coon – hind feet resting on the ground and looking a lot like those of a child, pattern sorta' black bear in miniature. The left hind foot appeared beside that of the right front foot...yep, I'm pretty sure it was a coon. Anyway, weren't much left of it. I knew I had to be careful. Cats are silent. They bound more than 25 feet and jump 15 feet into the air. And the attack – that's the cool 'stuff'! They surprise you from the back, knock you on the ground and tear away at your neck. Claws like knives! Wham! Bam! Can a' Spam!"

"Anyway, it was about dusk - they like to hunt at night you know. It was no more'n 50 feet away - eyes burning and mean as snot. I'm sure it was waitin' for me! I pretended not to see it then - BLAM!"

The spookiness of the Indian's delivery and the sudden outcry startled 'RC'. He dropped his cup into the fire; and issued a sudden profanity. He was immediately ashamed of his fearfulness; and busied himself trying to fish out the cup from the ashes and embers. He could smell the low fire scorching the sparse hair on his arms; and hoped that Bob did not notice either his unease or the smell of burning hair.

Bob turned away – he did not wish to embarrass the young man by watching his predicament. He pretended not to notice; and then pulled the blanket up around him convinced he had made an impression. The wind picked up as if in merry conspiracy and fanned the heat.

RC watched the embers attack the cup. A layer of ash overflowed from a burning log and fell over it, intent on burial.

Bob could hear 'RC' poking at the fire and searching through the ash. He felt sorry for him – and remembered that he hadn't finished his story. Without turning over he continued, hoping to allay the young man's fear and desperately ridiculous attempts to procure the cup. He would drop some of his formality – it seemed cruel; and he was certain 'RC's heart was an open one.

"Anyway...when I shot it, 'RC', I heard the bullet thump into the chest. It was a clear shot. I saw the lion drop and knew I had killed him. But then I saw him get up and run away into the brush. I ran forward to follow. But when I reached the rock – he was there – pretty damn dead too. Then, sumthin' told me to pray. You know, things speak to you if you listen...."

Aware of the repetitiveness of the statement, 'RC' stopped poking at the fire. He was certain the Indian's conveyance was meant to be instructive; and he recalled the night with Old Joe and the raccoons. The harmonica had stopped...and Old Joe was whispering to him again from the past,

"My music done spoke to you – and I ain't hardly said a word."

Bob continued,

"I realized I had seen the spirit disappear. I knelt over the body and thanked its spirit for giving me a clean shot – and not taking my life. It was now part of 'wakan oyahe'[7] – makin' its way back to light – cleansed, grateful."

'RC' stopped fishing for the cup. The ash had tried to cover it; but he could see it in the fire – it was half-full. He would wait until morning. Now he felt uneasy – as if something he could not see was watching just beyond

---

7   Spirit world

the perimeter of the firelight. It made him question whether all fear was based on event.

"I gave the meat away and took the pelt home for a rug. Now it's gone again...." Bob kept on.

'RC's eyes were wide, "The spirit?" he asked.

"No. My cousin took it. Said his wife thought their floor was too cold. Oh, by the way, them lion's – they don' like fire." Then he pulled his bedding up to his throat; and yielded to a vanquishing drowsiness.

'RC' poked at the embers again with a stick; and thought about 'mita-kuye oyasin'. He was no longer thinking about the cup in the fire. Instead, an emotion had been sparked by a curious and surprising thought - he wondered whether the taking of a life was any less favorable than the plundering of a soul. After trifling with the thought and coming to no conclusion, he fell asleep – thinking that perhaps, he didn't know as much as he thought he did.

INVISIBLE

The likelihood of actually having a fire and warm drink waiting in the morning was something 'RC' never expected – especially from 'Bob'. He couldn't imagine him 'deciphering' the mechanics of a percolator.

It had been a fitful night and 'RC' was dreaming...dreaming of orchids and the secrets they held...cygnets swimming around flowers, careening into each other; and crashing like falling empires...moonlight resting on Lunaria seed pods in a night garden. The dreams were nonsensical. 'RC' tried to hang onto them to see if there was more, but then suddenly awoke to the rattling and clanking of pans and crude camp silverware. He had to pee.

Bob had not disappointed him. The percolator was lying on the ground in pieces. He had used a pan and some old cloth to sieve out what looked like tea leaves. The water at the bottom of the pan was a green and translucent.

It was early morning; and the mist drifted through the woods – looking like an unfettered band of stealthy spirits determining their shapes and then, suddenly undoing themselves. The welts on his skin commemorated feasting mosquitoes. 'RC' scratched vigorously.

"Want some?"

Bob's indifferent tone vaguely reminded 'RC' of a roommate he had once tolerated.

"It's not much on taste – but I kinda like it...course you probably like your 'shee-shee' lattes."

'RC' wiped his eyes and stretched. The cold hands of 'mist ghosts' caressed his face as if to implore association. The quiet morning was interrupted by the sound of dogs howling somewhere in the distance. Their soulful sound seemed to bounce somewhere up into the gray cloud-mansard.

"Uh, thanks. But it doesn't smell like coffee."

"It isn't."

'RC' brushed off distractedly; and then walked over to a nearby tree. When he was done, he returned to the modest fire that Bob had started. Though he was sure he was awake, the mournful cry of a dove sounded like an eerie panpipe; and made him think of his dreams again. A nearby gander cried out loudly to its mate; and then fished, bottom-up in waters. In and effort to be hospitable, 'RC' took a steaming cup that Bob had offered; and swallowed a bit of the bitter tasting green liquid.

It was then that Bob walked casually over to 'RC's bedding. With a single, smooth motion he picked up the wallet that 'RC's had left there and threw it with intensity – directly into the fire. The fire crackled and sparks burst forth as if a monster had suddenly been fed.

'RC' only had time to declare,

"WHAT THE...!"

Horrified, he watched – as money became smoke; and his credit cards and ID's began to melt and morph into unrecognizable wads of plastic. He rapidly emptied the remainder of the cups contents into the fire – cursing as if possessed. With empty cup in hand, he attempted to dig the remnants of his wallet from the fire, scraping at the coals with a fervor to which he was unaccustomed in the early morning. Agitated and in shock, he could only turn around and stare at Bob in disbelief – wondering if he was crazy...and angrier than he had been since meeting the man.

"Guess you ain't real pleased with me...."

'RC's ire would not be so easily appeased – a fierce look overcame him. Were it not for his efforts to pull the disintegrating wallet from the fire, he would have rushed the man with as much force as a conquering army – he so wished to strangle him. He decided that he would not satisfy Bob's desire for conversation or atonement. In reckless despair, he pulled the fragments of his wallet from the fire, continuing to access all manner of vulgarities; and feeling a heat that did not just come from embers.

Bob was resplendent in quiet observation. He knew the question that 'RC' most wanted to ask; but would not. That question lay just below the surface like a tube of sand that had been solidified by a lightning strike. After watching for a few moments, he settled on his approach. He would provoke the difficulty of a conversation with a comment that might be humorously attired.

"Guess I got some 'splainin' to do..."

'RC' turned slowly. He was flushed with anger and would not divulge any trace of familiarity. He thought of the Indian's previous terse comment about 'knowing a lot about him' – and wondered if actions were a test of some sort. Perhaps the employing agency was challenging his resolve. His fingers curled and dug into his palms like a bull digging into the dirt – bent on charging. Observing his anger, Bob realized his opportunity.

"No currency, no identity, just something existing, something that is passed but not really seen. We do this everyday to each other and things that we touch – and that touch us. Maybe it'd drive us crazy to recognize them all...yeah, maybe that's it. Maybe you can't...maybe it'd make you go insane. I dunno.

We walk on things, throw rocks, lean against trees; ignore everything that doesn't have a name like 'Fred' or 'Jane' – even ignore the 'Freds' and the 'Janes' from time to time....Maybe this is what being invisible is all about. Somethin' that's right before you...unnoticed...underfoot...dully felt. Ain't it strange – all this life and we miss most of it. Maybe this is what we need to track this here 'cat'.... Just know that nothing' else has been workin' here. That wallet's about as valuable as a plate full of air. If you want to understand things that ain't like you – even understand yourself – gotta lose it all, get down in the dirt with everything else.... Yep, complacency...it's a kind of blindness..."

'RC's anger was boiling over,

"You recalcitrant, fool..."

Bob had called forth the conversation he sought.

"Hmmm...big words...tryin' to help you out here. Just remember, I got old bones – likely to explode like a box of talcum powder, if you attack me."

'RC' responded, "I'm not going to waste the calories on you!"

Bob shook his head in agreement, "Yeah, know what you mean – dinner was kinda 'light'."

'RC' extended a finger in the air – in response to the crocodilian behavior.

"Not very 'Christian' of me – was it?" Bob said.

"What would you know about Christianity – you're probably a 'frickin' pantheist."

"Ah...now that involves some of the consummate spoilers of any religion...and the height of irony for Christianity, particularly. Not that I'm pickin' on Christianity – there seems to be enough fault to go around. Religious fanaticism doesn't seem to restrict itself to any one team...."

"I don't give a damn about that! I want my damn wallet back....?"

"Well...since you asked..."

'RC' was tiring of the Indian's psychobabble and dalliance in religious theory. He was already trying to determine how he would replace what had been lost in the fire.

Unexpectedly, a quiet calm overcame him. He stretched and then tilted his head back to see the remnants of a small star in the morning sky – one he hadn't noticed before. His nerves were 'shot'. Then, he idly poked at the fire again – trying to procure what was left of his wallet. But the calm was momentary. He had not realized how intensely angry he was. How could he get paid with nothing to prove his identity? All of his contact information, banking information, medical information, driver's information, and identification had seemingly disappeared up in smoke. When he could stand it no longer, he rushed the native man as hard as he could until he had backed him into a tree. Holding him by his collar, he began screaming at him – nose to nose.

Bob's reaction was consistently stoic, if not, nonchalantly cynical,

"Made you blink...."

"What...are you insane?!"

"Everything's based on your identity, Rowan Chamberlain. That ain't gonna help you out on this assignment.... You're in a cage. That where you want to be?"

'RC' released him roughly,

"If it's all the same to you, 'Chief', I'll be the judge of what I need and don't need. And I'm reporting your butt..... There has to be a reason they lined me up with such an incompetent nincompoop. They must want us both to fail!"

Bob dusted himself off; tucked his shirt back in; and straightened his coat,

"I don't want you to fail."

"You threw everything that's important to me in the fire?!...."

"Because you need to be free..."

"From what....what are you - a child of the 60's!?"

"This animal is different, man. Nothing you got in that wallet is going to help you catch anything out here. And your arrogance is going to get us both killed."

"Arrogance...? What arrogance?"

"You see anything else out here with a wallet? That's a human thing. Maybe you need to just be invisible for awhile...forget yourself...who you are, who you were, where you come from...maybe take a page from your surroundings? You're still you – just not anything that anyone cares about. How can you find anything when you ain't even seeing half of what's out here...?"

'RC' wheeled around muttering and raging expletives; then, spat in the fire. Though he would not admit it, there was only one thing from the wallet that he really wanted. It was the photo of a young woman whom he had met in school. Now her image was floating somewhere in the smoke; and soaring out of sight like a wild bird. Oddly it made him think of the transient nature of the morning light...and wonder who he really was.

THE WRONG CAT

Despite the troubling morning and the lingering feelings of resentment that 'RC' had for the Indian's actions, his restraint had endured. He felt more determined than ever to appear calm. He had swallowed one more cup of tea than he could tolerate. Bob revealed that it was 'hemlock tea'. After laughing at 'RC' trying to spit it out, he explained that it was not the poisonous tea of Socrates fame. The philosopher's tea had been from a plant called the 'water hemlock' which grew abundantly along riverbanks – not the tea the Indian had made from the bark and needles of the hemlock tree. Though the information was consoling and revealed that the man was more educated than 'RC' had imagined, the incident squelched any desire he might have entertained regarding an extended breakfast with Bob. They 'saddled up', knowing of the rough ground and remote trails that were ahead of them. Such trails would not accommodate vehicular traffic – or resentments.

Bob rode a mild-mannered – though uncooperative – Appaloosa. He had to sink his heals into the horse's tough hide in order to prod it along. The horse was unmotivated and pitched its head forward and back making rasping sounds; and causing the Indian to wonder if the bit was too tight, or whether its teeth needed to be floated[8]. He scolded,

"Get movin', Cortez, or you'll be going to the glue factory."

"Interesting name," RC commented. "Distant relative...?"

Bob gave him a languid glance. "No...Spanish explorer – he' gone now."

"I didn't know Indians were fond of the Spanish given the genocide they exacted upon past native populations..."

"We happen to love the Spanish – especially over toast. Besides in 1518 Cortez introduced horses to us – 17 of them."

"You all had horses in this hemisphere – but you killed them off," 'RC' rebutted.

"Yeah...we did, but they were scrawny little things – about the size of pigs. Imagine saddling one of them up for a war party – or a romp across the prairie."

---

8   filed down

Hours later the heat had moved in; and Bob and 'RC' were on a rocky upward sloping trail. Bob was particularly concerned as he didn't believe 'Cortez' had been properly conditioned for the task before him. There were signs that the horse was becoming exhausted. The animal seemed to have little interest in its surroundings. Its eyes seemed dull and glazed and its ears hung limply. They stopped for a few minutes and Bob emptied the better part of a canteen into his hands, but the horse would not drink. They needed to 'push on' to stay on schedule, so he mounted 'Cortez' again and gently spurred him. The animal responded obediently but sluggishly. Bob decided that the pace needed to be modified and poured some of the remaining water from the canteen over the animal's neck and head in an effort to cool him. He had just determined that they needed to stop for the day when they arrived at a small clearing with sparse trees on the mountaintop. Bob immediately dismounted; asked for 'RC's canteen and poured some water into a small container. The horse sniffed the water and then looked away, so Bob moved him into the shade of a low tree that was nearby.

While their horses rested from the wearisome trip, Bob and 'RC' sat on a large rock and examined their surroundings. The few trees were stunted. Their branches looked like the tightly curled and primped hair of a beautician. A few frisky squirrels chattered amidst the sparse evergreen vegetation and dove for cover at the slightest movement of either man. There were tufts of hair that had been left on low-lying shrubs – evidence of some animal's passage. Knot holes on some of the trees provided burrows; and seemed to stare back at the men like stern, weary denizens. Scattered slabs of rock remained from the earliest state of upheaval which had forced the elevation on which they rested. A knightly table of round and particularly flat rock was positioned on one side of the summit as if inviting a feast of brisket. The contents of any such imaginary feast would have, no doubt, been blown away. The wind preferred a sparse communion. Storms had scattered the thin dust of the rocky top like it was a pastime. Dispersed loosely about the woods were bushes whose berries were dry and far from abundant. Tasseled seeds had been blown up from lower climes. In places, the trees clung to the edge of the mountain in vassalage – irritated by but accepting of the toughness of their predicament. The spine of the mountain caught the wind and occasionally uttered a sort of musical modulation commanding the low trees to murmur in imitation. Bewitching vapors of pine scent wafted about while a few ground squirrels quarreled. The hard, compact opaqueness of a string of trees in the corner of the mountain's apex seemed to baffle the flow of breezes like a formula for protecting the cap of the mountain; and freeing part of it for domesticity. The trees' hue trimmed one edge and provided a welcomed screen from savage elements. It was becoming cool on the mountaintop.

Within the tree screen, the wadded bulk of something was frozen in place. Both men rose from the rock on which they were sitting and walked slowly over to the perimeter. They had ridden for many hours in search of the great cat which now lay before them in the clemency of death.

'Deleterious species' – that was the government term. As 'RC' looked at the crumpled carcass, he could hardly believe the words would be associated with the animal. It looked almost kitten-like from malnourishment. So this had been the mountain lion that had claimed the life of a jogger – a mother of two. Someone had shot it. The death seemed unfair. The animal had only done what was natural for it.

"Tell me again, why we're here?"

But Bob was not listening. He was poking about through the leaves with a stick, prodding the body of the cat, here and there. Then, lying down on his stomach, he faced the animal nose to nose and pried open its mandible. Accounts of mountain lion kills indicate that the kill is swift – almost painless. The cat pounces on its victim and tears away at one of the most vulnerable parts of the body – the neck. It severs the spinal cord often causing its prey to lose consciousness or, in effect, strangles it.

"We're here...because they got the wrong cat," Bob replied.

DISTRACTION

Bob's conclusiveness provoked a deep-seated distrust 'RC' had of human fallibility, in which he was certain the native excelled.

"You can't be serious. And you learned this by looking in a dead cat's mouth?"

"Elementary, 'Watson'," Bob responded derisively.

"It's the classic 'bait and switch'. The animal's size indicates it hasn't eaten in weeks. There are marks in the brush and tufts of hair that reveal that it has been pulled through the area – no footprints from either the cat or its captors. They've concealed every footprint by dragging something back and forth through the dirt. There's no sign of a den or kits; no sign of the remains of the jogger's body. More than likely, the body would have been buried somewhere along the trail in some remote location. Despite traversing the mountain, I've seen no evidence of a cache; and no signs of vultures circling to indicate a cache. We could assume that this might be the cat's normal territory. There were scratch marks and the orange stains of urine on rock fungus. So the cache would have been somewhere nearby – because cats mark their territory.

There were hoofed prints before us on the trail; and though the carcass has been dead for days, there's no sign of predation or scavenging of the cat. Yep, I'd say this animal has been planted; and – oddly – the other animals have left it alone, as if they were uncertain of something.... Yep, it's either been planted...or perhaps, illegally killed and left for the vultures."

The sparse beams of remaining daylight had suddenly lit the native man's face like the paradoxical image of a Flemish painting. 'RC' briefly admired the odd lighting. He had underestimated Bob again. He felt humbled by his own lack of observation and artlessness; and sheepishly changed the subject. He did not begrudge a warranted apology, but the tethers of his own modest ability left him momentarily paralyzed. After a few seconds and suddenly unencumbered by that realization, he felt a small bit of freedom. But, and like anything so confined and just freed, he lacked the dexterity of an unruffled segue. He awkwardly blurted out.

"I've never understood this 'hunting' thing with you Indians."

Bob's pensiveness was unexpected. "It's a sensible universe."

"I mean everything is supposed to be so damn sacred. How can you rationalize hunting and killing an animal? This seems like an odd profession for an Indian to be in...."

"Maybe life and death are like dreams. We know freedom best when it's juxtaposed with some form of censure."

'RC' looked at him somewhat cockeyed.

"So you're saying that you think when you kill something – you're 'freeing' it?!"

"It's a theory that comports with the belief that life is circular; and that we are not frozen in a linear path that leads to non-existence. E=MC squared. The docking of one's life doesn't have to mean that all life ends – just that another form of existence begins."

"Hey, I 'get' that – 'no matter is lost in the universe'. But your attempt to catapult from physics into some sort of religious theory seems a little 'hokey' to me – if not an excuse to ignore the sacredness of life."

Bob looked at him sleepily,

"How interesting...never thought I'd hear you talking about the sacredness of life. Anyway, 'I have great faith in a seed'. That's Thoreau, by the way...."[9]

'RC' paused, struggling to find a way to express the cynicism he felt. Then he said, "Not sure I buy your theory, 'Chief'."

"Got a better one?"

"Then how do you explain Hitler? Was he just 'freeing' souls? Why did he do what he did?"

"That's easy – he was a homicidal maniac."

'RC' hesitated, almost afraid to ask the next question. "And the lion that you killed...?"

Bob's reply was cool and direct,

"It was a rite of manhood and... I was a selfish little 'shit'."

"But you still hunt?"

"I like to eat."

"Ever heard of a supermarket?"

"Ever heard of 'free range'?"

"Well, you could be a vegetarian!"

"Roots make me 'toot'."

Bob returned to the previous direction of the conversation. "Maybe 'life' is just one big distraction – to keep us from seeing something more real..."

---

9   *"Walden"* or *"Life in the Woods"*, Henry David Thoreau, Published 1845, Boston, Ticknor & Fields

"Nothing gives up life willingly, Bob. Life is the 'real deal'." 'RC' retorted.

"Maybe we transcend to other things..."

"Yeah – freezers..."

Bob continued, "Really...we're nothing but a mess of particles held together by will."

"Ah, quantum physics...now that's a field filled with debate."

The Indian persisted, "All of this bothers you because you really don't believe in prayer or the sacredness of any life – not even your own. You've shut down your feelings."

RC's passion was beginning to boil over. He was sick of the lecture; wanted his wallet back; and felt entrenched in deficiency, if not exposed by Bob's illusiveness and allusions. He stood suddenly and pulled the hood of his coat roughly about his head.

"And what exactly would you have me 'feel'?"

"Gratitude," was the reply.

'RC' turned abruptly and stomped away from the Indian and over to the edge of the mountain with its overhanging face. He looked forth to the horizon. His thoughts drifted to the neighboring range where they were blown clean by the strong wind that swept over the crags and then ricocheted back to him in a white wave.

A storm was upon them; and he was suddenly being pelted by sleet. It was forming pockets within the rough crags that had been previously excavated by the wind and creating hoary strands upon the mountain face. A thousand undulating voices screamed in the wind. The accumulating iciness attempted to wrap all things in a shroud as if to prepare them for a long sleep. In the distance the sun seemed to swell in obscurity; and then fall over the horizon. The sparse spindly trees bent under he weight of the accumulating snow; and the horses snorted and huddled together.

On the flat rock where he had left him, Bob sat like a brown cork barely containing explosive thoughts. The pelting storm did not seem to concern him. He was pondering the death of the mountain lion; the folly of their undertaking – and was staring intently at a fork of trees and listening for a clue.

PARALLEL SOULS

Those who had found the body of the unfortunate jogger had claimed to have undeniable proof that she had been killed by 'felis concolor' (a mountain lion). The body was badly torn, quite decomposed; and partially buried so that the great cat could feed on it later. The location and entrapment of the cat that had 'committed the crime' was now the paramount concern. It had proved to be quite elusive – and a number of hunting parties had been consigned to track and possibly kill it.

'RC' and Bob had bedded down for the night amidst the screen of protective trees near the precipice of the mountain. They had built a small fire. Drawn together around it, they watched as the body of the cat that had been shot, became a marbled sculpture in light snow, under the starlight. The native man had spent a great deal of time examining the animal and the perimeter. He continued to be curious regarding the unmolested remains of the cat before them; and was certain that they had found the wrong one. They had thought they were so close; but he was sure that the 'killer cat' remained free and was seeking its next meal.

'RC' thought of the circumstances that had befallen the victim. Gruesome as they were, he could not see the cat as a killer. The animal had only done what was consonant with its nature. It needed to feed itself. Melancholia swept over him; and suddenly he felt ashamed at the 'inhumanity' of the thought; and sickened that his emotion for the woman and her two children seemed base. Worse, he realized...he felt jealous.

Alarming as the thought seemed, he believed the jogger was lucky. She had managed to cross over into something else. She was no longer enclosed by the worries of this life and uneasy at the mystery of death. Like a bee-bee pellet that had ripped through a glass pane, she was on the other side of an invisible barrier perhaps, looking back. Maybe she wished to return - now knowing more and wanting for her children. Her freedom must be boundless. Impeded only by the inability to revert to a previous state, the victim knew what it was to 'once be'; and 'RC' resented that oddly mellifluous feeling – but wondered why.

Some god-like will had determined that this was the way it was to be. He wondered whether – were it not for pain – many might not choose 'exit'. Then he shuddered at the power behind the notion and finally reconciled his thoughts by being grateful that his will exercised some measure of control. He soaked uncomfortably in unrewarding thought. Was there something greater than all of us? Was the possibility of eternal darkness or hell fire so frightening a prospect that we willed ourselves to live a dull and often unrewarding existence? He thought he had seen evidence of that fear everywhere; and frankly, it wasn't much of an argument for life.

It seemed to him that some 'blew through' life grabbing every speck of enjoyment they could; and never seemed to care about others. While some sat with head and hands bent; trying to absorb as much religion as possible in order to petition for protection. Others wrapped themselves in the mediocrity of everyday thoughts – which seemed a pointless façade.

The last category was the most unfortunate to him. They would be overcome by terror at the moment of death – having believed in nothing but 'Argonautic' myths; chasing the 'golden fleece'; and not seeing the monster lying with one eye open at the base of the tree. He remembered how deeply he had once cared for someone. The sudden realization that he might very well be in the third category – now bothered him immensely. He wondered again about the girl he had once met who knew about literature and seemed to understand him so well. She had made him feel the electricity of that thing called 'life'.

It was then that he looked over to see the Indian staring at him again. 'RC' immediately thought of two things: Perhaps, a treachery had brought him to this cold summit; and - at that instant – he was overwhelmingly unhappy.

He looked away and upwards to the sky. The moon had risen from its slumber. The bedding of clouds, that had hidden it, was being swept away by the wind. In the distance 'RC' could hear the bay of a wolf that seemed lonely and seeking a mate. Lying on his back in the sleeping bag, 'RC' bathed in the speckled light. He was surprised by the moon's brilliance. The moon, in return, seemed to bask in his favor. He gazed at it for awhile as it moved imperceptibly through the sky. He imagined it being a beautiful woman making her way slowly through a night garden - seeding the darkness with stars. The exaltation of night had begun.

Then, he drifted into semi consciousness underneath the lantern of the night sky; and the darkness seeped into him. In the distance, he could hear the squall moving rapidly across the land. A succession of images appeared to carry his body along. Through heavy-lidded eyes – his sense perceptions obscured – he was certain he was dreaming; and wandering along a puzzling path, will-less. In what seemed to be the remnants of the day, he saw a wedge of lilies at a wood's edge. The trout lilies showed through the disappearing light; and had a rusty, sepia-toned appearance which glowed softly. As he thought about the girl he had wished to know better, his dream was suddenly interrupted.

"Hell of a moon up there, don't you think...big and sort of dull orange – like a possum's eye. Hopefully, you ain't getting' amorous on me – as I'm already spoken for."

The native man had pronounced it in his usual deadpan way; and 'RC' quietly cursed him. He hated to admit that he found Bob's company reassuring. The man's words had thrust him back to an easier and undisturbed condition. And his rough, weathered appearance had eliminated any unbridled ache of passion that 'RC' might have felt. He had returned abruptly to the ordinariness of his life – and its odd comfort.

For his part, Bob sensed that he had invaded a private thought; and that he might be dangerously close to extirpating dreams. Not knowing exactly what to do, he climbed a little deeper into his own bedding as if to shake off the cold - then said,

"Damn cold – sure would love some hot coffee." But he perceived that the internal chill that 'RC' felt was not just from cold; and knew that the young man did not wish to discuss anything.

"I'd rather have a shot of whiskey," 'RC' replied, evading any suggestion of sensitivity.

"Ever seen a wood lily?" Bob persevered deciding to dress his concern with nonchalance. "Odd little flowers, find 'em unexpectedly on the forest floor, speckled – looks like you could crawl right into them. Who knows what you'd find..."

The insight into his dream startled 'RC'. It was awkwardly intrusive; and caused him to speculate regarding the shelter of his thoughts. He glanced away and up to the sky again. The moon had fallen slightly and the constellation Virgo was now apparent – its bright star, Spica, seemed to beckon, as if attempting to communicate the yearning of a parallel soul who was looking at it.

Meanwhile Bob's own thoughts were drifting. He was thinking of Louise cooking dough balls in the kitchen; and remembering a vision that had once lifted him on the wind and introduced him to the young 'RC' and others whom he was sure would be part of the journey in which he now found himself. He smiled, both because of anticipation of that journey; its incompleteness; and because he thought the concepts 'time' and 'conscious-ness' seemed relative...and oddly human.

And, he was quite sure that the young 'washicu' would eventually find what he sought – if he would allow himself.

WITHIN REASON

The following morning the horses seemed to have recovered. The sun was brightly debilitating; and the sleet and snow which housed within the crannies of the mountain had become melted puddles – now running away. Bob and 'RC' saw no point in staying on the precipice or burying the carcass of the cat. They decided to return from the mountain. Small scrubby patches of sagebrush ringed the narrow trail that they descended. The air was light and crisp; and the horses breathed easier. Dispersed along the landscape, Bob saw the burrows of small animals; and thought the mountain much more abundant with life than most would notice. Blood sucking insects took advantage of the warmth and buzzed about the head of the patient quadrupeds as they carried the men downhill. Desert mice scurried about seeking food. The occasional prairie dog thrust its head up from a hole, looking like an anxious student hearing a school bell. The tousled mopped patches of goldenrod hauled in quantities of insects with an invisible net of nectar. The insects plunged like seagulls into the golden ocean of blossoms and then surfaced again. The quiet clucking of nearby grouse could be heard as the birds charged through the low brush.

The wind had increased; and with it, brought an unpleasant memory. 'RC' thought of the mass of cold air that had blasted into childhood and robbed him of his friend, 'Old Joe'. He flinched at the thought and then shook it off – determined to consecrate the man with happier memories. For a few moments, he allowed himself to dream lazily and wonder about the universe, his place in it, and who or what had made it. As he was apt to do, Bob interrupted 'RC's thoughts with a comment.

"Do you ever wonder if someone is lookin' back? I mean, sometimes I think the 'night' is like a woman with diamonds in her hair...and billions of wormholes that offer passage to other places."

"Frankly my dear, I don't give a damn," 'RC' replied mockingly.

He looked briefly at the man ahead of him on the trail. The shred of sensitivity and wonder had surprised him, but Bob's notion seemed demented – and he was rapidly tiring of a conversation whose inclination seemed insincere. He pursued the terse statement with an acrid comment,

"This 'humanizing' of everything in nature seems like a bunch of 'hooey'."

Bob replied, "But seriously – do you ever think about it...or do you just subscribe to the 'Hooey Theory'?"

"Nope – don't think about it."

"Man of a few words huh?"

"Yep"

Bob teased, "Is that because you can't remember many?" And then he continued, "Seems like nothin' ever leaves – just collapses into somethin' else...a bit of beauty in that."

"Getting into your 'child of the universe' mantra...?" 'RC' had intended the pithiness.

"Fuzzy atoms..."

"What...?"

"Yep, that's it...fuzzy atoms. We're like fuzzy atoms in the body of something much greater, but still part of it."

"Sounds like 'fuzzy thinking'."

"You would say that," Bob responded. "Wizard stuff - you know, you get the wand and I get the pond...and I better not crawl out of it."

The wind was suddenly concussive; and scattered nearby nesting birds. The chirping of their young became an uncontrolled choir. Bob heard the distant rapping of a 'tree surgeon' testing diseased wood with its bill and realized that they had descended to the tree line. He looked about until he finally located where the noise had originated. He could see the red cap and zebra-patterned back of a red bellied woodpecker hitching up the trunk of a nearby tree, its stiff tail bracing the bird as it ascended. Such birds were usually found in different environments. The woodpecker rose to a selected limb where it tapped on the dead part of the tree; and then plucked out larvae. It rapidly left with a dipping up-and-down flight through stunted trees – proof that the year had been dry and the wind characteristically brisk.

The Indian stopped and cocked his head. He only had time to catch a glimpse of an immense shadow as it melted into the low trees of a deep bowl on the gentle incline. The profundity of the sighting troubled him. It seemed to portend the darkness of an omen of which he had once heard. He rapidly dismounted and – holding up an eagle feather – began to chant to the four directions.

"Keep your day job, Chief," 'RC' remarked.

"Not meant to be on the list of the 'Top Ten' – meant to 'ground' us... speak a better world into existence."

"Ya gotta be kiddin me! Bet you think that actually works...."

"Did for Martin Luther King...."

"What happened – did you see a 'ghost'?" 'RC' had meant his query to be impertinent.

"Not quite." Then, Bob mounted his horse. After a brief suspension of speech, he said,

"Evidently, you think my convictions are groundless..."

"No, not groundless, more like a mime trying to prevent a traffic accident..." 'RC' sneered.

"...So you think they're ineffective."

"Just sayin..." 'RC' retaliated.

"Maybe you shouldn't be so quick to dismiss the power of prayer."

"You can think what you want, Bob. I believe in science."

"I believe in science as well. I also believe in prayer."

"Never been much on religion..."

"I guess you have your system for explaining things; and, I have mine, then."

"Ours is not a 'religion'," 'RC' pursued. "It's an organized way of explaining the universe. You know, and the four forces within it: Gravity, electromagnetism, weak force, strong force...ever heard of them? Or is everything a 'vision quest' with you?"

"Yours may be more of a process – mine is a procedure..." Bob replied.

"What's the 'diff'?"

"You're looking for an end point..."

"I believe that is the purpose of most scientific studies," 'RC' dissented. "But I suppose you have a problem with that too."

"No," Bob responded. "...I just don't believe in end points – more like a journey."

"Then you 'do' have a problem with my approach!"

"I don't believe in your approach, 'RC'...seems like every process can benefit from prayer."

"Told you...I'm not a religious person."

"Don't have to be religious to be spiritual. Maybe all reality is spiritual. Regardless, bet there's enough room in Physics to accommodate prayer. At least there seems to be enough room to accommodate chance...."

"Yeah, well I've never been one of those 'get on my knees'; 'cup my hands together'; and 'pray for a miracle' types."

"Not to go all 'Billy Graham'[10] on you – but I don't think prayer re-

10   American evangelical Christian Evangelist, born November 7, 1918 as William Franklin "Billy

quires that. Some prayers are just about gratitude; others about thanks and appreciation. It's really about recognizing that there's something greater than us."

"Uh-huh. Well, that's nice. But I still see 'religion' and 'science' as mutually exclusive."

"You're just saying that you don't believe prayer has any place in science."

"That's right – seems like utter 'bull' to me. Why pray when you can prove? Prayer isn't like reason...can't guarantee anything with it, so why waste your time?"

"Can't guarantee some things with reason either..."

"Yeah...not everything, but you keep trying. You don't 'rule out' anything; and eventually you'll get there."

"Sounds like a very logical approach," Bob acknowledged. "So then, why 'rule out' prayer?"

"Okay, 'Chief'. Then why 'rule out' Tarot cards?!"

"Well...you have a point."

"I rest my case." Though content in his victory, 'RC' would not admit he was annoyed by how close he had come to losing the argument; or that his approach might be assailed by any sort of impairment.

Bob continued down the path on the appaloosa. He was reflective – now questioning his beliefs. Though it disturbed him, he began to wonder about the remote dream he once had; and wondered why the warm wind had carried him along with it. The man who currently challenged him – was the boy he had seen in the sleeping bag in that dream. The reflection caused him to speculate about the others in his dream: the young Mediterranean woman, Sophia; the young man named Sincero; the nun; and the boy who spoke the strange tongue. Was it simply a dream? Was it meant to remain unfinished? 'RC' had engaged him in mental fisticuffs.

The one thing of which he remained reasonably certain...was that he was probably on a journey of his own.

Graham", Jr.

RELATIVISM

The following morning, Bob and 'RC' packed up their modest camp and continued the descent from the mountain. Though the trail was filled with the extraordinary sights that nature furnishes liberally and freely, Bob hardly noticed. He focused instead on following the path downward. Like anyone who has had their convictions challenged – and believes they lack sufficient explanation – he was troubled. It bothered him that someone, whom he believed would profit from his experience, might have found flaw. It wasn't that he wished to be without blemish – rather he felt a state of dissonance. In the end, he decided that dissention was nourishing. He had been too sure of things; and such certainty was imprudent.

'RC' felt moderately triumphant, but noticed Bob's atypical behavior. Having marginally won an argument, by causing Bob to consider what he saw as an absurd progression of his thinking, he had hoped to take pleasure in the victory. It now bothered him that he felt skeptical of the conquest; and he wondered if the victory had been cheaply won. He concentrated instead on the assignment and speculated about Bob's assessment regarding the cat. Had they really found the carcass of the wrong mountain lion – or was Bob wrong?

Meanwhile Bob temporarily questioned the meaning of his dreams – or whether they had any meaning at all. After much contemplation, he was certain that he and 'RC' had been thrown together for some reason; and that the reason would eventually be revealed. The coincidence of their pairing; and the prophetic nature of the dream convinced him that he must suspend any muteness – that their conversation was important. He had been thinking of the young Mediterranean woman – one of the people in his dream – when he decided to interject a comment into the stunning silence.

"Isn't it odd that 'logic' is based upon a set of principles laid down by Greeks and Romans – and that they thought they could deduce practically everything in terms of those principles?"

The comment startled 'RC'. He felt uncomfortable about continuing any abstruse conversation, but was discontent with the overripe stillness.

"Well…it is a fine set of principles."

"Yes, but it doesn't explain a great deal of existence – does it?" Bob was wary in his response.

'RC' was suddenly suspicious of the motive of the conversation and responded unfavorably, "I think it explains quite a bit."

"But, what about 'ghosts'..."

"I believe most scientists would agree that 'ghosts' are as conjectural as 'angels'."

"Perhaps most scientists could benefit from an understanding of metaphysical philosophy..."

"I hardly think so – and that's a gigantic assumption."

"What's the assumption?"

"That 'most scientists' have no concept of metaphysical philosophy..."

"Well, I suppose so, 'RC'. But 'gigantic' is a relative term anyway. A flower is gigantic, if you're an ant. We look at it while they can actually crawl into it. There's always something greater and something smaller. I think where we stand in all of that affects our viewpoint – and probably the structure of our thinking."

"I hardly believe that ants have much mental prowess...or that they think of much more than food, when they crawl into a flower."

"Yes, but 'how' do we know what anything really 'thinks' – unless we have some sort of psychic connection."

"Again, scientific principles...they explain the size of the brain in proportion to the body; and prove instinctual and chemical-based behavior."

"That's tidy," Bob replied. "But I suppose the ant is eminent in 'his' own domain. The way he views the world is based upon the limitations of where he stands; and his 'universe' likely affects the limits of the ant's understanding. But, there's more out there that the ant doesn't know, than it knows. ... Are we really that different?

For example, our society is based upon principles, laws, beliefs, cultures... the ant's world is based upon chemistry and instinct. Are our principles any less a product of the domain within which we stand? Just as 'good' and 'bad' exist side by side – is it any less likely that the physical and the metaphysical are so juxtaposed? Can we see outside of the flower? And if we see the field that the flower is in, can we really see much past that? Everything is connected somehow."

Then Bob stopped. He looked serious for a moment.

"Hmm...you were in love with that gal, weren't you?"

'RC' flushed as he realized that the Indian somehow had been trolling his thoughts; and he wondered how much more he might have perceived.

"She was the light by your side."

MIRAGE

'RC' and Bob had finally reached their destination. They had finished their descent; and a rough gravel road was before them. This was where they would turn in the horses; and report what they had seen to the main office. The smell of horses was chokingly pervasive and 'RC' could hardly wait to dismount, 'even up' with the rancher at the desk; and head for a warm shower. At that moment, life lacked any delicacy or ethereality. He felt like a lump of mud.

Bob was equally dusty and dirty; but none of what bothered 'RC' occurred to him. He had already dismounted; and was too busy thinking about things he didn't understand. He wondered about human commerce and looked back at the dirt path from where they had come. The royal sun lit up the sky with its gold vestments and made the papers that he had pulled out of his coat pocket, translucent. The wind had carried the scents of sagebrush from the low mountain steppes and it murmured something about how unusual human trade was – for the wind did not understand the need to bargain.

In a peculiar turn of events, 'RC' discovered that he was suddenly disappointed that they were nearing the stables; and that their travel together was ending. Their conversations had been vexing, but had also incited fresh thought. He would miss the verbal tourney with Bob – though he would not regret the Indian's spooky perceptiveness. Bob's uncanny insight regarding the girl 'RC' had met in school, bothered him. The insight had underscored his own intuitive shortcomings; and reminded him of a pain that he had wished to bury.

They reached the road and some semblance of civilization when 'RC's focus on the emotional ebb and flow of the trip was unexpectedly interrupted by a number of people who appeared to be a party of retirees. The group had arrived by bus; and was apparently out for an excursion. Intermingled was a ragged aggregation of men and women who appeared to be part of another tracking party sent to find the great cat.

The unusual juxtaposition of the dissimilar groups held his attention and caused him to think about discussions he and Bob had regarding prayer and chance; and the seemingly random way dissimilar people were placed together in life. It was clear that both groups had come to ride horses – but for very different reasons.

By comparison, the Indian's attention was not drawn to the groups at hand, but rather to three specific people within the two assemblages. The first was a brutishly large and ambitious man who appeared to have seen the spoils of war. A small patch on his jacket revealed that he was a member of a hunting group that participated in safaris; and that he was a seasoned traveler.

The other two were a couple. The man was older with an aquiline nose. His wife was middle aged, but interesting looking. She quietly hummed an operatic piece, 'Santa Lucia', to herself, while her husband looked on approvingly. Though she was older now, Bob recognized her as the younger Mediterranean woman he had seen in his dream. The two different groups had evidently arrived together. Sophia Angaros and her husband were directly in line behind the tracking party and the large man with the patch on his jacket.

'RC' glanced over at Bob. The native man's gaze had often seemed suffocating while they traveled together. He had once retorted to 'RC',

"I'm not staring at you - that would presume you were opaque."

The comment had bothered 'RC'. It was oddly metaphysical in nature and in keeping with the man's eerie behavior. And 'RC' didn't like to think of himself as 'transparent'.

The native man had also once asked 'RC' "why he believed he pissed Perrier and pooped bouquets." The criticisms, taken together, had severed their limited conversation for a period of time. The brisk memory of both comments left 'RC' stinging; and he thought perhaps, it was merciful that their trip together had come to a close.

He looked at the Indian again. Bob's gaze seemed fixed on the disjointed group of people who had lined up to rent horses at the stable. He had obviously resolved to find a new target for his criticisms. He was certain the man would latch on to another victim; and tear away at the heels of any sort of reason. The certainty relieved him - at least he would be free of any further abstract discussions regarding causality, truth, and existence. He would gladly depart from the realm of such unproductive social intercourse. However, and as he glanced away from Bob and back to the queue before him, he concealed a nagging thought - that perhaps it was such conversations which were entitled to attention.

The stables were abuzz with activity. 'RC' dismounted from his horse and led the animal over to an area where the bookkeeping was being done. From there, workers would collect and examine the tack; and decide upon the grooming requirements of the horses being returned. The business of pushing living things along in such a manner was an odd characteristic of any such employment. 'RC' now traded in the life that had carried him uncomplainingly to the summit and back. And though he responded to the pleasantries of the business conversation related to the animal's return, his thoughts were elsewhere.

He wondered how much the Indian had discerned of the arrested romance 'RC' had once had with the girl he knew as Anna. The glaring contradiction struck him. Perhaps he had not known much of the romance either....

But now, the wish to stare down the darkness – while in her embrace - seemed fresh, and achingly hateful. It so held his thoughts that he was hardly aware of completing the mechanics of the return of the horse. How could he have let love go? He wished to eject the pain of his longing; and concluded that – though love might be free – it was not without a price.

He looked back at the queue before him again. A middle aged Mediterranean woman and her husband were at the front of the line now, completing the transaction for horses. They bickered and laughed with each other. Before him, an autumn romance was occurring; while he still languished in summer, unable to move forward.

Suddenly aware of his obsession, it occurred to 'RC' that Bob might have completed the return of his appaloosa; and that he should at least talk to him before they parted. But, when he looked up, he could see the other tracking party riding away; and the native man had disappeared. 'RC' looked down the path toward them wondering if Bob had continued on.

It was only then that he was aware of a feather in his breast pocket; and was startled to see his wallet on the ground in front of him. It was the one that Bob had thrown into the fire – and it was complete and undisturbed.

CHANCE OR PROBITY

The tracking party - that had arrived in tandem with the busload of retirees - was now well on its way. The trail was hot and rocky. They were
miles from the stables and the frivolity of those who had simply come out for
a day outing.

Theirs was the tracking party that had discovered the jogger's remains and
which had set everything in motion. They started out now to find the animal; and to bring it back dead or alive - in conformance with humanitarian
principles...principles that would no doubt, be lost upon the mountain lion.

The wearisome task, the difficulty of the trail, and the rattling memory
of having seen a decomposing body - had all contributed to rendering many
in the group, emotionally numb. Slogging their way up the mountain, they
hardly talked. Their energies were focused on the task at hand. Uncomfortably
inharmonious, the group was composed of two disparate types: trackers with
a rudimentary education and scientists who had far too much schooling but
little practical experience. Bob wondered if they were capable of finding anything. His own self-recruitment had apparently gone unnoticed; and he had
blended in unnoticed by the group.

When, and after some hours, his presence was finally noted, it was by a
man with whom he had once worked and had differences. The lead biologist
was less than pleased with Bob's attendance, but decided that the additional
assistance might at least prove worthwhile. After some uncomfortable moments, he resolved that the native man could stay. When the group stopped
for a break on the trail, the biologist summarized for Bob, what was current
and important to their task; and underscored that there were to be no further
differences between them.

Marks in mud had recently been found on the trail. It was the paw print
of a climber. The depth of the prints revealed a heavy animal with front paws
composed of five toes. No claw marks in the mud meant it was an animal
that could retract them. The rear paws had four toes. There was relatively
fresh scat. Equally important, the ravaged carcass of a small mammal was
still bright with blood, indicating the cat had made another kill. One could

practically smell its breath upon the prey. Here and there in the brush, they had retrieved patches of grey fur; and a piece of the prey's tongue bloomed like a rose-colored mallow from the dark corner of a bush. There were indentations in the grass where the prey had been dragged and then partially buried. The wallow with death had ended and seemed a standard predator-prey story. The group knew that they were hot upon the trail of the killer.

Bob, however, remained uncertain of the ordinariness of the situation. He decided not to share his thoughts, but simply curled his lip; thanked the lead biologist; and then, looked out into the distance. The wind was blowing through the trees again; and – as he was apt to do – he would listen to what secrets the trees might reveal.

He momentarily thought of 'RC'; and regretted having not said goodbye to the young 'wasihcu'[11]. Instead, Bob had chosen to disappear into the second tracking party; and 'RC' had been suddenly called off on another assignment. But the native knew they would eventually communicate again. In the meantime, he was fascinated by the brutish tracker with the patch on his shirt. The man seemed surrounded by suspicion; and cast a large shadow.

Now, the trees murmured a message. It was something that had been carried from their relatives in a deep bowl on the gentle incline which he and 'RC' had previously passed. Bob struggled to discern the meaning behind the information, but his attendance to what the trees had to offer was suspended. The hunt for the cat had begun again.

The respite was over as the hunting party mounted their horses. This would be no mirthful sport of the countryside filled with bright uniforms, groomed horses and riders, the sound of a bugle, and quadrupeds thundering across land...something Bob had 'seen' in his dream. There would be no 'drivers' to flush the game from hiding. The tracking party was a disorganized band of animals yelping, pawing, sniffing, howling, and occasionally squatting to relieve themselves...and then there were the dogs, he chuckled to himself.

The hunt had initially begun freely and out of duty. Now, a queer impetus underlay it. The mechanics of finding the murderous animal had been feathered by the soft jingle of pocket money. That sound served to quicken any customary lethargy; and caused a slight stir of excitement – especially among some trackers. But to the brutish man who was head of the trackers, the interest seemed to be more than just a gilded one.

Winnington, a national gun company had pounced upon the story of the 'monstrous cat'. They had sent young men and women melded from a

---

11   White man

corporate culture into the local community. They were handsome, self–assured, and had winning smiles. The company had produced a squall of intriguing stories about similar attacks across the country. They had spoken informally with city elders and quietly poured money into local gun clubs who then, funneled that money to pro-hunting candidates.

The anti-hunting contingency fought back fervently, arguing that the cat was merely following instinct. We had invaded its territory; and it probably had kits to feed. There were well-intended vigils for the cat and sparse editorials. Ultimately, sympathy for the great cat diminished. Those in favor of the mountain lion were asked to consider their survival – or those of loved ones – when confronted with a killer. Would they shoot to kill? Their responses seemed fragmented and insincere; and industry's smooth, cohesive response had produced the odd polarity that Bob now saw in the tracking party of which he was a part.

However - and despite the onerousness of the task and the divisiveness of the group - the day was pleasing. And all days may be thought of as gifts. The side of the mountain, that the tracking party traversed, had received more rain; and there were certain areas of marshy land that gently opened to anyone who cared to observe. In places, the clouds broke and the sunlight fell down like well-groomed golden hair. Here and there, boulders and trees seemed to sit together in rows, as if in some godly quorum. The howling and yipping of coyotes somewhere in the mountains above the tracking party was a reminder that kits had recently been born. The coyotes were celebrating the end of a wild fast – certain that their hunger would soon be sated. The air was brittle and clear and promised to render a dramatic sentence for the day's end. The light would be pulled from the sky until it ruptured in color. Such was the public war between day and night that came and went regularly; and proved to all who watched that there was an odd balance to the world which was worthy of contemplation. The end to any day was a reminder that the greatest gold was the impermanent electricity from which all life was created. The beauty of the sunset was nearly enough to dispel a rumor that had been seeded within the group. That rumor held that money for the project had been provided from a mysterious 'power-couple'; and that they stood to gain from the hunt and the cat's demise.

A plan was constructed. The tracking party would split up. They would sweep the different entry and exit points of the circular gap. Their intent was to drive the cat toward a narrow ravine. They soon picked their way carefully through trees, briars and boulders trampling anything stationary. An outstanding patch of 'Adders Tongue' lilies with aubergine speckled petals was soon pulverized underfoot. The flowers sank into the soft earth which seemed willing to assist in their anonymity.

The trackers had spent a good deal of time scouting and prescouting to find where the forage areas and natural animal routes would be. They set off a canister of "buck bomb". If they could attract the cat's prey, they could get the cat. Though the less educated trackers were methodical, they had a practical understanding of the natural world that underpinned whatever they did. Some had brought along Matthew's bows – tight and ready for action. They looked for bachelor groups of prey and big sheds – to tell them if deer had recently passed. The reasoning was that the cat had taken the jogger by coincidence. It was probably hungry; and would now try for more traditional prey. They rattled horns to attract the large bucks.

It was not long before they saw fresh tracks – large and sunk heavily into the mud. The prints revealed retractable claws; and again confirmed the presence of a mountain lion. They were certain they were closing in - save one older man in the party. He heaved a sigh and said,

"We been drawn to this gap... don't like the looks of it. They's something strange..."

After much eye-rolling, snickering and sneering – questions clad in modicum of decency sauntered forth to challenge the errant observation. But the older tracker was resolute. He repeated his admonishment.

"Looks like a sacred place to me - the gap's one big circle....Maybe we oughta' wait for the cat to come out. Tell ya man, it's too easy – this cat's bigger than normal; and we could become a buffet."

But the loose democracy prevailed. They would flush out the animal. It would have to turn back and show itself.

The surrounding forest was beginning to 'close down' early. The abscission layer had set off a quiet alarm and cut off the water supply to the leaves. Carotene colors had begun to surface through fading green. The trees were protecting their water supply; and tucking in corners to prepare for a coming chill. The loss of the green in the leaves signaled the end of food production for the year. Diminished light would cause them to use up what excess food was in 'storage' and cause growth to stop. The stomata would close (one more corner tucked in) and the moderation of temperatures within its branches would cease with the rapid falling of the trees "green cooks" who worked in the trees' great kitchens. The trees would go into a state of dormancy until spring returned and slowly massaged the sap back into old limbs. The incursion of the woods was about business, though the period loveliness of the surroundings could not be disregarded by anyone. But...the changes were also a reminder that death was ever near.

Bob was conscious of the woods beauty. He watched it quietly; and – when he could - listened to the slow talk of trees as they communicated silent messages to the neighboring under story. As an observer, he was witness to the passage of time within the life of the woods. He thought he perceived that the trembling of leaves was more than just a seasonal affect. Parts of the trees conversation seemed to drop like hard filings. They were not happy; and suggested a transgression in the slow-changing regulation of their world.

When, at last, the tracking party stopped for the day. Bob chose a corner of the camp from which he could observe. His attention was once again seized by the brutish tracker with the patch. The man's darkness was extensive. He watched him mulling about the campsite. There was nothing fine about him. He barked out orders to the men in his group, as if he had led before; and intended the larceny of free will. His was a theatrical display of power. The big man directed that a fire be built and sat by it warming his hands and exerting a menacing psychology. As if in protest - or perhaps to underscore the man's darkness - the softness of the firelight only roughened his appearance.

The fire also aroused a flicker of thought in the Indian. Bob remembered where he had seen the man. He resisted the temptation to engage him, wondering instead about the unlikely encounter between the man and the husband of Sophia Angaros as the two stood in line beside each other.

Their juxtaposition had initially seemed serendipitous...but had lingered too long. Bob was now certain there was more than a casual connection between them. The artificiality of that chance meeting; and the coarseness of their interaction might have gone unnoticed except for one thing. Seconds after the conversation, Sophia Angaros had produced a white kerchief to her husband. He had been bitten on the arm by something; and the kerchief was needed to wipe away a few drops of blood.

Meanwhile -far from the tracking party and on his way to another assignment - 'RC' wondered what had happened to the Indian. And he tried to forget about a young woman who had once been his life's linchpin.

SILHOUETTES OF CHANGE

The dull ache of the day's tracking had pushed the group to exhaustion. Night had closed in and they had managed to set up camp. Overly tired, the thought of a 'Grendel' like monster[12] ready to spring out of the brush and sample humans as if they were canapés, seemed unlikely. And most were too tired to be concerned. They didn't even have the strength to resist a trend.

They tucked themselves into sleeping bags and tents and prepared to nest for the night. But some of the younger scientists continued to play with electronic gadgets while slurping camp stew or chewing on day-old bread. The scalloped leaves of a nearby tree swirled about the camp – another indication of drought, an advancing season, and the wind's neural omnipresence.

It was odd therefore, to hear the following banter among a few of the scientists who had gathered around a campfire. As if in unspoken agreement that the night should not end so soon – or perhaps bored by technology - their conversation seemed unordinary and incited by the grandeur of land they rarely traversed. One asked,

"Do you think trees have souls?"

"Do I think fleas are in my roll?" another responded – much to the laughter of fellow travelers.

"Oh...okay, I'll 'bite'. No, I don't!"

Another offered,

"Well, actually, if trees are connected – as they claim aspens are – they're really only one organism. That would mean they wouldn't each have a soul – just part of one!"

"Oh, sweet Lord...!" There were more snickers.

One, who was particular about definition or who had perhaps dipped into theological curricula, persisted in the discussion – unwilling to let it be suspended,

"I think it very much depends upon what one believes is the embodiment of a soul. Is it the 'spiritual' part of something as opposed to its physical form? Or is it the emotional part of something? Is it merely sentiment – or high

---

12   A monstrous man eating descendent of Cain slain by Beowulf in the Old English poem 'Beowulf'.

mindedness? Or...is it the disembodied spirit of something that has died?"

The half suppressed laughter that followed was an indication of those who were uncertain of their position in the world. That lack of certainty left the scent of insecurity. Few had really thought about the separation or meaning of something they took for granted. The group studied things – but did not seem interested in contemplating miracles before them – now they were out of the classroom and immersed in a nature that was far from 'textbook'.

Humans stood at the top of the pyramid and were therefore, closer to touching God. The inference was not without merit – we had the superior monkey brain. But despite the practical deduction, there were those in the discussion, who quietly conceded that they could never completely know the thoughts and perceptions of other life...that there might be a flaw in such premise.

How could we know? We did not live as long as other living things. And we could not run as fast; jump as high; or fight as ferociously. Neither could we apparently survive as easily. Humans were less adaptable; and had built up an artificiality of protections that often did not comport with the world in which we lived. Was our uniqueness superior – or was it simply unique? Some conceded that the concept of a human soul seemed cerebral craft or an exclusionary presumption to separate humans from other species. Maybe we just settled for what was comfortable. And while the conversation continued, Bob noticed the trees mocking lack of concern.

Another esoteric question came in quick pursuit; and the snickers of country trackers on the other side of the camp, became audible.

"Okay...so do you think a mountain has honor?"

Someone quipped,

"More than you, at least it's willing to 'stand on' something! But we won't talk about your forays..."

The questioner ignored the remark and continued,

"I mean...do you think we ought to use our surroundings for the sake of human consumption and survival – or should we use them for 'study'? Or should we 'use' them at all...?"

The 'quipster' - obviously too tired and cynical to care – followed up,

"Oh...for the love of...why don't we just wrap a big bow around our surroundings and 'teach the world to sing in three part harmony'..."

Someone else offered,

"Not with your singing – you have a voice that could clear a church!"

More snickers...and then, there was another interjection,

"I don't understand why the earth would even bother to 'splurge on the beauty of flowers'...must be less complicated ways to keep life going. Always seemed like a waste to me..."

"Bet he's a real 'Romeo,'" someone added. "What did you do on your last anniversary – show up with a wagon-load of hay and a box of cauliflower?"

Another remarked,

"Well, personally, I've always been amazed by the complexity of a single cell. The single cell is its own phenomenon - worthy of respect."

"Well, there's a flight of fancy that should be shot down and roasted on a spit..."

"Hey, I know it sounds crazy. But when I was a kid, I used to pretend like I was a cloud. You know – just to experience it...maybe float quietly, constantly changing shape... looking down on a herd of buffalo. Seriously – how cool would that be?!"

A young woman, who had been awakened, rolled over in her sleeping bag and said drowsily,

"Really...I only have one question, 'Who was cleaning up after the cloud – while he was drifting?"

The rest of the group laughed riotously. Remarkably the conversation compelled energy among the less sleepy and cynical until someone shouted out,

"Who started this conversation? I think it was Grady. Hey Grady, why you wanna know if a tree has a soul?! You gonna go psychic on us...able to read primitive minds all of a sudden...!"

Then they stole self-conscious glances at Bob, vaguely aware that they might have offended the only native in the party.

The conversation evaporated; and most returned to their palm pilots with intensity. Meanwhile, Grady, a short, stout fellow who had graduated with top honors in the field of zoology, and who had 'volunteered' to go along on the hunt and 'simply out of interest', was the butt of much negative attention. He was an easy target – both because of his stature and because he had 'no dog in the fight' related to saving, finding, or killing the mountain lion.

It was dinner time; and Grady's interest was decidedly more consumptive. He pulled out a special packet of dried food; and emptied the contents into a cook pot over the fire. Then he poured in a measured amount of water. A labyrinth of swirls inside the small pot curled into the air and the aroma wafted about. He methodically stirred the loose chunks of meat until they became moist; while he rocked back and forth to the music coming through his 'ear buds'.

His activity captured the attention of the immense hunter with the patch on his shirt. The man had emptied the rest of the corn dog crumbs from his pocket while his favorite hound 'snarfed' it out of the dust. He was not a man given to expression. A gale of contempt stirred within him.

One of the scientists shouted, "Hey Grady! How long's it gonna take? You goin' on sabbatical or are you just cooking dinner?!"

Grady ignored everything around him and poured a little Tabasco sauce in what appeared to be the drippings of gravy that was forming. It was just then, that the tempo of the wind increased. A sudden gust sent light pots flying and pushed a curtain of dust about the camp. Grady – who was unflappable when it came to food – covered the pot he had been stirring and put a flat stone on the top of it. His tent was nearby and he could hear the tent flap whipping about in the wind – making sounds like a backfiring muffler. He removed his ear buds; and ambled over to secure the flap.

Within seconds, a small, but intense, 'dust devil' had overtaken the well-ordered camp. Metal pots, cans and equipment were strewn about making the site look like a garage full of auto parts while many in the camp shrieked. From the corner where he sat, Bob marveled at the winds impartiality as it spared some things; and knocked over others. The tracking party scurried to save what they could. Only the powerfully built tracker rested in place. He gave his dog a pat on the head; unconcerned by anything the wind could do. He was watching as the short, stout man returned to the fire and fished leaves out of the stew that he had been stirring. Grady whined,

"Dammit! I got this stuff at a camp store. Very latest in dried food – a bit expensive too! ...A damn fine meal – "beef bourguignon'."

There were more remarks at Grady's expense. The large tracker had retreated further into the shadow of nearby trees. Bob watched him quietly. The man seemed to be assessing the chubby biologist. Without warning, he strode over; and stood before the pot stirrer – and looked at him menacingly. Collecting a throat full of spit, he sent it like a missile to the edge of the fire – close to the simmering pot. The fire seemed to crackle and explode. Then he scratched his stomach; and growled,

"Stuff smells pretty fancy for camp food. What the hell you call it?"

Grady responded, "Beef Bourguignon – want a spoonful?"

The big man bent over as if to smell it. "Seems like it needs a pinch of something to me..."

He opened up another pocket in his coat; and pulled out a small container. Then, twisting it open shook out something that looked like coarsely ground pepper; and scowled,

"Blend of my special herbs and spices – will turn this crap into something a man can eat."

Then he walked away insolently. The night was as dark as a spaniel's eye; and the chill was now acute. Bob sat nearly motionless. The wind had cleared the clouds; and the luster of the stars was visible. His thoughts sped like a comet. Things that hadn't made sense earlier – were coming into focus. This was the man with many feet behind him...a powerful man he had seen in his dream. Bob was thinking about the dream and what it might mean; when he noticed the voice of the trees seemed altered and somewhat disturbed. He slowly looked around him and realized...the forest didn't seem 'right'.

His mind now raced through centuries of research gleaned from college curricula involving trees and the evolution of flowering plants. Trees had differing requirements. Some had a narrow distribution – like the Yellowwood – while others populated widely and with ease. The Live Oak followed the coast; and some southern trees reached northward up the river valleys, such as the Bald Cypress. The Red Spruce was a native tree that extended southward along the mountaintops. It was a rivalry that the trees spoke to each other about, sometimes in warring words that only they understood. And it was a competition that only men who knew the secrets of certain types of husbandry - were acquainted with.

The trees that had seized Bob's attention were not typically 'known' for growing in a stand. They were solitary, thirsty trees that sucked water with ferocity; and which did not belong in the environment in which he found himself. The native trees rapidly uttered remarks – it was uncharacteristic for them to be excitable.

Bob speculated that perhaps someone had planted them as a test – but why in the middle of what appeared to be a virgin forest? He was aware of tensions between locals and government employees in the area. Residents had jack-hammered fossils out of public lands and shot at conservators. Publicly held meetings sometimes seemed to incite – and were often on the border of riot.

Could it simply be human interference? But these trees were not endemic. He wondered how they could have survived a climate that actively resisted them. Something had rammed into the native ecosystem...and sent it sprawling. And he knew – that when something like this occurred – a monster was often born within the lightning.

His thoughts flew back to the day and an earlier siting that he had dismissed. He had been so intent on studying the brutish man that he had forgotten an aberration he had observed.

He remembered now. At first, he had barely noticed the silhouettes. The trees were far in the distance. The branches swung back and forth in the wind, looking like the manes of running horses. Their limbs seemed sinuous. They were clumped together; like they had marched forth from a boat...to lay claim to a land that they did not recognize. Their branches whipped wildly in the wind. Their trunks seemed to have penetrated the ground, deeply intent on remaining in their new found altitude. They were assertively out of place, like neighbors who had advanced onto property to which they were not entitled. These were willow trees; and their dark images incised into the blue sky of the day as they drew the sparse water out of the ground through surgically precise root systems.

At that particular instant, he felt a sudden slap on the back which nearly sent him sprawling. Bob caught himself less he be propelled into the middle of the idle conversation of those who continued to chatter among themselves around the fire.

"Howdy, chief."

The native man righted himself; and looked back to see the very large man with the patch on his shirt, his hand extended.

"Name's Gregor – what's yours?"

They were far enough away that the introduction failed to attract the attention of the others. The large man had come up behind him with amazing speed and the quiet agility of one who was accustomed to living out in the woods. The slap on the back had been friendly but strong – like that of a man who took his physical strength for granted.

Bob introduced himself. Brushing away the dirt on his palms, he shook the man's hand. The strength of the handshake was enough to convince him that misfortune surely lay in the path of anyone who he might oppose.

"Sorry about the surprise...I notice you always take the edge of the camp." The man had obviously been mapping his movements.

"I don't blend well." Bob quipped.

Music from one of the younger biologists Iphones momentarily distracted the man. He sneered a little and then returned his gaze to Bob; and spat in the dirt.

"You a tracker too, chief..." Then he used the edge of his thumbnail to clean a space between his teeth.

"Yep..." Bob looked at the rough face of the man before him. He was not unfamiliar with the face – he had seen it years before in his dream. It was the face of the man who had stood on the horizon, surveying a tranquil village below him; and wondering what might be there for the taking.

"Nice to meet ya'.... Maybe we'll find that cat...and maybe we won't..."

He said it as if he were a dog who had sniffed the essence of the Indian; and now, knew him. His comment regarding the cat seemed more wishful than uncertain. Then he suddenly turned around; and – taking a willow limb that he had obviously snapped off earlier - appeared to idly drag it behind him through the dirt, as if to eliminate any trace of his having been there.

Their meeting startled Bob almost as much as the enormous man's departure. The merchandise of thought related to the misfit trees no longer seemed worthy of purchase –his attention had been captured. This was no gentleman. Gregor had an expansive and generous brutality worthy of a kenneled dog. He seemed to feast on fear and surprise. There were some men whose iron blood could be smelled through their pores as if they were wearing the skins of something else. They scoffed at sophistication or subtlety; and came from areas of deep woods where spoken words were distractions. They were sentient beings who shunned the volley of conversation, instead curling in rocks...waiting...venomous. They longed not for quiet, self-contemplation, but for the benefactions of time – resting in place for something to go by unaware. The gravity of their darkness was basic and something with which the native was familiar. He shuddered like a moth trying to shake off a spider.

But, for all of this, there was a surprising comfort in the understanding of this man called, Gregor. His motive was oddly pure – self survival. He would take the advantage before becoming sacrifice. Though the motive was corporeal, there was also a fundamental ethic in its intent. The contradiction left Bob a bit uncomfortable; as did an obscure verse which unexpectedly came to him,

"C'est le serpent, dit-elle, je l'ai ecoute, et il m'a trompee."

For some reason, he thought of the young wasihcu. He wondered when and where he would see 'RC' again. And then, he thought of a young girl who had been plucked from mud. Both had been part of the dream that had propelled him forward in his journey.

Earlier in the day, a bed of adder's tongue lilies had been trampled by the tracking party. It was then that he remembered his dream long ago in the sod hut with Louise. This was the flower that the wind had left on his chest and to which he had awakened. He had peered deep into the flower's small funnel as if it were a vortex to another sphere.

Finally, his thoughts wondered back to the puzzling stand of trees. Bob lifted his head to the wind, but could only discern its bohemian dance among them. The native trees seemed restless but – if there was information – they were holding it together in trust, unwilling to share confidence. He wondered what the alien trees had displaced. Something was off balance; and it meant that there would be anomalies elsewhere. Something would die in order to hold the secret.

It was then that he also remembered the dream at the sod hut again; and the vision of a young man named Sincero who he was now certain would be part of 'RC's journey. Now...the wind was high in the clouds.

On the side of the mountain where the tracking party was camped was evidence of grazing. The land had probably been leased out for such purpose. Or perhaps, stray cattle had made their way to that spot in search of better grasses while local ranchers pretended to fix fence that didn't need mending. The cattle had created twisting trails that resembled artificial boundaries – a sort of bovine gerrymandering. A warm, hellish wind increased in velocity and distributed dry seeds that had been loosely secured to plants; and waiting for the right moment. The seeds scattered about as leftovers from a late summer that frequently begged for the nourishment of water. In the sky there were brief flashes of – what some referred to – as heat lightning. The sky seemed angry, bent on vengeance – but not willing to grant rain. Querulous thunder would not set aside difference. Its sound rumbled across the heavens with a heavy measured tread while the lightning occasionally revealed plush purple velvet above the campsite. The welfare of the tracking party was not in any particular danger despite the theatrics.

Those camped around the small fire's edge watched to make sure the fire did not ascribe to the celestial gusto above it. Otherwise, they continued to play with their technology. The fire occasionally responded to small blasts of air but never intruded beyond the rock border. It seemed to understand its destiny, feathering about the edges but never producing the seed of a spark beyond where it was intended. It produced strong shadows that made any certainty seem quaint.

As Bob sat musing one of the shadows captured his attention. It was another species of tree with a most unusual quality that adjoined the campsite. The tree had the leaves of a gingko but did not branch. Instead, there were strong terminal shoots – not branches. It appeared to be a deciduous tree with coniferous growing habits. Genetically speaking, it was either a mess or a marvel. How could he have missed it?

He thought back to his studies. Conifers had developed approximately 200 million years ago – about the time that dinosaurs ascended – while deciduous trees had developed much later and near the great lizards' extinction. To have such divergent characteristics on the same tree seemed a collision of biology. He marveled at it and then rose to take a closer look.

Like linoleum in a cathedral; it seemed a profanity. He wondered, 'were there really constructs that governed reliable inference'? He was more uncertain than he had ever been. But what bothered him more was the speculation that such changes might impact the sacred path of wandering souls – something he deeply believed in.

He had seen enough for one day. He looked up to the sky and noted the small orphan star called 'Spica'. Many miles away, a young woman named Anna gazed at the same star. She sensed that she was not alone in her admiration at that moment...and wondered 'who' shared her intuition and 'why'. Bob sensed her wonderment.

Returning from the edge of the camp, he slid into his bedding. Thoughts of parallel reality and the wedding of life and death now kept him awake. The trees were speaking again. They laughed at his confusion – he who simply had a 'gnat's lifespan'...in their eyes. But their laughter was more measured. Their own existence was brief when compared to those of the ancestor stones and the stars. Just then, the wind blew down across the trees; and they carried a stern message to the native.

"Humans could never understand the language of the stone ancestors. The ancestors' speech was far too deliberate and with no reference to time. To the human, it could only be the interface between story and history."

And the trees laughed until the rain began to fall - content that there would always be secrets.

The profundity of the statement moved him. What was left? The buffalo herds, swarms of passenger pigeons, the great rafts of scaups in the bays – all had disappeared. The thought did not decimate him for Bob believed that nothing was ever 'gone'. There was an invisible code that held things together. Rather, he was in awe. Was 'how' and 'what' ever as important as 'why'? He was certain that though faith might demand – she would never explain...and he was content to be part of the great mystery.

The light rain had awakened him. His attention was captured by the area in which he lay wide awake inside of his sleeping bag. The land would not let him sleep. Just as the trees had conveyed...the spirit rocks by which he rested had an ancient history. He understood that there were stories in every square foot of earth. And he felt the presence one often feels in abandoned places – a great sadness, and the lost joy and hope of prior lives. What he felt must be the ancestry of man and all other living things that had crossed where he lie...a cemetery of events, about which the stone spirits understood. But now...it was 'old people's crap' as the young ones called it. Ancestors had moved from the trees to savannah; and left those instincts behind that did not seem to walk easily upright.

Across the land on which he lay, had been the heavy steps of ice age prey and the swift footfalls of Neanderthal. The feet of settlers had once trod – chasing their futures across the mountain. Here, where he rested, the flight of slaves...running and hiding – had played out. The fox and rabbit had both hidden there. But, more recently, something 'wild' had marked its territory; and had ejected the contents of what its stomach could not digest – then lapped it up again. Even the light steps of the brutish tracker named, Gregor... had been felt by the stone ancestors. This was as much as the trees would convey from the wind's conversation.

He wondered at the magic; and how no one – except the child - seemed surprised anymore at the great magic. Why should wonder be sucked out of us? Though questions were important, perhaps watching and waiting for answers to be revealed had equal merit.

Finally exhausted by questions that he could not answer, Bob sat up and scanned the horizon. Moonlight revealed a bank of clouds sitting on a nearby ridge, hanging over it like a loose vale. Small diamonds of light twinkled through the moving branches of nearby trees. What good was it to know all the words of a language if one could not understand its poetry? This was the wisdom of the stones – and they inferred that something was changing the poetry of the land.

He turned his head just in time to see the brutish man, Gregor, bend down in the shadow and pick up something. Just past the firelight, he watched the large man's silhouette pull back and send a stone hurtling toward the heavens.

CAT CAPTURE

Because most had not slept well or comfortably, the following morning arrived too soon. The rigors of a day of riding and tracking seemed a 'tough sell'. Eggs frying in a panful of lard – that was the first things they smelled. It was just enough to pardon the interruption of their sleep. Fragments of eggshells thrown into a sluggish fire randomly divided the hot ashes and crackled as the remnants were consumed by flames. If there was poetry to dawn, the birds spoke it while conducting their affairs – meanwhile fastidiously administering the guardianship of nests. But they seemed incredibly unconcerned by the pans of frying eggs. They flitted about seemingly without purpose; and sometimes, soared along on hollow bones with the wind currents...their floating, at times, angelic. The older tracker in the party cocked his ears to the wind and then mumbled a worry from the previous evening,

"I don't like this. It don't feel right. Sumpin's funny. I tracked animals before and this one don't seem normal. I swear it just don't seem normal...."

In the middle of the eastern sky, the sun shone brightly. Daylight had restored some of the group's confidence - as light was apt to do. A few of the trackers derided the older man.

"Sam here says somethin' don't feel normal. Whatcha think about that? Damn cat's got him spooked."

The older man continued,

"It's done doubled back and kept us busy the better part of the day and night. I dunno – this 'un's smart. I know we saw claw marks on a big log back there, but I felt a pair of eyes up in them trees. I think it just' plain ran back and forth across the log to fool us. And they's somethin' else..."

There was more sneering disapproval.

"No! Really, I aint a kiddin'! I done felt those eyes. 'Member how the dogs done lost the scent? I think the damn thing marked the log and jumped into the tree near it. We're just followin' our noses. We don't know where the hell it is. And them cat tracks...they don't seem right, don't seem like they 'sposed to be..."

His placid countenance had been peeled away like it was a tangerine.

"...The print's like a cat print – ain't no visible claw marks, 'cause the animal done pulled them in. But them tracks don't line up one behind the other. This one is joggin' side to side – sorta like a dog – but not really...and its feet done sunk deep in the mud – big sonofabitch."

Then he glanced at the large tracker, Gregor, with a worried look that no man should have.

"So what – it's probably injured. The jogger must'a hurt it before it killed her."

Gregor's voice was emotionless. As if in recognition of his tone, the wind pushed an icy cloud over the sun; and the light was momentarily held in place.

Could be – but there's somethin' else.... The cats walkin' and runnin' on its feet – not the toes! That ain't the way cat prints are 'sposed to look. They runs on their toes. This thing's hittin' the ground with full feet – sorta like it's learnin' to run."

Then the older tracker looked over his shoulder nervously - wishing that he hadn't said anything; and feeling exposed. Caution dictated that he must not admit to any other such sensitivity. It could be read as a weakness. Tracking had been good pay; and he needed money.

The intricate interweaving of something esoterically referred to as 'life'; and its mysteries were not subjects that the group of country trackers spoke of. These were topics reserved for poets and Indians. Such conversations were irritating, weak, and incomprehensible to men who had bills to pay and needed to put food on the table. Feeling vulnerable and foolish, the old man momentarily regained his composure by stirring the eggs over the fire – until the crackle of a random spark caught his attention.

The energy of the fire caused the spark to shoot high into the air and pirouette. The old tracker saw it cut across the strand of a large web hanging from a tree above them. The spider that 'owned' the web was provoked by the tremor. It clambered quickly toward the vibration. But the web's imbalance could no longer hold its weight. It plummeted earthward into the mouth of the flaming pit; where it fizzled and died. When the old man looked up again, he could feel Gregor's eyes burning through the cloud shadow like a warning. He returned his attention to eggs that were already overcooked; and then quickly doled out 'camp slop'.

After the tracking party had eaten, they discussed the logistics of the day. Some furtively drank beverages they thought might relax them; while listening to instructions with diminished acuity. They were certain they had chased the mountain lion into a ravine that had a single entry and exit. Outside of the ravine, a deep hole would be dug. Strong netting would be placed over the hole with leaves and other light debris scattered over it. A sizeable carcass had been placed in the hole as bait. It would be laced with poison in case the trap didn't work. The lead biologist – who had assessed the combined mental prowess of the trackers – advised Gregor to have the men take frequent breaks and to keep them well-fed. It was a thinly concealed attempt to prevent the bungling of a mission that he was now tired of.

The men worked like a colony of insects. Camp cooklery that had dried overnight was gathered and stowed away quietly – to avoid any distracting noise or scent that might startle a 'skittish' animal. Bedding, tents, and dogs were removed and taken farther away. The mashed grass and any evidence of fire were obliterated. After a period of time, the trackers had finished. Exhausted, they sat, drank, and watched as small, quiet animals started their own day of searching for food, while being careful not to become such. The wind blew across the wild grasses and up to the feet of the trees. It gently nudged the dew back into the ground or carried it away. And as the sun crawled into the sky, the heat whittled away any remaining morning mist; and late cicadas buzzed like busy merchants.

The biologists in the party had tired of watching the trackers work; and some had 'pitched in' to help in the grimy task. When it became evident that their efforts were neither welcomed nor appreciated, the group had left the ravine to follow a small footpath and idly study the complexity of the ecosystem in which they were immersed. They noted the botanical aberrations that Bob had previously seen; and were discussing it in some measure...when they heard shots that sent them running back at full speed.

The baying of hunting hounds further insinuated what all had been waiting for – something had been tree'ed or trapped. As complement to the baying, the trackers were making their own abundant noise – much like people who had just discovered the restorative power of soap and water.

By the time the biologists had arrived, it was clear that a large cat had fallen into the trap that had been dug for it. The tawny mass of prey was seething about in the deep well – teeth bared, vehement – rage exceeding capable description – and making jumps at the wall. Though the animal had not made it to the bait, it had fallen meanly. It was now frightened and angry. A single shot to the buttocks sent the mountain lion into more of a rage. Miraculously, the sedation had been well-administered by one of the trackers.

The biologists cajoled the onlookers into quiet; and gently insisted that they withdraw from the cat's sight. The cat roamed about lazily until its body gave out. Ten to fifteen minutes later – and after a few meager attempts to jump – it fell into sleep. Almost immediately the more experienced biologists jumped into the pit. They moved quickly to the great cats head and checked for signs of salivation. Telazol mixed with atropine had been used in the darts and they needed to check for signs of an intact pharageal reflex and make a decision whether to intubate the cat. Timing was essential. The cat's vitals were checked; and a cage was lowered to prepare it for transport. Its wild cells were caught up in a wave of sleep that would be just enough time to cage and prepare it for a trip down the mountain.

The cat's eyes were still open when the cage was pulled from the bottom of the pit. Bob looked into them. The bright tapestry of flattened cells beneath its retina bounced the light off and back onto the retina. It was the familiar glow that one sees when shining a light on a cat at night. As he looked into the animal's eyes, a reflection of his face was just visible in them, but something bothered him. The retinas seemed slightly different than normal.

The trackers enthusiastically celebrated the capture. There was much whooping and back-patting which they followed up with bottles of shared 'hooch' and elaborately dull stories and comments about how each had come mortally close to danger.

"I done thought it was a joke…'til I heard the first snarls."

"Damn thing looks like the devil – don't it?!"

"Ain't seen nothing like this in Calvinsville!"

"Poke it – see if it's still breathin'."

"Shoo…, I AIN'T startin' up no fire, man!"

"Hey 'Rog'…ain't you interested? Guys! He's back there – cool as a cucumber – just takin' a smoke!" The large tracker with the patch seemed only mildly interested in the capture.

"I think I done saw it move a bit. You think it's wakin' up. Maybe we ought to shoot it again – whatchu think?"

Bob sat next to a stump – looking quietly at the animal. Its eyes looked intelligent. His attention was drawn to the lead biologists. The man looked as tired and ragged as a potato field. Like anyone who had been out too long, he craved the warmth and companionship of the family he had left at home. He pulled a flint out of his pocket and struck it to restore what fervor he had lost during the day; and – as humans had done for 16,000 years – managed to create a fire. Rubbing his hands together over it, he shuddered in a personal cold; and then asked,

"Anybody seen Grady?!"

DESERT SKULL

It was early evening. The city lights in the distance produced a faint glow in the sky that seemed to be momentarily supported by the black bedrock of an unfathomable horizon.

'RC' was fresh into his new assignment; and had found nothing. He didn't really understand why he had been sent to the middle of the god-forsaken desert. The assignment seemed insubstantive; and was 'privately funded'. He thought of the native tracker, Bob. He was irritated by the man's certainty and the assertion that they had found the wrong 'cat'. It seemed like another failure in his life. He cynically wondered if the second tracking party had benefited from Bob's abundant personality deficiencies...and whether they had found the mountain lion that had killed the jogger. Perhaps the native had seeded doubt there as well. And he wondered at the trickery of how the wallet – that he had thought was consumed by the fire – had suddenly appeared. Still he was grateful to have it back.

Their conversations still bothered him. He tried to motivate himself by being grateful that confidence in him had been restored – the central office had sent him on another assignment. But the nagging doubts, which were the remnants of his pairing with the native man, left him terminally resentful.

Looking up again at the night sky, he could see that the three quarter moon was swaddled in darkness and gently glowing like the halo of the Christ child. He searched the sky until he located the constellation, 'Bootes'. 'The Herdsman' was just barely visible in the heavens; and was keeping watch over his imaginary flock - striding the vast heavens with a pair of hunting dogs.

'RC's new assignment involved the report of 'mysterious bones' in – what some considered – a 'vortex' area. He had studied paleontology; and was reasonably certain from the accounts that the bones were those of a dinosaur. But, searching for inspiration that evening had proved more elusive than searching for bones.

Coughdrop, Nevada, was a ghost town with a dry spring – and not on any of the state maps. Could the name have been more appropriate? It was a town that seemed to have dissolved; but the search for it still left one with a dry throat. He was camped near the ghost town. That alone was enough to make him miss even the native man's impertinence. And he was sharing the area with desert 'hit men' whose tell-tale rattle alerted any hiker to back off or face consequence – something that seemed strangely civil. Everything that could be stolen, used, or taken as a souvenir from the empty town, had been. There was not much left to it other than a prankish sign that said 'Gringo Go Home', a half-eaten bag of potato chips, a few dozen empty beer bottles, and the remnants of what appeared to be a gas station. Barely a litter-clad phantom of another time, the town had never seen the likes of a mall or movie theater. Sad, sun-baked memories remained – memories which had been ground by sand; frozen and melted again; dried into vapor; and then, lifted away by the dry unpredictable wind that served as the desert's pallbearer.

Only one noteworthy remnant of adversity had been discovered. It was a faded piece of paper in the corner of the gas station's remains. Once nailed to a wall, the paper had been blown down like its author. It seemed an odd testimonial to human struggle; and read as follows:

The feed bags are all gone. The desert moans. Salt sits on the land. Brave women and men stood like trees, exalted by dreams. Left only with thirst, now balled-up in earth, they call from graves while the coyote plays. Since deceased, and waiting to be released from their beds of sand and pillows of stone, their starch-white bones long – not for a glimpse of hearth and field – but for a Heaven that arrogance once keenly concealed.

'RC' turned the paper over to see if there was anything that might lead to the identity of the author – there was not. He would head home tomorrow, empty-handed. He had found no bones; and there was nothing to discover here.

He mused briefly about the poem's meaning, before turning off the small flashlight that he kept by the bed. As he lay on an uncomfortable RV mattress something appeared to flutter past the window. Pulling himself up, he peered out; and thought he discerned a large moth making its way in the mulberry light of an enveloped moon. What could it be heading for? It disappeared over a slight rise before reappearing on the edge of a small hill that seemed covered in a bed of flowers. How had he not noticed that hill during his two day encampment? He chalked it up to the mysterious speed with which the desert could suddenly come alive. Like an apparition heading for a mirage, the moth and flowers seemed to melt together and then fade. He fell back down on the hard mattress wondering if it was merely a mirage and if he was more tired than he suspected.

When he awoke the following morning, his nasal cavities were dry and irritated. The last line of the poem that he had found in the abandoned gas station...had remained with him through the night; and he wondered about his own arrogance. He hadn't slept well. Outside, the wind was blowing dust and sand about.

But more surprising than all of this, was the presence of a small flower that he found lying on his chest. It startled him. He recognized it immediately as a trout lily and wondered how it had come to be there, for it was neither endemic nor suited for the area. He finally reasoned that the wind had picked it up and carried it from afar, before blowing it inside. A nagging thought compelled him to look out the window toward the small hill that he had seen before going to sleep. But the wind had shifted the sand; and the landscape seemed different. He looked deep into the vortex of the flower and wondered at the power of the wind.

Then, he prepared a meager breakfast and resentfully resigned to the poem's power once again. He twirled the flower around in his fingers and placed it gently on the counter. After swigging the last bit of some old coffee, he cleaned up with a small bit of water.

He had just put the keys in the ignition and was prepared to leave, when he stopped. 'RC' thought of Bob again and how the man had mercilessly teased him about his shortcomings. Perhaps it was the desire to annul any such inadequacy – or wanting to prove the actuality of what he thought he had seen shortly before going to sleep – but something compelled him out of the vehicle.

The sun was higher in the sky and the day was warming rapidly, but he felt a renewed sense of vigor and focus. He strode with purpose out the door of the RV. He would not allow Bob to impugn his character or make him feel defeated. He would find the damn bones that he had been sent to find - if he had to resurrect someone. And so, he started out.

He had walked for nearly an hour before it occurred to him that he was very tired and hot ...and possibly, lost. More than likely, he had been walking in circles. 'RC' sat on the ground barely aware of the sandburs; and feeling quite discouraged. Then he made a silent promise to himself that he would never go outdoors again without a portable GPS.

Though he felt like screaming, there was no point. There was no one within miles; and he needed to save his strength. The top of his head was beginning to feel like it was on fire. He cursed for having not thought to bring a hat; and had just prepared to stand up – when an unexpected fortress of shade fell upon him. It lasted only an instant – and was too quick for a passing cloud. It was also too quiet for a plane. 'RC' looked up just in time to watch it sail over a small hummock and head downward – a bird of immense size. It must be a vulture.

Hitching up his gortex pants, he sprinted in its direction with as much energy as he could muster. Even if nothing else was over the crest of the hummock, he would at least glimpse upon a bird that had to be 'a record'. But, as he neared the rise, he saw its shadow disappear again over a nearby sand hill. He would have felt quite discouraged had it not been for the scattered remains of bones, now white as a wedding gown on the low ground just in front of him. The large bird had, no doubt, come back to feed.

He slowly descended from the hummock – out of breath, exhausted, but with increasing curiosity. As he neared the low area, he could see that its perimeter was loosely defined by a circle of stakes that appeared to be monument markers. In the center were scattered bones...and the cranium of an exceptionally long head that seemed to have belonged to an adult of remarkable stature. Though the cranium would need further forensics, it appeared to be a very large hominid. Unearthed by the same desert wind that had partially buried it, the skull was well-preserved. 'RC' picked it up and held it to the light while examining the subtle cephalic tissue markings. It was heavy; and he was reasonably certain that DNA evidence might be extracted from a core of bone that seemed to have not been fully ossified.

A sandy mixture poured forth as he tilted it. He righted it immediately and heard something rattling inside. He recoiled immediately and dropped the cranium. Snakes were likely to find the hollow openings of a skull an attractive place to rest. Ever so cautiously, he picked it up again. The sandy mixture continued to pour out like rough sand from one of the sockets. A large shadow soared over him once again; and caused him to fumble and look up. He quickly laid the large skull on the ground; and shaded his eyes. But – whatever it was - had faded into the zenith.

Bending down, he picked up the skull once more; and turned the head back and forth. The rattling started once more. It sounded like a 'rain stick'. Slowly he revolved the large cranium. With a free hand, he pulled out a small white handkerchief from his pocket. Taking both hands and giving the skull a forceful shake, seemed to free its contents. He watched a stream of darkish granules about the size of coarse pepper pour forth.

Picking up a handful of the granules, he rolled them around in his hands, feeling their irregularity. Their coarseness reminded him of the uneven sand at a shore break. He held up the cranium again. Despite the hollow darkness of the eye sockets, it seemed to release light back to the sky. Though he had not planned on an archaeological dig, he was now so excited that an aria was playing inside his head. His lack of preparation would not sway him. He briefly surveyed the area for small tracks – or worse, the curving smear of an 'S' like pattern, that a rattlesnake was apt to make. Seeing nothing, he began the delicate search for the rest of the body, removing the sand carefully around and near where he had discovered the cranium. A half an hour later in the blistering sun, he had discovered what he had hoped he would find – a radiating ring of bones attached to the top of the spine. It was the rib cage. Something had violently dislodged the head from the spine. He gently brushed away the sand until he could see more detail. Blowing away the remaining sand that seemed to interlace the bones, it became clear that the head had been snapped off.

'RC' pulled the skull close and eye-measured the distance of the skull to the breastbone. From lips to larynx, the distance of the typical adult throat was about six or seven inches. But this appeared to be twice that size – suggesting again that the skeleton had belonged to something of remarkable stature. He returned his attention to the skeleton. The length of the human head was typically about an eighth of the length of the body. This head was far larger in proportion. 'RC' wondered if the brain had been proportional in size. It baffled him; and he was concerned that he might be reading too much into the serendipitous finding. More remarkable, the bones appeared hollow and light – as if the marrow had been eaten away. In weight and consistency, they were comparable to the bones of a bird.

Feeling cramped, he stood up. The light fell hard upon him; and he suddenly felt weak. He realized that he had been too casual about preparing for a walk in the desert; and was now aware of the incredible heat. A determined wind had sprung forth. It blasted across the land, flinging sand about; and the sun felt like a furnace. Shielding his eyes, he peered into the distance and could see a bilateral mass of heated air and dust alternately whirling about and seeming to sink into the ground in an almost listless way. As it approached, he realized the twin-bodied wind would soon cover what he had labored to dig away. The 'dust-devil' was gaining intensity as it spiraled toward him, its pace absurdly quick and wobbly eccentric.

'RC' bent down and quickly tried to pick up a few of the longer light bones in the sand. To his dismay, they fell apart and poured through his hands. Looking at the roiling clouds in the near distance, he was aware that a storm of proportion was rapidly approaching and might cut off his return to the RV – if he could even find the RV.

Without thinking and with nothing but instinct, 'RC' jumped to his feet. Grabbing the cranium like a football, he began to run as quickly as he could – pumping his legs for all they were worth. The wind now flung mighty blasts of sand that had become needle-like shrapnel. Grit pushed into his mouth and eyes. Four more exhausted bounds sent him stumbling fortuitously into the perimeter of where he had parked - he was much closer than he had suspected.

He did not stop to think about his good luck. Instead – and with the results of his inquisition firmly tucked under his arm – he grabbed the door handle; and then released it immediately. It was as hot as an iron. Rallying his resolve, he reached for it again; yanked the car door open and dove onto the floor of the vehicle. Instead of finding relief, the internal temperature of the cabin made him feel like a baked potato. With all of his remaining strength, he pulled the door shut; and started the RV just long enough to roll up the windows. The sweat rolling down his temple and barely able to breathe, he listened to the screaming fury of the storm outside; and prayed for it to be over. He immediately despised himself for believing in the power of prayer; and, after awhile, fell soundly asleep – fully exhausted.

When he awoke the storm had passed. The last bit of daylight shined through gaps in the sand dunes; and created intense shadows. The sky was a rose-colored candle. He rolled down the windows and could see where the sand had buffed the body of the RV and etched into its windshield. The stars were beginning to appear in darker parts of the sky. The new-found calm and crisp air was enough to irritate small night animals out of complacency; and he could hear them foraging about. Cacti looked like trolls silhouetted against the sky. A tarantula was making its way slowly across the ground carrying a clutch of eggs on its back. The wind had blown back the sand from a small vein of rocks; and a chorus of birds took respite there chirping and clucking. The rose sky had developed greenish tinge in one corner where sand seemed to have been swept. Imminent smoky black in the east had begun to appear like the slender legs of something – creating a classic Western sky with bands of light. The landscape seemed sparsely operatic in its beauty. Cirrus clouds looked like the smears of lipstick across a holiday napkin; and the sounds of a few buzzing insects whirred as softly as a crude machine.

The sun disappeared quickly. The depth of the night sky's indigo had replaced the light as if it had been moved into place by a derrick. The fortune of night was devil to day. Night had adroitly set up her shop with stars that sparkled across façade as if to announce a prophetess who could deduce any destiny. It nimbly painted the landscape in muted colors and created deep shadows in the lower places with the genius of one who had always been an artist. She danced across the earth and sang in low tones.

'RC' looked at the enormous cranium lying on the floor of the vehicle. He would take it to a forensics lab and have it examined.

SOPHIA AND ARCHIBALD

Many miles away, a house sat, crouched like a crustacean on the edge of a beach. It was on a slight rise where tides were barely felt; and where the water belonged to a cove. Murky rocks with long locks of brown seaweed were made beautiful by the teal water surrounding them. There were flecks of small fishing boats bobbing in the distance. Spits of brown sand - littered with rock, seaweed, and beach debris - lent an unmistakable smell of coastal property. It was never totally silent at night. Distant bells or the gentle 'putta-putta-putta' of motors winding down as they approached the marina kept the bay from being too quiet. Added to this panoply of sound, was the soft rustle of the wind fingering its way through the sea oats; and the rhythm of tiny waves lapping the beach and forming a petticoat of froth at shore break.

What Sophia liked most about the area – was the darkness; and how countless stars kept the infinity from being too abysmal. To say it was night-time, would be to impose a schedule upon the night. She had long tired of timetables; and preferred to think of the moment as another bit of time in a flawless continuum. The area reminded her of her childhood.

The young Mediterranean woman was someone Bob had seen in his dream at 'the soddie'. But she had matured and was now middle aged. This was also the woman he had seen standing in line behind the second tracking party. The native man marveled at how dreams – like time – often did not seem to have clear chronology.

He sat on the stump and listened to the lead biologist who was still worrying about the missing man, Grady. The country trackers continued to re-count bigger and bolder stories about their brush with death and the captured cat. He was grateful therefore, to have inserted himself into the details of Sophia Angaros' life; for he still wondered about the connection between the couple and the dark man named, Gregor. His only regret was that his psychic ability had not allowed him to determine that connection. And so he dreamed...unencumbered by the space he was in; and now intrigued by the couple before him.

The patterns of her life were pleasant. Sophia preferred to fix Archibald's supper and then to excuse herself quietly to her coastal perch. There she would watch the ribbons of color disappear; as the visual purple of the sky theatrically revealed the evening star.

She had never been beautiful like her sister. Her eyebrows were a bit too heavy and arched rather than having 'that pencil-thin look' that would have made her more feminine in appearance. But she had a distinctive looking face – a face that showed incredible warmth.

She had the good fortune to 'marry into wealth'. He reminded her of her father; and 'Archie's' annuity had allowed them to live comfortably; and to have anything they wanted. They had furnished the house finely. She was comfortable there, but perhaps, more 'at home' sitting outdoors; and just breathing in the salt air. She liked the cove's unpretentiousness; and found the air exhilarating.

But tonight, even the iridescence of the marine plankton failed to arrest her attention. She sat, staring out at the cove, and thinking of the recent road trip they had taken. They had ridden horses up a mountain trail with other 'tourists' and it had been an adventure. But the chance meeting they had with the 'tracker' while standing in line to register – somehow, seemed more than circumstantial. And there had been a change in her husband since that time.

The change was slight at first – but had manifested in ways that now seemed monstrous. She couldn't stop thinking about meeting the large tracker with the patch on his shirt. He had bothered her, much like a dark moth fluttering just outside of a clear window – distracting and trying to penetrate into the light. Neither could she forget the small and unexplainable wound that had occurred to her husband after that meeting. Indeed, she still had the handkerchief spotted with Archie's blood.

She stared up at the moon, trying to distract herself from bothersome thoughts. The moon fascinated her. She had just read an article that discussed a fringe theory. The article had indicated that there were scientific studies which asserted that – if there were no moon – earth's winds would have been too strong for humans to learn to walk upright. Perhaps, she mused, when the wolf bayed it was asking the moon to leave...that the wolf wanted to run free again. Then, she let it go - like she did all such silly thoughts.

Distractedly, she played with a rosary which had been given to her by a nun; and which she wore around her neck. She spent several more minutes gazing at stupendous constellations before gathering up her apron and walking slowly toward the warm glow of the house. As she turned to leave, she saw the bright smudge of a star plummet to the earth. It caused her to think of the serendipitous nature of all life.

It was way past time for dinner. She walked back to the house. It glowed like a candle in the darkness. The kitchen door had blown open; and was slightly ajar. Thankfully, the old screen and a breeze off of the water had kept bloodsucking insects to a minimum. Entering the kitchen, she paused briefly in front of a small window with brocaded curtains. They were her favorites because they allowed the light in; and just enough privacy for the rare passionate kiss or the awkward listing of two older people trying to dance like teenagers.

There was a small bouquet of flowers on the counter that complemented the floor tiles; and seemed to practically tumble from the vase. Day-old coffee with a pitcher of thick cream beside it, were the remnants of an afternoon snack. She gazed at the tiles – blue as the Mediterranean Sea...and thought of home.

She had married Archibald – hoping to find the comfort that had been lacking in her father. The nose and the smile were the same, but the relationship hadn't really been what she had hoped for. There were many 'ups' and 'downs'. She had fancied him to be attractive even though he was older. She ignored his cheap pants and the 'car salesman' persona that others seemed to see. Her girlfriends laughed and quietly referred to him as 'Lester Polyester'. She overlooked the dated penny loafers and embarrassedly looked askance when he insisted on taking ketchup at a restaurant and cleaning the coins he stuck in his shoes.

But they had lived together long enough that – even though the relationship was not what she wanted – thoughts of independence or true fulfillment had long-since evaporated. In and odd way, the nuances of comfort and predictability were food enough for her soul. And, despite his idiosyncrasies, he was like an old shoe. Her life was comfortable – filled with predictable dinners and the occasional night out at a local bistro. Of course, she wanted more on anniversaries, but she quietly consoled herself. Such desires were simply 'young thoughts'.

Hair had sprouted on his back; and the thick black hair on his head had become gray and sparse. Pants were worn higher to hide a belly cistern. Still, she was devoted to him. She knew that true hearts drink whenever love is available.

Archibald had changed his name to make it more 'American', but he was also from the Mediterranean. He had the same sense of life and culture. He felt like 'home'. Though they had different impressions of how life was to be, she felt comfortable; and liked the lilting way he spoke; the richness of his baritone; and his deep-set, sad eyes. .

And he could do something that Sophia found intriguing. He could purse his lips together and whistle. She had never learned how to do so – and found it curiously masculine. He could whistle for a taxi; and whistle at a well-made point in a soccer match. But, beyond all of that – he could whistle "Santa Lucia" in its entirety in a rich operatic way that seemed profound... but, strangely bird-like. It was what had drawn her to him. She laughed, thinking that they had only met because of their 'musical interests'.

Many years ago, she had heard the operatic piece resonating off a con-servatory ceiling; and resolved to locate the source of the fantastic 'aviary'. Armed simply with lips and a space between his teeth, he had drawn her to him. Almost in a state of hypnosis, the sharpness of choice had been sheathed by chance. Their coincidental meeting had introduced an irresistible force in her life. Neither suave nor debonair – but agonizingly persistent and primal – she eventually succumbed to his proposal. The weight of his flirtations had crushed any defense.

But now it was Archie's hypoglycemia – not his lips – that consumed her. She felt selfish. His health required regimented feedings at one to two hour intervals to sustain his blood sugar levels. Once, when visiting a friend at the hospital he had wanted to put on some bravado; and had neglected the requirements of his body. Instead of bravado, he collapsed in a hallway next to a set of hospital elevators. Had they not been lucky enough to be near someone knowledgeable, he could have lapsed into coma. A piece of candy had resurrected him.

When Sophia looked back, the young woman she wanted to thank – was nowhere. A small daffodil with another piece of candy had been left on a nearby counter. The young woman had disappeared as quietly as light passes over a hill. It seemed beguiling that a simple and well-intended gesture had so easily determined the favorability of two destinies.

Though she hated herself for thinking it, she wondered if her personal circumstance would not have been improved – were it not for the chance intervention. Feeling horribly guilty, she had spent much time praying for forgiveness for the errant thought. But she could not dispel the memory. It lingered like gasoline on clean hands; and made her finger her rosary for redemption.

Even now – and odd as it seemed – when she looked into the funnel of a spring daffodil, it was the only remembrance she had of the young woman who had saved him. Inside of the daffodil, she also saw a whirling vortex of ce-lestial light. It reminded her of the vigorous struggle between desire and duty; and she secretly marveled at the dichotomy of the small bright narcissus. Like a half-moon with part of its disk shining and part of it in blackness, there seemed to be two sides of nature that could be fed. And sometimes...she wished she had not chosen the light.

Now, she heard him – suddenly plaster-cast in senility – the man had become child. He was whistling "Santa Lucia" over and over again like a re-cord with a scratch in it. The comparison seemed slightly humorous to her; and she mused that he was – at the same time – both 78 and an LP. But, after awhile, the thought ceased to amuse her; and the whistling slashed through her tranquility.

Archibald seemed to be fighting to hang on to mortality – one foot in the grave and another on a banana peel. It had happened quickly; and she felt sorry for him; and angry at herself for thinking mean thoughts. She pulled at her rosary, wishing it would open a trap door, then thought – if religion was to be reveille, belief should not simply share a room with need.

As she prepared the evening meal, she turned on the television – trying to escape the operatic rant. The world was becoming obscenely crazy. The news reported that '70 % of what was produced as food was from genetically ma-nipulated crops; and the human genome had been found and deciphered'. It only made Sophia certain that the poor thing was probably dying of boredom somewhere....

She pulled at her rosary again and wondered why there wasn't a prayer for sarcasm. Her Catholic upbringing had landed her in a familiar mental torture. There was only one thing to do, put a pan on the stove and start din-ner. So she put some butter in a pan and watched distractedly as it swirled around and danced like a hellion. Her mind ran through activities of the day – mundane, predictable – not even notable if put in italics. Gray hair had squashed desire. Age spots had crept into her hands. She rubbed them like Lady Macbeth, realizing that vanity had now 'jumped into the fray'.

Bristling, she switched to another channel; and was somewhat relieved to find a program about solar power. It rallied her interest, but only because the handsome presenter cleverly introduced the concept of solar nanotechnology. He poured the nanocells out of a tube, whereupon they disappeared into the pores of his hand. It transfixed her; and she could not stop laughing. She wondered if he would shine at night in the bedroom – and then felt guilty for the thought.

The earth's 25,000 mile circumference could not contain her restlessness. There was not distance enough to help her escape her wish to be somewhere else. Then, she did a tally of the spices that she had pulled out on the counter; and wondered: If she licked each one, would it provide the spice that was missing tonight? If she swallowed a bottle of sage, would it make her wise? All of a sudden - she realized she was having a personal summer.

Regaining her composure; and with concentrated industry she began once more to make the evening meal. She found the task to be more work than usual. The world was twirling about with incredible speed while she was trapped in the kitchen operating at three quarters time.

From the nearby room, she suddenly heard it. The repetitive coughing was slight at first. It was Archibald. She needed to go check on him. He had probably fallen asleep in his recliner – and 'swallowed the wrong way'. The ocean of blue tiles seemed to waver before her – the dream was over. The deluge of memory that had sustained her earlier had been dammed. She sighed; and then quickly shoved nostalgia into a corner.

By the time she had traversed the kitchen, the coughing had become severe. Her pulse quickened. She feared that he might be suffering from some sort of diabetic attack. The coughing insinuated the need for action. Without hesitation she rushed into the room quick enough to make the dust fly. She could never forgive herself if she didn't do all she could to help him. She heard the cry,

"Sophia....So...Sophia...Help.... me...I'm... choking...I....!"

Now, she was sprinting – motivated by a fear that she had rarely experienced. She bounded across the room dodging a settee. The mind has curious and patterned priorities even in crisis – instinctively she scooped up a fallen couch pillow as if she were heading off a grounder in a baseball game. Then, grabbing a vial of medicine from a nearby table, she dove to his side, both of them gasping for air. Her instincts told her that this would indeed be a battle. But she was not prepared. He was wearing a tank top t-shirt. The white contrasted with a series of pink blotches that were spreading rapidly across his arms and shoulders like a running horde.

She let out a momentary gasp before springing into action. He must be having an allergic reaction. Feverishly she grabbed the directory from a nearby shelf. Simultaneously she held his head up and worked her fingers down into his mouth – looking for a blockage of his windpipe. The tongue was in its proper place. His breathing was shallow. She threw the directory aside and dialed '911'.

Meanwhile Archie's flailing had become more intense. Had she been in the middle of deep water, it could have been no worse. She fought him off like he was a drowning man; all the while barking out orders to somebody on the phone; and pinpointing their address with the speed and accuracy of a GPS. Even if the ambulance was coming from Russia – it would find them.

Then, she crashed the phone down in its cradle; and toppled over. Archie had tried to stand but had collapsed from his own weight. Like a large tree, he had taken her down with him. His breathing had become more labored. The pustules were moving quicker than triage; and he writhed on the floor.

Perhaps, it was her childhood training...perhaps lunacy built by desperation, but she found herself thinking about musical fugues and canons - mesmerized by the way the patterns of blotches were forming. She quickly dismissed the thought – knowing that she needed to concentrate. Her brief volunteer work at a local hospital had familiarized her with the body's response to foreign material.

His eyes were now red and bulging. The rash was spreading rapidly. Why couldn't she command her thoughts? She tried to rally herself. He was gasping. A few seconds passed before she realized that she was screaming hysterically,

"TELL ME WHAT TO DO, DARLING... TELL ME WHAT TO DO!!!"

It must have been something he ate. And as her husband writhed on the floor, she directed her gaze about the room. It occurred to her that the culprit might be arthropodan. The lawn sprinkling systems had brought a scourge of bugs to the area. She scanned the room quickly but could discern no intruder; and the blotches had covered his body so rapidly that she would never be able to find a tell-tale bite. She thought of mosquitoes – but again, could not possibly ascertain the likelihood of a bite and it seemed a foolish thought.

Now she was sobbing. Not knowing what to do, she grabbed him around the waist and tried the Heimlich maneuver. Maybe the blockage was further down the throat and she just couldn't see it. His strength was amazing. He exploded in fear – like a wild animal being held against its will. He broke free. His surprising strength sent her catapulting across the floor until she was stopped by a nearby wall. He was writhing again; and foam was coming from his mouth.

She screamed...how could she have imagined this? Why had she not seen it coming?! A reddish flush on her skin alerted her to the presence of an ambulance – its light coming through the window; and the siren screaming. She pushed herself up from the wall and tottered to the door. Instinctively she suspected two things: that Archibald's demise was probably a 'fait accompli'... and that some treachery must be afoot.

THE CALL

A nd suddenly it was quieter than she ever remembered. Archibald was gone.

Between spasmodic bouts of depression, she reflected about the odd 'tapes' that frequently play in life – things we do not remember or learn, no matter how many times they are rewound and played again. She thought of the practicalities of day-to-day life; and how they eventually slam into things we cannot understand.

Sophia was experiencing love's great irony. Sooner than expected, those who love stare down at someone who is frail, unrecognizable, and gasping – or perhaps they are memorialized in stone. The great sun in our life has been extinguished. Perhaps, they stare down at us – and we feel the responsibility of one who can no longer 'be there' for them. It always seemed to end the same.

Love was never free. It might help us sail through tempests, but eventually it led to a deep blue sea where we float alone. And there was nothing we could do about it. No amount of thought could make sense of it. We were suddenly halved. We would cry outwardly as if tears might make love grow back; and we would cry inwardly as if to cleanse the heart and soul. There was no preparation, no formal schooling, no traditional teaching, and no learning at the knees of a master.

If we were sensible, we might open ourselves to others. But we are rarely sensible in matters of the heart. Like children we long for explanation. Oh, this thing called 'death'. We can see the husk, but continue to hope that it will render something from inside. If not voice, pulse or heartbeat – then seed. Wanting to see something floating like a milkweed seed...lighter than air and sailing like a silken angel ready to start anew. More than likely, we are like the waiting hill of grass basking in dewy mornings of dappled light...never thinking of winter until the snow is upon us.

Sophia now tasted this sweet bitterness. She had somehow missed her footing; and was looking back in disbelief. Like waking from a dream or too much sleep, she felt the grogginess of a day that had come before she was ready for it – a day that she did not recognize.

Archie's body had been overtaken by something so quickly that the body was indiscernible. The coroner could see no advantage in having her view it; and a well-intentioned priest convinced her that she should simply remember him the way he was. But even this did not prepare her for the grief she felt when – just one short day after being put in the morgue – the hospital called to say that the body had been 'lost'.

Their apology was rehearsed – a purse was at stake. The call was quick and formally polite. As minions of the court they had learned not to let things linger; and never to admit culpability. Sophia had to reconcile her feelings once again for the man whom she had learned to love.

Somewhere outside a bird sang like a cantor. It sounded artificial. She pulled at a mesh cap that she had worn for too long, because she did not wish to wash her hair; but could no longer tolerate the oily strands hanging in her face. She was a caricature of herself. Gazing up at the stars, she saw Cassiopeia fading as daylight advanced. She didn't care – she was howling louder than she knew was possible. The sound echoed off the walls of the house which now seemed cavernous.

She smashed a nineteenth century painting of a cabriolet; and threw about operatic records that she had once treasured. When she had screamed and broken enough, she calmly pulled out a dustpan from the closet and - in a fit of senseless duty - began to clean. Then she poured a cup of coffee; turned on the television; and rubbed lotion into her bruised and blistered hands.

She had broken the rosary around her neck; and watched idly as the beads tumbled about on the floor. Then slowly she got down on her hands and knees and picked up the beads that she could find; and put them in a small vase which she kept on the fireplace mantle. Without dignity or senti-ment, she had decided that any religion associated with them was now his-tory. They were objects of scorn and she did not know why she had saved them – Archibald's ashes should be in their place.

She sat down again; leaned forward; and put her head on the counter – wondering if things would ever be 'good'. Her thoughts drifted to their first kiss; and she began mentally cataloging every significant event that had happened in her life with Archibald. Why should she care? Did anyone care?

Then, she began to obsess. What if she missed some event? What if there were gaps in her memory? She thought of the trips they had taken; and the home they had tried to build together. Finally – and at the risk of being seen – she went to the window and peered out to see if she could find the bird that had been singing.

But she saw no bird. Slowly she returned to the living room; and found some records that she had not broken and thrown away. Praying hadn't worked – her gut was steering her now. Perhaps music would help. She gazed outside from a dark house. The garden was unkempt. Before she knew it, hours had passed and philosophical questions about life, death and purpose – had crept back into her thoughts.

It was dinner time; and she realized she might be hungry. Unable to endure the thought of eating alone – she turned on the television. The distance between what her life 'was'; and what it had 'become'…seemed incomprehensible. She slammed her fist on the counter and cursed the cruelty of love. Pitching old photos into a nearby trash can, she wondered about the meanness of time; how it only seemed to rob and spoil. When a stream of scarlet ran across the blue tiles of the counter, she realized she had injured her hand.

She had just stood up to go retrieve a bandage when she saw it – an enormous bird perched just outside the nearby window. Within seconds it had flown toward the ocean; and disappeared into mist. Its cry was barely audible, but sounded like a peculiarly shrill interpretation of 'Santa Lucia'. She must be slipping into madness. Weakened by the realization, she sat down again – her heart pounding hard enough to rock her body.

She barely heard the phone….

A rough, cultivated voice spoke into her ear as if the speaker had smoothed out the 'nicks', in order to show sympathy. The voice slid out in a smooth cadence and stopped briefly before her, like it wanted someone with which to walk. There were questions,

"When would be a good time to come over and discuss the remains?"

"Had she noticed anything peculiar before the episode of sickness?"

"Would she be available for a discussion with him – standard police procedure?"

His words formed pools on the counter. She wrote the questions down distractedly; and then – without response – quietly hung up.

QUICKENING

The wind pressed its way softly over a hillside of daffodils. It scattered yellow pollen, dusting the sepals and petals of adjoining flowers. Sophia walked by teal waters and then, waded in. She slipped into sleep; and – quietly as a grebe with children clinging to its back – sailed into the dark waters of a dream from which she hoped not to return.

When she awakened the season had changed; and it was winter in her heart – a cold, quiet, empty, slow, dormant time. Her nerves sat ceremoniously as a tomb. Her spirit was like a crippled bird, sitting in the brush... aware of its injury; and hoping not to hear the sudden snap of a twig.

But, before long and early that morning, 'a twig did snap'. Her trance was interrupted by a strong knock on the door. It was a call back from the hypnosis of loss. The world was there – staring like an unwelcome and amused audience. Letters had piled up. Flowers had wilted. Food, which had congealed on the counter, now entertained lines of ants. They looked like customers at an ice cream stand; and ignored her grief in favor of colonial activity.

A chilly wind blew in from a window she had left open. It was an indifferent justice and the tonic she needed to feel the quickening life demanded. She suddenly wished for the pleasure that only a warm and pulsating shower head could give.

The knocking persisted and was louder.

Would the intrepid guest just leave?! She didn't feel like moving from the couch – and had just lit a cigarette that was only partially finished. She had long since given up smoking ...but didn't care anymore.

The house looked and smelled like a cave. Once the 'queen of clean', she sat amidst squalor brought on by loss. Finally – a "Dammit!" had flown out of her mouth. If the world wouldn't leave her alone, the world had better be prepared for a fight! Like an angry bat, she would fly in its face – and scare the hell out of it.

More persistent knocking – louder now; and a disembodied puppet voice yelling through the door. The phone was blinking – musty with messages. She yanked it from its perch on the wall; and pulled out its battery heart, feeling temporarily victorious.

"Mrs. Angaros! Mrs. Angaros!! Are you there? I need to talk to you. Please open up Mrs. Angaros. This is Detective Tweeter.....Mrs. Angaros! MRS. ANGAROS!!!!"

Who the hell was this man?

She peered through the curtains to the outside. The remains of a monarch butterfly had been caught in a spider web – and blocked her view. The monarch had struggled with something that was hungry. Had the magic of its beautiful metamorphosis been severed ...or simply brought to a different inception? Unwilling to wrestle with the distracting thought, she headed for the door.

The voice had become more powerful. Even in vapid grief, she realized that – whoever was behind the shouting would not be ignored – that it was the same voice that she had heard earlier on the telephone. Slowly – and like the first daffodils that push up through the earth and feel the cold – something inside told her it was time. She pulled her house coat snugly around her – and prepared to greet 'whatever' she found on the other side.

He stood there waiting to be let in - looking a bit like a golden retriever. His eyes registered concern. Probably, she reasoned, the look was meant to display a feeling that he did not truly possess. She immediately regretted having opened the door; and realized how tired she was.

She was tired of the neighbors and friends who wanted to sit like restless pigeons 'cooing' out vacuous words while looking at their watches. She was tired of those who felt obligation rather than sympathy. She was tired of worn-out advice from those who had gleaned their wisdom from newspaper columns and self-help books. She longed for something fresh...something real. This large, lumbering man couldn't possibly give a damn about a middle-aged woman. Had she really admitted that to herself?

There was a secret in his dark eyes that intrigued and yet, irritated her. She often found men to be as incomprehensible as fence posts...and frequently, less interesting. But this one was different. He had an 'uncivil' civility – one that had obviously been hardened by investigative work; and which strained to come forth because of some sense of decency.

She said nothing – but just stared at him like a disturbed cat – her arms folded in front of her. Then she noticed that someone had left a small bouquet of daffodils at her door. He quickly scooped up the flowers and handed them to her. 'More deformed sympathy', she thought.

"...You Mrs. Angaros?"

"No," she replied. "I'm the neighbor 'hood' – I was just planning a heist in my bedroom slippers."

The wind blew his immense warmth toward her – something that she begrudgingly noticed.

"Um...yeah...Mrs. Angaros, my name is Conley Tweeter. I'm an investigator with the Police Department. I need to ask you some questions about your husband – if you have some time."

She saw him glance past her to the inside of the house. She was aware of how the house must look; and what he must think. His transparency provoked another cynical response.

"I have a lot of time, Mr. Tweeter – that appears to be about all I have these days! Do come in. Have a seat - and take a load off...."

She stepped aside and he prepared to 'barrel in'. Why was she doing this? Suddenly, she put up her hand to stop him. Then, realizing how ridiculous that must look, she blurted out,

"Wipe your feet! We're very 'upper-crusty' in this neighborhood."

It was a close call, but she had managed to resurrect some bit of dignity. Though obviously in a hurry, the detective took a good deal of time to clean his shoes on the outside mat; and then asked if she would prefer for him to take them off. She had to admit that he was accommodating. Even though she wanted to dislike him, he had an odd grace.

Detective Tweeter stopped inside the foyer and then, spoke carefully, almost quietly.

"Um...yes, ma'am, "I'm sorry to have to bother you, but to tell the truth, some of your neighbors were a bit worried. I mean, uh... after the funeral and all, they kind of expected that maybe you would need some help. But no one has been able to reach you for awhile."

She secretly looked him over; and immediately felt guilty that she should find anyone interesting – after all, she was still in mourning. But the detective had unexpected physical warmth. It felt refreshing after having spent days alone in a dark house. He had the start of a small pot-belly – probably not a 'tea toller'. He was an adequate man, solidly built – a little rough around the edges. His forearms were muscular; and a trellis of hair seemed to crawl up from underneath a white tee shirt - visible because of his open collar. He wore a light suit jacket and a shirt that was only moderately interesting – no tie. Pants and shoes were the sort that blended with anything.

His heavy eyebrows and 'sad-dog' eyes were unexpectedly amusing. She guarded her feelings. It was disrespectful to her late husband; and she very much cared that, in some way, Archibald might see that she respected him – even in death.

Self-consciously she buttoned one more button on her house coat; and then wondered why she had bothered. She was an oily mess; and no one could possibly find her the least bit attractive. Feeling foolish, she brushed her hair out of her face; and then blushing slightly, barked out,

"Coffee...?"

"Yes, ma'am, if you have some made."

"Since you're my first real guest, I'll go to some trouble. I have 'instant'. Cream... sugar...?"

"Black, please."

"Of course..." she thought as she disappeared into the kitchen.

Microwaves made life easy – in less than three minutes, she had brought back two strong black cups of coffee. Tweeter was looking at a mantel picture of her late husband. She thought, "How very 'Bogart."

"Well, obviously you're not a Mormon intent on converting me," she said directing her attention to the coffee.

"Beg your pardon, ma'am?"

"Never mind, it was a dumb thing to say..."

"Um, yes ma'am." Tweeter was getting uncomfortable and shifting from one foot to the other. He took his coffee from her; and began to slurp it nervously – staring at the picture on the mantel again.

"Yes, I loved him, Mr. Tweeter. We weren't what you would call 'a glamorous couple' – but I loved him anyway. Truth of the matter is – he could be pretty damn frustrating at times – but I didn't kill him."

Tweeter looked at her as if he had discovered hidden candy.

"No one said anything about a killing, Mrs. Angaros. Why would you say ...?"

She interrupted him before he could finish.

"Oh come now, Mr. Tweeter! They don't send out investigators after a funeral just to cheer up middle-aged ladies.

Then, suddenly she was angry again. She had admitted to a stranger that she was no longer young.

"Well, ma'am, the death was a bit sudden n' odd. Did you notice anything unusual? Uhh...I just want you to know that no one is a suspect here. Uhh...did you make him anything unusual – that was quite an allergic reaction he had...?"

Then he quickly looked at the floor – better than to face her stony stare. She tried to rally herself; and wondered if she shouldn't be more introspective. Immediately it occurred to her that introspection was a futile exercise – how could the mind ever truly examine itself? And would it really give an honest assessment? She sighed and said,

"Mr. Tweeter, are you familiar with 'contrapuntal'?"

"No ma'am. Can't say that I am....Is that a terrorist group?"

"Hardly – you're a very literal person – aren't you?"

He snapped back,

"I deal in the facts, ma'am. I don't try and imagine things. What moves police work is, observation and documentation! Being literal has its advantages."

"Yes, Mr. Tweeter, I'm sure it does. I can imagine you opening a box of cereal in the morning...with that 'literalness' of yours. 'Pull at tab', 'press down' and 'flip over'. The gymnastics alone would keep you from making it to work on time..."

"Ms. Angaros – let's us stick to the details of this investiga...uhh question and answer session of ours. Now what can you tell me about this Contra Poontal group?" He was practically growling.

She rolled her eyes – no longer in the mood to put up with a lout whose education seemed to be in street crime. He had obviously identified her as a suspect in her late husband's death! She continued,

"Did you obtain your degree in law enforcement through a home study program? Contrapuntal is a musical term...."

Tweeter reddened,

"Mrs. Angaros, I'm here doing an investigation into an unusual death. I don't have time to 'tiptoe through the tulips'. Now, let's talk about your husband's last minutes."

She had won. She had cracked the puny, plastic layer of pity. She took a triumphant breath – sure that she was getting back on her feet. Fate had sent her an odd angel.

"Now that we understand each other, let me explain it to you. 'Contrapuntal' is a term describing a kind of music found in fugues and canons."

She could see that she was losing him.

"...It is a common operatic style, a composition that features two or three parallel voices that follow slightly behind each other. Remember the old 'Row, Row, Row Your Boat' song in elementary school?"

He seemed confused.

"Okay, then what about the tavern songs – '99 Bottles of Beer on the Wall'?"

He nodded.

"They're both examples of contrapuntal, Mr. Tweeter...parallel voices or rhythms that follow each other, with one voice or rhythm slightly behind the other. The music seems to 'fold back into itself' and start over again. They call it an endless fugue. Believe me, anyone who has ever dealt with kindergarten children can identify with an 'endless fugue'...."

It was just then, that an unusual thought occurred to her about Archibald's death – the thought involved a 'tracker' they had both met; and a comment the man had made. She would not share it with the detective – but continued,

"When I saw Archibald's rash, I thought to myself 'contrapuntal'. I know it must seem odd to you – but it was different than any rash I had ever seen. I could see the blotches forming – following each other in a parallel fashion – one or two slightly behind the other. I watched them turn back on themselves – so to speak. Musically speaking, they resembled a contrapuntal."

She looked at him for feedback – and could tell he thought she was crazy.

"Listen...I love opera. It's not that strange – just another way of looking at things...."

She was still not reaching him.

"Okay – another way to look at this – a sort of spiraling ladder returning in on itself."

He looked like a glazed donut.

WINDOW

Where was he?!

'RC' lay on the ground – convinced he had been hit by a truck. A ringing noise inside of his head made everything sound like 'chipmunks singing Christmas carols'. His nasal cavities were on fire; and he was way past thirsty. There were many adjectives to describe the way he felt – all of them profane.

Slowly his memory was coming back to him. Someone, or something, had hit him from behind. He rubbed the sore knot on his head; and decided to try and retrace his steps. But those first 'steps' brought him back to some meaningless childhood verse – an obvious fit of delirium. He scratched away at it until a discharge of memory erupted. Slowly he was returning to his senses - if anyone could ever claim that.

He remembered the dry air of Nevada...an assignment there. But that was weeks ago. He had returned with a mysterious and most rewarding find – a gigantic cranium that he had found in the desert. He had immediately turned it over to the central forensics lab for analysis. The large cranium was a bewildering prize that needed further investigation and research. Now, his own head ached so much that he wondered if he might not have turned in the wrong skull. He gently rubbed the knot on his head. Blood had clotted in his hair. 'RC' felt sick to his stomach; and wondered about a concussion.

More thoughts were coming back. The forensics lab technician who had checked in the sample cranium for analysis – had initially seemed smug and slightly bored. 'RC' noticed the man's interest was only kindled when he told him of the small granules that had tumbled out of the skull and which 'RC' had saved in a handkerchief. The attendant suddenly seemed very curious, rapaciously interested – if not a bit creepy. The memory evaporated. 'RC' strained to turn his head and look at the terrain that was now before him. He obviously had set up camp somewhere and was on another assignment.

But, the site had been turned upside-down. Everything had been kicked over, torn, or crushed as if a large animal had taken it apart looking for something. Blood trickled down the side of his face. He struggled to remember where he was. A crumpled piece of official letterhead was stuffed in his pocket and he labored to retrieve it. The letterhead logo was outlined in red and had the bust of a Spaniard and indigenous man. The seal seemed to reinforce his legal entry and approval for travel. He realized he was now in Mexico - somewhere in the Chihuahua Mountains...a name that seemed more than a bit ridiculous to him. Someone had told him that a couple with 'well-line pockets' had funded the trip; and it involved breaking up a smuggling ring involved in the trade of exotic animals and animal parts. But that was all he could remember before his senses left him again. He was suddenly cold; and the altitude was making him nauseous.

An extension of the Rocky Mountain range, the Chihuahuas were well known for a variety of archeological sites and a series of large mountains including the Sierra Madre. He was on a high plateau. Mesquite was strewn about. Here and there Ocotillo plants dotted the sparse landscape – their red flowers looking like drops of blood. He could hear the rummaging of some animal in the distance; and suspected it to be a boar foraging for food. A rat crawled out from nearby food that had been scattered. It wouldn't be long before rattlesnakes came out to dine.

A fat black beetle crawled slowly in front of him. It looked like a scarab that had freed itself from a piece of jewelry. Various cans from the campsite had been stomped, crushed, and thrown about. Nearby bushes were dotted with them; and the cans glinted in the sparse light looking like ornaments. There were ruts in the dirt that he mistook at first for old carriage tracks. Then – and seeing the tread marks – he realized that something motorized had made its way through the area...not long ago.

A gust of wind picked up an old map of the local roads. He saw it sail past him and over the side of a ledge. Then, an updraft lifted it briefly. It twisted in mid-air before plummeting again – like a cartoon character. The limbs of various small desert bushes had been snapped as if something had given them a haircut or they had been browsed recently. His crushed tent undulated in the wind as if liquefied. Small bunches of desert grasses seemed lined up at the horizon. They were catching the last bit of sunlight. Their amber tufts seemed clipped, but beautiful. Liberated by receding light, the first stars had begun to appear.

'RC' bent his arm stiffly; and licked a cut on his hand. He wondered where his first aid kit had disappeared. The cut oozed gently. He didn't feel any pain – just the warmth of the blood trickling down his arm. He felt very mortal; and hoped that no predator or scavenger had picked up the red scent - certain he would not be able to defend himself. Looking up, he could see the sky was changing rapidly. The moon had come out of hiding. Once cuckold, a nighttime romance had brought it back; and it was gaining lunar strength.

He pulled at some nearby grass and chewed it. Hardly able to move, he was hoping to find a band of moisture in the plant that would quench - what now felt like an overwhelming thirst. A particularly bright planet at the meridian gleamed like a jewel in a cummerbund. It was a stunning competitor for the moon.

Then, he cupped his hand over his ear. It seemed an odd remnant from childhood, but he could hear the wind whispering. He sought explanation – what could it reveal about his predicament? He tried to move. It was an impetuous mistake. The pain was unbearable – he screamed out. Yes, he had been badly beaten. Something might be broken. Then he gingerly searched for keys in his pockets – they were gone. Slowly he leaned back against what were the 'trashed' remains of some personal effects. More memories were returning. One – maybe two nights ago – it had all happened.

It had been cold. He had been staring at the stars of the northern hemisphere and the bright 'Strawberry Moon' as Bob, the Indian, called the full moon in June. He had made plans to drive to one of Mexico's nearby national parks to investigate an archaeological site; and to look for traces of exotic animal trade.

Nevada and the cranium he had found in the desert now seemed like a drunken dream. In half-conscious stupor, he wondered if anything was ever 'real'. Perhaps he was dreaming again. But memory exclaimed its presence - thoughts were weaving their way back.

He had been wearing a thick furred-hat – the rest of him was cold despite his preparation. There was a young man – more than likely a guide from the local area. The guide had very little in the way of clothing; and seemed disinterested in any sort of conversation. He huddled near the fire as if he was attached to it. After watching the guide for some time, the cloak of guilt had become a heavy garment. 'RC' pulled out a spare coat; and asked the guide – a young man named Sincero - if he would wear it. The guide seemed perplexed but, after a moment, wrapped himself in its warmth; and then pointed to the sky. In broken English he remarked that a large shadow had sailed over them.

'RC' immediately wondered whether the man had become too cold, but remembered his own vision of the same...that had drawn him to the cranium in the desert. He pondered the coincidence. But the guide seemed grateful for the coat; and they had started a casual conversation which ebbed and flowed – before things suddenly went haywire.

Now, blood trickled down into 'RC's mouth. It was from a cut on his forehead. Its strong iron taste was repulsive to him. He had only tasted blood once before – and it brought him back to that time long ago in the barn when 'Old Joe' had suddenly died.

Trapped in a barn with a dead man and a hissing wind, he remembered being crazy and afraid. When Joe's son, Angus, had finally managed to open the barn door, 'RC' had bit hard into the older boy's hand. He didn't understand why he had done it. The bite did little for their friendship; and had given 'RC' the less than savory local name of – 'wild boy'. It was a memory he did not cherish; for remorse bites back twice as hard.

His thoughts crackled back to the present. At the moment, he wasn't certain of anything other than that he was looking up at thousand year old light coming from distant stars – stars which seemed to dance in the night sky. A nagging internal pain made him wonder how badly he had been hurt; and he again tried to remember everything that had happened.

While he was unconscious, the wind had decorated. Litter was strewn about with nothing but a 'directional' design. He wanted to limp over to the edge of the plateau to see if there were clues to the melee – but his body would not cooperate. A dull ache in his gut subdued the desire; and drove him back to prostration. A wound on his side was oozing blood. There was a catsup-colored stain on his shirt. He ignored it, hoping it would bleed out any infection.

His thirst had returned and he was suddenly quite hungry. A diminished ability to move had made him restless; and perhaps – in balance to the present situation – the restlessness pulled in more ancient memories. He was dreaming again...

"Look at them theah stahs, 'RC'. You done evah seen anything that purty?"

It was 'Old Joe'.

"They look like sparks from a fire!"

"Maybe they is! Maybe it's God's fire." Joe had responded.

"I don't believe in God!"

"Um huh... thet a pretty big statement fo' a little fella."

"I'm not little – I'm almost 6 years old! And I know there isn't anything out there."

"Well, how you think them stahs got theah?!"

"I think they fell off a flag!"

Joe chuckled,

"Well you sure DO got some BIG ideas, 'RC'!"

The pain was now squeezing his body like a vise. He was very tired;

and his vision seemed distorted. 'RC' was certain he had lost a great deal of blood. He stared up at the stars again. He could discern the fishhook shape of Scorpius. Just to the east of Scorpius Sagittarius hunted the scorpion monster that had fatally stung Orion. Scorpius had been sent by Jupiter to kill Orion, for Jupiter had tired of Orion's bragging.

Sagittarius, half-man and half-horse, was on a centaur's quest – to 'right' a 'wrong'. The scorpion must pay. Saggittarius would chase it across the sky. His arrow would 'pin' the dangerous tail of the scorpion; and he would slay it. He would bring back the tail and large claws as proof. After receiving his reward, the half man/half horse would gallop down a path of sparkling diamonds – and disappear into the night forest of the sky. The heavens – save Jupiter – would forever honor him.

The story would be repeated for centuries; and each time denizens of the night sky would twinkle in approval. Stars were the 'superheroes' with which ancient children played. Their stories would be repeated and embellished with flourish. Ancient children would dream of quests they might take while watching the only medium available to them. The thought caused him to wonder about a falling star that suddenly streaked across the sky. Oddly, it felt a bit like a doppel ganger. He thought he must be delusional.

Now, more recent memories that had been packed away...came tumbling out. The intensity and confusion of the raid had stirred him from sleep. He remembered the shouting, the scuffling, and the rending of tent fabric. He heard the muffled sound of his guide screaming. There must have been a brief chase. Shots were fired. Someone had beaten and slashed 'RC'; and he lay bleeding. With that memory, he fell into unconsciousness – but continued to dream. In his dream, he was a moth, fluttering elaborate wings as it descended into the inebriating nectar of a night-blooming plant. Then he was falling – and when he landed, should have split apart – but the force of love had kept him together.

It was hours before he awoke again. When he did, he could see his breath escaping. The weather had suddenly changed. For the first time, he realized that he was half-naked. His body had begun to blanch from the cold. By all rights, he should be deader than Stalin. He carefully rubbed his eyes. They felt like frosted olives in a cold martini. He had the visual acuity of an alcoholic.

That was when he saw 'it' – though he couldn't be certain. It sat like a great vulture on a near boulder – hooded, monkish and silent, waiting, and observing the partially clothed creature in the light falling snow...no doubt dreaming of a feast. 'RC's breath had congealed; his nose had 'run'; and icicles had solidified over his top lips. It gave him a frightening appearance and

– when he finally moved his mouth – some of the frozen water slid down his throat. Tears had started to wriggle down his face, but froze in place. The wind would show no remorse. It pummeled him with stinging snow. He looked down at the ground and could see that he was framed in his own blood. The animal on the boulder moved slightly as if it was observing some sort of trinket...was it advancing?

He decided to usher every bit of energy that he had left. With Spartan effort he pulled himself up and heaved his body across the ground. He realized that – though the gash on his side had been 'sewn together' by the cold, the weather had not meant him to excommunicate himself from the area where he rested. He screamed as he separated from the bondage of his congealed blood - uttering words that were far less than ecclesiastical.

He needed to find warmth, and protection from the curved beak of a carrion-hungry monster that was, no doubt, waiting for him to drop; and would feed upon him the first moment he lost consciousness. An enormity of will – and the desire not to be something's pudding – pushed him forward. He crawled to some nearby bushes and looked for a place to burrow in; and, perhaps a stout stick. He no longer doubted the clarity of the guide who had reported seeing a large shadow sail over them. In the craziness of near-death, he remembered something 'Old Joe' had told him long ago when he saw him playing on an icy ledge. It seemed silly,

"Make sure you lets the snow fall, 'RC' – not you!"

His strength was rapidly waning. His head was firing messages to neurons that now routed pain throughout his body. He was almost at the bushes, when he realized that the creature had moved quickly, quietly, and much nearer to him. He had not even heard the rustle of a feather. Boulder-brown and hooded, it stood before him and seemed to open its great wings. It was expectant, confident, and perfect in its predation.

He lunged at it with as much force as he could muster. A loss of coordination sent him reeling head-first into the snow. With that final bit of energy, he lapsed into the unconscious. The mind's organization of psychic material – which was never available in clarity – now, lay before him.

A lithe red animal bounded forward. Its features were sharply canine; and it had a white-tipped tail and russet coat. The tell-tale crucifix marking on its back allowed 'RC' to know that it was the 'cross fox' that he had seen long ago from the window of the barn where 'Old Joe' had died. The fox now whispered to him,

"Find the fish, the adder and the dog together; and utter the holy words given to you."

The message was brief – and made no sense. Then another image transcended it. Here now was a glacier – slow, unstoppable, and leaving permanent chatter marks on the rocks in its path. The rocks - that it did not mark – it devoured and spit out as powder. Suddenly, it spoke in a low, powerful monotone.

"How question? Why answer? You ask 'to whom does this beautiful dream belong…"

Then – as if to answer itself – the glacier rumbled through powerful clenched teeth,

"You can seek the beginning of this cold current that forms my unbreakable' ness – or you cannot. I can be melted easily within the smile of a star. Is everything connected or does something stand apart – at a distance from everything else? Nothing wasted in nature…reducing all to the complexity of its simplest form… a purity which intuits rather than inquires…that 'is' rather than 'seeks'.

Small, but great light, I wait to join thee.…"

And then, a clattering soliloquy,

"Spigot where this cold current begins…consciousness spewing dark and light…great experiment in choice…blessed with formidable offering…definition without end…within and without…triumph and tragedy of a predestined choice…unfathomable structured, chaos…reincarnate to your purest form…join us."

'RC' thought he understood something of the ancient glacier thoughts; and – for a moment – saw himself as everyone, standing at the perimeter of journey. In this thought, he took to the glacier a small bunch of violets; and then watched them melt into a sunlit bouquet of daffodils that brightened until they were blinding.

Then, he quietly stroked the side of the glacier's cold face – pocked marked by centuries …and understood it to be his own.

JEFFERSONS

'RC' awakened to the sound of feet padding along a path and the feeling that he was being jostled back and forth. The air was much warmer than he had remembered; and the snowy sky had disappeared. The sparse plants of the high-altitude plateau – where he last remembered being – had been replaced by a wild land overgrown with dense, rank vegetation. He was being carried down a green tunnel of little breadth which had glistening leaves, silvery and dripping. The hot narrowness of the trail and the silvery foliage made him hallucinate. He envisioned a thermometer; and half-expected a torrent of mercury to shoot up and engulf him. The slope of his carriage made it seem obvious that the descent was steep. Was he still dreaming? Had his dream returned him to the moment of birth? Suddenly, he felt encased, as if he had crawled into the receptacle of some large, tight blossom. His head was buzzing.

Sick to his stomach, he could feel warm blood oozing from a wound. It was puddling around him. After the crown of his head had stopped aching, he understood he was being carried in a makeshift gurney; and that the jostling was caused as those who carried him shifted from foot-to-foot.

His thirst was extreme; and he was being pulled in and out of consciousness. Occasional breaks in the heavy vegetation revealed the sun which had a ring about it. Floating in a grayish roiling sky, it seemed like a donut in boiling oil. As his eyes began to focus, he was able to turn his head slightly; and was surprised to see traces of residual snowmelt.

The snow, which had almost killed him, now seemed to beckon. He longed to taste it and quench his thirst. Just out of reach, it blanketed and protected things, gently releasing water as it thawed. He marveled at nature's engineering. Plants - which had few leaves to transpire excess water and were vulnerable to uprooting - were being held in place and sustained by the slow release of snowmelt into more solid ground.

Harnessed tightly in the gurney, he could not move. He had been stripped of everything and felt like a prisoner. 'RC' remembered the predatory figure he had seen before his collapse on the plateau; and wondered what had happened to it. The scent of sweat, leaves, and decomposing vegetation were added to the bin of information – as he tried to discern where he was and where he might be going. There were floating heads with long dark hair just above him – as he fell in and out of consciousness. He felt heavy – and embarrassed that those who carried him were working so hard. The mist of delirium was clearing; and the straps of the gurney rubbed against his sore body. Frenzied and delirious from the pain, he imagined a large snake tightening its coils around him while blood poured from his nose. The perfume of a spice plant was the last thing he remembered before again falling into unconsciousness.

When he awakened, he could see the signature light of an evening sky; and watched it dance around a nearby tree – lighting it up like a lamp finial. The tree canopy filtered the sunset; and gave it the appearance of a candle flickering through faceted glass. 'RC' strained his head upward – feeling a tremendous need to see who was carrying him.

There were four men led by a tall figure in a hooded robe. They did not speak but, occasionally cast quiet glances. Their stoicism revealed nothing, but the difficulty of his transport. Had he been able, 'RC' gladly would have changed positions and shared the weight of his load. His mortification at being carried as dead weight was directly proportional to their effort. The men continued through the evening – heading for some destination that seemed mapped in memory. A saber-like wedge of wind had begun to push at their back, but their grips on the gurney remained resolute.

The 'hiss-singing' of cicadas and other insects harmonized in the darkness and seemed to follow the rhythm of an imaginary band that played for a dance older than the millennia. Liriope-like tufts of great plants rustled along the path as if in silent applause; as the wind fanned and cooled. He realized that he had lost his camp, his freedom – and nearly – his life. And now, he felt a strange fraternity of madness with the moon which seemed to whisper to him with familiarity.

The hooded figure that led the group turned briefly - and looked back at him. It fingered a rosary and seemed to pray in the slim light of early morning. Even in the darkness and under the veil of a hood, the sparse locks of hair and bald face revealed a tall capable woman whose visage was as certain and determined as a crocodile. The boulder-brown robe that she wore was Franciscan; and gave her a winged, predatory appearance. Turning away from him, she continued to lead with the certainty of one who had traversed the area many times. Sister Frances was as comfortable in shadow as she was in light.

An irony occurred to him. He had assumed his role might be to restore balance to a world suffering from environmental degradations and corruption. Now, he had no notion of what 'balance' was. Indeed he was incapable of restoring his own. He resigned himself to the notion that such a role might not comport with - or even be needed - in universal law. It was he who seemed to need protection. The swaying motion of the gurney stirred more memories – things he had not thought of for years.

Long ago, his family had bought a failing farm. And that was where they had met more than one 'Jeffersonian'. The Jeffersons were a local family of substance and generosity; and consisted of: 'Old Joe' – as he was known locally – his wife, Trudence, their son, Angus; and their daughter, Earnestine. The Jeffersons had freely provided advice to the newcomers; and they had become friends in a southern area where men planted tobacco; planted themselves in seats to watch horse races...and were eventually planted themselves in graves marked by gothic-looking headstones. The Jeffersons had their own family cemetery of wooden crosses which they carefully maintained.

Remote memories in the anesthesia of time surfaced. He was ten – an age that was particularly memorable because of its vulnerability. After that, much learning had been closed off in favor of memorizing facts and conversations... but no longer experiencing flight.

It was a dreamy, naked time when the sun always seemed to be in the west – a time that is given to us and which is most fetching. 'RC' was comfortable believing the world did not extend much further than the farm. He felt positive and calm. His belly was full. Centuries' worth of rich soil lay before him; and there were promises of future heroism. His own heredity had bumped up against the heredity and stories of others - just enough to expand his sense that the universe was more than what he saw. The lighting was prankish and yet, real. Ketchup-red suns sank and signaled the world's daily, predictable fast. For 'RC', the night was never dismal. Nor was it an end. It referenced a time of discovery and the sensibility imparted by 'Old Joe', a man whom he had befriended; and whose family loosely defined the parameters of his remote adolescent world.

Joe's son, Angus, was older. He didn't seem concerned with a skinny boy from the city – he was interested in books. His wife, Trudence Jefferson – or 'True' – often scolded her son...though she was secretly proud of him.

"Boy get yo' hed outta that book and help yo' daddy! We don't need no one holdin' down no chairs heah. They ain't gonna fly off nowhere!"

Angus was doing well in school and might be the first in their family to get a professional job. 'Old Joe' had decided to love the boy no matter what he did or didn't make of himself.

No one ever asked for True's opinion about anything. There was no need – for it was provided freely. Her honesty was customary; her reserve nonexistent, and her heart unquestionably sincere. She found all people interesting, saying simply,

"They's my species".

'Old Joe' was similarly conversant; and would give his opinion as easily as a sneeze – but only if asked. He was calm in temperament, as if he knew that everything bothersome in this world...really didn't matter. Someone had once remarked that he had "colorful speech"; and the young 'RC' had gone back and told 'Old Joe' that 'listening to him speak was like hearing a rainbow'. The old man laughed for hours, whistling through a mouth that was missing two front teeth. He related that he had once been a 'shoeshine boy'. And, in response to the boy's grimace, simply said,

"You can learn a heap by sittin' at the feet of great men." He smiled, but had never explained what he meant. Now, he was gone....

The daughter, Earnestine, was cerebral, and only faintly social. She had no interest in 'RC' or her brother but took copious and clinical notes about every part of her well-ordered day. She would refer back to them from time-to-time as if she was a scientist.

Few have families that are as interesting to them as the families of others. 'RC's interest in the Jeffersons defined the limit of his world at that time – particularly his interest in its patriarch. For 'Old Joe' appealed to both the truth-seeking and dreamy side of the ten-year old. He knew 'stuff'; and could provoke reveries.

His favorite place to hunt was along the railroad tracks where the 'hogs' built burrows in ready-made banks; and came out to chew. He related that 'groundhog stew' was best with a turnip or two.

He told 'RC' about the lynx. They had once extended down into their valley. He had seen one scraping moss off of a tree limb to entice a small deer.

"Real smart animal, boy. That ole cat knows where and how t' hunt. Waits outside of the burrow of most of it's prey. When the animal come out the fron' door – nabs him real good. Even knows the time to sit 'n wait for it."

Joe told him of the 'Cross Fox' – highly prized because of the black band of fur which circled the chest and shoulders and went up and down the back and stomach to form a blackened cross upon the red fur.

"Mos' folks say it ain't nuttin' but a relation of the Red. But I say it ain't that simple! We all related in some way. God done put it there fo' reason – maybe to remind us. But they done kill it outta this valley. Ain' none more bein' born."

And he spoke of squirrels that flew. "Them thin's ussa be so plenty, they cross paths in the sky flyin' back and forth. South'n ones eats nuts, one's in North like shrooms."

"Only one animal done bother me, boy. That be the 'painter'. Some folks call it 'mountain lion'. It likes bein' alone – lives in the darkness. Scream like a demon...and can take a man down! Jumps on you and tears away at the back of yo' neck – so as you cain't move. Don't never turn your back on one."

"Sounds mean," 'RC' remarked.

"Ain't sure it's mean – just know it ain't scared; and it thinks jus' like you and me."

"Am I dreaming, Joe?"

"Sometimes we dreams things, boy. Sometimes it make us see better – kinda like pushin the hair outta yo eyes. Sometimes it like ridin' a wild horse...an' we don't know where we done begun or lef' off."

And with that, 'RC' opened his eyes. He seemed to be back in the present - no longer strapped to the gurney. He had been deposited on a dirt floor in the middle of a rough hut. Those who had been carrying him were gone. He was no longer in the Chihuahua Mountains. He had come out the other side of the long green tunnel. The campsite in the mountains, the beating that had left him practically lifeless; and the young guide to whom he had lent a coat were so distant in his memory that he wondered if they were real – or had he also dreamed them?

And the 'silver sand' that had spilled from the cranium in the desert – and which he had carefully wrapped and tied in a bandana...had also disappeared. Why was it so significant - perhaps enough to kill for. He wondered what had happened to the guide, Sincero, and why sometimes, the most unsettling predators have two legs. Then he fell away again.

SISTER FRANCES

"No, 'RC'. They's farmahs. Jus' like me. They cuts into the bark of a healthy tree just to grow them some bugs. The bugs sees the scar. They comes to the tree – an' latuh on the bird, he come back and harvest the bug. They smartah then we think they is. I seen 'em do it. Indians'll tell ya'."

It was 'Old Joe'. He was talking about the pileated woodpeckers. 'RC' was now crying because of the powerful memory of the loss of an old friend. Once more, he saw the 'cross fox' running away in the distance – far from the barn. In an instant, a man who had been so important to him in his childhood; lay crumpled on the floor while the wind hissed like a snake in the corner.

'RC' shook himself awake; and wiped his eyes. Rain had been falling on his face through a crack in the roof of the hut. He could not sort out which were his tears; and which was rain. He thought of the slim difference sometimes, between dream and reality. He quickly eliminated the notion as distastefully irrational; and of the sort which produces trolls and angels.

A storm was passing overhead. He was lying on his back – staring up at the sky through a crack in the roof. After awhile, the clouds passed and the vision of a fox with a cross on its chest seemed to run across the sky; and suddenly turn into a flame of light. Alone in the hut and feeling incredibly weak, he knew his bleeding had stopped, but was afraid to move. The loss of blood must be contributing to his delusions.

There were sounds – faint at first; but they seemed to increase in volume. Small voices pulled him sinuously through a stream of visions until he surfaced like an errant leaf that had fallen into dark water. The ringing sound in his ears had stopped and been replaced by the laughing of nearby children. Was it real?

Then he heard the buzzing of a fly. It was making its way in bomber-like dives toward his face. It angered him; and he snapped at it with his teeth. But the fly rose easily up to the ceiling of the hut as if caught in and updraft – and unconcerned with the slow movements of an inferior creature from whom it had been licking salt.

His back ached. 'RC' slowly rolled over and felt his elbow hit the side of the rough wall of the hut. A small shaft of sunlight came through the space between the sparse slats; and he strained to see what was outside. The area was tropical. Smoke hung low in the air; and the leaves of nearby plants swayed gently as the storm passed. In the near distance and up a slight rise, was the mud-stucco façade of a building with a formidable wall. Flowering vines encased it.

Children played a game in the dirt with sticks and pebbles. A vigilant elder woman ground something in a small pot, and worked over a campfire. The image caused 'RC' to remember the native guide – and Bob's proclivity to 'read the fire'. Mildly irritated with the memory, he wondered where the crazy Indian was; and whether he was still hunting the illusive mountain lion which had killed the jogger.

His eyes slowly focused just beyond the mud-walled structure. He could see what appeared to be a row of votive candles flickering in a dark arched window. The building had a sharply pitched roof with a crude cross. The church seemed to grow out of its surroundings.

As he studied the details of the building, a shadow momentarily obliterated the ample sunlight. He would have dismissed it as simply a cloud passing over the sun, but the dark image had disappeared too quickly. It caused him to shudder slightly and wonder about his mental state. The elder stopped her stirring; looked up; and 'shaded' her eyes. She had seen something as well. Then, she returned her gaze to the pot; and continued to stir calmly. She looked into the fire - as if by doing so, she might understand the soaring shadow.

Just past the circle of dirt where she worked and the children played their games, were loosely built huts that had been slapped together from whatever could be found in the surrounding jungle. Theirs seemed a frugal but happy existence where time was modestly spent...and rarely on worry.

Suddenly – and as if the fly had returned and plundered a pearl of sweat from him – the hair on the back of his neck seemed to stiffen. He felt something watching. His weakened body would not allow his customary response. Instead he mustered what little strength he had; and rolled over to face whatever it was.

What he saw – surprised him. It resembled the predator that he had seen on the cold plateau; and it was staring at him from the trappings of a sharply hooded smock – silent and imposing. From the vastness of supposed solitude she had appeared without sound and was in frightening proximity. The sight caused him to draw his breath. Startled at being watched and feeling the need to restore some measure of self-control, he blurted out,

"Who the hell are you?!"

He immediately wondered whether he should have been so cavalier - given the compromising position in which he found himself. Her response was casual but strong - and direct,

"I am Sister Frances."

The tone was highly disapproving and in an equal measure to his own. She placed a walking stick that she had been carrying next to the door of the hut and removed her hood. She was a large woman with a strong core. Her porous face gave away no sentiment other than stern resolve. Her hair was sharp, straight, and damply flat; and it fell upon her shoulders – shoulders which were more than adequate. The nun's hands were generous, rough, and slightly soiled. Labor had manifested itself upon them. She wore a large metal cross that pointed in four directions like a heavenly compass; and looked as if it could be used either for exoneration or as modest weaponry.

"Yeah...well you look like you're part of a coven. Do they make you wear those hoods so you won't scare too much of the world – or so you will?!"

He was proud of his rejoinder, particularly given the disadvantaged circumstance. The fly had come back and was buzzing around him again but he would not deign another snap at it with his teeth. He did not wish to repeat any clumsiness in front of an audience.

The nun didn't break at all at his comment – she was accustomed to insults. Her face was completely lacking in expression as she responded,

"You're not looking awfully well yourself."

"Cut myself shaving," 'RC' responded

Her response was an instantaneous,

"Must be an old wound, judging by the look of you....I'd say you haven't seen a razor in at least a year. And that shirt could probably walk out of the country if it had a passport - but I think we'll just burn it."

"Yeah, well, I'm not one to spend much time in front of the mirror..." he volleyed.

"Small wonder – there's not much to hold your attention there," she replied.

"By the way, we took the liberty of attending to your wounds and the rest of you. Both are slightly less grotesque when fully dressed – even in those clothes."

Quite by surprise...he decided he was beginning to like her. He hadn't expected a sense of humor in one who looked so reptilian. She took a pan of 'mud' over to his side and said in a voice that reminded him of an army sergeant.

"Now roll over – I have to dress more of those 'shaving cuts'."

With a free hand, she quickly caught the fly that had been buzzing around him; crushed it; and threw its body on the dirt floor. He was surprised by her agility. She simply said,

"Dear me - hope it wasn't a friend."

'RC' felt the first slap of dressing hit his open wound. It stung more than he anticipated and he cried out. The nun rolled her eyes. Earnest in her endeavor – and very much aware of 'RC's attempt to hide any compassion or fragility – she enjoyed pounding away at his arrogance. She seemed intent on inspiring him to a higher purpose – a notion he was anxious to dispel.

"Is that a cry of pain or – are you just happy to see me?"

Before he could respond, she barked,

"Oh, never mind – just shut up and drink this."

'RC' took one sip of what looked like a tea. It tasted like a hot, bitter dagger. Practically choking – he coughed out,

"Were you sent here to kill me...because there's an easier way!?"

"Sadly, I no longer own a gun...." she smirked.

The conversation was 'heading south' – and he was enjoying it. He would find a way to throw her off balance.

"I think you just frightened, 'Jake'," he quipped while looking down at his anatomy.

"Honesty might demand that you call the little fellow, 'Shorty'," she retorted with a slight trace of annoyance.

He decided to ignore any spiritual illumination that she might conceive to imbue upon him. But he could not deny that the tea and salve had nourished and sustained. His memory of why he had been sent to the Chihuahua Mountains was beginning to return. The assignment involved the investigation of a sophisticated smuggling ring which was bringing rare animals and animal parts into the United States. He remembered that he had been gazing at the Strawberry Moon shortly before the attack had happened; and rolling around in his hand a few of the granules of 'silver sand' that he had retrieved from the great skull in the desert. They had a metallic sheen under the moonlight, but – like the moon – held no light of their own – only reflecting what was provided.

In an unusually introspective moment, it struck him that the description was uncomfortably close to what someone had once said of him. The thought seemed to temporarily dislodge his arrogance. It was also then, that he realized that – shortly before he had been beaten – he had dumped the mystery granules into a coat pocket...the same coat that he had mistakenly lent to the guide who had disappeared.

Suddenly, he heard chipmunk voices. Had the moon finally insinuated its lunacy? 'RC' thought he could hear what he had awakened to on the cold plateau. It was a musical composition of humorous character with high pitched voices singing carols. It was as if images and sounds on that plateau were revisiting him. Sister Frances noticed his slight disturbance - and temporarily ceased her disparaging quips in favor of explanation.

"Yes, you're hearing what you think, Chamberlain. We have 'movie day' occasionally. We only have one film - but poor children don't seem to mind. It's probably the twentieth time they've seen the singing chipmunks."

He was grateful for her explanation; but his suspicion would only allow a modicum of comfort. A further inquiry was necessary.

"...So, Sister, - you must 'eke' out a pretty good living here!"

"I survive," was the curt response.

"How did you know my name?"

"We found a receipt in your clothing."

"What generosity...to take in a perfect stranger."

"Perfect" – is not a word I would connect with you...but, none are strangers in God's eyes."

"You know what I believe, Sis?"

"What a relief, I had my doubts that you believed in anything."

"I believe," he continued, "this is a sham...you know, this whole 'humble nun brings faith to the savages' routine?" It was an effort to throw her off balance and gain a foothold into understanding what had happened to him on the mountain. He was certain she must have some part in his undoing.

"Think what you want...the church site was a piece of rock hard ground that had been torn up by 'investors' doing lumbering. The fools didn't realize that the rainforest has a very thin layer of soil which must be replenished constantly by native vegetation. The land was sterile after that; because the soil wasn't good without the majestic trees and vines that built it. Church took the wasteland over... even planted some daffodils. Miraculously they've survived and it gives the kids something pretty to look at every year."

She paused..."So what brought you to our fair country, Chamberlain? Had a 'yen' to see the Chihuahua Mountains, did you?"

"No. Here on business."

"My...how obscure. Care to share, or does the balance of the free world rest on your shoulders?"

He decided to trust her. "Looking for smugglers – animal stuff..."

"Interesting – how do I know that you're not a smuggler? No, you're obviously not...I've seen a few of them wandering through. You don't look the type."

He admired her courage.

"Um, yeah... thanks for that – came here to try to stop the illegal harvest of rare animals – to stop them from being imported."

"What an unusual term...'harvested'. Sounds like an agribusiness – all about commerce is it? Why not just protect them because God put them here?"

"...Beg your pardon?"

"Don't beg for my pardon – I didn't die for you."

"Listen, no offense, but I'm a scientist," he continued.

"Oh – I see. Well then, I suppose there's no point in exploring any theological line of discussion. Yours is obviously the physical and material world – not too very different from the commercial one, if I may say so."

"Not into 'religion'."

"Ummmm...nothing is 'real' to you unless it's 'proven'...?"

"And this is a 'bad thing' because..."

She looked at him as if she was astounded,

"Because it's imbalanced...and it assumes that there is no magic to the world."

"I'll take method over the madness of 'faith' – any day!"

"Well I'm certain you would. It's the biggest trick of the brain – 'that all may be explained through a process developed by intelligent apes'."

"It is... an 'intelligent' method."

"...And we're still apes," she replied.

'RC's mind deviated from the discussion – it was beginning to bore him; and he was looking for clues. He thought of the daffodils that Sister Frances had mentioned – common flowers that he rarely noticed. Then why had a memory surfaced about him presenting a bouquet of the flowers to a girl he couldn't seem to forget? He angrily eliminated the thought and sprung back into inquisition mode.

"...Little odd isn't it that a 'creature of the cloth' should believe in an evolutionary concept?"

"You really need to keep up, Chamberlain. The Church allows for some flexibility related to such things. Some of us subscribe to developmental creation... or theistic evolution"

"Meaning..."

"Meaning the world and all things created in it - material and spiritual - were created from nothing...and by the hand of God."

"Still not getting your point," he was enjoying the adversity of playing within her spiritual realm.

"If various life forms developed over time, it was at the impetus and under the influence of God. Their creation and development must be ascribed to Him. The church allows the possibility that man's body may have developed from other biological forms; and under God's guidance...but insists on the special and immediate creation by God – of his 'soul'.

"So, Sister, do I detect that you're begrudgingly admitting to the power and proof of science?" He was smirking.

"Ah...the fatal flaw, Chamberlain. We 'creatures of the cloth' know that methodical research if carried out in a truly scientific manner – and which does not attempt to override moral laws – cannot be in conflict with religion. The things of the world and the things of faith are derived from the same."

"Then, by your explanation, Sister, you've proved my point...it's not just a 'trick of the brain'. Carrying that point to conclusion, your God has allowed that all may be explained by so called, 'intelligent apes'..."

"Save for one itty-bitty point, Chamberlain."

"Yeah, what's that?"

"The humble investigator of nature is being led by the hand of God in spite of himself – for it is God, the conserver of all things, who made him what he is."

"I fail to see any conflict with what I've said. We're still gonna eventually 'peak behind the curtain' so to speak....Care to break down your premise for me?"

"Very well," Sister Frances replied, "You think you're in control; you're not; get over it...clear enough?"

"Sort of..."

"Method is, of course, not without value – but true faith is flawless."

"Faith is also 'blind', Sister...." He sneered.

"...And the arrogant are never aware of the limitations of their understanding or the boundlessness of their vanity, Chamberlain."

He was now becoming vexed,

"Seems to me that faith has killed more people than fact..."

She responded,

"Faith steadfastly follows the light. Killing is but a weak bargain made with a dark knight. Don't confuse the two."

"Lovely sentiment...you seem to be trying to say something 'important'," 'RC' smiled offensively.

Sister Frances seemed unconcerned by his cynicism.

"I hope this isn't some prophetic sign of your coming dementia. Regardless...let me spell it out for you. 'If you're killing simply in the name of faith – you probably have none'."

"So...what if you're killing simply in the name of commerce?"

She suddenly stopped and looked at him.

"Life shouldn't be considered a commodity, Chamberlain."

Outside, the light was beginning to disappear. The sky looked like a dark screen. The wind had picked up; and – by its invisible presence – seemed to portend some sort of change. 'RC' was beginning to feel better. The tropical evening seemed calming. He was at a dark podium before an audience of stars. Reluctantly he admitted - to himself -that she had made him feel better. Sister Frances reached for the walking stick that she had come in with.

"Gotta go....This old walking stick will support me in my little journey... but faith will guide me."

Then she turned again, intent on making a point,

"Science – or the scientific method - may not be able to explain everything. Maybe we need to challenge that very fundamental...just like we challenge everything. The brain may have found an approach that works for us... but it's just an approach; and not that different from the faith you readily disparage. Finding a blanket – any blanket...doesn't suddenly make the whole world warm."

"You don't talk like a nun." 'RC' observed.

"And you don't look like a savior..." she smiled.

With that, she opened the door and walked away. Moments later 'RC' saw the extensive shadow of something sail over the steeple of the jungle church. It occurred to him that -what he had seen - was perhaps seeking its own exorcism.

DREAM AND THOUGHT

The tracking assignment was over.

Bob had been paid; and had returned home to his wife, Louise at their 'soddie'. Even though he had enjoyed his 'journey' – he was grateful to be home. Louise grounded him. He had missed the open terrain of the prairie; the constant voice of the wind; the tasty stew that Louise made with dough balls; and their simple dinners together. The 'prairie pothole' was now filled with water; and 'old man muskrat' had been feeding on the cattail shoots. Bob had missed the dry heat; and the grasses burning under the sun. And he had missed the sound of crickets at night - and the vast field of stars that shown above him. The land was beginning to recover from the ravage of the winds that had blown through some time ago. He felt humbled and grateful by the earth's resolve; and marveled at the creative nature of 'wakan tanka'. Life felt uncomplicated and steady. He had just eaten supper and sat looking out at the pure and desolate Sandhills – sucking on a butterscotch candy.

But, to say he was happier than he had ever been, would have been wrong. The second tracking party had been nothing less than emotionally deteriorating and physically difficult. The lead biologist seemed weary; and it reminded him of his own fatigue and increasing age. He was sore from riding; and wondered how much longer he would be able to work such jobs. More than all of that, the celebratory tumult that marked the capture of the 'killer cat'...seemed premature and foolish. He had seen something in the lion's eyes that seemed intelligent and charismatic. And he again wondered if they had captured the correct animal.

On this night, he lit a pipe; and idly smoked while he looked out at the moon that had just surfaced above the Sandhills. As he was apt to do after dinner and under a vast sky, he leaned back on an old chair – and reflected on things while patting his full stomach. Meanwhile Louise busied herself with the repair of an old basket.

This was the time of day in which he was most able to accept the secrets that might be traveling on the wind. It caused him to consider just what 'thought' and 'dream' might be. Both were a succession of images and ideas;

and both were invisible and disarmingly powerful. He mused about it – playing with the idea that 'thought' more often seemed to have structure - like a box that holds a gift – while 'dream' might be like the ribbon that held the box together...and it was seen before 'thought'.

'Thought' was usually purchased during the day. 'Dream' was the sinuous wrapping that often took place at night. Then he quietly laughed about the allegory he had constructed; and wondered why some depreciated the 'dream' as being discardable and foolish – nothing more than unrestrained imagination. He was certain that 'dream' dressed up 'thought' and made it more special. It encouraged one to explore what was inside the box. He was also certain that – if the moon might choose to speak – it would allow that very little happened beneath it, which had not once been deemed 'somebody's foolish 'dream'.

It was at this very moment that he was aware that 'RC' was thinking of him and wondering whether Bob was still hunting the 'killer cat'. He laughed that he was in the young 'washicu's thought and imagined that 'RC' must be irritated. Some might call the timing coincidence – but Bob had always accepted that 'dream' and 'thought' were connected. Sometimes, the box and the ribbon were 'one'.

But – try as he might – Bob could not seem to communicate back to 'RC' in the same way he had received 'RC's thoughts. It didn't surprise him. 'RC' was unreceptive; and cynical regarding all such things.

'Such things' traveled through and rested in air. The young man could not accept it...even though his electronic devices worked similarly. 'RC' would not be called upon without a telephone. He believed in the box – not the ribbon. Bob yearned to communicate to 'RC'. He wanted to further irritate him - and to let him know that he was sitting on his butt - at home recovering from saddle sores...with money in his pocket - and a 'butterscotch' in his mouth.

He would tell him that the cat had been caught alive, caged, and transferred to a working lab to undergo tests. But the Indian was old and the boy was arrogant. No amount of literacy would seem to change either condition. Bob briefly pulled out his flip phone – then, resisting the urge - folded it and put it back in his breast pocket. Some day phones would no longer be needed.

Then he closed his eyes; and began to unravel the ribbon of dream. And from the box sprang the images of the lab to which the great cat – and the desert cranium - had both been transferred. Bob was 'traveling' again; drifting upon the wind. He closed his eyes and let it take him where it would. And – as dream and wind had done for millennia – they tested time until the boundaries of past, present, and future were blurred.

He traveled to a farm; and there again was the Jefferson family who had befriended the city Chamberlains. 'Old Joe', the man who had so influenced 'RC' when he was young, was surrounded by family. His wife, 'True' prepared supper; while son, Angus, read his books. The daughter reviewed the copious notes she had written about her day and how it had unfolded.

The ribbon of dream had brought Bob to the daughter, Earnestine. For it was the daughter who would help him understand the current narrative about what was happening to the great cat...and possibly, the desert cranium that 'RC' had discovered.

CAT IN A CAGE

"Earnestine!" the little bird man cried out on the telephone, "Bring my notebook and a pen! I'm going to the lab."

Within seconds of receiving the mission, she had returned with both. She was a serious black woman who rarely smiled; and stood a head taller than the little man for whom she worked. She had pinned her hair back on one side with a writing pen; and had made her way up the hallway so quickly that few remembered seeing her pass. It didn't matter as she rarely took time to engage in good-humored banter. She preferred – in the following order – research, equations, music and conversation. She held an advanced degree in chemistry; and the position at the lab had vindicated her regarding the expenses the Jefferson family had incurred by sending her to school. Earnestine was highly computer-literate and well-read. Somewhat emotionless and loveless because of her nature and a poor complexion, the rhythm of her heart beat more quickly to bits of information rather than to amorous advance. Her world was digital and pugnacious – and only occasionally colored by fantasy, when she allowed herself to close the day with a cocktail. Personal history had taught her that romance was over-rated. The last thing she had kissed...was a good book.

The little man was standing there – waiting for her expectantly. She handed the book to him and he toyed with the Chinese 'frog' that bound the book together – then opened it.

"Felis concolor..." he mused, before running off to the lab.

The great cat had awakened and was already furious to find that it was caged. This was the mountain lion that had been captured by the tracking party of which Bob had surreptitiously been a part. Instinctively it looked for an opening and snarled as if doing so would make the bars separate. Instead, the size of the cage seemed to shrink like wet leather. Feeling constricted, the animal paced back and forth and breathed heavily as if something had suddenly siphoned its air. It tested the openings of the cage and then proceeded to each metal bar, methodically looking for weakness. It made claw marks that seem faintly pictographic and it growled like Tallulah Bankhead[13]. After awhile, it sat and began to clean itself for a few minutes. When done, it stood up and prowled about again. Its gait was awkward – as if it had been injured. Occasionally it would pause as if flickers of memory had surfaced regarding the moment of its capture.

It had been running through the woods at great speed when it stopped at a streambed. Feeling the damp soil under its feet it lapped water under the moon. With only moments to lament, the fading twilight of its world had been chased away as it ran from voices – high into the mountains.

Suddenly, it was night again. The cat watched the familiar patterns of humans from a distant ridge. They were huddled around a fire eating. The lion wished it was there - warming itself like a house cat by a radiator. That evening, it had also seen the shadow of a large bird soaring in front of the moon - looking down...observing. It felt an odd kinship that was more than just 'wild' - as if both knew the same truth.

Finally, and in one weak moment, the mountain lion had traveled through the mud of a small watering hole and rested there too long. Its footprints had led 'the chasing animals that ran on two feet' directly to it. They had closed in and the cat had circled back on itself and fallen into a deep hole. There, amidst loud cries, it was trapped. It had a faint memory of once eating something domestic in a blood red sauce. But it had felt life in the wild; and that sense of freedom did not compel it to seek the shelter of men.

Everything had seemed new – as if overnight it had been transformed to a sentient being. When it sat very still, it could hear color creeping into leaves. Its eyesight was impossibly acute; and it could smell those who were hunting it from a quarter of a mile away. It could run and jump to such an extent that previous mobility seemed trifling. It felt indomitable and yet ...spooked by 'the chasing animal that ran on two feet'.

More surprising than all of these new senses, was an awareness of things of which it had not previously been conscious and for which it had no previous gauge. Voices in the woods had coached it along; telling the lion where to hide; and where bones had been buried. It had seen the winged animals that floated in the wind; rested on the boughs of trees - and which had such slight coloration, as to barely be visible. Lighter than air and floating as if there was more space than substance, they watched. Theirs was a quiet strength that was principled and free from malicious intent - and they spoke in light. There were also the shadows that exited from corpses; and which wondered among the living. Half-colored and flowing across the mountain disguised

---

13   American actress of stage and screen, 1902-1966

as mist, they seemed to stand on the other side of the wind - unable to pass. Beings - that blended in with rocks and trees -lived in the dark earth; and bickered over the water in stumps. But more than all of these things...the constant buzzing of voices that came from the rocks, trees, water, and plants themselves – were carried on the wind; and held the great cat's attention. They whispered secrets to the lion – some which it could understand. These were the things that had driven the cat and distracted it into the trap. All were unexpected; and made it forget the fitful entanglements, its pain and hunger; and a life constantly threatened by the nuisance of pestilence.

Now it was confined and the life that had been new to it was new again. It had awakened – though the animal was not certain where dreams began and where they ended. It growled and felt uneasy. And standing in front of it – separated by the hard thicket that would not part – was a wan creature with hardly any fur. It was watching intently and scratching at something with its naked paw. Small in stature and with eyes that seemed contained in ice, it made noises as it moved a stick. It seemed tasty - and reminded the cat of a moonlit dinner of lamb.

"Well, you're certainly not a two-headed monster..." the little bird man said, "but you're a killer."

The cat was suddenly 'spent'. It slunk to a corner; and – without warning – began to convulse like a skin-covered accordion; and wretch with intensity. Its abdomen shook; and its tail extended as if hung by a wire. It relieved itself – and didn't care that anyone noticed. Then, it retired to a corner – quite satisfied – like a politician who had given a paid speech.

From its vantage point, it watched the small man cautiously approach its cage. Nimbly, and with a single quick movement – the man reached through the bars and transferred the scat to a container. The specimen was ready for study – a potpourri for waiting lab rats.

Growling briefly, the cat sat down on its stomach; and stretched its hindquarters out like a tired tabby. The little man briefly observed the markings the cat had made in the cage. He suddenly turned around; stroked his pate as if he were wishing for something to grow there. Then he rapidly walked away.

"Judas!" he cursed to himself, "What bothers me about this animal?!"

He strode authoritatively down the hallway, pad in one hand – sample in the other. It was still warm. He walked to an office with red lettering on a frosted glass door. A second later he barked out an order to an administrative assistant – a woman who was often desk-prone and disobliging.

"I want you to take this sample to Ernestine in the lab – immediately."

She looked at him stonily – fresh from the fantasy of daily nap. Then, holding the bagged sample as if it was a kidney, ambled – with as much ambition as she could muster – down an adjoining hallway.

The little man strode into his adjoing office and looked out the window. It was almost evening; and the light was making its way through the leaves of nearby trees...with the might of busy commuters returning home.

LAB RATS

A hive of humans buzzed about the central laboratory. They examined the scat using electron microscopes and then, supplemented the test with more sophisticated technologies. Machines whirred and hummed in a lab that was therapeutically clean and shiny with potential. The light chased away niche shadows; and the expansive room was rife with the reflection and sheen of buffed metal. Even those who worked within it had a clean, sharp look. They wore white starched lab coats, sparkling eyeglasses; and had hair that was ferociously clipped, capped by a hairnet - or had been long since buffed away by time. Straightforward research, experiments defined by boundaries; and the unique madness of those only interested in method – was what mattered.

The animal's fecal matter was split into different containers of gleaming glass; and the samples were spread throughout the room. Scientists probed; pulled apart; and sliced minute sections for examination. Cellular microscopes drew the structure down to its most basic level. Slides were preserved using a flash program and then 'blown up' for study and discussion. Printers ejected graphs, tables, and DNA sequences bursting with color.

Petri dishes with agar had been scored and scarred. The chemical components of the scat were summarized with great speed. The process was fast, certain, informational; and detached. They would determine if the contents of the cat's stomach matched any of the DNA of Homo sapiens – particularly the dead jogger.

A lead technician pecked at computer buttons like a bird searching for grub. When the tasks were complete, the results were fed back to Earnestine who reviewed the 'work summary'. She read it slowly – stopped – and suddenly looked up. She pulled off her glasses, whisked a cleaning cloth out of a drawer and applied it. Putting her glasses back on, she looked at the report summary one more time; and frowned.

She had been waiting for the tedious day to end; and the promise of a hot cup of coffee; and dinner at the local dive called, 'Chicken Lickers'. There she would eat by herself and worry quietly about her brother, Angus. It was all she had to look forward to - and she was achingly hungry.

"Betty Anne, how can this be? Do you want to see me laid out on a stretcher..." she said.

"Well ma'am, we don't really know. We just received the 'analytics' from the computer; and try to interpret them as best we can," the technician pouted. Her face had no color other than a splotch of bright red lipstick.

"But I can't believe this...you sure the sample wasn't somehow contaminated?"

The technician looked stressed, fretful, and helpless. Earnestine ignored her. She took off her glasses and twirled them around like a gunfighter. Her eyes hardened,

"D'ju let Dave coordinate either the 'analytics' or the interpretation?"

The technician toyed with some hexagonal stones that were part of a bracelet she had received from her fiancé. The pause was long enough for Ernestine to believe that Mercury had completed its three-month orbit of the sun. Then, she whispered apologetically,

"Um...no ma'am...but he was on the team."

The man was not one of Earnestine's favorite employees. Indeed she didn't like anything about him: not the smell of his cologne; not the lexicon of his technical writing; and not the milk glass coffee cup that seemed to leave a ring on every counter it came into contact with. She was aware of his 'extra-curricular' exploits; and that he had been earmarked by the Director for special assignments – such as the analysis of a gigantic cranium recently brought to the lab. She worried that his insolence was communicable.

"Look here, Betty Anne, this is no hayride. If he was involved with this at all, he'd better be sure of his part of the project – or more than one head is going to roll. Y'understand? Now go back again and ask him about his data."

She watched the technician walk away hastily – a bracelet full of Nevada silver jangling as she moved. Then, she decided that perhaps it was time for her to make an unscheduled visit to the lab. So she took off her lab coat; put on a precisely tailored power jacket; and walked briskly down the hallway. The shock of her arrival caused one of the technicians to drop a vase full of liquid just outside of the lab – a bouquet of flowers lay sprawled across the bleach white floor of the corridor – and looked like a painting by Jackson Pollock.

"Clean up that mess!" Earnestine commanded.

The technician scurried away in search of towels and a trashcan.

Earnestine stopped at the door of the lab, aware of it being the boundary between contamination and sanitation. She motioned for the team. They rose from their seats and moved forward in purple hospital booties. Then her voice became uncharacteristically sweet.

"Hello. Team, I must ask you once again if you are certain that all of these tests were carried out correctly and under the strictest guidelines. We don't want to make this a classic textbook failure." They all nodded in unison and shuffled uncomfortably.

"Have there been any nanotechnological 'glitches' in our forensics?"

She shot a harsh glance at the man known as 'Dave'; and noticed him smirk and then quickly glance down at his feet. The technician, who had delivered the results to her office, pouted slightly – her red lips looking like a rosebud ready to unfold. Then Earnestine 'geared up' for a lecture of the vexed staff before her. The technician was paler than normal. Smiling, she said almost affectionately,

"'Snow White' here says that the tests were done excruciatingly well and with the precision of samurai. That's good – because we simply can't have any holes in our conclusions. But the tests did not yield effective results. Sadly, we must try again."

The technician beamed. She appreciated the affectionate nickname – especially from someone who was not known for her warmth. Ernestine quickly regained her composure and stood a bit straighter as if in executive capacity. Her suit fit her well and gave her an authoritative, professional appearance. The bright lights of the laboratory shined on her. She gleamed with the power of angelic resolve. Then, she lifted her head a little more as if her voice needed to carry to the back of the room and focused on the expansive whiteness of the lab and its shining silver technology. A distant window revealed fading sunlight and a crisp day that everyone wished to be out enjoying.

"I will not tell you that you have to stay, but simply will say that those who do...will be 'noticed' for their fine work. Thank you, all."

With that, her bright smile imploded into a characteristic stoniness. She turned gracefully and walked back toward her office – sure that she had put a limp in any sort of lust for rebellion.

Thus, began the second lab analysis. Though Earnestine had felt somewhat victorious in her delivery, it was tempered by what her father had told her long ago. She remembered 'Old Joe' once saying,

"The big fish in the pond only eats if the small ones do...and remember, they's always something bigger'n you."

She had no desire to trample her staff or to deny them 'potty breaks'. Her own career had been wrought through many hours. She remembered the startled technician and the shattered vase with flowers on the floor. Though she would not contaminate the laboratory by returning to it, she felt badly that the staff was confined on such a glorious day.

Feeling slightly guilty, she had pots of yellow daffodils delivered. They were set outside of the lab on ledges in order to balance the starkness of the room; and so the technicians could enjoy some color. She allowed her staff to have longer breaks and insisted that they take time to call anyone who might be missing them. She ensured that anyone needing metro or cab fare had it; and a water cooler was installed just outside of the lab.

Skin creams and various toiletry items were provided in the restrooms; and she had soothing music pumped into the break areas. Earnestine was not looking for adulation; but only wanted to be the grommet in a sail that kept everyone on course. She understood that an iron fist in a soft glove was necessary to ensure the excellence of any team effort.

The staff followed up like detectives on any residual clue. At the end of several more hours, most of the test results were in. The only thing remaining – other than prayer – was the 8 to 24 hour wait for the trays of agar to yield results; and the review and interpretation of senior staff. Scientists and technicians sat around tired and anxious – hoping there had been no 'ghosts' in the machine - that the next set of results would yield 'juice'.

During this period, they distributed themselves throughout their floor of the building – but never very far from the stage that had brought them together. Some watched movies on Iphones. Some read 'research papers' that had accumulated. Others engaged in 'horseplay'. A few took advantage of the time to learn the latest scientific application. Some read books online. There was idle conversation in the break rooms; and calls to family and friends. Online games and directives tested minds that would not be idle. They lined up for the company's shower facilities and took advantage of the toiletries that Earnestine had provided. They went into 'quiet rooms'; put in ear buds and hummed along peacefully to songs. A limitless supply of 'comfort food' had been provided by the company. They snacked; idly perused the outside from large windows in the adjoining hallway; and canceled previous commitments. Some simply got well-earned sleep...but, no one left.

Outside, nature had its own unspoken vetting process. The weather had changed suddenly and the wind had picked up. Weakened branches tumbled from trees as if to reveal the detriments of excess growth. There was a mild snow flurry that marched through so quickly that some were not sure they had seen it. A remote twinkling planet beckoned from the heavens. The wind pushed against the building – sometimes shaking it; and seeming to demonstrate a ferrous resolve. Something seemed to gestate inside of the wind – the warmer wind had been cast aside with great force. The cold wind seemed to speak through the glassed mezzanine to those who watched. It demanded deference and had a great hunger. The sights and sounds suppressed any mutinous thoughts about being outside. Those who had been watching from the windows retreated to break rooms and napped rather than face a stormy sentinel.

Finally, the tests and review were completed again; and presented to Ernestine. She read the report; sat still for awhile; and then – abruptly left the room 'muttering French'. She walked purposefully down the glassed-in corridor toward the Director's office. Outside the wind had started to pick up; and was rifling its way through nearby bushes and trees –looking like a bandit seeking entry.

Earnestine strode past the sleepy administrative assistant; and – after several crisp knocks on the door – entered the office of the little man who had collected the 'sample' from the cat. He sat behind a large desk and an oversized pair of wire-rimmed glasses. He looked expectant and tired. On the desk, and in front of him, was a small vase of yellow flowers. He removed his glasses; loosened his tie; and pushed aside a stack of papers he had been examining. To either side of him and on the wall were paintings of former lab directors who looked more like minions.

In a small, dry voice he asked,

"Ernestine.... finally... what did you find out about our predator? The trackers believe that the woman died within the time frame necessary for us to examine the contents of the cat's stomach. Did the fecal matter confirm anything?"

She looked at the floor; and wondered where and how to begin. Then she sighed and pursed her lips.

"Two separate tests were done on the animal's fecal material – and under a strictly controlled environment. In most cases of predator/prey kills there are some distinctive patterns. We can look at the carcass and evidence contusions and tears created by the prey's flailing – an attempt to escape the jaws of its predator. We can discern an approximate time of death from the clotting strength of the blood and rigor of the body."

She paused,

"We also examined what was left of the victim's carcass. There was evidence of hemialgia – that is to say – the partial paralysis that sometimes occurs in stroke victims. Unlike the stroke victim, this paralysis seemed to be confined to the lower part of the body – starting just below the waist – approximately at the lower abdomen and continuing all the way down. Of course, this is not out of line with the predation by a great cat. Though it's customary for the cat to surprise its victim from behind; tear away at the neck or spinal column; and to thereby render its prey immobile, an incomplete arrest of prey could produce the partial paralysis found in the victim."

She made a dramatic tearing motion with her hands to add force to her delivery.

Usually there is evidence of neuralgia content in the stomach or intestinal tract of the predator – if such an event has occurred. We have examined the fecal material of the predator and did not evidence such material. We did find non-adipose fish content – perhaps a herring – which makes no sense…and there were other odd results. We could, of course, carry out a more invasive and complete procedure – upon your instruction, sir."

The director tapped his pen with intensity.

"What are you saying, Earnestine?"

"Van, we…well, we didn't find the typical scatological content, not what we were expecting…" Very seldom did she address the little man by his first name.

"We must have missed something. What were the specific results? Are there other directions to pursue? Other clues…?"

She took another breath,

"We did nanotech experiments – of course manipulating the samples on molecular and atomic scales – and studied some of the quantum mechanical effects of the samples we had…but…. Well, unless there's a law against stalking 'beef bourguignon' – we should let the animal go."

The little man stood up – his rising barely perceptible.

"Are you quite sure?! Something isn't correct. The animal or the tests must have been compromised. Was the hunting party absolutely careful in the capture? Were they 'professionals'…someone must have sullied the results."

Earnestine responded,

"We did find one example of a slightly divergent DNA – from the animal's intestine – or at least we think it's the animal's intestine. It seemed odd to us because it was as if the structure was building back upon itself somewhat resembling a counterpoint."

He stared at her – disappointed.

"Uh, sorry sir…anyway, we dismissed the divergent DNA because the results didn't make sense. It's probably a contamination issue – not by my lab folks, of course!

And, there's more, sir. Some of the hunters sent in samples of hair that was found in the bushes near the kill. The hair is close – but it doesn't match the cat's hair or the victim's hair – it's sort of um…a derivative."

"Well whose hair is it, Ernestine!?"

"We don't know, sir. But it appears to be some sort of genetic modification – unprecedented...."

The little man idly picked up a Rubik's cube[14] from his desk and began to 'play it' with ferocity. It was what he did when he was nervous; and it seemed an uncanny evolutionary adjustment – as if he were twisting and shaking about worry, like it was prey. He worried about the direction of the world. He worried about the lack of results that he expected. And he worried about an appointment he had later in the day with a 'flatfoot' named Detective Tweeter. One of the scientists had not come back from the tracking assignment; and the detective had some questions. The little man wondered how on earth he would explain the missing man...he couldn't even explain it to the man's family.

Earnestine continued,

"The hair samples don't match up with anything in our genomic database."

Then, she stared up at the light – partly out of exasperation; and partly, to show her displeasure with the conversation. She was embarrassed by the intensity with which the little man was playing with 'the cube'; and wondered what might happen if he got nowhere with it. He obviously needed a 'win' – and she had not been able to present one. It suddenly struck the little man that she was quiet and he put back the cube on his desk – slightly self-conscious.

"The hair sample has probably been contaminated," he asserted, trying to cover his temporary madness.

"Well that's just the problem, sir. It's ..."

"Another problem..." his eyebrows arched slightly. "Take the results back and test them again."

His frustration was slightly visible; and his certainty compelled her parallel interest in perfection. Nonetheless, she felt obliged to defend her staff's scientific rigor. Besides, his order seemed to reflect badly on her.

"Sir, if I may, the technicians are all highly qualified. They tested it twice." It was more than she felt comfortable saying; and already seemed like a risky insurrection.

"Well then it must be the laboratory itself. If we have to rip it out, we'd better start now."

She twitched slightly - her response had made it worse.

"The lab and the chemicals are top-notch, sir; and we've followed the

---

14   A 3-D combination puzzle invented in 1974 by Hungarian sculptor and professor of architecture, Erno Rubik

strictest standard operating procedures."

She had pushed him to his limit.

"Well then...your 'operating procedures' need to follow a different set of standards. Do all the tests by hand; run the tests backwards and forwards if you have to. Make it as painful and methodical as it has to be, but get me some defensible results. The press is already crawling up our butts; and they want some sort of explanation that makes sense regarding the death of the jogger. The woman had two kids...."

He saw her reluctance and followed up,

"I don't need a bunch of over-educated worker bees that are afraid to get dirty. If you have a problem with anyone...let me know."

He had stolen back his self-control with the ease of a kleptomaniac.

A FINAL TEST

Just twenty four hours later, Earnestine returned to the Director's office. Like anyone who endured a serially repetitive assignment and minimal rest, she felt its mind-numbing effects. Worse, she was profoundly unhappy at not being able to render results that she knew would make the little man happy. She felt tormented by a lack of closure – but had an ace up her sleeve. Her stoical face – an adaptation to past disappointments – now, seemed a particularly comfortable defense.

How could she have known it would take hours of training to get the staff to the point that the Director expected. Through a 'hands-on' approach and rotational assignments, all had learned more about the dirty secrets of forensic science. It was something they could add to their resumes. But, Earnestine felt uncomfortable in the attendance of the technician she called, Dave. His shifty ambition was menacing; and she was certain that he must be reveling in her weariness...waiting for her to drop.

Another review of mountain lion's scat had been accomplished. Far from an alluring task for either the animal or the scientists and technicians – a rotational oversight of 'experiment' and 'analysis' had ensured the system of checks and balances needed to be defensible. As instructed, the laboratory staff had taken apart the remaining fecal matter. They had been insufferably methodical and exacting in their approach.

But she was not happy with what she had to report; and knew the little man who was the Director would be agitated. She reasoned that – if she propelled her results with a strong, positive approach – he might swallow the medicine that integrity demanded she deliver. Thus, she entered the room robustly.

"We did it. We took apart the fecal matter and examined it by hand... piece by piece...if you will."

The light-heartedness of her delivery was quickly snuffed out by his serious look.

"And what did you find?"

Suddenly, she felt like she was using her father's favorite hoe – but continued,

"Well, sir... (She cleared her throat)...the results were the same. We... (She took a deep breath)...did every viral and bacteriological test possible. We re-examined the DNA sequencing. There was nothing out of the ordinary with the first set of tests... (Now, she was rambling...)"

He interrupted,

"There's a mystery to this great cat, Ernestine. I feel it. We have to unravel it. The animal's not what it appears to be. We must be careful with our tests – so that we can better understand it; and, in turn, understand more about ourselves..."

It was an unusual ending to a brief rant. The little man looked out his office window at the panorama before him. The far mountain peaks held the remaining light of the setting sun. Shadows were already dancing up from their bases. Briefly, the little man daydreamed; and his thoughts were tumbling through the violet shadows of the base – trying to bounce toward the lighted peaks. Almost imperceptibly he shook himself in time to see the light falling like an amber mop of hair over the mountain facades. At the same time, he could discern the sonata of a gaggle of wild geese passing over the building. They made honking sounds as they flew toward the last bit of daylight. He wondered, 'could they feel the wonder of what lay ahead of them; or was theirs just some primitive bond of light and weather?' But he buried those thoughts deep inside – not willing to show a more sensitive side.

Then he remembered the flowers that Earnestine had set along the corridor. He had passed them often; and while inspecting the activities of the lab. The jonquils readily absorbed the light. Money did not interest them; the law had not established their right to be anywhere; and thievery could not steal their perfume. For a second he marveled at the magic; and wished for another life. He immediately rejected the thoughts as something others might see as 'childish'...and swallowed them.

Earnestine stood before him, shifting from one foot to another – she had noticed his discomfort. She cleared her throat; knowing that she had some news which might ameliorate his opinion of her. And she realized that while time was rented, reputation could still be purchased.

"We did find one difference from the previous tests; and we've isolated it."

His curiosity allowed him to shed the dream in which he had been momentarily encased. He waited for her to feed him the next line.

"We found a marvelous bacterium – but can't determine whether it exists naturally in the gut or is part of what the animal may have eaten. It's like a virus; and seems to need living cells to survive and feed on. When it's reached its fill – so to speak – it begins to pupate and goes into a dormant stage of very little duration. It has a sudden metamorphose that transforms it into a DNA sucking machine. It seems to travel throughout living material transforming the DNA. Then it stops; produces others like it; dies – and the process starts all over again. It doesn't really 'act' like a normal bacterium..."

He was stupefied by her response; and walked over to his desk and picked up the 'Rubik's Cube'. Then he put it down suddenly. He was thinking about the implications of what he had just heard; and trying to see if he could parlay her results into something palpable for the press.

"Are you sure of the results?"

"Well, we're not absolutely sure. We still have a few more tests to perform. Frankly, we've never seen an organism behave this way."

The little man flushed a bit. She continued,

"The bacterium seems to have a crystalline structure of sorts that is dog-toothed in appearance – not unlike the Erythronium, or calcite crystals called the dog-toothed spar…it's very curious."

He appeared reflective; and then said,

"We may have to examine the animal's stomach contents – there's a chance that the remains didn't make it completely through the intestinal tract."

"You mean cut the animal open?"

"That is exactly what I mean."

Ernestine looked at him dourly; and then said,

"You know we'll piss off every animal rights organization on the surface of the earth."

The Director trembled slightly. He was whiter than a tea rose. Then, he asked,

"Do you like American Ragtime…?"

SINCERO

The combined features were the arithmetic for an angel. The sensuous curve of the neck could only be rivaled by that of a beautiful woman's. White feathers were comparable to the purity and softness of snow. Long slender wings were gently curved and beat as rapidly in flight, as the heart of a lover.

The swan was fleeing something. It moved rapidly through the air - its shiny obsidian eyes focusing on an invisible path. Something sought the warmth of its blood, and its incomparable downiness. It flew straightly and quietly as a feathered arrow; and could not have imagined that the impulse would take it directly into the path of the eagle – waiting ravenously with steel claws and horn-curved beak. It was midsummer and the constellations of Cygnus and Aquila were visible as they approached each other head on. Dinner would be served.

Sincero spent a long time sitting in the brush; and staring at the boundary that separated two countries. In fact, he had sat all night under the Thunder Moon. He was paper-thin and had a long dark mane of wavy hair that seemed to counterbalance its absence on his countenance. He had trifled with the idea of cutting his hair; but decided longer hair made him look older and therefore, more employable. He was fond of bathing and liked to take care of himself. It irritated him that he had not had the opportunity to do so since the beginning of the enterprise in which he now found himself. This was the young man that Bob, the Indian, had seen in his serial dream.

Frightening memories of the bedlam, overturned camp, and the shots fired – still resonated. Sincero hoped the man who called himself, 'RC', had survived; but was too afraid to return to the mountains to discover the man's demise. The coat 'RC' had lent to him had helped him endure the cold nights since he had fled the thugs who had trashed the camp. He felt ashamed and angry that he had not stood by in defense of the man.

In his desperation to escape, he had nearly lost the small cross that his mother had given to him long ago. He had hurriedly thrust it into one of the coat's pockets. The cross was the only material thing he had by which to remember her. Now, as he sat underneath the moon divinity, he was thinking of 'El Dia de Los Muertos'; and wondering if he might soon be joining his ancestors. He looked over the river to the United States and wondered about borders...including the border between life and death. The thought caused him to fish around in the pockets of the coat for his mother's cross. He found it and fastened it around his neck. It was also then, that he discovered something else.

Sincero pulled the package of small granules out of the coat pocket, wondering at their origin. Surely they were worth something or the man at the camp would not have kept them; and put them in the coat pocket. How could he return them? He emptied some from the packet and rolled them around in his hands. They had the luster of tarnished coins – and Sincero was in desperate need of money. Then, he put the granules back in their packet and considered what he should do.

The coat was not his and neither was what was contained in it. He had left someone defenseless; and the cross now reminded him more than ever of a duty he had not fulfilled. He stretched out his arms; and looked at the moon imploringly. He was certain his mother was looking back. Then he looked down and prayed for answers regarding what his responsibility should be and what plan he might make. With hair falling down across his shoulders – and with his outstretched arms and head bent – he seemed as some exotic crucifix. The answer that came back to him was a surprise.

'Though money might be in his hand – love, birth, and a flight home would be his quest.'

He did not understand the message, but prayed that its meaning would eventually be revealed. Then he fell asleep - mesmerized by the power of prayer. When he awakened, the simmering heat of day was upon him; and sweat rolled off his brow. He was sore and the ground was as hot as a barbecue.

Long ago, the philosopher, Aristotle[15], had reasoned that there were three basic types of government: monarchies, which eventually became aristocracies; which eventually became democracies. Monarchies became tyrannical. Aristocracies centered influence and power among a few powerful elite. Democracies became selfish factions that were unable to come to agreement. Then, the cycle repeated itself – giving rise to monarchies again.

Sincero's head hurt. He knew nothing of Aristotle...only that his country seemed to be in a dark transition. He sat staring across the river – feeling like a plant pulled toward light. His own country seemed to be festering from within; and his heart told him it was time to leave. He had spent months working

---

15   Greek philosopher, considered the father of science 384 – 322 B.C

for money; and planning an escape. He had been unsure; but the incident of the overturned camp and the men who had chased him away with guns; had confirmed that it was time for action. Though he felt guilty that he had not returned to help the man who had given him the coat, he also believed that he was at the precipice of his own survival.

He again pulled out the packet of granules from the coat pocket; and rolled the packet around in his hands. The granules shined as if they were wet. He was now certain that the men who had chased him were looking for what was in the coat. Though he didn't understand their significance, he knew that someone deemed them to be important. He concluded that it was far more desirable to execute a plan than to face his own execution.

Then he thought of a distant conversation with a cousin. She had put her hand on the side of his face before he had started his journey as a guide,

"You look worried, Sincero – what bothers you?"

"I don't know if I can do it. I'm afraid, Perdida. I don't even know what to take with me."

She smiled and said,

"Then only take care, my dear." And she kissed his forehead, "Vamos con Dios."

Now, he watched the great river from a distance; and he was afraid again. The current seemed swift and dark. He peeled off his clothes and threw them aside with the coat that 'RC' had given to him – they would only weigh him down. He secured his mother's crucifix around his neck. Other than the cross, he was naked as the day he had been born. In his hand he held the packet of granules – knowing he could not risk losing them. Then he took a deep breath; opened his mouth; and swallowed the packet whole.

FLIGHT

He sat on the bank for a long time, looking at the water rushing by. Sincero put his hands to his eyes to shade out the intense sun; meanwhile scouting for an entry point to the rushing river. He was lonely and without hope. Maybe this was a mistake.

Years ago, he had been hunting with an uncle. He remembered the steamy day and a jungle dripping with humidity. Quietly, the two of them had come upon a river when his uncle stopped. Putting his finger to his mouth, he motioned to Sincero for silence; and then whispered,

"La bas – grande rata. Se dice 'nutria' in ingles."

It was the biggest rodent in the world. Waiting by the side of the water – without warning – it splashed forward as if it had heard a nearby predator. Its eyes seemed intelligent. They watched as the female bested the current; and its babies crawled upwards to suckle the nipples on the mother's back – hunger would not be sated by uncertainty. After much struggle, the nutria arrived safely on the other side of the river. She crawled up the muddy bank. The light glistened off of her tubby body; she shook herself; and the young crawled back under her carriage.

And with that memory...Sincero slipped into the deadly water. The current was stronger than he had anticipated. When his head bobbed back to the surface, he spat out water and quietly prayed as the current rapidly carried him downstream - he could barely swim. The sun had not impacted the icy fingers of mountain snowmelt. The excessive heat he had felt when he had awakened was suddenly pushed away by the breath of a cold giant. He looked skyward and briefly caught sight of the pale moon that earlier, he had called upon. It was now just a phantom in the sky. Sincero paddled with all his might. He again thought of 'El Dia de Los Muertos' – determined that the boundary crossed on this day...would not be an abstract one.

Glancing downstream he could just make out a jetty of thick vines that had tumbled from the far bank. Still attached to the land, they bobbed in the rushing water. He turned his body toward them and propelled himself forward with as much force as he could muster. He hoped the tangle of loose vines was within reach – it might save him. His breath was labored and his strength had settled like the land under the blistering sun.

Above the vines and the bank to which they clung, the country was wide and open. It looked like a welcoming port. The watery froth in which he floated was noisy and danced with the careless abandon of a white wedding party. It carried him as easily as a lesson learned. Sharp pellets of rock and sand stung his feet like fire ants and reminded him of the deadly bottom current willing to suck him under. Surrounded by water – but thirsty only for freedom - he neared the tangle of vines. With the thought of 'Los Muertos' resting upon his shoulders he lunged for the vine-covered projection grabbing as much of it as he could. Then, pulling his weary body upon the bank, he lay there – panting, resting upon a raft of vines; and thankfully reciting a prayer.

When he had rested enough, Sincero sat up and looked about. He had drifted much further downstream than expected. He crawled up the bank to higher ground; found the protection of some small shrubs; and then, peered intensely from his hiding place. He was looking for a certain part of the tall fence that was above him. Clearly, he was not where he should be. He must follow the fence line back up river; but would have to do so as stealthily as possible.

And so he began picking his way quietly through the low brush. Barefoot and naked, he felt exceptionally vulnerable. The wind had picked up – it blew his hair about his face and flung the land's heat about him like a furnace. Soon he heard high voices, brass instruments; and the distinctive shrill plucking of guitars. He furtively approached the fence and looked through a crack in it. He had arrived just in time to see the band making its way toward him. Nearby guards had become captives of commotion. Denizens of a border crossing – their duty had obviously been compromised.

The elaborate festivities were borne as much from spontaneity as plan. The music was loud and brimming with Latin spice. The costumes were unscrupulously colored; and the dancing participants seemed like vibrating color wheels. Hands and hems were raised frequently in response to the passionate music. Smiling eyes glowed like embers. The band had billed the event as the celebration of an obscure saint.

His cousin had been correct. There was much drinking and revelry. The Maharachi band and its dancers passed around 'refreshments' from brown paper bags. The women were flirtatious, cute, and persistent. They amused and confused the guards with their spirited dancing; and punished them with sacramental flirtation.

A generously sized young woman took great pride in their embarrassment.

She would start out with a flirtatious song reinforced by the pulsing music. Then, running her hands lightly across her chest, would offer the guards liquor that miraculously appeared from underneath her raised hem. One guard, in particular, seemed to 'catch her fancy'. She pirouetted around him – the yellow frill of her dress looking like the curled trumpet of a nodding daffodil.

But strict rules forbade drinking while on duty. The scent of alcohol could easily be written on skin and behavior. However, 'playing cards' could be carried without notice – like a pack of cigarettes. The guard was anxious to get back to a winning hand. Losing patience with her flirtation and yearning for a chance to win easy money, he pushed her away roughly. He could have any woman he wanted if luck was with him - and he was certain that the lady was well within his court on this particular evening.

Hopped up on alcohol - but realizing the futility of competing with an ephemeral suitor - the flirtatious girl seemed only mildly offended. Tipping a bagged bottle to her lips, she gulped down the remaining liquor in a suggestive way; and then tossed the bottle high over the fence. On the other side of the enclosure, Sincero saw the bottle plummet – and wondered whether he should risk trying to catch it.

But one of the guards had been very attentive and seemed to understand that the impropriety was a risk. He put one hand on the holster of his gun; and looked about the perimeter of the fence line. Then, he gave the flirtatious dancer an unpleasant look and pushed her away. The celebration was attracting a crowd of 'onlookers' just beyond the duty station entrance. It was time to end the celebratory activities and restore some order. Hearing something, he looked back to the fence briefly. Sincero quickly pulled the bagged bottle into the brush; and then sat – as motionless as a woman who did not wish to be noticed at a dance.

When he was comfortable that the guard's attention to the perimeter of the fence had dwindled and that he was safely out of earshot, he opened the twisted neck of the bag and quietly pulled out the contents. The bottle had cracked - but had not shattered. He turned it upside-down. Just as had been discussed, a packet had been hidden inside the highly indented bottom. A false, flat clay bottom had been constructed over its recess; and sealed with a layer of glue. The bottom of the bottle had been decorated with a label; and ribbon had been twisted around the entire vessel as further decorative deception. Sincero attempted to pry the bottom of the bottle away, but the glue held fast. He was concerned that it might shatter in his hands. Seeing a small stone by his feet, he pushed the bottle back inside of the bag. Up-ending it away from him and barely breathing, he waited for a distraction.

The band had started again – persuaded by an excited crowd just outside the perimeter of the gated compound. Reveling in attention and moved by the beat...the dancers again began their teasing rhythm.

With several quick sharp blows, the bottom of the bottle cracked open; and the contents burst forth. Sincero stopped and waited – he wanted to be certain that no one had heard. His heart was pounding. Then he gently emptied the contents of the bag - more assured that everything was going according to plan. His money had been well-spent.

Inside the bottle's hidden compartment, a micro fiber, dye-stamped material was concealed. Sincero unraveled it. Then, looking about the border of the fence for any sign of movement, he quickly stood up...and pulled a web-thin dress over his head.

He marveled at how light it felt and how it stretched to fit his frame. It was like wearing the wind. A manifestation of vanity caused him to brush back his long hair; and adjust the dress to fit him better – it felt more comfortable than he had expected. He quickly shook off the thought as being pathological - and then, concentrated on his plan. He would jump the fence and sprint as hard as he could, to freedom.

The music had started anew, but was now a different composition and style. It was music that had been born thousands of years before; and played on pan-pipes – centuries old 'ghost music'. The dancing had slowed. The music's origin was a derivation that had descended through time. Its modern connotation was proof that there was a selection process – even in the phenomenon of culture. Eerily enticing, the melody caused Sincero to long for the past. It momentarily distracted him from the boundary that he intended to cross; and he wondered if he had been prudent.

As the tempo of the music increased and from the sidelines of the accumulating crowd that had now stationed itself just outside of the station gate, a throaty voice cried out,

"DACAPO! DACAPO! DACAPO!"

The small Italian woman – whose eyes were closed tightly – was listening to the music and shouting with enthusiasm. Sophia Angaros had been swept away by the music and the moment. It was not the normal operatic style of music to which she was accustomed, but it seemed to leave her almost breathless. For the first time since her husband had died - she was thoroughly enjoying herself. It was just enough distraction for Sincero to get closer to the fence.

...Meanwhile, and many miles away, Bob and Louise had just finished an early supper. Bob got up from the table and walked toward the door of the soddie, when Louise caught his shadow out of the corner of her eye,

"Where ya' going, old man...?"

"Goin' out to the porch, Louise....got something to do." He had heard an ancient music that seemed to have traveled hundreds of miles in the wind.

"Ya' got some dishes to do – too! Get 'em when you come back." She knew that she shouldn't interrupt 'the dream', but she was no fool either.

Bob sat in a favorite old chair and lit his pipe. He stared out at the late afternoon sky. It was quiet other than the rasping sound of grasshoppers in the dry grass. His last 'dream' had taken him to the lab over which the woman, Earnestine, presided. The 'churring' of the insects now reminded him of its humming machinery. The lab's forensics had indicated what he suspected all along. The great cat that the second tracking party had captured...was not the one which had killed the jogger.

He closed his eyes and drifted into what seemed like a yogic state. After a few minutes, he was certain his soul was traveling. He could 'see' the young man, Sincero, contemplating his decision at the fence line.

Further away and south of the young man, a bell had tolled in a jungle church. He could 'see' the young washicu named, 'RC'. He was now sitting upright and eating. He had gained some strength back; and his wounds were binding nicely.

A tall, capable woman who was dressed in a hooded robe watched cartoons with children – while 'RC' sat and wondered what had happened to the guide with whom he had traveled before the camp had been overturned. He was plagued by thoughts of some 'silver sand' that he had mistakenly left in the pocket of the coat which he had lent to the guide; and he was certain that the package of granules was significant. Whoever had overturned the camp had shown intention – and it was the 'silver sand'...the metallic granules... that they were seeking.

As he had done so many times before, Bob tried to communicate with 'RC'. He hoped that 'RC' might finally be receptive to the spirit side of himself. This time a message came back to him. But it was not from whom he expected. Bob shuddered slightly – wondering how the man had interjected himself into his thoughts.

BAREFOOT FREEDOM

Sophia Angaros' joyful outburst had momentarily stopped the band. An accompanying friend – similarly widowed – tried to comfort her and diminish her embarrassment. She realized that the music was the first bit of bright warmth Sophia had felt since the death of her husband, Archibald. For her part, Sophia now understood that she had dwelled far too long on the man and had forgotten how much she missed music.

"Sophia, just relax and try to enjoy the band. It's quite 'cultural'," her friend prodded.

The composition had a kissing syncopation which was intriguing; and the Maharachi band had become manic. The dancing – refreshed by the pause of Sophia's unexpected outburst of enthusiasm – had become electric. The piquant yipping of the band would have made nearby felines nervous. Castanets snapped like click beetles. Colors swirled about. Hot pepper and onion dresses rose and cascaded in roller coaster circles while the dancers' feet pounded the earth and stilettos pierced the ground like cactus quills. The dancing raised dust to the sky as if beating out the dry grime of labor and sadness. The bang of a tin'ish drum twisted through the piece like a Bacchanalian vineyard. Black and white skeleton catrinas were hoisted to the air; and mandolin-like instruments let out zippered sensuous sounds. Bilious clouds of dust formed in the nearby horizon as if to cover the blue sky and entreat rain. Now the air was so heavy with vapor that fish might spring from it and swim toward the zenith.

Then it happened. The big girl - who had been flirtatious with the guard - began to slow down like a large wind up toy. Her face turned ashen. She whirled halfway around swinging her hat. Her skirt, which had been ballooning from the activity of rapid twirls, began to deflate. She stepped once slightly...attempted to pirouette...listed like a large colorful parade float...and crashed into the dirt. The clay tarnished her outfit – giving her the appearance a wilting peony. The wind which had been absent up to this point - picked up slightly; and blew dust upon her like powdered sugar on a cake. Then the wind left abruptly...seemingly called off in another direction.

An astonished Sophia Angaros prepared to run towards the fallen woman when the shadow of something large moved across the spot where she was standing; and caused her to look up. 'Perhaps', she thought, 'it was an angel'. But she rid herself of the notion immediately. Only God could dispatch angels – and the occasion would not have merited such heraldry.

The coiled crowd had erupted into barnyard madness. Musicians, dancers, and onlookers, gathered around the large girl who was now as green as an olive. Someone shouted,

"MARIA ESTA INFERMA!"

The crowd pulled her to her feet and dusted her off. She moved like a giant drunken moth – fluttering slowly...stopping...making its way toward the light...and then, falling again.

The shrieking crowd had brought the guards' initial paralysis full circle into a pathological frenzy. Now aware of the jeopardy to their reputations, they ran towards the sickened dancer – convinced that their presence would call the crowd to order. They awkwardly addressed the 'situation' – uncoordinated, emotionless...robotic.

"Ma'am, please step away!"

The guard, who had arrived first, seemed pale and faded as a wax statue. Sophia, who was now kneeling beside the fallen dancer, looked at him with as little interest as if she were looking at a vending machine. He was sweating profusely; and the light seemed to be melting him.

"It's about time you got here."

He demanded,

"Do you have medical training!?"

She rolled her eyes; removed a handkerchief from her handbag; and unfolded it. Then she daubed the woman's forehead and responded,

"Does veterinary medicine count?"

Then, she folded the handkerchief back into a neat square; pushed it inside of her handbag; and looked keenly into the woman's eyes, to see if they were dilated.

The guard stammered for a few seconds trying to unearth an appropriate response, when another guard appeared from behind him. More forceful than the first, he ordered,

"Please step aside!"

He had blue eyes, a mop of blond hair and a chubby boyish face - for which some sort of authoritative compensation was obviously necessary.

"I think she's dead," Sophia responded; and took great delight at seeing him blanch.

Then she immediately followed with,

"Not really...but we need an ambulance here right away – so get one! Could be heat stroke...."

The crowd buzzed like cicadas.

"She needs to have her feet elevated. I think she may be going into shock." Mrs. Angaros said calmly. "Here! Take this!" She lifted up one of the woman's legs and let it fall into the arms of the first guard who had been admiring the curve of her ankle.

"Ma'am!!!" The chubby boyish guard was shouting; and he took the leg out of the arms of his comrade and dumped it on the ground. It bounced with the tension of a heavy spring; and the large girl moaned. He shouted again with greater intensity - and stood above Sophia, waiting for a response.

"Yes, I heard you already. Whad'ya think – I'm deaf? Go see if you can catch someone trying to smuggle something."

Then she turned to look at him. Seeming quite surprised she queried crisply,

"Are you even old enough to catch a cold...?"

The rapid flush of his face signaled the guard's growing impatience. He vigorously intervened,

"Step aside, ma'am! She needs air!"

Sophia had also become impatient; and responded with equal force,

"Well she's got a whole sky-full of that! Do you fancy we're sucking away the earth's supply?!!"

A breeze, as if on queue, brushed across the face of the lethargic girl. The guard's anger had become visible. He raised his eyes for a second away from Sophia Angaros looking intently for the origin of a sound he was sure he had heard. On the other side of the fence, Sincero withdrew rapidly – and worried that the shards of the broken bottle might have attracted attention. He froze in place – his breathing arrested. Before the guard could act upon his curiosity, the other guard grabbed his arm and swung him around, saying forcefully,

"Man we gotta do something!"

It was just the moment she needed. Sophia Angaros yelled out to anyone within earshot,

"...some help here! We need to get this woman out of the sun!"

Those who understood calmly lifted the girl; and carried her to a nearby structure. There they hovered around waiting to see if the meager shade and the infusion of water from Sophia's handkerchief would resurrect her.

The rookie guards had arrived at their station and retrieved their phones. One guard was red and breathless – the other white from fear.

"We're gonna catch hell for this, man! I don't need any more demerits. What are we gonna do?!"

Meanwhile the crowd was bent over the sick girl – looking very concerned; and muttering in low tones.

Sincero had been watching everything from a crack in the fence. When he felt the time afforded his best opportunity, he stood up and – saying a quick prayer for the ailing dancer - then, bounded across the dry landscape. He reached the fence in seconds. Jumping as high as he could, he caught its razor'ed top; and then threw himself over. He fell to the ground – bleeding but determined that he would focus on the advantage rather than the cuts on his hands. He pulled the bright red of his own blood across his lips, hoping it would lend more to his disguise.

The crowd suddenly turned their attention away from the ailing girl and toward Sincero. Their excited conversation alerted the guards who stopped what they were doing. They saw Sincero sprint across the open ground – long hair and skirt flowing like banners. The more nervous guard started to pursue, but was stopped by the other.

"You're getting ahead of yourself, man! We don't have time to chase anybody – the border's a sieve anyway. Gotta figure a way out of this mess...the MPs will be here any second. How bad you wanna get dressed down...?"

The crowd immediately thronged together and absorbed Sincero. Shoeless, bleeding, and knowing the danger he was in – he was on high alert. In the meantime the large girl seemed to be recovering. The color was returning to her face. She lay against the side of the building where they had carried her; and idly played with a flag that had been carelessly propped there – daubing her face with it occasionally.

A drummer pumped out a beat and the pounding rhythm slowly ignited the band. In the intervening time, the guard station had become an apex of excitement as the men barked orders to each other as they attempted to restore order. They turned off a radio; threw bottles away; doused cigarettes with water; and stowed the playing cards at the bottom of the trash can – tossing the remains of an earlier lunch on top of everything.

But they were not as cunning as the one who watched them from the side of a building. She fully intended to expose their bungling even if it would bring only one minute of harmony. She had experienced enough discord... and that particular music did not please her.

Suddenly the guards caught sight of Sincero running for the entrance. The dress was liquid color. His hands were bloodied. Confused spectators stood with jaws agape. He shot past the guard booth and out the gate – heading for freedom, burning a colorful path along the parched ground.

"Oh, man! Now we got an illegal! We gotta get her! If she makes it to the park our gooses are cooked!"

The other guard immediately severed his inclination.

"Let her go! If we don't get this mess cleaned up and get that band outta here – we'll both be living under a bridge!"

Their eyes swept the area like it was a minefield. Within seconds, the booth was cleaner than a sanitized crime scene. They escorted as much of the band as possible out of the area. Sweat dripped from their foreheads and arms.

Sincero continued running hard. The wind was at his back and seemed to push him along. A flotilla of emergency vehicles gave credence to his decision to leave rapidly. He was certain there would be questions and requests for identification. He jogged past a nearby pizza parlor where patrons barely took notice of him.

Back at the guard station – and in the midst of confusion – Sophia Angaros stopped to look up at the sky. Squinting hard she could just make out the shadow she had seen earlier. It sailed over the horizon. She glanced away from it and back to the large dancer who was still leaning against the wall of a building; and daubing her forehead with the flag. Then she quietly prayed for the young girl who had run past the booth – thinking how frightened she must be.

When the emergency vehicles arrived, she was fanning herself as if she were gravely ill and clutching a small bouquet of yellow flowers that had fallen from the hands of one of the band's performers. She knew it would render her more noticeable. Feigning slight illness and leaning against the guard station, her intent was to draw attention to the buffoons. And then in a voice that was not know for its fragility, she said in a feinting tone to approaching medics,

"Oh please, please! Don't bother with me gentleman."

Then pointing,

"It's the other lady over there that needs help. I'm fine really. I'm just not use to celebrations. You know, in my day, men in uniform were so meticulous. They rarely celebrated with the crowds. Oh! What am I saying? I'm an old fool. Smelling champagne bubbles when it's really probably just the smoke from the guard's booth that got me a little light-headed. Things happen here, you know, disturbing things, oddly improper things.... Oh dear, I really shouldn't be telling you this – I'm fine...just fine."

She assured them one more time that she was well; flirted a little; and then watched out of the corner of her eye as the police walked rapidly to the booth where they found two guards trying very hard to look as virtuous as cub scouts. They looked like little boys; and – for an instant - she wished she had said nothing.

Meanwhile – further away and betting on the safety of the distance he had put between himself and the guards – Sincero finally stopped. His heart was beating harder than it had when he crossed the river; and he felt sick to his stomach. He lay down on a nearby rise to rest. It was then that he noticed the shadow of what appeared to be a large raptor circling above. Even from a distance, he could see that its talons were perfectly capable of determining the course of events of anything it chose to hunt.

...Many miles away, the smell of dough balls, cattail shoots; and a bit of meat – pulled Bob, the Indian from his dream. Louise was cooking again; and his pipe had gone out. He thought of the young man named, 'RC'; and wondered if he would ever be able to communicate telepathically with him. He sneered as he remembered that he had barely been able to transmit his thoughts face-to-face with the young 'washicu'. But he wouldn't give up hope. Perhaps 'RC' simply didn't possess 'the gift'.

But something had interposed between his dream and any communication, as if holding an opaque object between the light and his eye. It had stimulated a dark thought within him and cut him off from the sky. He remembered dreaming of Sincero's swim across the river; and the young man's run to safety.

But now, there was something looking back at Bob from his dreams. It had burning eyes – and begged to be identified. He slowly rose from where he had been sitting; and stretched his neck up to the sky to see the stars. The constellation 'Draco' was thrashing about as if looking to avenge.

He had meant to cross the threshold to the 'soddie', but suddenly stopped and turned around. The waxing moon seemed to be calling him. It was then that he realized what had interceded in his dream. That which had communicated with him was not 'RC' - it was a large, dark shadowed man who he had once seen on a mountain top – looking at village...eyes full of plunder.

It was time to do some dishes...

WOUND AND WISH

The screaming of ambulances momentarily caught the attention of a group of men who played 'beer ball' in the park.

They had staked out their territory much earlier. Some were xenophobic – or simply wore the dark vestments of war and lives that hadn't been that for which they had hoped. All had felt the hard side of life; and many had long since forgotten the transformative power of a smile. They did not wish to exhume the bones of emotion; and were solitary men who didn't sleep much...and who had few relatives or friends. Alcohol was sovereign or had only recently been deposed. The brutality of conflict and a common rank of 'survivorship' had created deep, uncomfortable camaraderie. Happiness was an illusion which was as unbelievable as the 'Easter Bunny'. They had sickened of directives and orders that had nearly killed them. Some were clean; some were mean; and some days they hated everyone...especially themselves. Most had lost more than just time. Some were disfigured – with the worst scars inside. They were men who had been bulldozed to flatness - but there were deep holes. Behemoth rehabilitation sometimes worked. Many insisted instead, that mankind needed to be made over. Some had souls that had been braised to tenderness – for others the heat had been left on for far too long. If they had faith, it was good. If they had no faith, they walked through life, already dead.

Immigration was a common concern – especially when jobs were already scarce. In this border town, immigrants had shown up as 'the great unwashed masses'. Impoverished hordes were willing to work for less money. But there was one among them who had come back from war with more money; who had married finely; and who was one part of a 'power couple'.

This evening, the men had a field to themselves. Nothing else seemed to matter. Glory could be attained momentarily by simply standing on a raised mound of soil; rather than storming up a hill. It was time to play rather than plot – time to 'bust some baseballs'.

Clement, was 'batter up'. He was a disreputable man – something that had escaped from the lab of human character. He was a plumber by sunrise;

and a trader in exotic species after the sun's descent. Given the opportunity to go to school under the GI bill, Clement had decided that knowing a trade was less important than knowing how to. His uncommon abilities had fostered a seedy dream which – at its base – was supported by a pet store rumored to be a 'front' for all things illicit. His dark dream had feet; and he had made money. Nefarious activities did not involve a 'leap of conscience'. He was not particularly scrupulous – and had a conscience that was legless.

For a moment, he stood at the plate – as if he sensed there was something different in the air...something like, intent. He looked skyward but could see nothing. Never one to be sensitive to abstractions, he immediately ignored the sense; and began to swing his bat back and forth in order to 'warm up'.

He thought of himself as 'a survivor' – one of the few GI's who had returned from a skirmish alive with all body parts. There were those who knew of the craziness of war; and secretly wondered about the veracity of his 'sole survivor' story. But his story was now formula; and – like any formula must be disproved or accepted – even begrudgingly.

This evening he had stood at the batters cage thinking about things other than baseball. His little business was known in selective circles for its exotic species – some advertised and some not. Yes, he sold the usual parakeets, turtles, fish – and even a few dogs and cats if he could get his hands on them. He sold the required gravel filters for aquariums, pet food, cat boxes, and a variety of grooming materials. He had expanded his trade to include animal parts; for there were those who preferred to get their supplements from sources other than vitamin pills. And he had a voodoo contact who believed that health, well-being...and magic would be determined by animal remnants and the secrets locked inside of them.

If he was lucky enough to get an occasional Hyacinth Macaw, it could easily fetch about twelve thousand dollars – a two to three month salary in his world. Some of his best trades had been with those 'south of the border' who were trying to keep themselves above the muck of poverty. Some wanted money. Others were seeking entry and nine little numbers – in order to start a new life. It didn't matter to him. He had access to such things; and the trade in 'exotics' was keeping him afloat. He had even tried the occasional trade in plant species. Orchids would command the most handsome price, but some of the forest lilies were also heftily rewarding - and interesting in their genetic makeup. The hunting populace had also recently become a lucrative 'market'.

Clement never thought of his 'business colleagues' as equal. He chuckled at a secret joke that he 'kept close to his chest'; and out of 'marketing' circles. He believed that all of his business partners were simply, 'species trading other species'. It was a hard belief and one not based on respect.

But - like most life – he sought to continue and possibly, reproduce. Like a strong tree, his taproot went into darker places; and like a bird that flourished in that tree, he would feather his nest with whatever abundance he found. The deals that he struck; the shiny things he bought; and the wealth that was his – had a natural principle at their core. He was just doing what everything else did –save one fundamental difference. He had been schooled in conscience and choice; and therefore wore the darkest of all tarnishes.

Clement had worked that tarnish into luster. There had been snags along the way. He almost 'lost his shorts' on the pink boa constrictor – but the deal was now legendary in his own mind; and in the darker trading circles. Two smugglers had transported the snake from the Amazon jungle. It lay practically immobile amidst a crate full of winter vegetables. Clement had previously arranged payment with the driver – a dependable partner. Once past the border, the 'partner' would stop at an agreed upon location and 'lose two crates' of 'produce' in the brush.

The strategy had worked perfectly. Clement found the crates as planned. The crated boa, now warm from the sun, was taken back to his shop – but not until the driver completed a detour. The other crate would be dumped into the swamp where appreciative locals would devour its contents with gusto. The remains of the second smuggler having 'disappeared' in the gut of alligators, allowed the more reliable partner to walk away with twice the money and a valuable bargaining chip...a social security card. Clement smirked as he thought about the plan's simple perfection.

The memory of the 'trade' made him feel immortal and capable...he needed that. He reached down and ceremonially daubed his hands in the batting plate's dust like it was holy water...and prepared to hit a 'homer'. Picking up two bats, he swung them back and forth. It had less to do with 'warming up', than showing prowess and power. Then he dropped one of the bats to the ground; beat the plate with the remaining one...and fondled himself. It was a rude display of masculinity and an attempt to 'psyche out' the pitcher. The game was being played more with beer than aplomb.

The opposing team – neither opposing nor a team – was only mildly interested in the game. It had become a social event and an excuse to get together. They admired the fading tracks of jet trails in the sky; and waited to hear the 'crack' of the bat. Really, they just wanted to sit down and drink. Their faces had reddened from exertion and generous amounts of beer; and they made frequent forays into park's deeply wooded area - to urinate.

That area of the park was a protective fringe of trees and bushes that had been left in place to shield nearby houses from noise. The thinking had backfired. The area was both a hangout and hideout for those who wished to engage in any activity. Metaphorically speaking, it was not much more than an outdoor bathroom, receptacle – and den of iniquity.

The players had learned how to lean into a ball; and swing at it hard as if they were part of some powerful mechanical swivel – often knocking balls out of the park. Their locomotion was far less impressive as they stumbled around bases. And they traded stories about landmark games. It was a bonding mechanism that did not involve getting too personal. The games were filled with catcalls and broken bits of profanity. There would be things to talk about – bombastic words related to plays and failures.

Failure was a particularly sensitive issue with Clement who had recently broken up with a steady girl. It hadn't been a happy coupling and the separation reflected it. She had thrown his clothes out on the front lawn. He knew that most 'knew'; and had considered not coming to the game. At the last minute, ego prevailed…besides, he needed a drink.

Flowers and one 'two-layer' box of chocolates had not been able to resurrect his doomed relationship. He was out of a house; out of money; and out of a relationship – which he ranked in that order. It angered him that he was spending his time with a bunch of burping baseball 'wannabees'; questioning whether women were 'worth it'; and rolling the bat around in his hands as if he were feeling the sensuous arm of a woman he had lost.

The outfield had become inpatient; and the tempo of their insults had started to increase.

"Hey! Play ball, man! Whaddya need a 'frickin' break – or some Little League practice?!!!"

And then,

"Stop lookin' around…ain't no 'groupies' out here – just hit the damn ball!"

The profanity increased. The field was hot…and none of the players were young – so the 'cage-rattling' was not entirely uncalled for. But Clement – or 'Clem' as he was known – now wished he had not come. He should have kept the box of chocolates. He could be home watching a real game on television while gorging on sugar and leftover beer. There were more insults. Someone had finally penetrated his reptilian skin. Despite his best attempts not to appear disturbed, he fired back,

"I'll knock the crap outta this ball! I hope you dumb asses got somethin' to run in other than heels!"

There were more attacks. He spat on the ground; scratched himself again;

and eyed the pitcher with a rancor that he hoped would give him advantage. It was the way any good game was played.

The light from the sky had come barreling over the trees with momentum. It momentarily distracted Clem whose interest was piqued by the beauty of it against the gray sky. He would not let that appreciation show – it wasn't manly. The wind had picked up. He noticed the wind first on his beefy forearms; and then in the vigorous rustling in the trees.

The players in the outfield looked up wearily; but also grateful for a breeze. Birds rapidly soared for cover. The players looked to the horizon – none of them wishing to be deterred by rain while temperate glory was still possible. They opened and closed their baseball mitts; occasionally pounding them with anticipation – until they beat the dust out.

Nearby at a guard's booth on the border, Sophia Angaros had also noticed the wind increase. She dropped the roll of paper she had been using to fan herself; looked up; and thought of the young woman she had seen running away past the guard station. She wondered what had happened to her; and felt a little embarrassed about the guards. They looked like boys outside of the principle's office. She thought that perhaps she had been too harsh; but had enjoyed her role as a 'material witness'.

Back in the park, Clement had received an assault which he did not expect.

"Come on man! Hit the ball – a goddamn storm is blowing up!!!"

It was Roger Gregor – part of the power couple. The two men had always been rivals; and their competition extended off field. It had started long ago over their mutual interest in a bull-headed young woman.

Cynthia Gregor had porcelain skin, honey-colored hair, and painted red lips...from which tittered the laughter of a gull. She smelled like honeysuckle; was exquisitely slim, neat in appearance, and had hard red nails that belied a fawning nature. Many were interested in her. In an unordinary role reversal – the 'prey' had culled the 'predators'. Only Roger Gregor had survived courtship. Now encapsulated, he was the seed to a powerful woman with a hard velvet hull.

Clement felt the wind pick up again. The dusky sky was streaked with orange and purple 'mares' tails'. The wind knocked a few caps loose in the field. The pitch had come much too soon; and he was unprepared for it. There was a sudden rush of air as he hit the ball in a lopsided way. It connected with the top of the bat; and immediately he felt sick. It would be a high-flying pop-up which would land in someone's open glove as idly as a yawn. He watched it spin up to airy heights – knowing the ball probably wouldn't even clear the 'short stop'. He took a few lazy steps toward first base - full of beer and in no mood to run unless the ball's trajectory took a different turn.

Then – as if it had discovered life – the ball began to fly. An unexpected air current sent it spinning 50 feet into the air; seemed to deliberate regarding what to do with it - and then handily delivered it much farther away than he expected. It slammed to the ground on the other side of the fence – bouncing a few times only feet away from Sincero who was passing by. There the ball stopped.

Seeing his fortune, Clement tottered around the bases, full of beer and empty of any thought except vindication. The outfield was raucous as they made a mad scramble to retrieve the ball. They had not noticed Sincero until that instant. He had now become the object of their drunken disapproval. They whistled, shouted; and some pulled at themselves showing the carnal disrespect that one might expect from a group who had too much to drink.

On the other side of the fence, Sincero's brief rest had given him the energy he needed to carry on. The previous sighting of the large circling raptor; and the piercing whine of ambulances had reinforced the critical nature of his need to escape and find shelter. He quietly prayed to himself and decided to ignore the outfielders' drunken overtures – believing they were unlikely to cross the fence that separated them. He didn't really understand some of the defiling remarks...and had forgotten that he was still wearing the disguise of a young woman.

But vulgarity had long since proved its remarkable quality – it could leap past linguistic and cultural boundaries. Sincero was well on his way when he was intercepted by particularly crudity that had been prepared with a dash of wine; and served up with hatred and a relish of intonation. Momentarily lacking presence of mind, he returned the insult.

The players stood in disbelief.

A ceiling of clouds was beginning to form and the sky was blackening. The war of words and gestures had escalated. Impropriety had no zenith when propelled by drunkenness. In a fit of anger, Sincero picked up the errant ball and hurled it as hard as he could. It hit a man squarely in the head; and the man crumpled to the ground. For the first time in his long journey, he knew he had made a misstep.

Though startled at first, the drunken band quickly recovered and made their way toward him at a dog-fast pace – one of their own was down. Even with the anesthetization of beer they were determined to chase the quarry. Their expletives enveloped him like a snare. And, for the second time in his life, Sincero was trying to run in a dress.

He raced away – praying that he would find either cover or protection. The pack had managed to cross the fence. His feet propelled him rapidly, though he didn't know where he was going. He could hear brisk footfall not far behind. The stretch of street before him was murderously wide and open; and he opted for a narrow alley hoping to find security or cover. The swiftness of is turn nearly sent him hurtling into a tree. He sped away from light – seeking the cover of darkness. The alley opened up before him. There was a slight rise with notched steps and strewn rock. The remnants of an old fence convinced him that he might find cover in a structure nearby. Perhaps he could hold off his pursuers or at least find something to crawl under. His legs were already weak and sore from his previous flight past the border fence.

Then he realized his mistake. He had looped back and returned to the park again – and was now in a dark ravine. Doubling back he ran toward the street. The pack had split up; and he wasn't sure where the other half might be. He ran into the wide street, feeling vulnerable but aware that his pursuers were breathing hard. Perhaps he might evade them by running into a more congested area.

It was then, that one of his bare feet hit a renegade piece of metal – remnant of an earlier car accident. It pierced his foot deeply. The pain was intense; and the blood began to flow rapidly from the wound. Sincero gritted his teeth. In a second he had pulled out the metal. Then, kicking his feet and legs as hard as he could – blood streaming out of his foot - he ran with as much strength as he had left. With every step, he slackened. He was leaving red prints on the pavement. Nearby he could hear one part of the pack of men closing in; and felt a strong push that landed him face first in the middle of the street. He tried to right himself and was flung to the ground again. To his horror he heard one of the men growl,

"Let's take her back in the trees."

Someone began to tear the back of the light dress. Another voice snarled, "Hey man not here!"

Horrified, he remembered his disguise – and knew it had been too perfect. He prayed for some sort of deliverance. Quite unexpectedly, a monarch butterfly flitted around him. It landed on a cut, seemingly attracted to moisture. The men smacked it away roughly; and the monarch darted off. Gaining in height it seemed to head for light that was being held by the clouds. Sincero watched it disappear; and wished for a freedom he was sure he had lost forever....

The pack of men had reunited. They lifted him into the air and roughly carried him - the force of their collective strength binding, despite his struggles. Within moments, they were in the park's dark fringe; and his fight had become ineffective. Semiconscious – but understanding his mortality – he fought back with what little strength he had.

The pack threw him into the ravine; and pulled him by his long hair... further into the brush. The overwhelming smell of alcohol barely hid the stink of the dark swale. He felt the dress being torn. No courtesy would arrest them – a vise of powerful hands around his neck assured it. He breathed in the heavy smell of alcohol, sweat and the filth of the swale...then heard their surprise as they discovered he was not what they thought.

It did not matter. The durability of their anger combined with inebriation would not be sated except by the undoing of something. Beaten close to unconsciousness and surrounded by stench - he wished that the river had taken him. For the river meant no injury to life and virtue - it merely was.

Miles away, the young tracker, 'RC' was quickly recovering. Occasionally he thought of Bob, the native, and the cat they had tracked. It seemed long ago. The gurney he had been carried on had been rolled up and stored against the side of the shack that he now thought of as home. He felt optimistic. Something 'told him' that a lost love was closer than he expected. And he was hurried - he wished to get on with life; and was no longer bothered by the jurisdiction of Sister Frances. Unexpectedly, on this day, she had come to his hut; and made a pronouncement. He would accompany her on a trip back to her home.

..Meanwhile – and much farther to the north of 'RC' - the native tracker, Bob, had 'seen' the carnage in the dark area of the park. He shook his head and – in his dream – prayed for the young man named, Sincero. He marveled at the wishful nature of all who held hope.

SUE BEE

'Sue Bee' had just placed the end table by the sofa. She sat admiring it, but wondering if she had paid too much. She wasn't really sure why she had bought it, but imagined it had something to do with the salesman who was wonderfully tanned; and looked good in jeans. A cricket - that had somehow made its way inside - was singing its fool head off in a dark corner. She needed some 'balance' in her life; and the end table seemed harmonious with an umbrella stand at the other end of the sofa. Emotional balance could be had later - she was looking for a quick fix.

She thought of the salesman again. The antique store had proved that it could make more than just an excellent selection of furniture. The young man was sitting cross-legged in a window. He wore a snappy shirt and tie; and the light from the window shone on him. It seemed to create a halo of light around his handsome head.

"Yes ma'am, I think you've picked out a fine piece there – something that will only increase in value."

"Um-huh...really..." Sue Bee responded casually.

He continued,

"You never know where some of these pieces of furniture come from. People are still finding stuff from President Arthur. You know, they say our 21st president sold 26 wagonloads of White House furniture for a mere $8,000 dollars! Sure would love to get my hands on an 'Arthur'..."

The checking on his shirt was slightly raised and the sleeves somewhat blousy. When he stretched his arms out, it gave him the curious appearance of having wings. She was tiring of his smart look and insincerity - but bought the table anyway. She wanted it; and he had worked hard for the sale. Now she was home questioning her purchase and life in general. She was no happier than when the day began.

Suddenly there was the 'THRREEEEPPP!!!" of the phone. A moment of vanity had been interrupted – her dark mood had been penetrated by a gadfly. It was Louisiana Anne Crofton. Her father had named her, but her mother – refusing to bend to the idiocy of naming a child for a state – simply called her, 'Lu Ann'. It also 'rolled off the tongue' better.

Sue Bee bent over a nearby coffee table and scooped up a handful of small candy hearts. She would need the energy for the conversation. She rolled them around in her hands as the voice on the other end of the phone shot conversation at her in rapid monologue. Despondent – she threw the candies back into the dish. Messages like "Be Mine" and "U R Cool" had been replaced by "Text me" or "Tweet me". It made the candies seem impersonal and not from a century with which she identified.

She glanced over at the ficus tree in the corner. It was glowing green again – the latest craze and a biotechnology breakthrough. Experiments with the green constituents of jellyfish genes had enabled nurseries to sell certain houseplants that glimmered green when they needed watering. She wanted something to talk to her – not glow at her; and the damn thing would sometimes 'turn on' at night. She had tried to drown it. Now, she walked over grabbed a 'mister' – misting it just enough to see it turn itself off – and then spat on it for good measure.

"You there, Bee...you there...? HELLO!"

Lu Ann's shouting punctured her eardrums. She jerked the phone away from her ear and considered whether or not to throw it across the room. The voice was strong and chirpy – enough to blow off a hat.

"I'm here, dammit! I'm here!"

"Hope you got plans for that chiffon dress this evening, Ms. Bee...!"

"Honey, the only plans I got are to take a load off my feet; sip a lemon 'pick-me- up'; and admire this brand new purchase I done made in the interest of promotin' the 'economy.'"

Lu Ann continued her monologue but Sue Bee was barely listening. She had found the source of the chirping. The cricket was just barely under the counter; and stroking out its exoskeleton rhapsody. She picked up the only bug-smasher within reach – a remote control – and accidentally turned off the television. Muttering to herself, she turned it on again. There was an interview with an older woman about her role as a musician. It was a January/July interview. The older woman was offering the advice of generations to a young musician in the prime of his life. Sue Bee thought of her mother and wondered how she was doing.

Then she brushed off some water from a lacquered tray – the 'mister' had worked. The ficus was no longer glowing, but the water wouldn't do much good for the tray. She went over to a cupboard and rifled around looking for tea; and found a packet of sassafras. It had been in the cabinet for quite some time and was slightly tattered, but still had a sweet licorice smell. She pulled it out of the box; dumped it in a teacup; and put on the kettle. Her stomach was upset and she needed something to settle it. The lemon 'pick-me-up' would have to wait – she needed an inoculation of comfort.

Lu Ann's tongue was still wagging and her speech had become more exaggerated. Sue Bee went to the window and played with the vines of a sweet potato that she was growing in a tray of shallow water in the kitchen window. Then she looked under the kitchen sink for some bug killer; found it; and turned it over to read the warning label. Would it get rid of the pitifully unmelodic cricket with its insistent serenade? The ficus tree had kept her awake for far too many nights for her to care about other life forms.

She returned to the television – they were having a documentary on illegal immigration and border towns. Pro-immigrant groups were fomenting a local protest. And Lu Ann – her uninvited 'motivational speaker' was still on the phone – distracting attention from everything else.

"You hear 'bout that woman that fainted at the border station? Big girl! She an illegal – sho' enough! Sue Bee...SUE BEE...! You listenin' to me?"

"I'm here, Lu Ann! Whatchu want girl – applause? Watchin me some T.V.!

"Sounds to me like you already sippin' on somethin', Bee! Ain't it kinda early?"

"I'm makin' tea – and sipping on some leftover coffee – not that it's any of your business."

"That this mornin's coffee... you still drinkin' that stuff?!"

"Naww..chewin' it."

There was a hearty laugh on the other end of the phone.

"C'mon Bee, this is girl's night out. And you know what that means..."

There were others near the phone and they were laughing with Lu Ann and making rapid comments.

"I ain't interested, Lu. I don't feel well."

"Hmmmm. Sounds like MAN trouble to me."

"Naww. I just don't feel well."

Lu Ann solicited the opinion of someone else at her end of the phone. "Bee says she don't feel well, Linda, what you think?"

Sue Bee heard an, "Um! Um! Um!"

There was apparent agreement among the girls about her mental state. She ignored them but was suddenly aware of a chilliness in the room. The wind had crept through a crack in the door. Sue Bee walked over to the far wall and edged the thermostat up a notch – then looked through the window to see if a storm was imminent.

Another call was coming in.

She put Lu Ann 'on hold'. It was 'Herman' – a Marine Corps friend. Though he irritated her and was a hopeless 'rum head' – she knew he was a well-intentioned. He lived in a rusty old Quonset hut and sometimes played baseball with the rest of the vets at the park...but he really preferred playing Sondheim. Herman was a curiously dysfunctional mix who had seen things in war that he 'couldn't talk about'. 'Wasn't like he made sense half the time anyway'...Sue Bee told herself.

"Sue Bee, this here's Herman. They done beat up some woman in the park."

GIRL'S NIGHT OUT

She was multi-tasking – fighting off boredom and frustration. Herman's call had not helped the latter. She had Lu Ann on one line and Herman on the other line; and was sitting on the sofa 'channel surfing'. The television featured a 'special' on the Pope and it seemed oddly juxtaposed to the conversations on the telephone. Sue Ann checked back to see if Lu Ann was still talking and could hear her going on like a repeat rifle. She returned to the catastrophic conversation with Herman deciding it was more interesting than listening to Lu Ann - who really didn't expect a response anyway.

"What the hell are you talkin' about, Herman?"

They done beat up some Mexican woman purty bad. I wasn't there but heard some of 'em talking about it. You want me to go down to the park and check things out?!"

"Nawww, Herman! You stay right where you are! What you think we got cops for?! You get your fool head cracked and then I have to go out and look for someone else to work with me. Use some a' that sense God done gave you!" She would never admit that she liked the man.

"But Sue Bee, I don't feel right about..."

"Dammit, Herman! I got another call comin' in. Hold on!"

She cut him off and returned to the previous conversation with Lu Ann who was still going on in her absence...despite the fact that she was its subject matter.

"Shore enough does sound like man trouble... Don' worry bout it honey. I hear they got an extra chromosome – makes 'em screwy.

Lu Ann always knew the latest gossip. It intrigued Sue Bee mildly – especially if it was about someone she knew. Her peripheral vision had caught sight of something moving. 'Better not be that damn cricket' she thought to herself and looked for a shoe. The wind had come in through a gap in a window that she had left open; and it was moving a mobile wildly back and forth. Disgusted, she went over to the window and slammed it shut hard enough to almost take the weights off. She sat down on the sofa again – but realized that the telephone conversation with Herman bothered her. She felt guilty about her response, but really wanted to hear gossip.

Lu Ann continued,

"Speaking of screwy, did you hear about Colette's little problem?"

"Girl, I don't give a crap about Colette – or her problems." Sue Bee was dying to hear the news.

The comment was too 'obvious'. She knew that Lu Ann would aim right for her curiosity, with a big glob of gossip. The woman was relentless.

"Well you may not care – but that jes' make it twice as GOOOOD!"

"Look, Lu Ann – I got a headache." Sue Bee reached inside the fridge for a slice of bread; and turned off the whistling tea kettle.

"Not as big as the one Leroy done got after Colette done parked a plate on his head."

Sue Bee noticed that an ugly plant someone had given her – they called it a 'night blooming cereus' – was languishing like it had been caught in an oil slick. It obviously needed water.

"What?!" She was thinking of her conversation with Herman again; and really needed to get back to him.

"Yeah, girl! Sure enough she did. Caught her man on the run; and the fool done give her a diamond where the bottom part be GLASS! Took it into a 'fraction' expert – when she decided she done had enough – and he done confirmed it! Um, Um, UM!"

"You don't mean…" She couldn't stop thinking about Herman's phone call – maybe she should call the cops.

"And after she done had those Botox shots! Got all puffed up in the face for nothin'! By the time she finish cryin', face look like a 'retread'. And all this time she be sayin' she a natural beauty."

A potted maidenhair fern in the corner seemed to be half dead. Sue Bee reached for a glass of water while balancing the phone on her shoulder and eating the bread with a piece of bologna.

"Well I feel sorta sorry for her."

"Shoot. Natural beauty nothin' – she a natural disaster now….Hey! Harriet done told me that some nun got reservations at the Hillcrest!" Lu Ann had switched to another topic of gossip as easily as a trombone slides into a note.

"What – that flea-trap!"

"God is my witness! Say she done made reservations for her and a MAN! Whatchu' thinka 'bout thet?!"

"Maybe it's a relation…"

"Yeah…and I a 'boy scout'!"

Sue Bee took the phone outdoors. She gazed at the distant landscape. A strip of wild sunflowers could still be seen in a nearby vacant lot. A complementing strip of red and pink poppies was just below it. The land was a laminate of lipstick colors.

"Anyway, I don't want to go out, Lu Ann." Then she added, "Girl you got more dirt than a dump truck – where you hear all this stuff!?"

Lu Ann responded,

"Now don't be actin' that way. I know when you use that tone of voice and talk about not feelin' well ... it shore enough spells man trouble to me."

Sue Bee was just about to walk back in when she heard howling. At first she thought it was the wind.

"Yep, it's man trouble."

She barely heard her – the howling had become more intense. Sue Bee looked down a nearby alleyway...probably some tomcats fighting with each other over garbage. She was suddenly sleepy and wished the call would end.

The howling became louder.

"Girl, what's thet sound?! You gotta ambulance nearby – or you watchin' 'Wild Kingdom'?"

Sue Bee's stomach hurt – she wished she hadn't been diverted from the licorice tea. She looked up at the sky just in time to see something large sail over a nearby hill heading for the park.

"Damn cats in the neighborhood got spooked by something..."

She suddenly thought of Herman – he had hung up.

"Come on, 'Bee', slip that chiffon dress on and go out with us!"

"I hate that dress." Sue Bee knew there was no point in arguing – it was just a temporary distraction.

"Well it is a little old – but it looks good on you! Shows up your attributes - .you should thank your momma."

"Momma had nothin' to do with 'em."

An hour later she was on the road with Lu, Linda and Fran – and some dumb corsage they had pinned on the white neck of the yellow chiffon dress. She felt like a lemon meringue pie.

NEAR DEATH

"When are we going to be through with this little venture?" Sue Bee was in the front seat of a car that was hurtling through time and space. She was already bored and counting the trees along the road.

Lu Ann corrected her,

"Adventure is the word darlin' and you makin' it sound like dental surgery. I wish you'd get over that mood a' yours!"

Then she took a spontaneous poll of the car population.

"What time we going to 'call it quits' girls? We have someone up here needin' her beauty sleep."

A wine-colored glow could be seen from the car window – the neon light of a local dinette blended finely with the evening sky. They sped past the dinette – uninterested in food.

"Oh Lu, shouldn't we just retire ourselves at 11:30 post meridian – as is customary for woman of our stature?" Linda was mocking the 'dweebish' prep school ponies that they had met in a similar foray the week before.

"Oh shut up, Linda, you don't even know what 'post meridian' means," Lu Ann chided.

Sue Bee wasn't listening she was looking out at a small pond that seemed to be 'pulling' bits of moonlight into it. The water rippled slightly. Meanwhile, she continued to search the sky. The last bit of daylight mattered to her. They were close enough to water to possibly spot a large bird – if indeed, that was what she had seen earlier during the day. Whatever it was, the cats in the neighborhood were not happy.

Meanwhile, Linda was busy bragging about a new job she would be starting.

"It's all about import and export," She explained. "Odd things comin' into this little country of ours...not that I care that much, but it helps to have a career!"

Lu Ann was busy trying to 'connect the dots'. "Whatchu mean, 'weird things'?"

Linda responded, "Oh, they mixin' everything up these days...breedin' this with that...and then, lettin' it loose. Call it 'genetic engineering'...I just call it one big mess. But them boys with their guns, they like to hunt somethin' a little different."

Lu Ann rolled her eyes; and turned to Sue Bee. "Ain't Earnestine involved in somethin' like that, Bee?"

"More involved with that little man she work with...but don't start me to lyin'. Anyway...said they just done a case in the lab - somethin' about a mountain lion...supposedly killed some woman. Started lookin' at its DNA – but it don't match anything they got. Don't know what to do with it. They afraid it might pass into somethin' else if they let it loose – so they just sayin' nothing in the meantime."

Linda broke into the conversation, "Long as it don't bother me on my time off...."

Lu Ann crumpled up a cigarette pack and sent it sailing her way. "Oh hush up, Linda. We're here – and I feel lucky. Don't jinx me. Good thing they don't have a tax on dumbness – you'd be workin' the rest a' your life!"

They pulled into 'The Roundup'. It was a typical Saturday night – young bucks standing out on the patio underneath the party lights – their shirts open and wearing intravenous jeans. The local 'dingalings' were there to – teased hair...and more legs than a bucket of chicken. Still, it was one of the few mixed bars where the only color that mattered was green.

Sue Bee was becoming uneasy. Was this really what she wanted? She was still thinking about the call from Herman and feeling guilty. Cigarette smoke came out of the doors of the bar and floated up to the single streetlight. Paper lights were strung about in faded Christmas colors. Some drunk was standing on the bar doing Karaoke.

She looked up to the sky at a constellation that had caught her attention momentarily. She didn't know what it was; and barely cared. The constellation, Lyra, 'The Lyre', was quietly plinking away at its chords. It had weathered everything from Greeks to geeks. But tonight a chord seemed to have been broken. 'The Lyre' cast a light down from a dark indigo sky. The season of plenty was over – and the moon was ripening.

Lu Ann was 'herself' – looking for good hair, anything with a full set of teeth...and screaming out the window. Sue Bee slammed her arm,

"Lu Ann, have you no self respect?!"

Lu Ann shot back.

"Respect...girl, that's so Aretha! Come on let's head for the bar!"

"Lu Ann, I'm gonna stay here – I don' feel well."

"What are you – ninety?! Come on! Opportunity don't come on a stick!"

"You're nuts! You call this 'opportunity'?"

"Well, what you callin' it?"

"Leftovers..."

"Hey, listen! I'm goin' in there and kick up my feet – just give me a sign if you stop breathin'."

"This is your plan?!"

"That an' alcohol." And then, she opened the car door.

Fran chimed in, "Let's leave Miz Poison Ivy here – shall we?"

Lu Ann grabbed her keys,

"Not without my car keys! Next thing you know she be in China."

"I wish you'd dropped me off at that dinette we passed."

"Come on, Sue Bee!"

"Sorry – I ain't got the itch..."

She stared out the window. The moon was drawing her in. She didn't feel romantic and wished she could just chop it out of the sky. A passing reveler threw confetti into the car. It landed in the cup from which she was drinking. She pitched the drink out of the window.

Lu Ann was sauntering as if she meant business. The other two girls were eyeballing anything that had a hat on. This would not end well.

"Lu Ann! Stop it! Get your skinny butt back in here!"

It was becoming restless at "The Roundup". Sue Bee pulled off the damn corsage and threw it on the floor. She jumped out of the car; and immediately lit a cigarette. Someone had to keep an eye on everyone; and it might as well be her. She strode over to the open door and then pulled up a seat next to the bar. There she continued to smoke like a forest fire – trying to appear nonchalant.

A chubby red-faced rock of a man, who had started out with a mixed drink, was getting loud. He didn't feel good – something was bothering him. He ordered a stiff dry whiskey. The bartender asked,

"You wanna pony – or a jigger in that?"

"Wassa difference, Manny – I can howl at the moon with one drink or two."

The bartender smirked. "One tablespoon of whiskey, Clem' – and a few bucks..."

Clement pushed himself against the wall – the light bothered him.

"Make it a jigger."

"Gray kinda' night out there – ain't it?"

"Dunno – been workin' my butt off most of the day...too damn tired to tell." He had just started a part time plumbing business to supplement his pet shop venture.

He rolled the whiskey around in his tongue as if to savor it.

"Trace of bitterness in this damn drink."

"Hey man...it don't come with flowers."

Clem finished off the drink, picked up a scruffy hat; and stood up. He was puffy and inebriated but feeling more cheerful.

"I better get on down the road. Hope there ain't no deer out."

Then he licked a cut on his hand and tried to get it to stop shaking. He was waddling toward his truck in a pink pair of snakeskin boots when someone yelled out.

"Hey 'Porky', where you goin' – barbecue ain't warm yet!!"

A handsome, red-talon'ed woman with honey-colored hair was snickering in the corner. Clement knew who she was immediately. Cynthia Gregor was having a night out with her husband. Clement kicked a trashcan – he was still reeling from taunts of the previous afternoon's ball-playing with Roger Gregor.

He yelled back, "You tell your wife about the woman in the park!?"

Gregor wouldn't be silenced; and he was equally drunk. The large man darkened and then growled out a warning,

"That what you call a woman?!"

It was enough of a remark to catch Sue Bee's attention. She mashed out her cigarette and headed for the car. She looked over at the Lu Ann and the girls. They seemed fearful; and had stood up – prepared to make a hasty exit. A brawl seemed to be in process.

'Dammit!' she thought 'Herman had been right.' She was already on the cell phone dialing his number. Her guilt was now in 'full-gear'. Why hadn't she listened to him? If the woman wasn't dead, she must be near to it. She had to check. The park's neighborhood had a reputation; and the police seemed to put it on the bottom of the list – if they visited it at all.

Lu Ann, Linda, and Fran had returned to the car hastily. Their fear was visible; but they were disappointed. They had been counting on the 'girl's night out'. Sue Bee was still trying to reach Herman and hoping he would be available. She was afraid to risk going to the park at night alone; and didn't want to further frighten her friends.

"Let's go girls. This place is making me sick".

Lu Ann glared at her. She had worked hard to get the group together. She knew men 'talked big' when alcohol was involved. Though she wanted nothing to do with a brawl, she had been looking forward to some well-deserved downtime. Sue Bee turned away from her and said,

"Come on, Lu. Turn this buggy into a plane and let's get the hell out of here. I mean it. I'm really feeling sick. If those hoodlums hurt someone, we need to find out. You want this on your conscience!? Now go, girl!"

Lu Ann replied, "You can't be serious!!! You know these guys ain't nothin' but talk!"

Sue Bee bucked back her head suddenly, "I hope you've got a bag, Lu Anne, because I'm about to hurl chunks!"

The car abruptly turned 180 degrees and tore out of the parking lot. Lu Anne was cursing to herself,

"Not in my car you don't. I only hope whatever come out goes with your dress – you gonna have to catch it in your lap. I just had this car detailed! Why dontcha catch it there anyway – humph! Ain't caught much of anything else lately!!!"

There were moans coming from the back seat. The car sped off; and an anesthesia of silence took over. They were headed for a park; and it was almost midnight. Sue Bee's stomach had calmed; and she rolled the window down to get some air. They passed a cow pen and watched as the landscape opened up. Here and there were fat cacti that stood in peerage by the highway.

Linda was the first to break the silence.

"Ain't it pretty? I think it looks like Camelot."

"Sure nuff smells like a camel lot – or is that your perfume?" Fran quipped.

They were laughing again; pantomiming in the back seat; and taking off their shoes in order to shake the sand from them. And Lu Ann didn't care about the car's detailing.

Sue Bee had finally reached Herman – he would meet them at the park. It was the right thing to do.

RESCUE

Anti-Semitic words vandalized the rough trunks of scraggly trees and the ashen remains of a few fires were evident. The ravine was sometimes a haven for the homeless. Here and there, pigeon feathers were left and bits of tiny spit-cooked bones were strewn about. A truant rhyme was written on various parts of an old fence that shyly poked out of burgeoning kudzu. Random hypodermic needles and the leftover parts of some motherboard were evidence of a previous drug-related computer heist. An old country western CD hung from a cut limb - it shined like a Christmas ornament in the dim light. Broken children's toys gave the dark fringe of the park a dumpish appearance. It seemed as if some old house had been abandoned and sucked back into the earth – and rubbish was all that remained.

Sincero was barely conscious. He had been lying for a long time in the park's ravine. Chiggers had crawled into his skin; and he itched all over. The dress was badly torn. He was bruised; and could not tell if anything was broken. There were pieces of garbage lying everywhere. The sweat and rancor of men had been left on him. He turned slowly and realized he was lying in some unfinished 'fast food'. Hearing voices, he jerked his head up and felt a stinging pain. He could just see the silhouette of a snake slithering up a tree. It was full from a meal of rodent that seemed to be melting into its body. He rolled to get away from it; and immediately realized his mistake. A head wound began to bleed down his neck and it nearly caused him to vomit. A dull pain came from his gut. He bit his lip hard and tried to pull himself further into the brush – certain he heard voices.

Quietly he tried to sit up and restore what was left of his ripped clothing – trying to cover his nakedness. He tried to right himself but could not – he had been badly beaten. He felt blood oozing from his bottom. His movement alerted a roaming animal which grunted and then scurried away. The brutality of his beating and the pain he now felt made him wonder if any plan was worth what he had endured. But he was alive...at least, he thought he was.

He considered suicide. There must be worse things – then, remembered... his life had been lent – not purchased. It was an odd consolation that his mother had said to him, years ago. He suddenly thought of the packet of metallic granules he had found in the coat lent to him by the man named 'RC'. He had swallowed the packet; and now, hoped it was still safely inside of him. It might very well be the only thing of value that could help him survive in this new land...or help him return home.

A warm wind opened the canopy of foliage above him. The moon sent a gentle light down and it glowed like a spring flower in a night garden. He was nauseous and weak. He cast one more look at the moon; and began to have the thoughts of someone who was slipping away. There was a kerosene lamp coming toward him and he could smell perfume.

Barely conscious, he could feel someone dragging him out of the brush; and hear expletives.

"Dammit, Sue, these shoes were expensive! If you weren't my best friend..."

"Leopard skin looks good with a little bit a' dirt on it."

Sue Bee was studying Sincero,

"Wonder why he's wearin' a dress?"

She could see that they were on a very narrow trail – no bigger than a rat path going through the ravine. Herman was lighting the way...'his usual help', she thought. She smoothed the hair out of her face and realized the senselessness of her vanity. She had smeared mud (or worse) across her forehead.

Linda snapped a switch of dead wood as they passed under a tree. It startled the group.

"What n' hell you doin', Linda?!"

"Protection..." she whispered.

"You couldn't take out a fly with that dumb stick!"

"You'll be sorry when I'm the only one that comes out alive from this 'Friday the 13th' place. I don't need no date with a ski mask!"

"Damn! They done treated him like a streetwalker," Fran uttered in her normal delivery. "...you think he was part of that Maharachi group the border guards done kicked out?! Said they interviewed some 'Eyetalian' lady; and she done did some sorta expose on the guards down there..."

"You think he 'terminal'? I don't wanna be haulin' around no dead body – don't care how cute he is – not in my car! Why you think he wearin' a dress?" Lu Ann said.

"Lou, shut up and get him into the car. Did you guys notice how swollen his stomach is? If I didn't know better...What am I sayin?"

Sue Bee looked up at the night sky just in time to see the shadow of the large raptor she had seen earlier in the day. It sailed past them rapidly and into the ravine...moving as quietly as the wind – as if it were seeking remains.

SUE BEE AND SINCERO

When Sincero awoke, it was to the reverberations of a music medley. His eyes were swollen and he tried to focus. His head felt like dropped glass. He was lying on a mattress on the floor.

"Guess you're lucky they left you alive...though they probably didn't mean to. Well, boys'l'b'boys...or somethin'."

Sincero tried to turn his head but couldn't.

"Yeah, I know," Sue Bee said coolly, "Welcome to the Holiday Inn."

Sincero started to dry heave. Sue Bee quickly grabbed a nearby trashcan and ran it over to his side.

"Nothin' to give – huh...where are the cheerleaders when you need 'em? I think your arm might be broke. You were pretty much of a mess when we found you. Habla Ingles...no matter, I'll just talk. Yep...gotcha right before the biggest damn vulture I ever seen made a snack outta you."

He studied her for a moment; and then – aware that he was wearing someone else's clothes – felt ashamed. He focused instead on the corner of the room where a small spider – which had digested the inside layer of its skeleton – was now making pumping motions with its legs in order to shed the remaining part of its old body. A molt was in process. The insect was heading for a new beginning. Then he turned his attention back to the husky-voiced black woman. She used too much makeup - but had a large, pleasing frame.

"A bunch of us girls found you in your little outfit and brought you here. Didn't know what else to do – you was pretty messed up."

Sue Bee shivered slightly, then got up and slammed a window shut.

"Damn draft..."

Sincero was beginning to feel at ease with her – she was exorbitant with conversation – and her honesty was pungent. She was wearing a yellow chiffon dress; and full shaggy dark hair fell about her shoulders. Her eyebrows were cleanly plucked; and she had eyes that were heavy lidded, and set off by enormous eyelashes laden with mascara. Her lipstick was gold-colored. He wondered why humans were the only animals to wear a face not given to them. Her appearance seemed oddly incongruous with the integrity of her interchange.

Sue Bee looked at him and said,

"You look like ten shades a' hell."

She stopped. It wasn't fair to tease – he had already suffered a horrific beating. Then, she added,

"We'll have to find you a new dress – the other ones too tore up. Tell ya... folks sure can hurt your heart, cain't they? Dontchu' worry none – we git you fixed up and on your way again."

Then she flipped her hair like a wild horse – pretending not to be bothered by the sight of him; and began to primp. She was in control and liked it that way.

Sincero looked away – he was afraid of offending her and losing the munificence that had been granted. He needed to recover; and must try to 'play his cards close to his chest'. The selfishness of his motives immediately made him uncomfortable. He scratched his head and realized someone had washed his hair; and nursed a head wound. He felt the binding obligation that sometimes comes with gratitude.

Uneasy, he followed the line of the shoe molding against the floor. At his feet lay a pair of shoes with a rally of daffodils pushed inside of them. His foot wound had been cleaned and bound. Sue Bee observed him – all the while primping, and not pretending to see anything else,

"Young lady left those for you. I don't really know who she is. Said her name was Anna. Was out there star-gazing in that damn park where we found you. She helped us get you into the apartment here and gave me her shoes and some flower she done picked. Said you looked like you needed 'em more'n she did. Walked away barefooted...I think she probably crazy, but well – she a 'good crazy'...if ya know what I mean. ...Best go put them flowers in water before they dry up like a town drunk in the ' slammer'."

"What park name...bad hombres there?" It was all Sincero could muster out of a bruised and sore mouth. He felt his teeth with his tongue – they all seemed to be in place.

"My God – it speaks! ... They calls it 'Frances Park', darlin'."

The CD was beginning to play again. Sue Bee turned it down rather abruptly – a call had come in.

"This is Sue Bee!" she chirped.

"Yeah, he better. Naww, honey, I don't wanna do it. I already done seen them things they call 'waterfalls'. Mos' men pee more'n that!

Gotta stay here with mah boy. Oh, he's good. But his insides seem to hurt him. Okay, well thanks for checkin' in. Bye now."

Sincero had turned back toward her. "Who was this 'Frances'...man in war?" He noticed Sue Bee's strong hands and reasoned that she was a working woman, probably cleaned houses or motel rooms.

"Newwp. 'Frances' some woman who a nun. Someone donated money for a park; and they done named it after her. Lord knows a nun ain't got no money like that..."

Sincero tried to make conversation – it was all he had to offer.

"You know her?"

Sue Bee appreciated his efforts but found the questions annoying; and believed he needed rest. "Naww.... Listen, honey, I'm enjoyin' the conversation – but this ain't no game show."

"She – Christian woman, then?"

Sincero felt obligated to somehow 'pay' for the trouble he had caused her; and was certain that she was concerned about him. He felt better and did not wish to impose. He was also uncomfortable about the compromising position he had put himself in - it was better to take the focus off of his identity. The woman might have strong opinions regarding someone who had entered the country without papers.

"Lord, I don't know! Whatchu think I done read an autobiography?!"

"I sorry – no talk to anyone in much time...it make me feel better." Sincero responded anxiously.

"Well if that's a polite way of tellin' me I gotta big mouth – I'll take it! Once you get wound up...it's hard to get you to stop, boy!" She suddenly realized she had made him uncomfortable and stopped. It felt like she had committed an offense.

"Name, Sincero...you?" He implored, not wishing to offend her.

"Sue Bee! Nice to meet ya', Sincero!" She could see they were coming around to each other.

"You good woman, Miss Sue. You no have to take me in. Gracias, gracias... Sincero remember your kindness." And he meant it.

"What a cute name – fits!! Anyway, to answer your question 'I ain't certain whether this Frances is Christian or heathen now. But if she dead, she probably rollin' around in her grave. The park ain't no more than a garbage can – if you askin' me. Though it do have a nice fringe of daffodils. I think that be where you girlfriend plucked them things stickin' inside your shoes."

The wind suddenly blew open an unlatched window. It traveled along the floor knocking things around much like a dog padding along and creating mayhem. Sue Bee muttered an expletive; rose from where she was sitting; walked over; and slammed another window shut.

"I don't get this wind," she muttered. "Cain't see it; ain't got no body

– but touches everything! The devil ain't that damn good!"

Sincero looked perplexed. He didn't understand her, but smiled. Then he took a breath and continued,

"But what this woman named 'Frances' do, Miss Sue?"

"Good god! Would you jus' let it go?! Nothin! She done nothin'! She just be herself!"

"But why they make park for her...if she no hero? Sincero persisted politely.

Common courtesy required an explanation.

"They a lot of quiet heroes that no one don't know about...this one just got a park named after her. Probly done more than most folks who got plaques on they walls. Some local woman put up money for the park and insisted they name it 'Frances Park'."

Sincero fixed his eyes upon her for a second – then said,

"Loco!"

Sue Bee turned to him and responded,

"Yeah? Welcome to 'Crazyville'. Hummmph! Listen, boy...some a' the best flowers grows by the side of the road. You know what I mean...?"

Outside a low mournful howl came forth, as if a big dog was expressing its disapproval with the wind. Sue Bee howled back. Sincero was quiet. His insides hurt and he wondered why the packet of granules he had swallowed had not come out of him. Then he said quietly,

"I think you grow by road, Miss Bee."

She turned away from him...it had been a long time since she had felt tears.

Then, Sincero turned away. A frightening flashback from the park had come back to haunt him. He was remembering a behemoth man who seemed darker than a shadow – someone he had seen in the Chihuahua Mountains.

A BONE TO PICK

Within seconds he was there. It irritated him how the seedy side of life was dominating his own - Detective Tweeter was at another crime scene. But of all the people he had interviewed, it was Sophia Angaros whom he could not seem to forget. He was remembering the lilting way she spoke and the slight accent. And frankly, the case was unusual – from the death of her husband to the morgue's admission that they had 'lost' the body. Though he would not admit it to anyone, he earnestly wished for a life that was stable, clean, and unsullied. He had seen enough dirt to last a lifetime.

Out of his breast pocket, he pulled the small sketch of a daffodil that a child had drawn and given to him, some time ago. The sketch was crinkled now, and hominy white. Its lack of sophistication made no difference to Tweeter. It had come by way of hand and heart – unrehearsed sweetness with no expectation attached. It irked him how the mother had left the child easier than an encore. He folded up the sketch and gently put it back in his pocket - wondering what happened to the special needs child.

The agency thought of Tweeter as a 'dinosaur', begrudgingly recognizing the quality of his work and its usefulness. But really, he was 'frozen in place', like some ancient exhibit. He didn't really care. Instead he concentrated on his work. So it was odd to him that on this particular day that he could not appoint his thoughts to the task at hand. He was distracted by the interview with Sophia Angaros...and couldn't stop thinking of her. Though the rind of the woman might be tough – he believed that it belied an inner kindness. The thought made him feel foolish and adolescent; and immediately he discarded it - wondering if he was becoming one of those 'overly sentimental types'.

There was no time to dream. Flipping an old cell phone shut, he stepped through an embellished doorway and into the 'crime scene'. It was everything he expected. He pushed past the motley collection of geezers, peepers, and 'media vultures'. Local authorities were already there. He fired some questions – they fired back. He viewed the corpse briefly through the body bag and pushed his way through the rest of the house. Then he suddenly stopped. There was something on the floor. Using the end of a pencil, Tweeter carefully lifted the specimen and put it into a clear bag. A young policewoman passed by at that moment. Rolling her eyes, she quipped,

"Ever thought of wearing a glove?"

"Not unless, I'm feeling romantic...." he responded dryly.

He held the specimen at eye-level. He had never seen anything like it. It was a cylindrical piece of paper with the remnants of several long strands of dark hair. The paper appeared stressed and browned – as if it had undergone some intense heat. Putting it down gently on a nearby coffee table, he scrutinized the rest of the apartment while the authorities readied the body for pick up and transfer to the morgue.

Forensics was taking pictures from every angle. Tweeter walked over to the kitchen area. He examined the stove for evidence of ashy deposits, melted paraphernalia, or discolored areas – nothing. He strolled towards the window and examined the panes – searching for the direction of the sun. It had been a scorcher of a day. Finally he tapped along the wall and found a lever. He released the spring – and nearly wet himself as an ironing board fell forward with a bang, from its walled compartment. He examined the ironing board for use – nothing again. He snooped around the different outlets trying to discern any faint odor burning. He went over to the fireplace and felt the hearth. It was cold. There was no sign of ash. Finally he opened the individual storage shelves within the kitchen looking for some sign of an oil burning lamp – no clue. Baffled, he returned to the body in time to see them lifting the body bag – ready to take away the corpse.

The afternoon light had now passed to a nearby window and was shining directly on the wood floor when Detective Tweeter noticed something odd. The prints of the animal were very large – and the faint points of its claws were barely visible on the varnished floor. The earlier trajectory of the light had not rendered the prints visible before.

He asked the men to put the body bag back on the floor and requested that they open it. They unzipped it halfway down. The throat had been torn away and one of the arms very badly mauled – as if the victim had been attacked by pit bulls. A manicured hand had nearly been severed. More surprisingly, the body was quite pale. The remnants of hypodermic needle marks to major arteries confirmed that – though the victim may have suffered a horrific death at the hand of some animal – her blood had been siphoned, as if by a phlebotomist.

Tweeter had seen the victim's face before though he was not sure where. She was a pretty woman. He mused about the irony of being in police work. Everyone seemed familiar – but no one could be close. He thought of Sophia

Angaros again – his mind seemed willing to conspire against him. Not wishing to entertain any further thought about her, he suddenly put his hat on and headed for the door. He had seen enough.

Minutes later he rolled into the station parking lot and climbed a flight of stairs to his office. It was a warm evening and he had left the window open. An insect had come through a hole in the screen. The male katydid was rubbing the rasps and ridges of the base of his outer wings – playing his 'summer violin'. Females would be listening to the performance through 'ears' on the upper part of their front legs. The animal suddenly stopped 'playing' – perhaps aware of Tweeter's un-amorous disposition.

Tweeter paced around the office. Tired from the day, he collapsed into the seat at his desk. He emptied the bag's contents out on the desk and studied it, lifting it gently again with a pencil. What would cause the unlikely marriage of materials? The paper had a faintly 'chemical' smell; and seemed to hold a secret. The hair looked human but he wasn't sure. Frustrated and out of guesses, he finally decided he would take the sample to the forensics lab. It was really the last place that he wanted to go. The lab had been a hive of activity recently with the arrival of – what the media called – 'a killer cat'.

The wind had picked up as if to incite another performance by the katydid, but the animal was 'laying low' and would not honor any such applause. Then – as if suddenly bored with efforts to obtain more of the insect's music - the wind pushed through the screen and sent a bin of papers flying about. Tweeter closed the window; picked up the papers; and put them back in no particular order. Then he put on his coat and hat; grabbed the sample; and headed for the nearby forensics lab – hoping to get there before a storm blew up.

He arrived at the lab within minutes; and tried to swallow his pride. He was envious of the rising generation of professionals. The studiousness and ponderousness of past investigations was rapidly being eliminated in favor of millennially-born techniques and forensic science that was dominated by computer assisted development.

Vapor-collection systems could determine the presence of culinary activities related to the 'cooking' of amphetamines; and was an industry standard. There were also vest-mounted computers equipped with digital cameras, laser range finders, and global positioning systems that could ostensibly pin-point the hair on a gnat's behind. A microchip could process DNA samples at the crime scene. Camera-enhancement techniques restored old or damaged footage from videos. Every modern lab had the latest fingerprinting technology that could detect nicotine and cholesterol levels.

The forensic lab's budget was balanced by a computer program. The lab used an artificial intelligence (AI) application to highlight problem areas within electronic spreadsheets - and to recommend fiscal economy. The application was also being integrated into field work. Analysis by humans was rapidly becoming passé. The AI application was connected to a massive investigatory data warehouse with the ambitious name, 'InterplaNET'.

In the words of its new chief who seemed hardly more than an adolescent...

"People are the primary liability at a crime scene."

Tweeter cringed every time he recalled the squeaky voice. The man had a somewhat tyrannical disposition when working with his staff. He was slimmer than a whisper and had a long pointed nose that looked like a beak. Some called him the 'little bird man'. His deputy – a black woman named Earnestine – was the only person who seemed to have enough forbearance to work with him. Tweeter had never learned to like the man, but begrudgingly admitted that the technology he brought to the lab was impressive.

With the support of devices such as the electron microscope and the ultramicroscope the world of forensics had been changed. Images that had been confined by old technology now used electrons rather than visible light to produce images on an extremely tiny scale. Such devices used high-intensity illumination to shoot light out and capture small floating particles visible only by the diffraction of light blocked by their microscopic densities against a treated dark background.

There was talk of obtaining a scope that could reveal and record the chemical changes in substances – molecules which lost electrons to other molecules during a chemical reaction. There was a move afoot to call the newer computer technology simply 'derivators' – or 'DRVs. They had artificial intelligence coded into them and could deduce rather than simply compute a mathematical formula. The word 'computer' was becoming obsolete in forensic circles.

The molecule was replacing the silicone chip. Everyone would have a 'derivator' some day. The development of nanotechnology might soon change our impression of where technology ended ...and we began. Chips could be inserted into the body.

Though Tweeter was a 'throwback', he read profusely. Those on the forefront of the information age had already predicted that technology would eventually assist the limitations of human deduction 'from the inside out'. The probability of cerebral implants might link us to one another thereby increasing deductive capability. Our thoughts would be secured and authenticated by chemical matrices unique to each individual.

Really, the world was changing more quickly than he wanted. It seemed dispassionate. He felt like an outdated contraption – a flint and steel solution in a millennium where the ubiquitous storm was technology; and the temperature was 'arctic'.

But today, the lab had the energy of an exclamation. They had broken the code to a high profile case that had been played as skillfully and with as many dodges as a game of chess. The 'kingpin' was dead and – virtually speaking – lay on the board like an overturned castle.

The 'bird man', who was not known for his mirth, had allowed a bit of sport within the lab. Someone was playing 'Catch the Wind'[16] at full blast. It seemed oddly timeless. A small flock of birds darted gaily about the outside windows. The normally austere nature of the sparse confines had evaporated as quickly as an expletive around a child. An entire body of forensic knowledge had been employed to trap a felon who had eluded them for years. The man had bound himself in a losing throw of the die; and his substantive plot had finally become mush.

Two or more rambunctious young men did a celebratory wrestle in a nearby hallway – releasing the energy of weeks of strapping work. Tweeter avoided the reveling melee. He was tired; and the thundering noise bothered him.

All he really wanted was a hasty answer to his question about the specimen he had found at the crime scene. Afterwards, he would retire to his office; pour over some paperwork; and enjoy a cup of noodle soup in his 'solitary confinement'.

He strode down an adjoining hallway trying to mentally adjust his attitude. Every step seemed heavier. He kicked a piece of trash in the middle of the hallway and sent it sailing down to the next set of starched white doors. Then he blew a big gob of spit into a nearby trashcan; and took a few deep breaths – wondering if the cameras mounted in the hallways had caught his errant disrespect. The pine scented deodorizer he kept in his car was lingering on his suit. It had seemed like a good idea at the time - now he felt like Christmas had thrown up all over him.

Suddenly his thoughts were interrupted by a commotion. From around the corner, there was an explosion of sound and energy. Coming down a hallway – which was long enough to be a landing strip - a small 'lap dog' was running at full throttle; and carrying a bone in his mouth that was larger than he was. A 'lab coat' was in full pursuit...and a hard looking, beautiful woman was chasing the two of them.

The man yelled, "Come here, you prancing little idiot!!"

The woman was screaming hysterically,

---

16   A 1965 song written by Scottish singer, songwriter, and guitarist, Donovan

"Buster...Buster! Come back, sweetie! Come back..."

Tweeter prepared himself. He knew that he could scoop up the little dog – unless it doubled back. 'Buster' looked hesitant but instinctively weighed his options. He seemed to think that his chances were better to make it past the old guy with bad knees rather than the screaming entourage behind him. He held on firmly to his prize – he had an impressive head start on his pursuers. Instantly his passage had been blocked by the detective. He darted with as much determination as a little dog possesses.

Tweeter's large hands arrested him by the scruff of the neck. The large bone fell to the floor with a clatter. 'Buster' snarled; wriggled like small child; and bit into the meaty hand of his captor – drawing blood. Tweeter growled out a profanity but held him tight. His owner had just arrived; and was panting like the subject of her adoration.

"Let go of him, you big lump! He doesn't mean you any harm. I'll...I'll pay for any damages!! Let go of him!" She was fine looking woman with honey-colored hair and bright red lipstick. She smelled like honeysuckle.

"God damnit, lady! If he doesn't mean any harm, then, why is my hand bleeding?! I'll probably have to get a shot!" Tweeter released his hold on the dog's neck. It snarled at him - and smelled like it needed a bath.

"Poor baby..." She petted and cooed over the dog, while the lab technician, who had been first in the pursuit, continued to heave – fresh out of breath.

Tweeter pulled a handkerchief out of his pocket and wrapped his wound. The he turned around to find what the dog had dropped. It was laying on the side of the hallway still in one piece...a cranium of enormous size. He picked it up and rolled it around in his hands, examining it with much interest.

The frustrated technician now seemed awash with embarrassment. Grabbing the bone out of Tweeter's hands he quickly stuffed it under his arm like it was football that had been used to win the Super Bowl. He turned abruptly to the handsome woman and said,

"Cynthia, we really should be getting back..."

Tweeter's curiosity began to grow as quickly as his annoyance. The wound would be fine, but the woman's honeysuckle perfume had started to compete with the pine scent from his car. It had been a long day; and he wished to wrap it up. Still, his curiosity compelled him,

"Pretty big bone – is it human?"

The technician snapped back, "Probably not."

The answer was too quick – something he had been trained to spot when questioning suspects. The technician could sense Tweeter's suspicion; and quickly added,

We believe it's some sort of large primate, perhaps a mountain gorilla."

The woman whom he had identified as Cynthia suddenly tapped Buster's collar impatiently and interrupted.

"You know – it is late...and I have an appointment."

The technician seemed uncomfortable,

"Yeah...uh, sorry to keep you so long...I really appreciate you coming in to help us out."

The woman pulled gently at the technician's arm and pointed to her watch. The two excused themselves and hurried down the hallway. Tweeter watched them leave and then, examined the bite on his hand. The woman's offer to pay for any damages was disingenuous – she had left no contact information. He watched the two disappear through a set of double doors farther down the hallway. He would wait a few minutes – and then, pay an unexpected visit.

He walked a few feet and turned aside into a 'break room'. There, some vending machines were sitting like pigs in linen just off the starch-white hall-way. He slid a few dollars into one of the machines and it spat out some Columbian coffee. Then, he walked over; sat down at an uneven table; and 'killed' the hot drink within a minute. He rubbed the last bit of the coffee into his cut hoping it would act as a sterilizer. It was time to go find out more about the cranium and the nervous lab technician.

Tweeter rose and strode confidently down the hall. When he reached the set of double doors, he didn't bother to knock. His abrupt entry caused the technician to jump slightly.

"Well, hello again! Darn, must have taken a wrong turn...Dave." He had observed the man's name tag.

The technician quickly regained his composure. Removing the cranium from a solid oak desk at which he sat, he nonchalantly entombed it in a deep drawer on the side of the desk – as if to clean up.

"Did you have a question?"

Tweeter decided that he didn't like his condescension. He would have some fun with him.

"What happened to the girlfriend and the pooch?"

The response was firm,

"You're imagining things – we have purely a professional relationship. She has an Associates and I'm doing some mentoring."

The technician sat in his chair – trying to look as authoritative as a news anchor. He had a cynical smile on his slightly pocked face. A small desk clock ticked off seconds. There were some tennis shoes and small hand weights shoved under the desk – an attempt to knock out some light exercise during 'slow moments' at the lab.

He looked up slowly from his desk and a bologna sandwich he had been attempting to finish. He opened a top drawer of his desk; pulled out some gooseberry jam; pulled the top off; and lathered it across the remains,

"Needs a little 'something'..." he smiled.

Then, he put the jar's top back on; and shoved it into a drawer that had a collection of condiments. Light from a nearby window rested upon a straggly plant that seemed to be marking time. The technician remarked,

"It's a calendula. If you want, you can rub some of it on that wound – an old time vulnery, if you will. At least that's what folks say..."

An announcement suddenly crackled over the building's intercom – there would be a brief ceremony to celebrate the close of the high profile case that had just been completed. The technician stood up; strolled over to the opposite side of the room to retrieve his lab coat; and put it on. It was just enough time to create a distraction. Tweeter peered down into the wide side drawer of the desk – the large cranium was barely peeking out from it. The technician turned around as if he was bored,

"Well, duty calls...time for another ceremony with 'the man' and his dreary assistant."

Tweeter smiled at the reference to 'the bird man' and his assistant, Earnestine.

"Gotta lock up shop..." He motioned Tweeter towards the door.

Minute's later, Detective Tweeter's long legs had carried him down the hallway and out of the building. He was thinking about the sample that he had pilfered after the announcement had come on. He had stuffed it in his breast pocket; and felt slightly guilty at not having 'followed proper procedure'. The tag from the large cranium simply read 'Unidentified Cranium – Cough Drop, Nevada'.

He placed the tag back in his pocket remembering that it was the same pocket where he kept the small drawing of the daffodil that the special needs boy had given him. He immediately pulled it out again and transferred it to a pocket of his coat when two startling things occurred to him: First, he had forgotten the primary purposes of his visit – to have the lab analyze the sample from the crime scene. More importantly...he remembered where he had seen the victim in the body bag. She was the mother of the child who drew the picture.

He reached for the drawing in his breast pocket again; unfolded it and wondered about life's serendipity.

EZEKIEL – 'SHOOTING STAR'

"**I** BROUGHT PAINT!!!" Anna shouted jubilantly. Meanwhile her mind was ringing with bothersome memories.

She was remembering a disturbing conversation she had heard some time ago on a hill outside of her neighbors' bedroom – the night she had identified the small star, Spica. Since that time, she had seen the neighbor - a large man named Roger Gregor. He seemed to sense something...as if he knew of her accidental impropriety.

There were also occasional odd stories from locals about the sighting of some fantastic creatures. Though she was not prone to believing such things, they still bothered her. Worse, the rumors had been echoed by some of the children in a local facility where she worked.

More immediately disturbing, she remembered the badly beaten young man whom she had helped rescue at Frances Park. He was barely conscious and grasping a flower in his hand. She didn't really know why; but she had taken it from him when they were bathing his wounds. Perhaps as some sort of reciprocation, she had earlier picked a cluster of daffodils at the park. Deciding that it was the fair thing to do, she had left both the cluster of daffodils and her shoes with the black woman, Sue Bee, who was caring for the young man who was shoeless.

Much later, she had opened a flower identification book and managed to identify the flower that she had taken from the young man. It was a 'trout lily' that grew in low, moist areas – he must have retrieved it somewhere in the park's dark tree fringed area.

All of these thoughts bothered her. The town seemed to be changing – and she did not like its metamorphosis. She longed for the comfort of a love she had once known. Then, she tried very hard to remove any negative thoughts from her mind.

Today, she would focus on a small, brilliant star in her life. He would become the new monarch of her memories. She had just caught site of him – he had expected her visit to the facility. His brown eyes had narrowed to smiling 'jack-o-lantern' slits. When Zeke was happy, his body was luminous.

The light infused him as if it had found home. His short brown hair seemed to dance about. His mouth widened to reveal a broad toothy grin; and his encumbered limbs vibrated with excitement. Though a slim, frail boy with crutches – at such times he shone as if any quest for gold surely began and ended with the discovery of his joyful exuberance.

Anna swept past the front desk casually waving to the receptionist as easily as she would brush hair from her forehead. The woman at the front desk was sopping wet.

"Havin' my own personal summer here – don't just wave at me. Get me a fan for God's sake... or turn into one!!!"

"Hi True! Has my main squeeze been behaving himself – or is he still telling you strange stories about 'Big Bird'?"

Trudence Jefferson bellowed forth her answer, "Oh he been a handful today, Miss Anna! Watch out for him!" Then she continued, "God get me a great big banana split...or an igloo...anything cold! I swear I'll park myself right in the middle of it!"

Anna gave the thumbs up to several others boys in the hallway who watched her like she was a celebrity; and quietly drank in her perfume as she walked past. Then she stopped in front of Zeke and gave him an affectionate hug with one arm – while balancing the can of paint with the other. He melted in her embrace. Anna asked,

"How ya' doin', 'sweet stuff'?"

One of the boys that she had passed - hissed and rolled his eyes, 'green with envy'. Zeke radiated a grin and then replied,

"Iaaaahayam Fiaaahhhnnn, Aaahnaaah.....Hwow awwww roooohhh?"

"I'm fine, sweetie! Don't have a humbug left in me – now that I'm with you! Look what I brought!"

She held the can of paint in front of her like she was presenting a meritorious pin. The boy looked at it as if he were examining something totally foreign – and then stared away. It was part of the distraction that Anna noticed appeared to be symptomatic of his cerebral palsy. Zeke's attention returned momentarily; and he made an 'up and down' gesture with his hand and said,

"BAINTT!!!"

Then he reached out to her – his body rocking slightly and his arms flailing. She grabbed his hand and cradled it between her own. He bent forward balancing on the crutches; and gave her a 'peck' on the cheek. It was so awkwardly endearing that she almost cried. He was easy to please. Even with his frailty and being a ward of the state, he had a commanding energy. The mechanical sound of his devices combined with his awkward playfulness

- made him seem like an adorable wind up toy. She wondered how anyone could have abandoned him.

She remembered True's rambling as they did 'intake' for the boy at the facility.

"Hummpph – don't make no sense! Sum folks only interested in perfect – got contempt fo' things that ain't quick an new. I'd sooner have heart than smart. That boy got his own shine!"

The memory evaporated in an instant – a large shadow had passed across the window and momentarily distracted her. It was so quick that she wasn't sure she had seen it. Gliding planes had become popular in the area and so Anna dismissed it as such; but the sighting brought back a nagging memory.

When she looked back at Zeke, he was beaming a large smile at her. She thought about the accidental nature of life. How could she have ever imagined that she would find herself through the chance encounter with a parentless child? Very briefly she allowed a regretful memory for the parents she had lost. Then she focused back on her remarkable gain – the boy with the bright smile standing on crutches before her. They had things in common and it only made him more endearing.

"Woooeeee gonga baint wall?" he asked expectantly.

His hand patted up and down excitedly on the paint can top which had a swatch of color on it called 'Spring Daffodil'

'Yes, Sir! We're going to paint those ugly old walls today – just you and me – give you a room to brag about! Let me see if I can chase down another paintbrush."

When she returned, he was smiling even broader than she thought possible. He shuffled over to her as close as he could. His gait was like the waddle of a bird; and the mechanical clicking of his braces made him sound like a slow moving crab on linoleum. Anna quickly picked up a few of his plastic toys and threw them into a series of bin-like containers along the wall of the room. Then she spread out a small drop cloth in front of the first wall.

"I even brought an old sheet. You gonna help me roll it out? It'll keep paint off the floor."

Trudence Jefferson passed by at that moment,

"And this here what we call Phase One of a disaster..." she muttered.

A small crowd of boys had congregated outside the room. Anna unrolled more of the sheet. It had been used before and had splotches of paint that made it look like a large Rorsarch card. She gazed at a nearby window...an intense storm had blown up.

True passed by again – on her way back to the front desk.

"Take cover or getcha net...fish gonna start fallin' from the sky..."

The rain pounded the roof and plunged over full gutters to the ground. A vortex of dark angry clouds swirled around. Anna could see Zeke's concern. The storm momentarily caught his attention, but the smell of the paint distracted him. He moved back to Anna's side and ignored the rain that was now covering the windows with a thick glaze. She teasingly pulled his hood over his head. Outside the thunderstorm continued to roil and 'pinged' the roof with light hail. Zeke looked to Anna for reassurance and she hugged him again.

"North Wind's a blowin' out there – you gonna keep me warm?!" He huddled near her; hugged her back; and 'made a muscle'. Then, rocking back and forth asked,

"Cooounnn hmaahh fweh..fweh...fwehhhyund wasjhhh?"

His friend, 'Jimmy Mack', zoomed up to the front door. 'Jimmy Mack's' stubby arms could barely reach the lever that steered his wheelchair. He was a tough little product of congenital birth defects and bullying.

"So, woman, you finally brought paint – 'bout time this dump got a face-lift! The boys and me was gettin' embarrassed. Hey Zeke – you choose the color?"

Before he could respond,

"You see that 'big-ass' bird that flew over? Damn vultures must be circling this hole like weight watchers lookin' for a candy bar."

'Jimmy Mack' looked at the paint can,

"This stuff is girlie lookin' – some little old lady pick it out?" Then he looked at Anna, "No offense, ma'am."

"None taken, 'Jimmy Mack', - wanna help?"

"I got places to go chickadee. I can't be standin' around here with you rollin' slow-folkses. I gotta go where there's some action!"

He stuck out a stubby arm and hit a button that spun his chair around. Another touch – and he was whizzing off in a cloud of institutional dust – unable to admit that he had a 'crush' on her.

Anna returned her attention to Zeke.

"Let's start painting!"

He clattered over to the nearby wall almost losing his balance. Anna grabbed him around the waist; and then, secured his crutches. Supporting his thin frame, she lowered him in front of the wall in one smooth motion. He watched her stir the paint like she was a Madonna. She reached over with a free hand; pulled up a utility stool; lifted him; and sat him down gently.

"Don't fall off, handsome – or I'll tell True to cut you off at two glasses of milk."

He beamed – so anxious to get started that Anna had difficulty keeping him balanced.

She handed him the roller; but noticed that he held something tight in his hand.

"Whatchu' got there, partner?"

Zeke frowned and jerked his hand away.

"Come on now, you don't want to keep secrets from your girlfriend – do you?"

He continued to frown. Anna reached out and gently opened his hand. Inside was a small stop watch – dainty in appearance.

"Zeke, honey, where did you get this?"

"Miz Cymfia."

"That the night nurse?"

He shook his head slowly up and down.

"Did she give it to you?"

He shook his head left to right and looked down.

"Well, honey, we can't take things that don't belong to us. We'll have to give it back –okay? Now give it to me."

The behavior was uncharacteristic.

"Iaaaauhhh sowwee. I bour baint on my head," He made a motion above his head and frowned like he was sucking a lemon.

"Well, that won't do. I can't have a punk-rocker for a boyfriend!"

She grabbed a few strands of his black hair and smiled at him.

"...So, you're gonna punk out on me huhn? You gonna get a Mohawk too?! Kinda like you the way you are! Oh well, when you go on tour with the boy bands, I'll tell them I knew you when you were a famous 'painter'!"

Then, she gave him a can opener. "Gotta get paint on this wall!"

His flailing was becoming more erratic. She watched him ply the can as best he could for a minute, before he began to look unhappy and frustrated. His hands simply weren't steady enough. Meanwhile 'Jimmy Mack' had sped back down to the room to assess the situation.

"Geez, man...you still working on openin' the can? I thought you'd be done paintin' the room by now!"

Then he whizzed away again – happy that he had a glimpse of Anna. She glanced at Zeke and said patiently,

"Zeke, how about you takin' over for me here and spreading the sheet on the floor a little better...I'm havin' trouble with it. I think I can handle the paint can. It would be easier for me than this silly old sheet. Can't seem to wrestle that darn drop cloth – I think it needs a man's touch."

Zeke bounced naturally to his next assignment. She watched as he erratically pulled the drop cloth across the floor. She followed behind him, quietly straightening the cloth and tucking in the corners. She wouldn't risk destroying his happiness.

Then, she opened her hand and looked at the stop watch again; before putting it in her pocket. The change in his behavior was sudden and it concerned her. But there were other things. Deep inside, she longed for someone in the past – longed so much that it ached. And she had a vague and distant dream of flying with him through the sky, like they were two 'shooting stars'.

COLOR ON A BLANK WALL

When the paint can had been opened and the drop cloth had been tucked in corners, they began. Soon the wall was streaked with color. It was clear that Zeke was having difficulty coordinating his movements. But his clubby motions would not diminish his joy or erase the smile on his face. It was this energy that made time pass quickly whenever Anna was with him.

She continued to dip his brush in paint; and then, gently but firmly, handed it to him. He attacked the wall with the energy of any ten year old. The palsy would only allow him to make wandering swipes at it. Anna thought about how much she took for granted and suddenly felt guilty. She could never really be angry with the boy – even though the theft of the pocket watch bothered her.

The wall was everything to him. Metaphorically it was a symbol of his daily challenges. Zeke could not have been more determined than if he was painting a chapel; but his movements had become more erratic – and he began to look tired. Those at the facility had tried to discourage Anna from having a child with cerebral palsy come anywhere near a paint bucket. It only made her more determined. She believed she owed it to him. Though it made her sad to see his awkward attempts, she knew that she was doing the right thing.

After a half hour 'True' appeared in the doorway. "Jimmy Mack' says you got some old lady color for our boy here..."

In an instant she changed – she could sense the discouragement.

"...You know I always done said that 'Jimmy Mack' ought to pace his mouth more with his head. He don't know what he talking about – this here is beautiful!"

Zeke was too focused to notice her presence. He was now stirring his brush around in the paint as if he was making a homemade soup; and drooling slightly. Anna wiped his mouth; then, motioned to True; and followed her out to the hallway.

"Be right back, pretty boy!"

Outside and out of earshot, she let her guard down.

"Been a weird couple days, 'True'...I'm worried about him."

'True' gave her that 'I-told-you-so' look.

"Unhhh! Unhhh! Unhhh..." was all that she said. "And I gotta explain this mess to that hussy, Miz Cynthia, tonight."

"I know, 'True'. But I can't bear to take the paintbrush away from him. He would be so unhappy."

She heard a clatter in the room and peeked around the corner to see one of Zeke's crutches fall across the room's entryway. He had knocked it over. True rolled her eyes again.

"Miss Anna, thet frown dance across his face as quick as a shadow. He get over it."

Anna quickly glanced into the room again – to make sure the boy was okay. The light was streaming in through the window and seemed to be heading for the painted streaks on the wall as if the pattern were intoxicating. Zeke was smiling broadly. The light seemed to circle him. True looked at Anna and smiled,

"Hmmmphh...trouble is you cain't stand it. That boy found a home in yor' heart. Now ain't 'True' right?"

"He's got spirit, True. It's stronger than anything I've seen."

"Boy's definitely golden...."

Then she put her hand out and gently stroked the hair away from Anna's face. They stood at the doorway. There was more clattering in the adjoining room. Zeke was trying to pick up his crutch; and balancing precariously on one foot. 'True' rolled her eyes again and looked in the room quickly, as if she were trying to decide whether rescue was in order.

"He nothing but a little mess...You know you oughta 'dopt thet boy. And thet's the truth. You likin' him too much to let go."

"Can't do that with a part-time job, 'True'."

"Sure wish you was workin' here, Ms. Anna. That Ms. Cynthia sooner read a book and paint them expensive nails a' hers, than pay any 'tention to these kids! She paused and took a breath. Well...gotta do me some checkin' on some of these rascals round here."

Then, she patted Anna on the shoulder and muttered, "Swear...if I don't have me enough gray hair..." And then she hurried up the hallway and ducked into a room where an annoying clutch of boys were rough-housing with each other.

Anna peered into Zeke's room; and saw him trying to paint the wall with his hand. He seemed determined to accomplish the task – and looked content. She turned around; and went back into the hallway. There, she leaned against the wall and gazed through a nearby window. The sun had turned tonsil red. Outside, the storm had passed but the wind continued to blow things about. It seemed to reflect the chaos in her life. She fingered a tiny cross that her adopted mother had given to her; and reached into her pocket – where she found a piece of candy. She hadn't eaten anything all day. The television was playing in the 'rec room'. 'True' had managed to restore order – the boys were quiet again. Outside, the clouds formed fabulous monsters that made no sense. She walked back into Zeke's room.

He had paint in his hair but was fine otherwise. She left him and walked up the hallway past the goldfish bowl of boys watching television. 'Jimmy Mack' was entertaining them with jokes – and stories about how he used to smoke. She stopped at the front desk in front of Trudence Jefferson, to continue their conversation.

"True, he looks so tired – is he okay? I mean has he been bothered by anything lately? He used to have those awful dreams about his mother. Is the hospital taking care of him?"

"Whatchyou think ahm here fo?! Decorashun?! Thet boy get treated better than I used to treat my own!" Her response was indignant.

Anna was apologetic. "I know, 'True'. I don't mean you. I mean just...well he looks so tired? Is the night nurse up to snuff?"

True rolled her eyes, "Hummph! Don't get me started 'bout Miz' Cynthia, now."

She paused,

"Well, he been havin' some dream – about someone he call 'Miz Needles'... swear the boy got more imagination than he do sense! Anyway, only person tired aroun' here is me. That Miz Cynthia, wearin' me out...spends mo time on her reports than she do on patients. Don't care if she do got degrees comin' outta her butt. Tired a 'pinch-hittin' for that two-timin' hussy...sure she seein' someone on the side. And perfume stinks worse than a cow pie. She call it something like 'Honeysuckle'. I think she fell into a bucket of it."

Anna didn't wish to assess anyone's character on the basis of gossip; and she still had the stolen stopwatch in her hand. She whispered,

"Please, 'True'. Not so loud..."

Trudence Jefferson ignored her,

"Yeaaahh, she's here at night, all right! Hummpphh! Darn good thing – probably burn up like a vampire in the nekkid lite a' day. Thet woman had so many face lif's she look like a' extra-terrestrial! Says she know someone who into nanny technology – whatever that means. Ain't helped her none – cain't even take care of a barn cat! Management hire her cause a' them degrees."

'True', she can't be that bad. Now you know 'Old Joe' wouldn't have wanted you to talk like that...."

True put her hand up as if to stop her,

"You right 'bout that, Miss Anna. God rest his soul – still miss the man. But I'm country; and I know when a skunk parade done passed by. I ain't havin' nuthin' to do with her brand a homemade sin. Don't care if management like her or not. Proof's inna' pudding; and that woman ain't peddlin' nothin' but slop."

It seemed impossible to keep 'True' on the subject of Zeke's health – much less silence her opinion. Anna heard another clatter. She rushed down the hallway – and walked into the boy's room again. His hands had paint all over them and he was trying to clean them off with a rag. He had tried to stand; lost his balance; and was now trying to fish a partially finished sandwich out of the paint tray. He had rubbed his eyes; had paint on his eyelids and eyebrows; and was trying to clean himself with part of the drop-cloth. When he saw Anna, he smiled – but looked like the victim of a drive-by painting. The wall was streaked and practically dry. There was wet paint on the floor. Anna exclaimed,

"Hey there, buddy – did a drone take you down. Gotta watch out for those space invaders!"

The boy replied, "I wub baintin...!"

"Yeah! I can see that – especially your hair!" She smiled at him. He was straining to get up.

"Yoouuuu wike myaaaahh wall...?" He asked – pointing to the streaks.

"Looks like a treasure trove of beauty to me! You like it?"

"Smellsa gooood!"

"Let me give you a hand there, little man. We need to finish this before we have our 'grand opening'! You're getting to be such a big dude! I can barely lift you!"

She came up behind him; lifted him up gently; and encircled him. Then she gently guided his hands.

"Glad you left some for me – I was feeling a little 'left out' – you know what I mean?"

He beamed his wonderful smile, "Whooaahkaay, Aaayaaaaa. Iaahh mmm..mmmm.mmmaaake whooo veeeel bewaahhhhh!"

Anna steadied his faltering arms and gave him the hugging assistance he seemed to need. They painted together. She could smell his hair and feel the beating of his heart. She rested her chin gently on his head; and brushed away a tear. The boy was happy – and she wondered if he knew he might never see more than the facility or the wall with which he wrestled. To Zeke...everyday had a rainbow.

The wall was coming together. It looked like a large field of warm wheat; and she imagined the two of them happily walking through it toward sunlight. But she would ask him to return the pocket watch himself; because she believed any journey might be ruined if it started with a misstep.

ILL WIND

At the back of a large sport fishing boat, Sue Bee busied herself examining jigs and baiting hooks for tourists. Occasionally she looked at the lace pattern the boat's wake left in the waves...dreaming of calmer waters. It was another ridiculous part-time job that she had snagged for herself and Herman; and she needed the money now more than ever – because she was supporting Sincero, while he recovered.

Her father had taught her a good deal about fishing; and she had used that knowledge many times to supplement her salary. She felt obligated to Herman. The man seemed to look out for her. He had told her about Sincero; and assisted in his rescue at Frances Park.

Sincero's recovery was remarkable. Though she hated to admit it – she enjoyed having someone in the apartment to fuss over, even if it did mean another mouth to feed. She worried about him even while she obsessed about getting the lines set up for people who had paid to catch more than just sunburn. All the while she kept an eye on Herman who was less inclined to work than he was to socialize. Truthfully, the man irritated the hell out of her.

High in the sky above them, the ancient mythology of the sky had disappeared under the blistering noon light. It was the same story – a soliloquy that always began with a rattling hiss; and a voice that was low...and crept through the silence eerily.

"I know what you have come for Perseus.... I can hear your thoughts. You are hiding – but you seek my head. Its magic is the only thing that can vanquish the monster they call, Cetus."

The light deflected off her reptilian scales. Medusa could hear the hero's hushed breathing. Her coarse voice whispered,

Come...show yourself. I will make death most kind. You will barely feel the prick of my arrow....I sense your breath. Surely, I must be close..."

She has a presidio of confidence as she caresses the bow case and draws an arrow. She slithers along half woman, half serpent – a head that is writhing with snakes – and seeming like something that has evolved - precipitously poisonous. She pulls the bow tight, continuing to tease Perseus. Carrying a glistening shield on her back, Medusa calculates how many feet she is from her prey. Her wicked machismo is oddly feminine – and ancient.

The maze chamber is a mausoleum. It is so quiet and Medusa's hearing so acute that she can hear a drop of sweat fall to the floor. She pokes through it stalking the young hero and avoiding the light of the moon. She detests the moon because of its revelatory quality.

There is hissing; and the distant howling of a two-headed dog. Medusa continues her soliloquy,

"I used to be beautiful...as the one who waits for you – chained to the rock...fair Andromeda, I believe she is called. But now I am cursed...with a face so wretched that to glance upon it brings a stony death. Not so tragic though, handsome Perseus, for I will have your statue to gaze upon forever. Thus, you will be honored by Medusa"

She twists along sinuously – a part of nature that Nature wants no part of. Perseus readies a heavy sword, hoping he cannot be heard by her as she advances. He can hear the rubbing of her scales upon the floor as she moves forward. He prays to himself – and with a single powerful swing of the sword – severs Medusa's head from its trunk. The coiled serpents on the head writhe angrily. Even as he picks up the head, it continues to whisper in its awful hiss,

"You know not what you have done...you will be too late...touch my blood and feel the everlasting...."

The constellation Perseus is close to Cassiopeia in the night sky. The western most tip of his leg points to the Pleides. His arm, the southernmost part of the constellation, holds Algol, the Demon Star...the head of Medusa.

Far below in a boat full of mortals, Sue Bee continued her work knowing nothing of the great celestial tragedy taking place. The war among gods did not concern her. The sun was high in the sky and the constellations were invisible. Besides, she had sensed something more immediate...even before she felt it. It was the rush of wind that one feels walking along railroad tracks... like a train that has passed perilously close. It seemed focused...and had narrowly missed her. She had not seen anything, but the force was consummate.

Many miles away, Bob the Indian, also 'felt it' and, in an odd empathy, entered into the spirit of Sue Bee with appreciative perception. His people called the phenomena of the wind 'wanagi' – which in the language of the Lakota meant 'being in the presence of ghosts'.

Sue Bee momentarily stopped what she was doing and looked across the water into the distance. 'It' had caused 'goose bumps' on her skin – and suddenly, she felt frightened. Had something been shot? She hadn't heard a shot – and no one else on the boat seemed to be aware of it. She felt foolish – it was probably just the wind. She surveyed the sky to see if the weather was suddenly changing - abhorring the prickliness of uncertainty.

She thought of Sincero and wondered if he was okay. Why had she left him alone? She would never forgive herself if something had happened; but he hadn't looked well enough for a boat trip. Now she wrestled with that discomfort; and wondered if she hadn't inadvertently abandoned him at a time of great need. She felt horribly distracted – and had not expected the growing interest she had in him. Seeing Herman nearby, she shouted,

"Herman! Get me something to drink, will ya?!"

He scurried away to find her a beer.

When she was done with the lines and had ensured that a carload of life vests were on deck – she unwillingly returned to the eeriness of the moment. Not easily 'spooked', she was certain about what she had felt. The gust seemed almost...angry. It had made a "whoosh" sound as it passed nearby. She thought of a voodoo woman who had a shop near her apartment; and who had once referred to a 'devil wind'.

Sue Bee straightened her tank top and then, folded her arms across her chest. Something seemed sickeningly conniving and there was a chill in the air. She focused on the horizon to see if anything was bobbing in the water - it was not. The waves seemed as if they had been turned off; and the water was like glass. She pointed her chin into the wind to smell the sea breeze – nothing titillated her senses. Then, she turned back again to look at the comings and goings of the boat. High up in the sky she thought she heard a faint hissing sound.

Finally, dismissing the reflection as goofy – she thought of home again; and wondered how Sincero was. Then she looked about the fishing vessel to see if anyone needed assistance - they weren't paying her to dream.

Some time later after she had bounced about checking lines and offering help, she was aware that the sky had color in it; and knew it was time to turn the boat and head back. She surveyed the carnage of cups and plates. There were fish in various stages of death – some writhing and gasping in buckets - others on deck with a whitewall of film that had formed around shiny hubcap eyes. Anxiously, she looked up at the sky again; and wondered if the weather might be 'turning'. Herman was still socializing. She growled,

"C'mon Herman, they don't pay you for your looks. Get the lead out!"

He responded, "Sue Bee, you wearin' me out – I'm goin' out' tonight!" And then he walked over to her.

"The generosity of some women still amazes me..." she grumbled derisively.

"I'm particular about the women I go out with," he muttered.

"You'd kiss a chicken – if it paid any attention to you."

"What's wrong with you, Sue Bee? You goin' through 'the change'?" He rolled up the sleeves on his crinkled cotton shirt; looked away teasingly – and prepared to pull anchor.

"More than you'll ever know," she shot back. It was not the insubstantial nature of his discourse that bothered her – rather it was the memory of what had happened earlier. Perhaps the voodoo woman was right.

Herman moved slower than wet paint. It was a distraction that she need-ed; and gave her something else to think about. He was muttering to himself,

"I'm tired of examining the jig line of every tourist that comes here." He whispered, "They all want to know why they ain't walkin' away with state records…you know you got strong arms, Sue Bee…anyone ever tell ya you got strong arms for a woman?"

She was now sure she hated the man – after love, it was the next best emotion. The sun was dropping quickly.

"Dammit, Herman, get moving – we don't have much light left!"

She regretted the day that she ever come to know him, but preferred not to focus on the idiocy of negative distraction. Besides he had a decent streak; and had been a major help in rescuing Sincero. She felt an odd sort of pity – the war had not been kind to him. The pity she had been inclined to, had long since been replaced by a more balanced outlook: one that accepted mis-takes but expected responsibility. Like everyone, he was adjusting to a life that had been far less than perfect. But it caused her to reflect on her own foibles… and she secretly hated that. She kept him on – if for no other reason – because of something her mother had once said,

"Honey, all God's children got skin."

Herman was on the upper deck now. She could hear him being ingratiating.

"Hey man! You sure have been doin' some great casting! I've seen a lot of fishermen – but none who can cast like you! Fish must be nowhere – or I'm sure you'd have a record breaker. Bet that pretty wife of yours is aching to catch something".

The woman was under a leaf-green canvas canopy; looking as hard as a knot, bored, and cool as spring in Saskatchewan. Pretty, with long legs, and a filled bourbon glass, she seemed uninterested in conversation. The man be-side her was a beast – huge and threatening looking. He seemed uncomfort-able when Herman alluded to the woman sitting beside him as his wife. There was an obvious pale line where Roger Gregor had taken off his wedding band.

The young woman crossed her legs; looked away; and played with an Iphone. Ignoring Herman's chatter, she put down the glass she had been 'nursing' and returned to an unfinished plate of crab. Gregor licked a cone of ice cream to death; and seemed irritated by the woefully small catch that a day's worth of paid-for fishing had produced. An opened tube of sun tan lotion had foamed out on the deck.

Sue Bee looked away and continued to busy herself – keeping an eye on the sails. Her sea skills had taught her the importance of paying attention to the wind's change. She looked out at the vast water and thought of Sincero again – grateful for the companionship he brought. She immediately felt edgy – the recklessness of her feelings for someone she had just met, disturbed her. Sincero's heart had not been fully vetted; and she had been misled before.

Near the boat, a pod of dolphins had gathered. The energetic mammals surrendered any fear of the boat or its inhabitants. They were playful and amorously disposed. Most of those on the boat ran over to the side to watch them cavort. But Roger Gregor's attitude darkened by the second. He had spent a good deal of money; and had no game fish to show for it. The distance from shore was diminishing as was his time to catch something of significance. He finished the cone of ice cream; drew his line in; meticulously baited it with a smaller fish that he had caught earlier - and then cast it back into the ocean.

Sue Bee – who had been watching the activities on the boat – found the large man's actions to be peculiar: He had absolutely no interest in the dolphins. And oddly enough neither did a tall woman wearing a coif and veil – and who was sitting in the shade of the vessel's cabin. The nun was studying the large man named, Gregor, as if she recognized him...from somewhere long ago.

The dolphins had submerged again and those on the boat returned to their seats. Herman continued his specious conversations – quite unaware of any responsibility to assist Sue Bee. He continued to focus on the couple. Sue Bee was captivated by the nun; and wondered if she was the nun of whom Lu Ann had spoken...and who was staying with a man at the local hotel.

Suddenly, there was a motivated tug on the big man's fishing line. Gregor's face lit up with the expectation of what was most certainly at the other end. The animal ran with the line until it seemed to play itself out. Gregor could feel the line begin to slack even as the boat moved shoreward. He pulled the rod tip up hooking it deeper; and then reeled rapidly as he dropped the tip back down. The fish tried to plunge. Gregor stood and - with the aid of his harness – continued to exert a smooth reeling motion; alternately letting the animal play itself out and reeling it closer to the boat. He would not pull the fish on the boat 'green'. Those on the boat gathered around. Slowly the fish began to tire as Gregor tried to steer its head and pull it closer in while the boat's captain navigated the boat favorably. When it had tired enough, Gregor reeled his capture in. Gaffing it with one hand; and with the other grabbing the animal by the tail – with a single powerful pull, he threw it onto the deck.

A mortified crowd of onlookers gasped as the exhausted dolphin lay bleeding. It had been dumped on the deck as unceremoniously as a junked car. The hook was protruding from its mouth like a bauble. The dark fluke of a calf was protruding from the mother.

Sue Bee watched as the nun stood and made a cross. She was certain the woman had come on the boat for a daytime adventure – not expecting to see something as grave as 'The Pieta'.

Gregor rumbled out,

"Anything we can take to the market?"

The blood of the dolphin had begun to brown in the sun. The royalty of a birth had been interrupted; and the bridge between life and death - recklessly torn asunder. The captain of the boat would not allow its transport. Gregor dumped both mother and child overboard. Neither death nor birth seemed to interest him.

Sister Frances stood and abruptly left to throw up in the cabin restroom. She was now more certain than ever of Gregor's identity and where she had seen him before.

The shore suddenly seemed more distant. It was Herman who finally broke the silence. The nun had coincidentally returned and stationed herself next to a vacant jig line when Herman beamed a smile at her and said,

"How's it going, Sister? Never seen a member of the cloth leave this boat without a fish – or at least some ferocious bites...bet you'll haul in a whale before the days over –especially with your 'connections'!"

His timing had never been good. Sister Frances – who clearly had been disturbed by what she had just witnessed – was in no mood to be patronized,

"Run along before I ask my 'connections' to part the sea and leave you in the middle of it."

Sue Bee, heard the interchange called out to him,

"Yo! Herman can you help me here?!"

Sister Frances adjusted her coif and veil. Her habit – a sign of consecration, poverty, and membership – had been suitably modified for the boat ride. She was wearing 'deck shoes'. She fingered the silver cross around her neck and the rosary hanging from her sash – thinking of things she would discuss with 'RC' when she returned to shore.

The coast was in sight. The passengers were still horrified by the killing of the dolphin – their conversation had turned pedestrian. Some on the boat nervously played with their entry tickets. All were trying to forget the site of the dying dolphin and its calf.

Two riders at the prow tore up their tickets and released them into the air like confetti. Seagulls made passing swoops as if to repossess something that belonged to the sea. In the distance, the silhouette of a few of the larger buildings had begun to appear. The shuddering of the boat, rattled glasses and cups as it slowed and its capable rudder steered the vessel toward port. Gulls made impassioned swoops in search of anything that might be thrown overboard – their cries, stripes of noise, against a faded water-worn shore.

Sister Frances' stern countenance was evidence that her adaptation to the sea had been less than successful. She gazed up at the sky and appeared to say a prayer. An airplane had left a bright contrail that eventually puffed out like loose stuffing from a pillow. The spirit moon rose; and night birthed bright stars – much to the excitement of those on board. They seemed to forget about the earlier grisliness of the day.

The pier moaned as the boat's protective floats rubbed against it; and the boat's captain positioned the boat to disembark its passengers. There were conversations about where to eat. The twinkling of port lights and the soft playing music caused a tiring day to metamorphose into festivity.

Meanwhile the wind had moved in with the boat. It softly wailed seeming to meander among those who were already portside. Merchants, who had set up booths, labored to keep their products on the table as the wind pushed forth. They were selling everything – except dignity.

Sue Bee had secured most of the sails and was already thinking about dinner with Sincero. If he felt well enough, perhaps they would make their way toward the lights and music. Herman tottered toward her. He had made his 'strokin' rounds' for the day. There would be no more false encouragement, unsolicited advice, 'fishing fly' adoration, or philosophical discussions about different weight requirements of nylon – at least not today.

Sue Bee collected the life vests. It had taken nearly an hour to 'shore up' the boat; have the passengers collect their belongings; register what they had caught; and escape the onerous swaying of the water. They were a disheveled, disorganized, loose huddle of fatigue; making vague promises about 'getting together for the evening' and exchanging 'nice to meet you' and 'have a wonderful time' comments.

Roger Gregor gave the young woman with whom he had been with on the boat, a cool embrace and tight wad of cash. Then, they split up and went their separate ways.

Sister Frances – whose voice now sounded as if it had collected rust – grated out a few goodbyes. She had observed the separation. Now she would return to the hotel to soak her feet in a salt bath and think more about this gargantuan man who had murdered the dolphin and its calf.

And as the last passenger left...the wind picked up and played with the sails of the moored boats. It rustled through nearby reeds loosening their seed-bearing tassels. It blew off the hats of some who waited. Its seemingly inadvertent actions caused random strangers to speak to each other. It had traveled far through time and space. There was nothing it had not 'seen'.

It had caressed the sweat from the brow of the peasant who carried full pails from the milk barn. Its 'fingers' had separated the thick brush in order to touch the eggs of the quail's nest. It had shifted the smoke from steam engines on railroad tracks; and blown it in the face of buffalo. It had filled the sails of Portuguese ships and – much later - helped lift the 'barnstormers'. It had blown up the skirts of bashful women; and had danced across dark skies – watching the waxing and waning of the moon. The wind had pounded every inch of the Caribbean islands; but had also caressed daisies along country roads. The same wind had pushed those hanging at gallows, making them swing; and – a short time later – caressed the faces of schoolgirls who chattered as they walked home. It had plucked the hair of dogs making it stand up on their backs; and had squeezed through the open windows of penitentiaries – imbuing prisoners with a sense of freedom.

The winds invisible fingers had touched many things – and its motive and effects were never predictable. It had voyaged into chaos – and had created its own. And, in a way, it had forged the unconnected into a shared stream of consciousness that was deeper than the scope of human intellect.

It was the middle of the month. Sue Bee hurried home to Sincero – still wondering about the trumpet of wind she had felt on the boat.

In the northwest corner of Nebraska in a 'soddie' in the Sandhills, Bob the native tracker did not wonder. He had heard from the large cottonwoods that the wind was upset. The agreement it had held with trees for millennia – had been broken. The stand of willow trees that Bob had observed on the second tracking of the great cat – the aberrant trees that seemed out of place with everything else...had ignored the wind's request to carry their voice.

Tonight, the wind sought perniciousness. The idiom of its language might not be translated – and it sought the company of a woman whose lips were redder than murder – as if to feed its contempt. Cynthia Gregor was idly working on her nails.

SNARE

The weather had suddenly turned much colder; and a light snow was sifting through the sky. Nothing stuck, but it was a reminder that the quarrel between seasons has started again. Many of the leaves had been brought down in a swirling dance by the wind. It was what meteorologists referred to as an unexpected 'cold snap'. The crackling of branches and the light clicking of dry leaves hitting each other was neither easy nor agreeable. The leaves lay on the ground as faded evidence of a richer time. The skinny nakedness of trees would soon be revealed. What was left green – now stood out like expensive jade. Clouds had been ushered away and the night sky seemed cold and unencumbered as a conspiring divorcee with a hair full of diamonds.

She looks up – deciding whether or not to have a cigarette. Tracing a line from the Pole star through the West-end of Cassiopeia, the winged horse, Pegasus, can be seen. The 2nd-magnitude star Alpheratz, or Alpha Andromeda joins the two constellations of Pegasus and Andromeda. Pegasus has long been known – recorded as a constellation in ancient times.

But she's not looking at any of that. A football game is over and she has just turned off the television set. The wind alternately rises and falls. She has put off what she must do, preferring the warmth of the couch and to concentrate on her nails. The cigarette pack has been crushed and she is dying to have just one more.

Miles to the west and sitting on a chair in front of a sod hut, Bob, the Indian, takes the last puff of smoke from a pipe before he puts it down; offers a prayer to the sky; and asks for guidance. He too, wishes for a cigarette – but has long since quit. Instead he looks up at the sky and notices that Pegasus is upside down with its head toward the equator.

She goes into the bathroom and sits at the vanity. Her skin looks like iced porcelain; and her hair is honey-colored. She tells herself 'a girl has to look good' even when exercising. She pulls back the long tufts of curled hair and puts on a studded golden clasp to hold it in place. She smears lipstick on her lips like it is peanut butter and then gently licks off some of it. Bright red in color, it is just enough to give a hard but exquisite face the 'lift' that it needs.

Then she pulls on a 'frumpy' sweat suit – grateful for it, because she does not have to shave her legs. She applies a faint foundation and some rose color to her cheeks. She emerges from the 'powder room' like a spider from an elaborate web – then stretches as much as she is comfortable doing; and looks for jogging shoes. The shoes feel like they were built for a sport utility vehicle. Though she doesn't like their look, they make her feel less vulnerable.

She goes back to the powder room; administers a 'spritz' of perfume down her 'bra'; puts a pinch of talcum powder under her arms; and grabs some sunglasses. She wonders whether wearing glasses at night will make her look ridiculous; but she hates jogging and decides that the anonymity they provide is worth any ridicule. One more look in the mirror convinces her that her overall appearance is stylish enough to pass muster.

She is just at the door when the dog appears at her feet – looking up devotedly. She bends down and kisses him. 'Buster' sneezes – blowing talcum powder into the air. Then she grabs the 'protection' that she needs and heads out the door hoping that the same feet that felt comfortable in heels will adjust to the 'all-terrain vehicle' flats she is squished into. There's just enough time to pose and examine her form in the mirror. She looks good. As a final accoutrement, she puts on the sunglasses. It is important to be seen, but not recognized.

Then, she blows a kiss to 'Buster'; closes the door and enters the 'great outdoors'... something she despises. She makes one more attempt to stretch; rotates her arms and center as if preparing to spar; and readjusts her sunglasses. Hoisting up the sleeves of her sweatshirt, she begins her jog. This is her time to think and plan. There is only a little time left before she is due for her shift at 'the facility'. A little boy waits for her there; and she will pretend to care for him. But really, she intends to see Zeke only for the few minutes necessary. Cynthia Gregor – Miss Cynthia as she is known at the facility – would rather be immersing herself in the festivities of the port. The shift at 'the facility' is something that annoys her but that she needs to do. If everything works out as planned, it will be her final shift.

She jogs around the corner feeling closer to death than life; but will continue because she knows that a young man will exit a building by the time she rounds the fourth corner; and arrives several blocks away. They have made plans. A Pentex watch glistens against her skin. It is a substitute for the pocket watch that was stolen from her. She is already planning her rebuke of the boy named Zeke. It will serve to warn any of the other little thieves in 'the facility'.

Meanwhile, at the lab, it is just about time for him to quit. He has spent long hours in a low-lighted room surrounded by shade-loving plants; and completing research on the incredibly large cranium. Dave, the lab technician is excited about what he has learned; but still mystified by the absence of the tag on the bone sample. He wonders if it might have been lost during the visit by the nosey detective who called himself, Tweeter. Then he briefly ponders the fate of the man 'RC' – from whom he had retrieved the cranium. He assumes that his body has long-since been picked apart by scavengers; and strewn about the Chihuahua Mountains – particularly when he passed on the information about the 'silver sand' (which 'RC' had not provided with the cranium).

He makes out another tag for the cranium that reads, 'Unidentified Sample – Cough Drop, Nevada' and reattaches it to the sample. Opening up a desk drawer, he pulls out a late lunch – a bologna sandwich upon which he slathers gooseberry jelly. When he finishes it, he waters a suffering calendula on the shelf – not really knowing why. If the meeting he has tonight regarding his findings is successful, he will not need to return to the lab.

Dave, the lab technician is planning his departure and what he will say to the little Director who everyone calls 'bird man' and his assistant, Earnestine. The two never really cared for him. He laughs to himself. It is his turn to gloat over their misfortune and to celebrate his own. He has discovered something important related to the large cranium.

He looks at his watch and then frowns at the clock on the wall as if frowning will somehow make it move quicker. The two time pieces are synchronized. He wishes he could press a button to make the time go faster. He 'spritzes' some breath spray in his mouth. A 'hot date' requires a cool minty mouth. He can barely concentrate on anything but his date with Cynthia Gregor. They will talk again about the 'fundamentals' of his findings related to the blood he has drawn from the boy named, Zeke; and what he has discovered related to the cranium. Then she will yield to him.

He takes off his lab coat and replaces it with a sport coat, then walks toward the bathroom. There he fluffs up his hair; adds a bit of 'product'; and returns to his desk. He knows where they will meet; and has planned where they will spend the evening. Her husband is out of town. They will meet at a bar which bears a painted 'shingle' with a two headed dog. She has reminded him not to be late. They have timed the meeting with Swiss precision.

She has sent him an earlier note with puff of talcum powder in it; and her favorite perfume. The note is signed "horizontally yours, CG". The lab technician loves the mystery; and feels as if he is taking part in a romantic movie. He meticulously examines his teeth; pulls out some dental floss; and lightly flosses them. Everything looks in order. His pupils are slightly dilated with the anticipation of the conquest. He checks his wallet for a credit card. He doesn't care how much the hotel room costs.

He looks in a mirror that he keeps at his desk. One last sweep of his appearance reveals dirt underneath his fingernails. He had washed his hands – but they will not come clean. It is good enough for the evening's flight of fancy. And he is filled with itchy expectation.

He knows that he has 'opened a window' into tissue engineering research, based upon an old bone found in the desert – and blood samples taken from a 'cripple'. He laughs at the irony of the incidental forensics discovery built upon the language of blood called DNA.

They will languish over an expensive meal and drinks; and he will tell her about the fascinating and fertile implications of the 'nanotech' DNA sequencing he has completed. She has asked him to bring a 'thumb drive' so that she may try to understand his research – it will give them more to talk about the next time her husband is out of town. After the brief business of the night, he will take her to a secret place in town where they will spend a guilty night; and talk of future plans.

The technician exits the lab and locks the door – taking one more glance at the lab before he leaves. Then he picks his way methodically down the long hallway where he first met the nosey detective named, Tweeter. He has a piss hot secret about the boy's blood work and he is ready to explode like popcorn. He has already called Cynthia Gregor to confirm their date and the time; and hinted to her about the lab results which include a fruitful DNA sequence; and his thoughts about the role of the cranium – which had nearly been contaminated by that damned mutt of hers named, 'Buster'. Then, he will ply compliments, caresses, and kisses from her.

Leaving the building, he walks two blocks – nearing the bar and a night of risk. He looks at his watch and sees that he is precisely on time. A night blooming flower scents the air, filling the evening with the expectation of feminine encounter.

His peripheral vision picks up the sight of a female jogger coming towards him in frumpy clothes and sunglasses. He quietly laughs at her awkward appearance and the buggy sunglasses; and then crosses to the other side of the street to give her room. It is too late for a woman to be jogging alone; and he has no intention of being accidentally 'pepper-sprayed'. The street is dark; and they are the only two people on it. He can almost feel the quiet gratitude of the ungainly jogger as she continues down the opposite side of the street past him. He gives the incident no further thought. He is whistling to himself thinking absentmindedly about the woman he will meet at the bar;

the exciting results of his day; and a night filled with primal passion.

The 'frumpy jogger' suddenly turns back and crosses the street. Her footfall is soft. She is practically abreast of him. Her step increases in speed as she lunges toward the white of his neck. With a single swipe of the 'protection' she carries, she opens up an artery under his left ear. He barely has time to grab his neck. Within seconds, the blood pours forth. The steady red flow travels down his arm – staining his shirt and splattering on his pants. In agony, the lab technician realizes that existence – as he knows it – is quickly coming to an end. He cannot scream. The red river of blood will only allow him to gurgle. His eyes widen – something that suddenly understands it is prey. And then he swallows an iron cup of his own blood.

The jogger quickly pushes the unsteady man into a dark alley filled with trash. He rolls over several times in the 'confetti' of garbage – trying to defend from further assault; and to close up the gaping wound to his neck. After a few seconds, he lies motionless – no longer the admiral of his life.

Cynthia Gregor bends over him and fishes through his coat pockets until she finds what she is looking for. Satisfied that the man she was to meet is 'finished', she retracts the open blade and shoves both it and the thumb drive taken from him – securely into her bra.

She jogs away like a lioness; and leaves the unconscious man in a final plummet. She needs to let 'Buster' out to pee. Her eyes blink coldly. She glistens from the sweat on her face; and then, disappears into the night like a crocodile submerging in water.

In the darkness of her subterranean shop, an old woman sits just below the surface of the sidewalk and looks out of a dark window. She has watched most of the activity unfold. Her name is Yoruba. She runs a voodoo shop. She gazes upon the lifeless eyes of the technician; and watches his blood seep into the ground – wondering what guardian will take him to another life. Will he nourish the soil of the alley and become a night blooming flower. Then she speculates why the God who gives life, would allow it to be taken so casually. Did the withering of life by human hand represent His calculation – or portend the crossing of a margin?

The old voodoo woman named Yoruba simply smiles – and seems slightly bored. Then, she 'fishes' through her pocket for loose change. It is something that she has done since she was young. Long ago, she realized she had 'the gift'…no need to invest in 'entertainment packages'. The human race and its foibles were diversion enough – and commercial free. She looks at the dates of the coins and remembers the years that have passed. The currency seems to harness other-worldly thoughts.

She pulls a penny out of her pocket. It is dated '1989'. It has exchanged hands many times, but carries a story from the last person who touched it – something about a marred marriage and narcissistic tendencies. It is quick peep show into a life – but she knows what she feels. Yes, the last person to have touched the penny would most certainly be quarantined by selfishness; and die alone in a house she had traded for conscience. She throws the coin on the counter, and immediately feels the irony of asking, "A penny for your thoughts...."

The vision is quickly over and she snaps back to focus on the street and its many feet. Because of her subterranean shop with its high window to the walkway, her world is pedestrian – though certainly not prosaic. She has watched the feet pass by all day; and is familiar with each – but not the one of the female jogger in 'all-terrain vehicle' sneakers. This is a new set of feet that she is anxious to remember; because of the quickness of its stride and its determined nature. And such a lovely well-turned ankle! Each step screamed out. She fixes it in her mind – now it is memorized like a license plate.

She flicks the waste of a cigar she is smoking into an open saucer where it has already formed a small dike of ash. 'Ashes to ashes and dust to dust' she mumbles to herself. 'That is what we all are – until pulled back into the light'. She briefly wonders whose relative she might be dispensing; and then sneezes into the saucer...there seemed to be no point in restraint. Then she hikes up a comb that has begun to slide out of her wild hair; and wonders why she cares.

Did all audience require testimony? She sits in the darkness for some time, thinking. It occurs to her that she is audience to Time – yet it expected nothing from her. She chuckles at the notion.

No, she would say nothing. The world was filled with reflection – the purest coming from mirrors. With that Yoruba turned off the light and gazed into the distance where she saw the bar 'shingle' of a two headed dog...something that, no doubt, had more than one tale. The dew will be upon the dead man tomorrow. He has died with his secrets – but she senses that it will involve a woman who has come into her shop before – and who is now caretaker of a young man with his own secrets. No, she will not report what she has seen – she will wait for the police to ask... and for more of the story to unfold.

THE LANGUAGE OF BLOOD

It is nighttime at 'the facility' and the new shift has started. Zeke is dreaming; and the night mares gallop away with him. They strain at imaginary reins. Their muscles are taut; they puff heavy froth from their mouths; and gnash their teeth. Occasionally they whinny in unison – sounding like tenors digesting music. They gallop fast and hard leaving dust across the evening sky – pushing, pushing...as if toward some dark prize.

In the boy's dream, a witch is making her way toward him. She has a wart that pops out like a raisin from her face. She calls herself 'the Witch of Point Possession'; but he also knows her as "Miz Needles". She extends her hand menacingly – hovering toward his face.

"I must have your points!"

She reaches for his face with long bony fingers and hard nails. The boy recoils immediately. She screams at him,

"I must have them! Give them to me! A freckle or point that is anywhere other than in my possession cannot be!" Then she whirls around like a gyroscope and suddenly grabs his cheek.

The moon has dropped from the sky. It falls into a deep blue lake; and the fish curl around the floating luminous orb. Somewhere a bell rings. It is a single pure note that blows out votive candles in a nearby church and pushes into his heart where it resonates. The witch suddenly releases her hold. She cannot touch something that is clean.

Zeke is torn from the dream; and is now wide awake. He is wet from sweating; and has pee'ed all over himself again. His puny unstable arms do their best to wipe up the urine. He is aware that the door to his room is being opened slowly. The raw lighting from the hallway comes at him – sharp and sour as pickled cole slaw. The raspy voice – a smoker's voice - whispers quietly, entreatingly,

"Zeke....."

She moves across the tiled floor as quickly and easily as a serpent. The honeysuckle of her perfume is overwhelming. This is a nightmare that has run before. Even though he cannot see the face in the partial darkness he knows who it is. He rubs his eyes to make sure there is not more than one of her. Other shadows scurry across the room. The woman locks the door. The scent of his freshly painted room and the strong odor of perfume are disjointed – thrust together in error – an imposed and contradictory order bent on collapse. The boy wishes Anna was there. Then, there is the voice again,

"Zeke, we're here to see you...."

The boy plummets from his dream and rubs his eyes with hands that are already wet.

"Whaaaa tyme zit?"

"Let's not talk about the time now – we all have plenty of that." The woman with the honeysuckle perfume responds.

Miles away and in the middle of the prairie grass, the winds engine has revved. Bob, the Indian, is lying in the grass watching the boy's dream unfold – he has fallen asleep in the tall grass; but their dreams are syncopated as something singular. He 'awakens' – seeing clearly what is happening; and knowing that he can do nothing to help. He rises up on one elbow and sees the moon in the sky. It has witnessed many things; and from its outward point of view, advises that some pain simply must be endured. Bob too, rubs his eyes; and lies down again. He will join the boy in the 'dream' again.

Zeke also is looking at the moon through the window. He says,

"Iaaaahhmmm turrrstey... Can Iaaahhhabbb m-m-milluk?"

The husky voiced woman responds,

"Come now, I'm not a grocery store...and perhaps you should remember that the next time you steal someone's watch...."

"Buddd I'aaaammm turrrstey..."

The voice has suddenly become icy,

"Yes, my dear...but, by the looks of that wet bed, you don't need any more liquid this evening. We need to clean up your mess; and then I'll give you a little something to help you sleep. Now roll over, and let's get these wet sheets off the bed."

And then, in her next breath she mutters something derogatory. The smell of her perfume is overwhelming him. He breaks into a cough; and she scolds him,

"Stop your croaking now – you'll wake the others. You've got enough water on the sheets to keep a camel happy for a month."

The scurrying shadows appear on the edge of the high-intensity light that she has turned on. They are men with syringes and machines. The woman roughly pulls the wet linens from underneath the boy. Using alcohol swabs, she cleans a standing tray that she has wheeled up to his bed. It glistens under the light; and she places the syringes on it.

She pulls out the thumb drive that she has fished from the pockets of the dead lab technician – and inserts it into a tiny laptop computer. One of the men mutters,

"Apparently your 'date' was successful..."

She responds crisply,

"Very! I'd rather ride a horse than, well....thankfully, no 'riding' was necessary – the horse was 'put out to pasture'."

The man continues,

"Guess you'll get your office back at the forensics lab, then."

She responds, "Be assured, I'll clean it out tomorrow – and stow away the cranium for further 'testing'."

The boy wants to cry – but cannot. He vaguely remembers that the woman has given him a "goodnight pill" before. Now, she pulls out another pill from a stylish purse; and then rolls him over on his back. She wipes the hair out of her eyes; and pushes a glass of water to his face saying,

"Only enough to swallow the pill..."

Then she grabs the glass from the thirsty boy; pinches his cheek; squeezes his mouth open; and pushes the pill down his throat.

"Sleep tight...don't' let the bedbugs bite."

She feels mildly guilty, aware that she has been rough - perhaps languishing in thoughts of motherhood. The boy's mother has recently been killed; and all that is left of her are the vials of blood which they will mix with his own blood to continue their experiment. She speedily disavows any such empathetic emotion in favor of composure. He begins to cough; and she orders one of the men with her,

"Don't let him spit it out – we need to get another sample! The last one didn't take well. And we can't have him pulling the needle out or waking the others up!"

One in the entourage growls back something indecipherable. She hisses at him. They are like two cats fighting,

"Don't botch this one up, you fool. We can't have a lot of needles marks on him. They watch stuff like that around here!"

The man grabs Zeke's arm. The boy feels the rubber tourniquet make his veins pop. He sees the needle come toward him; feels its sting; and watches it like it is a mosquito becoming crimson and full.

From the lab coat of one of the men, a tabloid peeks out. It has a sensational headline that reads,

KILLER CAT STILL BELIEVED TO BE LOOSE!
ANOTHER CORPSE FOUND!

Sensing Zeke's interest in the paper, Cynthia Gregor says angrily,
'Give me that paper – it's interfering with your work."

She folds it up and stashes it inside of her coat pocket. Some blood has
been spilled on the standing tray. She lifts up the syringes and wipes it away.
It is a tidy and practical thing to do – to eliminate any loose ends.

She fishes around in her bra to readjust the 'protection' she used earlier.
The retracted knife has become uncomfortable and she wonders if anyone
notices it. Then she firmly shoves the knife further into her bra until it is resting there well-concealed.

There is a chair next to the wall of the boy's bedroom. She longs to sit
down after her 'evening jog'; but dare not separate herself from those she is
watching. Men could not be trusted. The window to the boy's room is open.
She shudders slightly as if the spirit of something has entered the room and is
seeing everything; and then, notices that the forehead of the man drawing the
blood - is shiny from sweat. It is a secondary concern to her. Things are going
well and the blood they need has almost all been drawn.

Deciding she can finally relax, she walks toward a chair that is next to the
wall. A segmented arthropod scurries across the floor; and Cynthia Gregor
crushes it with her foot – just another piece of filth. She wishes she were having a night out at the port listening to music, shopping and dining on pastry.
Instead she is 'pulling the night shift' at the facility. But she comforts herself
knowing that soon she will be working at the forensics lab again – she's had
her fill of working with 'the living'.

Then, she hears the man say,
"This should do it – enough for a couple thousand bio-bricks. Why do
we need to bother with this little 'cripple' anyway?"

Cynthia Gregor's response is severe,
"We believe that the qualities of the subject might affect the outcome
of our genetic experiment....probably affected the outcome in Coughdrop,
Nevada. Frankly, the boy is too stupid to be anything but 'pure'...."

The man releases the tourniquet; and mumbles something about mixing
DNA. Another man uses a restriction enzyme to cut the DNA into pieces,
separates it using electrophoresis; and fixes it to a nitrocellulose filter. The
third man exposes it to X-ray film and applies a modified polymerase chain
reaction process that has been adapted for the mobile unit they are using. He
looks up suddenly and exclaims,

"I'm getting an error message again. Damn DNA sequencer!"

He looks down and notices that some of the blood has spilled on the floor – then reaches down to swab it up; and bumps into the medical cart. More blood spills and he tries desperately to save it.

"Never mind – it's been contaminated! Now mop this mess up!" Cynthia Gregor's voice cuts through the quiet like a saber – she is feeling the pinch of time again.

She walks over hurriedly, grabbing a box of tissue on the way. Crouching quickly where the blood has spilled, she begins to mop up.

"Open the window more – it's hot in here!"

A man makes his way through the cluttered room and throws the window open further. The wind moves nimbly through and rests upon Cynthia Gregor's brow, like a fly preparing to deposit larvae. It devours the sweat on her forehead.

"Finally a frickin' breeze – I feel like I'm on fire! Let's get this equipment out of here before someone notices. Hurry the HELL up!"

With the speed of an acrobat she moves to the window; slams it shut; and returns to her previous position. The biotechnician is beaming.

"Error message gone – the DNA arrangement looks pretty promising – all the A, G, C, and T combinations are there – though their not completely normal. It'll copy itself – and reproduce thanks to the promiscuity of the bacteria culture. It should be a synthetic recombinant success. We should start to see the silver granules forming soon..."

Cynthia Gregor grumbles,

"Let's go before any of the other brats wake up. Morning staff can clean up this mess. I need a smoke."

The team packs rapidly and exits; leaving only two things: the scent of her perfume and an alcohol swab with a drop of blood on it – the proverbial medical calling card.

Now, the boy is alone again; and dreaming.

..The blood red color of the swab on the floor has been replaced by a vivid blue crayon. In his dream, Zeke picks it up and scrawls out something on the daffodil-colored wall. He realizes that – for the first time – he has been able to write his name. He suddenly drops the crayon. It flies back up – an indigo colored bird that flutters before him briefly before flying away. It is looking for someone else – he knows it seeks Anna. Then – and just as rapidly – the boy falls into slumber.

When he awakens, someone is stroking his head. It is just morning; and Trudence Jefferson is gently brushing the curls of his hair; and wiping his forehead.

"How you doin', Bustah!? You done made a mess uh this bed. You jus' like makin' work for me – ya little 'stinkah'."

Zeke smiles radiantly.

"Looka' that face – like you done seen the 'bluebird a' happiness'. Roll over now, honey, and let's get you cleaned up. 'Parently, you done been out to sea – wet as this bed is! Cold in here – you leave the winda' open? Dream of that 'Miz Needles' again? Will you looka this mess! That Miz Cynthia don't nevah clean nothing' up – what she do all night?!"

True glances down and sees the solitary alcohol swab on the floor,

"Hmmm...will ya' looka this...."

Many miles away, Bob, the Indian has also awakened. Louise is shaking him gently.

"Time to get up, Bob – what are you smiling about?"

PART V

FULL MOON

REUNITED

He was so 'over' the shabby little town. He wished he had not agreed to accompany Sister Frances. The nun's quarrelsome nature was proving more difficult than being with the native tracker, Bob - and the leads he had hoped would come to fruition, were proving frustratingly insignificant. Still he felt a sense of indebtedness to Sister Frances. After all...she had saved his life.

'RC' had come searching for clues in the animal trafficking assignment that had previously sent him to the Chihuahua Mountains where his camp had been overturned and where he had nearly lost his life. What information he had been able to piece together after that incident, had led him to the border town where he now found himself with the nun. It was a place where many types of trafficking were known to occur...and the promise of resolution to one of his investigations was the only reason he had agreed to go on the trip. But the 'leads' weren't 'leading' to anything; and he felt despondent.

He had partnered with a local investigator when he arrived; and sought his help in closing the case. The man, a Detective Tweeter, was gruff and hopelessly stuck in the twentieth century – but he was helpful; and connected to the lab where 'RC' had turned in the great cranium that he had discovered in the desert of Coughdrop, Nevada.

It was 'RC's hidden hope that he might also locate the metallic micro-granules which he had surreptitiously removed from that cranium – and which he had lost in the Chihuahua Mountains. He hadn't felt right about not turning in everything to the forensics lab; and felt slightly guilty about concealing his secondary intention from Tweeter. Now the granules were lost. They apparently held a secret important enough to kill for. How could he have been so slow-witted as to leave something that important in a coat pocket that he had lent to the guide named, Sincero?

Since he had left the cranium in the care of a lab technician - he had been through two countries and a number of states of mind. In short, he wasn't sure he knew what was right or wrong; and was just mad enough to want to return to another assignment with Bob, the native guide. Though Bob made no sense to him...the man seemed oddly ethical – if not eerily psychic. And oddly...he missed that.

For her part, Sister Frances had agreed to accompany 'RC'. She was searching for a member of her church who had also disappeared from the Chihuahua Mountains. Relatives believed he had traveled to the same area to which 'RC' going. 'RC' and Sister Frances had 'made their peace' and decided to journey together. He would assist her and she would help conceal his identity by pretending their companionship involved 'service work' or a 'membership drive' on behalf of the church. They were miles away from the Chihuahua Mountains where she had found him – nearly dead. Both were content not to discuss the details of their visit to the dreary little town.

The nun had decided to stay in for the night – and though it was a cosmic relief – 'RC' had no idea what he would do that evening. He had spent the better part of a difficult day with the detective; and nothing new had 'turned up'. Now he felt empty as a cored apple. He regretted the trip. But...serendipity is a virgin birth.

In the distance, he saw the orange and pink sign which read "Chicken Lickers". Hungrier than he had ever been, he told himself that - if the 'joint' wasn't open - he'd pull up the sign and fry it in his own secret blend of herbs and spices. He'd finish it off in the parking lot if necessary. He didn't care if he died and came back as a chicken.

He walked to the entrance and pushed the door open. The sound of a 'dime store' bell announced his entry into the 'greasy spoon'. It grated on his nerves and gave him a headache. Who would work the evening shift in a place called "Chicken Lickers"...probably some 'loser'. Though he had already decided his dining choice was a new 'low' – the scent of breaded chicken was not without virtue. He strode towards the counter – unsure whether the decision had been a wise one; but with an emptiness that propelled him forward. Though he had only waited at the counter a few seconds, it seemed like an endless period of time before he called out impatiently,

"HELLLOOOO!!!..."

She stood up from behind the counter – clearly startled. She had been wearing ear buds and listening to music, while cleaning the floor. Apologizing, she brushed the long hair back from her face.

'RC' was smitten. Her face was round, but delicate – and exquisitely luminous. Her voice was soft and assuring as a lullaby - but held a gentle determination. More surprising...she was familiar. He glanced down quickly – conscious that he might be staring; and now very aware of the clumsiness of the situation in which he found himself.

Unable to stop, he returned his gaze – hoping that he did not appear as awkward as he felt; praying that the flush he felt was not obvious. She was looking at him mischievously. He looked away again; and his eyes rested upon a bouquet of yellow jonquils on the counter. It seemed oddly inconsistent but somehow reassured him about the eatery. He had long forgotten about food. When he returned his glance to her, she was looking like she expected an answer – or perhaps an apology. But Anna was simply mystified at how love had come home to rest. Her longing was over – still, she could not resist playing.

"C'est le serpent, dit-elle. Je l'ai ecoute, et il m'a trompee." And then she smiled, "Did you ever really memorize Alfred de Comte Vigny, 'RC'?"

He could barely look at her. He was remembering the past, his recovery at the beach, and the bottle with the message in it – that had floated up on the beach. Shame and embarrassment caused him to stutter a reply,

"I found... uh, the bottle... and your note...I..."

She cut him off, "I'm not surprised – we were meant to see each other again."

But it did surprise 'RC' – he didn't believe 'one spit' in preordination. The wind rocked the door back and forth causing the bells to 'jingle' as if someone new had entered. He looked back self-consciously; and then returned his gaze to her. Then he said in a voice that was dry and barely above a whisper,

"Anna..."

She smiled at him again; and replied,

"What happened to our bet, Mister?" She said it jokingly, wondering if it disguised the hurt she had endured.

"Bet?!"

There was no way he could deny his self-absorption or the confused mess of his life. He immediately felt cheap; and wondered why he had leaned on pretense. If he could have subtlety bitten off his tongue, he would have done it.

"But, how sweet, that you remembered my name." Why had she said something that would drive him away? She stopped and winked – hoping it would soften the blow. Then quickly added,

"College...don't you wish life was like a Christmas chain and you could just work your way backwards sometimes - correct the mistakes?! Never thought I'd be working here..."

He wondered if she was married or had children...and was trying not to show any interest. Before he could respond, she asked him,

"You look hungry – would you like a leg or a breast?" Then she flushed and wished that she had learned another way of asking a question that suddenly seemed cheap.

"Um...either. Listen, do you have any soda? If you give me a cup, I'll just go get a drink."

She gave him a cup and he strode over to the dispenser. It would buy him some time from the guilt, discomfort...and lack of answers. When he returned, he felt stronger. His curiosity had far from diminished. It had been years; and he needed to know more about her. He looked for a band around her finger – not wishing to be obvious. It was as if she had read his thoughts,

"Still have my name...no children – you?" She said it as a matter of fact.

"No time for either..." He wondered if his answer had been to blasé.

"Looks like you've got a lot of 'specials'," he continued – looking at the menu board.

"Nothing special about them...." she mugged, happy to restore some level of comfort. She was admiring his longish hair, day-old beard, and sturdy frame...trying not to show too much interest herself.

"You told me that we would contact each other. That was six years ago - must have a very busy life." She hoped it didn't sound too accusatory – or desperate. Then,

"What happened, 'RC'? Guess I could have hired a detective...."

"I ...uh...I'm late?"

"Cute."

"Sorry..."

"Would it have killed you to write a note - couldn't find a stamp?"

"C'mon, Anna, do we really need to do this..."

"Just trying to throw a little transparency on all of 'this'..."

"Can't we just bury old mistakes - put some rocks on them?"

She smirked,

"They usually come back as vampires unless you put stakes through their little hearts."

He laughed. And then, the jingle of the doorbells signaled the entrance of another customer.

"Oh, I'm sorry, m'aam... We're closed...closed about a half hour ago." She pointed to the clock on the wall. "Can you come back tomorrow... promise to give you a discount." Customer music - the woman smiled and left.

"Want me to lock the door?"

'RC' dug his feet into the floor. "Thanks..." he said quietly.

He glanced again at the jonquils on the counter.

"You seem to like flowers."

"What woman doesn't like flowers?"

Then she bent over so that her lips were just above his and her hair dangled near his face.

"Wanna start over again - it's getting a little too serious here."

"Um, yeah...mind if I sit down, before you play detective?"

"Not at all, handsome," she smiled. "Try not to break anything else." It was an allusion to her mended heart. Then she brushed past him; firmly pushed the door shut; and turned the sign around to read 'CLOSED'.

He watched her stroll – a beautiful creature holding the light. And the light – like any lover - returned the embrace. She came back and sat down next to him – glowing.

"What are you doing tomorrow? Wanna see where I volunteer my time?"

It relieved him that she wished to see him again. Before he could respond she continued,

"I'd like you to meet my boyfriend."

It was as if he had walked in front of a truck. He looked away from her toward the clutch of bright jonquils that suddenly seemed to wither – apparently she had someone else in her life. Why had he waited so long?

"I'm - uh - sorry ...I ...uh guess I 'm sorta tired. I well - uh – sure that would be good. You know, I'm still a little hungry," he said almost apologetically. His eyes focused behind the counter,

"Very good drawing..." he stuttered. He was looking at a botanical sketch that someone had tacked to the wall.

"Woodland plants are so interesting. Have you, ever seen a Trout Lily? Some folks call them 'Dog-toothed Violet'...or 'Adders Tongue'. They intrigue me and I don't know why."

He was afraid to respond. His disappointment at her having a 'friend' was unbearable. If he spoke he would sound like a blithering idiot. She seemed to notice his discomfort.

"It's been a long time, 'RC'...did you keep up with your French?

He could hear himself muttering something about an advanced degree in a biological science. His voice sounded disembodied; and he was trying not to look at her. She would, no doubt, see through the ridiculous monologue – but he couldn't stop himself.

"Um...yeah, well, 'Trout Lilies' are weird...course they're also called 'Dog Lilies' or 'Adders Tongues'...ya know..."

She interrupted,

"Your French, 'RC' ...your French...did you keep up with your French and old Alfred de Comte Vigny??...Or was our time by the river totally wasted?" It was a reference to their romantic forays at boarding school.

"Uh - sorry - I'm uh ...having some trouble hearing tonight. God! I can't believe it's you..." he stumbled along.

She laughed; and he felt her warmth. It only exacerbated the pain in his heart – a heart that had awakened and was dusting off. Rather than admit any regret, he lackadaisically responded,

"The only 'French' I've kept up with is of the fried variety. The other stuff – well it's too elitist."

She ignored the comment,

"You'll love Zeke – he's a great guy!"

'RC' couldn't muster the venom he felt for the man. Anna's smile was too disarming. If he really loved her, he would meet this 'Zeke'; and be happy for her happiness. And though he told himself as much...inside he was mourning a great loss. After a few seconds, he managed to misuse an honest tongue,

"Can't wait to meet him..."

The silence was uncomfortable. He stared at a large potted palm in the corner of the restaurant; and she gazed out the window at the cheddar-colored moon. Both were subconsciously drawn to things that made no sense - other than that they might be places to focus longing. Finally, Anna stood up and straightened her apron,

"You'd better stay seated, 'RC'. You look as if you've had a rough day. I'll bring some dinner...chicken, a light salad, rolls, old coffee - sound okay?"

He nodded, not really hearing her. She wheeled around; turned off the outside lights; and then sped past him to the counter. The mix of his emotions was murderous,

'How could he have been so stupid? Why hadn't he tried harder to find her? Who was this devil who had swept her away? How could he rid her of the miserable bastard? He dared not lose her again...'

But his head resolved that his heart should remain hidden. He would not show either his longing or his envy. He would stuff any such feelings in a place that was green and remote – his usual response. He prayed for an excuse to avoid a 'meeting' that would surely cause a plummet.

Minutes later she appeared with a tray of food that he no longer had any interest in. He could barely concentrate on it – still upset that she hadn't 'waited' for him. But he had been the one to leave – how could he blame her?

He could barely tolerate his desire just to watch her move and be in her presence. She seemed to sail on air – illusory, yet pleasant...familiar. She felt like home; and it wasn't fair that he found her more beautiful than he had remembered. Ridiculous poetry in every step – even the smudge of grease on her nose only made her seem more real.

It was at that moment, that he remembered something odd that had occurred months past. Bob, the Indian guide and he had been sitting – minions on a mountain around a great campfire that kept out the cold. They were trading spars back and forth – two very different people. 'RC' had resurrected a memory that – at the time – made no sense to him. The Indian had been 'reading the fire' – something 'RC' found appallingly stereotypical and ridiculous. Bob had said something about 'great happiness and sadness being found in something backwards and forwards'. Why was he remembering it?

The answer came to him more readily than he wished. 'RC' realized that the name 'Anna' was a palindrome. It could be spelled the same both backwards and forwards. He shook from the cold of Bob's 'reading' – wanting to usher it away. Then he pulled the collar of his jacket up around his neck, as if the cold wind had crawled into him.

BEDFELLOWS

A nna was speaking to him,
"You know, 'RC' it's so odd that you were my very last customer for the night. I had just been thinking of you and our times together at school... and the first time you jogged by – ready to throw your book in the river..."

She glanced up at him aware he had pulled up his collar,

"Hey, what's with the high-collar? You decide to become a 'man of the cloth'? It isn't that cold in here!"

He was barely listening – thinking instead about the absurdity of love. An entire industry had developed around hearts and heart-shaped 'everythings'. But love was rooted in the brain – not the heart. Scientists had proved that the brain was the seat of all emotion. Some compared love to a kind of addiction; and speculated that monogamous pair bonding had the same implications of a brain reward system as any addiction. Losing someone you love was not really much different than going through withdrawal. The study had been based on a prairie vole that mates for life.... Still, it didn't seem to explain the distressing sensation he felt in the center of his chest related to Anna's news about this man called, 'Zeke'. He could barely tolerate thinking the name.

And while his heart continued to beat irregularly, his head – the said 'seat of all emotion' – was busy trying to control what he should say to her. Then, as if something had flown down and lightly touched him, he felt her hand on his shoulder.

"You look like you've seen a ghost, 'RC' – you alright?"

He was suddenly 'belly-up' – he tried not to stare at her but the head began to lose to the heart. Before he could stop himself, 'RC' was reminiscing about their times in school. He confessed how much he had missed her – he had thought of her often. Finally, and after a few minutes, he realized he had been talking too much. He stopped and looked at her. She simply smiled and told him she was certain he would like her 'friend'. He tried to muster a smile in the face of his torture.

Perhaps, there are odd things which pull us apart; draw us together; and make us realize something about being human and the many sides to our lives. A series of oddly unconnected images – they light up our thoughts that seem part of a play, most foreign. At this moment, they came to him as if in a split-second trance...oddly unconnected but gratuitous thoughts that had a common halcyon thread.

...the gray-brown of a dun in a field...the beauty of mushroom with a fluted top...morning light reflected by a cloud...pounding surf...sliding through reeds in a canoe...the crackle of the fire...the redness of blood...and long flowing hair.

The thoughts - drawn together as if in common purpose and experience – are the closest thing to humanity frozen in ice. And we, lunging past the mundane, sought their meaning outside of cloistered lives. We look past the hobgoblin of meaningless repetition...and run toward a light which seems to draw us back to old suns. Then - through a tunnel of light – we fall to earth again...grateful.

When he blinked the thoughts away, 'RC' realized he was staring at her lips – and she was staring back. He thought of their earlier times together. Her frailty, warmth, silliness, shyness, occasional aloofness - even her total disregard for anything other than the present – a trait both agonizing and pleasurable...and something he did not understand. Her strength was surprising. She seemed able to lasso his soul; and bring it back from a purposeless flight. He could not take his eyes away from her exquisite neck and the small brocade of flowers at the top of her blouse. His heart was fluttering as rapidly as the wings of a bird.

Outside, the wind had increased. It blew hard across the parking lot and knocked over the café's sign. They both looked up, started for the door – and then stopped,

"'RC', would you like to walk me home? It looks a little wild outside... besides, I've got a couple of creepy neighbors. I thought I saw them pass by earlier."

He answered much more hastily than he was accustomed; and hoped she didn't notice the pounding pulse in his neck.

"Uh... yeah, it's late – you must be tired."

It was only minutes before they had closed up and exited the building. The wind had diminished and there was a sweet palpable scent in the air. The power of the evening was upon them; and the subtle motion of darkness had restored the nomenclature of night. The darkness lent an equal valence to everything.

The wind had successfully muted the heavy smell of the eatery where they had been – and made it a pleasant aroma. Insects hummed and buzzed quietly about; and stars shone about the moon like jewels in a courtesan's hair. A tomato-red sign nearby blinked with intention. They strolled together hearing the occasional mournful song of a night bird singing for a mate and the sturdy echo of response. It was a quiet time when plans are made, and divination is most intense. They studied the constellations above them and conversed through the drug of evening. He doted on her every word – warmed by her presence. They passed a stand of goatsbeard – laughing and letting their hands languish and play amidst the flower umbels. It was a well-kept garden that seemed to require nothing but notice. He watched the dance of her hair in the breeze; wishing to be nowhere else. The night's warmth was lotion - he dared not ignore one drop of it. If enjoyment be his cake, he would devour great chunks of it until he could no longer move.

In her restraint, he felt happy knowing that her attention had not run from him. He sensed that she was waiting and wanting something that required time - and which must be built carefully. But how could he dare hope for something that now seemed impossible?

He slowly walked her home, getting as close as he could – hoping the walk would not end too quickly. She asked him if he liked the town. He lied – and she smiled, and told him as much.

"You haven't changed a bit, 'RC'. You're still an impulsive and conniving little boy." He would have been angry if anyone else had said it, but the criticism was fair.

"Don't pout." she chirped at him.

The shadow of a large bird sailed across the moon. It momentarily rallied their attention; then it disappeared like vapor. Both wondered if they had seen anything or if it was simply an illusion brought on by the inebriation of happiness.

Feeling her distraction, he reached out and fingered a pearl necklace she was wearing around her neck. Then he let it drop gently. Had he been too forward? When she said nothing he asked,

"Can't we forget about this guy you want me to meet?"

A small smile and then a response,

"You'll like him – what he thinks of you is another matter, of course." And then, a broader smile...

He would press on with his attention even though his stomach was rumbling. Unsure of what to do, he brushed her shoulder as if by accident and then stepped back a little. If she had no interest, at least he might discover where she lived. His mouth was now drier than it had ever been; and he wished he had a bottle of water. He practically choked out the name of a constellation; pointing to it - and feeling her draw near.

He was still looking at the stars when he thought he saw the shadow of the great bird they had seen earlier. He quickly looked to see if she had also seen it but Anna was looking at the street before them. There were children playing and she remarked how late it was for them to be out...something could happen. Quietly he wondered about the shadow he had seen; and meanwhile thought of how he could heal the gap in their time apart.

How could he steal her back? Why wasn't she speaking? He was sure that she felt something. They passed an area infused with the aroma of some flower. She caressed his arm just enough that belief might breed hope. And then he did something that he had dreaded – and yet wished to do since seeing her. He ignored the deception of his thoughts...and freely kissed her.

She was not surprised. Instead, she let it happen as if she had expected it. Nor did she shrink from him, but seemed comfortable in his embrace. And though 'RC' enjoyed the passion of the moment, he could not help but wonder at how easily she had allowed it.

What of this man called, 'Zeke'? Was he that easy to forget? Was he what she said he was – merely a 'friend'? He did not wish to think it; but wondered at the ease with which Anna could forget the man. But he could not stop. Instead he resigned himself to the premise: that he had disarmed her; and the conclusion: that he did not feel selfish about it one bit. She interrupted his thoughts,

"Good kiss, 'RC'?"

He made light of the first sample and demanded another. She willingly gave it; and the language that had been so critical in bringing them together simply became an accessory. Only propriety could interfere with ardor. Anna was the first to pull away – believing that they should continue to walk, though now - arm in arm.

Neither could understand why; but it seemed as if they had been connected for a very long time. They discussed it briefly as they walked. Though 'RC' felt the connection, he did not accept any divine implication. His mind and experiences caused him to believe that the world he lived in was not governed by anything that cared about humans – either in impact or outcome. Life simply was. It happened without partiality; and there was no rational sequence to explain it. But he hid those thoughts out of selfishness. He did not wish to lose either Anna or the emotions he now felt.

Slowly like the bud of a jonquil that peeks out of the snow, emboldened with a pretense of power gained from the heat of the sun, he had begun to open. For once - and he hoped forever - he would release the sedition of cynicism that had made him leave her before. But he could not tolerate the concealment. He started to speak when she put her hand to his mouth - as much to close it as to keep it from emptying himself of chance.

"Please don't talk, 'RC'."

As they walked, he felt how her body and gait complimented his own. She was the missing piece that made his life less puzzling. Would it be what they both wished for? The strangeness of it all seemed to creep forward like something wild and quietly watching from a footpath. The strength of his feeling arrested any danger and kept it bent over in the brush, denied of its century's worth of hunger. He would walk festooned with dreams. The world would be their park and it would be a merry stroll. Let it be a lie - he did not care whether it lasted as long as the pyramids or was as short-lived as a bubble.

They reached the house; he implored; she fumbled; and the door finally consented – and slid open. She reached for the light and he stopped her. They kissed the way they had always wanted; and danced slowly, drifting together. And in the warmth of love, his cynicism melted. They did not talk; and when they had played out what they had come together for, she laid her head gently upon him.

Seconds dripped away like blood from a sweet wound. He stared into the perfect darkness of her iris. Then, and after a few moments, he returned his gaze to her form. The curves of her body were as dear a landscape as he had ever seen. The lunacy of love had grown in him like a seed; and it had popped open and sprawled like a silly vine around an Italianate ruin. It repeated the pattern of its growth until the vine surrounded an imaginary temple and wrapped him in a soft leafy shelter beset by blooms. So this was love? He would have died in her arms. Rolling over to his side, he drank in the scent of jasmine. She smiled almost imperceptibly, an alabaster Madonna in the moonlight.

When the first shafts of morning light struck a large tree outside her bedroom window, he was still enjoying the memory of their night together...and trying not to think of the Indian guide's prophetic statement. It was a bright morning. She bent and kissed him. And like everyone in love, he had become an artist wishing only to paint her exquisiteness. How had it happened that he was so quickly enveloped by warmth? His conquer was complete. Ancient harbored thoughts tripped and fell away.

She stood up. A breeze came through the open window causing her long hair to float around her like vestiges of the evening. That single image had the power to cripple any negative thought. With a slight movement he swept an irritated 'Beauregard' off of the bed; and pulled her back to enjoy the warmth.

The cat shot a peeved look at him and then trotted toward the kitchen to find food and water.

Meanwhile the day burnished as softly as a sweet potato ripening in the sun. It was many hours later and he wondered what had gripped him so that he had missed the day. He did not mind that it was night again. Now he was staring out through translucent curtains at the moon. A warm wind parted the curtains and blew across the bed. It enfolded them. He watched the curtains waft as lightning bug lanterns floated about. A distant cricket played violin. She was sleeping as if she would never awaken – and he was unsure if she was real.

On the dresser, the flame from a candle danced in the breeze. It flickered and reflected pieces of diamond light from some tiny brooch. In the dresser's mirror, he could see the dusky reflection of the two of them – dreamlike and changing into ethereal shapes – looking less like shadows than pieces of light. He leaned toward her warmth. She stirred slightly. He would not awaken her. Instead 'RC' watched the flame of the candle burn down to its remains; knowing that the deepest shadows were those cast by our own thoughts. As the room darkened, the passive illumination of the moon revealed the smoke of a candle disappearing into the night to become something else.

Far upon the hill above them, a crude house crouched unnaturally. A single brutal security light cut through the night. Its harshness made the sacred evening seem incomplete. The Gregors were at home; and their bickering flooded the quiet oblivion.

...And 'RC' held Anna in his arms – wondering how to explain the night and his absence to an expectant and intolerant Sister Frances.

THE DAFFODIL SECRET

A nna and 'RC' spent as many nights as they could together.
It was not as frequent as he wished; but he was walking a tightrope.
He had constructed a lie that – despite her stony stare - Sister Frances seemed
to believe. He told her that he was doing night surveillance work with the
local detective who was helping him with the animal trafficking case. Though
the lie came as naturally as breathing, he knew it would fly to pieces under
scrutiny; and would probably jeopardize any further friendship with the nun.
He wondered whether she would continue to be his 'cover' after she discovered the truth. She had accompanied him with a mission of her own – to
seek a member of her church, a 'lost child of God' as she referred to him.
'RC' reasoned that was probably enough to keep her with him; and provide
a 'safety net'.

But he felt unfocused – barely able to concentrate on why he was in the
border town. His priorities had changed so quickly. Often in the trim nights
that followed, he would lie awake staring at the ceiling or watching the chintz
curtains blowing in the wind that came through the window to Anna's bedroom. He had never allowed love to come between him and what he sought.
But this time...it was love that he sought. He despised the distraction; but
could not allow himself to leave Anna especially when another man waited
for attention. Curiously, she rarely spoke to him anymore of her friendship
with the man she called 'Zeke'.

Often at night the baying of wild things in the distance drew his attention. There were reports of coy dogs and coy wolves in the area. It made
him think back to his time with Bob - and their search for a mountain lion
that had successfully eluded them. He wondered where the Indian was; and
whether the cat had ever been captured. All of that seemed to have become
lost in the black ocean of time. Nevertheless, there were occasional reports of
missing hikers; sightings of peculiar animals; and oddly, the desecration of a
local church.

'RC' questioned whether his time was well spent; and he felt guilty about
the deceptions in his life. The lies had all been summoned because of things

he wanted. He had kept the micro granules from the skull in the desert; and it had nearly cost him his life and the life of a guide in the Chihuahua Mountains. He had hidden that truth from a detective who was helping him on the trafficking case. Now, the falsehoods extended to the woman he loved and the nun who had rescued him as he had lay dying on a cold mountain. He wondered how he could possibly seek any felon - when the criminal within him seemed to grow.

And he felt a growing jungle of uneasiness. He was concerned by changes that he saw about him. The assignment on which he had been sent, involved the illegal trade in species. But something was evolving – a nascent field involving the artful management of biology and law. Current news articles about unusual changes in the world – both interested, but worried him.

Anna, on the other hand, did not seem concerned about current events. If she held any opinion at all regarding them, she hid it well. Peeling off layers of clothing had proved easier than peeling off layers of her past. He longed to know more about her. She had a favorable disposition and did not seem to obsess about much of anything. Wherever she landed in life she seemed happy in her own light. She had a propensity for lighted candles and fingernail bouquets. Though both things seemed oddly anachronistic, they were in harmony with her personality.

Contrastingly, 'RC' felt as if he barely had been pulled from darkness. He was hesitant, careful, and sometimes wondered about the soundness of his mind. Infrequently, he allowed himself to ask why he was 'here'; and what difference it made. The retort – immutable silence – only served to turn the question back on him.

Immediately following the charming, simple days of his rekindled romance with Anna, the media issued a series of articles that - despite his happiness - drew 'RC' into further misgivings about the capricious nature of virtue and the evolution of any sort of human path. Though it did not make him question Anna; the thoughts he held related to the moral nature of mankind and its sustenance – began to vanish.

The first article – an expose related to an evasive mountain lion – disturbed him greatly; and made him remember his time with Bob and their attempts to track the cat that had killed the jogger. He had wished to leave that time behind him, but now wondered whether they had squandered their time; and what he could do about it. The animal must still be on the loose. The somewhat textbook approach they had used related to its capture had not worked. As Bob had said, they 'got the wrong cat'. The public now appeared to be dealing with an animal that was more sophisticated and required a new set of rules.

Days later - and hidden among mundane news about local interests and developments – a clever piece about an unsolved mystery was put before the public. It was a syndicated article that bordered on 'yellow journalism'; and appeared to be the local newspaper's attempt to draw in an audience that got their news from grocery checkout lines. The article was in regard to the unsolved death of a woman's husband; and the swift and utterly complete decomposition of the body. Apparently the remains had been improperly disposed of as medical waste; and a gargantuan vulture had benefited from the error. Though the article did not specifically mention Sophia Angaros, 'RC' knew of the woman; because he had heard of her narrative from Detective Tweeter.

But on occasion, there were articles that made even a cynic like 'RC' somewhat waggish and want to pound the table in laughter. The third article was just such a composition. The account involved the artificial production of two genetically identical human eggs fertilized by artificially produced – or generic - gametes. The recombinant DNA process, like any 'off brand', was deemed a cheaper alternative than obtaining 'donors'. Two genetically identical boys had been born. The befuddled mother was unable to distinguish them. Part of the generic spermatozoa which had produced the boys had been taken from other simian sources, specifically a chimpanzee. Lawyers, filing on behalf of a relative, determined that the boys were questionably 'human'; and that her sizeable fortune might not be inherited by them.

When he was not becoming depressed or amused over the news, 'RC' continued to work with Detective Tweeter regarding the animal trafficking assignment with which he had previously been involved. Meanwhile, in her quest to find the 'lost child of God', Sister Frances shunned the services of the blue uniform in favor of a uniform with which she was more familiar. She firmly believed that the Vati'can' had been aptly named to reflect its attitude; and that prayer – though important – was secondary in effectiveness to church gossip. She would find the errant church member...with the help of the church.

The days were cheerful and drifted on, quietly unpredictable. Though Beaumont, the cat, would not reveal the secrets Anna had told to him in confidence, 'RC' gradually began to unpeel the layers of her life. She only became more real to him. The cat, on the other hand, continued to show his contempt at having been displaced from the bed. He ignored 'RC' and became increasingly reticent.

'RC' learned that Anna had been born in Vietnam - plucked as a crying child from mud and blood - as if she had simply emerged as part of the complicated landscape of carnage. No living parents - she had been adopted secretly and with very little paperwork. The Army nurse, who was connected to a religious order, had just enough money to buy their tickets and return home. Once state side, the woman had rented a small flat where she cared for and raised the infant girl. Though their lives had been sparse, she adored the child. Love made everything seem plentiful.

At the periphery of the building where they lived, grew a bed of daffodils. In the spring, they shone like tiny gold trumpets - seeming to proclaim resurrection. It was a favorite memory of her new home – and consistent with the ever-present adornment of such bouquets about the house in which she now lived.

Too soon there was college. When Anna returned, her mother had disappeared – and had left everything to her. A simple note revealed the woman's intent – to let the girl start a life with fate tipped in her favor; and unencumbered by an elder parent. The mother would rejoin the religious order where she could do more good. She would be absorbed in the great sea of religion where any land might be her home.

'RC' listened to the story with cynicism. It made him angry that Anna's mother had abandoned her in favor of religion; and he didn't know how Anna could believe it. His distrusting nature would have him believe it was just as likely that her mother was having an affair in Ontario. But he continued to listen.

It had taken years, but she had located her mother. The woman had started a mission south of the border. Anna explained,

"It was her choice and I finally came to terms with her decision. I know you'll probably think it maudlin; but I sent some daffodil bulbs to the mission so she could start anew and help someone as she once helped me."

'RC' assured her,

"I don't think it's maudlin at all."

Then, as with any story where a puzzle is completed, he had a secret that made him happier than he could almost endure. He quickly pulled her close; and kissed her. He knew there was more than just one purpose in their chance meeting – and understood why he must immediately return to the right and reverent Sister Frances.

Before Anna could say anything, he had dashed out of the door, telling her he would return shortly.

THE CELEBRANT

He could no longer deny the ecumenical nature of the church; though 'RC' had always resisted any such edification or connection. Now, however, his efforts were for someone else; and he felt as brittle as an eggshell. His morality had been independently constructed and under his ownership. It included an odd measure of self-control constructed to comply with his beliefs. Surrendering to any external influence had always been beneath his dignity. He decided upon most things through well-considered analysis; and was confident in that approach.

Initially buoyant about his discovery related to Anna, he unexpectedly found that he dreaded every step that he came closer to seeing Sister Frances. He would have to admit to the lies he had created; and he secretly worried that her reproach might shatter the bedrock of his personal convictions. More than anything, he wished he could be as ingenuous and trusting as the woman he loved - and on whose behalf he now came forward.

As chance would have it, he met Sister Frances as she exited the elevator of the hotel where they were both registered. The energy of her stare nearly electrocuted him. Before he could stop himself, a drivel of meaningless conversation began to pour forth. Her interruption was vigorous and wrestled away any control he thought he might possess.

"RC, I did not get up this morning purely for the purpose of bracing myself for another round of idiocy - get to the point!"

Though it was the type of interruption he had become accustomed to from a Catholic nun, it abruptly bridled any conversation. No scholarly approach to his dishonesty would keep it secret. The study of words had failed him. Before he knew it, he had blurted out.

"I've found someone who I wish to spend my life with..."

Her response was well-executed,

"I will give you a new heart and put a new spirit in you; I will remove from you your heart of stone and give you a heart of flesh."[17]

She stood in front of him, smiling. But it was not the response he

---

17   Ezekiel 36:26

expected; and only darkened his mood. He did not share her rapture. The consequence of telling everything made guilt swell. For the first time in a very long time he wanted to run. He didn't understand why; but he cared what she might think related to the legitimacy of his relationship with Anna.

"We've already spent nights together...she's...um, originally from Vietnam...."

Her response surprised him,

"Do you think you're the only one who's ever been young...you love the girl?"

'RC's relief was solid, "I've never been happier."

"So your little secret is out. That's good, because I have one of my own. It's not exactly going to please you...and, no, you won't be able to pry it out of me."

He suddenly felt as if he needed to sit down. The exasperation 'RC' felt regarding a response that he had dreaded all day; and the fact that she was now keeping something from him, made him feel as exhausted as if he had been wrestling a steer. The vigor of his newly found desire to be truthful had waned. Could he risk telling her what he had deduced in his conversations with Anna? Sister Frances' secret had reawakened the initial distrust he had regarding her.

But as eerie as he found the nun's response to be, he could not ignore the valor of his purpose or the right of Sister Frances to know the truth about something that affected her. He reasoned that the nun's secretiveness must have been born from the experiences in her life. He had always felt that her seclusion in an order that he did not understand was not unlike discovering some supernatural and capricious forest creature for which one has responsibility. He wondered if the secret she kept might be finally released, if he simply closed an unfinished chapter of her life. After some consideration, he decided that he could not say what he wanted.

"I'd like you to meet her."

She walked through the opening as easily as if she had expected such an invitation.

"Of course I will, but I guess you know that I detest sentimentality. Now I must go."

It had not been that long since she had saved him on the mountain; and 'RC' had no reason to distrust her intentions. Sister Frances might never have known love, but she had a heart that was equal to her stature. The nun scratched her head; readjusted her wimple – and then left abruptly without saying goodbye.

His credit with her had been secured. Sister Frances' appetite for the truth seemed to be boundless. He felt like a child in her presence. The only thing that remained was the leviathan task of arranging a meeting between the three of them and feeling the metal of that truth once the nun learned everything. And he feared the retribution of her sharp tongue.

Minutes after Sister Frances's sudden departure 'RC' left the hotel. He didn't know where he was going but knew that he needed to walk and think. Eventually he found himself sitting on the edge of town by a set of worn railroad tracks. He looked to the right and left of him studying the straightness of the tracks and wondering why he hadn't the sense to take them in either direction. It didn't matter where he ended up – anything had to be better than confronting the nun with more of the truth he had withheld from her.

When, at last, he looked away from the track, he saw a large swath of blue penstemons in the distance, being buffeted about in the wind. Their undulations reminded him of two things: a stream where he had once met a most incredible young woman; and the blue ocean where he had recovered the bottle with the note in it – and that gave him the hope he needed. He would set up the meeting.

The time that passed seemed to be part of a dream. 'RC' was aware that they were standard 24-hour days; and marked the approach of the meeting between Anna, Sister Frances, and him. But the affective state of consciousness connected with the event seemed unreal. Everything moved in three quarters time.

The breezes, that had initially blessed the union between Anna and him, continued to play, though there was a tension between light and shadow that he had not noticed before. The sun rose triumphantly each morning; and was driven back to its western shelter in the evening. It always exited leaving a long scarf of color. The web of a large garden spider held a collection of mummified remains in its loose embroidery; and the strands formed crude alphabets above a bed of zinnias that Anna had planted. At times, the dew captured the light in the webbing of the spider's home; and it glistened like newborn sea spray. Beauregard, the cat, had grown as large as a hippopotamus - the result of guilt feedings which now substituted for the attention he knew he deserved. Wild grapes had become as sparse as hair on a middle-aged head - the birds had found nearly all of the fruit. The butterflies, moths, and skippers merrily floated about looking for last bits of nectar. Birds' nests that had been dislodged by past storms could occasionally be found on the ground. A pestilence of spots had developed on one of the wild cherry trees; and the leaves fell, creating a small dam in the street's gutter. The season was rapidly changing....

The formality of the meeting he had set up between the three of them was on a bright day. It had progressed as painfully as the recitation of arithmetic. All of the lofty defenses he had prepared to explain his actions had begun to crumble. If Anna noticed his discomfort, she did not show it. She had put on some music and was busy dancing to the beat of it in the kitchen. He sat in the living room watching her and wondering at the lightness of her mood. He had previously spoken to Sister Frances who indicated that her attempts to find the 'lost child of God' were coming to completion. She was ready to return to the mission. Unknown to 'RC' – though Anna danced – she had not forgotten the young man whom she had helped rescue in Frances Park. She too, would soon share a secret that was bigger than Texas.

Evidence of 'RC's nervousness had manifested itself in the form of a sore on the inside of his cheek. He had bitten himself while eating. Though he had planned to be productive that day, a spell of laziness arrested any spark of activity with which the day started.

Sister Frances had insisted on walking from the hotel to the address he had given her. As the walk was a long one, he wondered whether her insistence had been an attempt to unbalance him or if she was expecting a medal. And then, the moment he had so dreaded finally arrived. She was standing at the front of the house looking as hot and tired as a driven horse.

Anna was the first to see her; and went rapidly to the door. She immediately embraced her mother - much to 'RC's astonishment. The meeting could not have been more pedestrian. Now, he knew the nature of Sister Frances' secret. The leaden stare of Sister Frances then fell upon 'RC'.

"A gentleman would offer his guest something to drink."

She had read him like a book,

"How did you...?"

"I'm a nun!"

"But Anna...?"

"I have more than one bead on my rosary, young man."

So, that which 'RC' had been dreading for days – went without a hitch. The size of his relief was briefly matched by disappointment that his worry had been embezzled. 'RC' imagined that Sister Frances must have discovered the location of his nightly forays; and the two of them had played a keen trick on him. Only later would it be disclosed that finding her daughter had simply been 'another bead on her rosary' as the nun had put it – and another reason for her accompanying him on the trip.

Reuniting Anna with the woman who had adopted her, had some built-in unease, but also served to strengthen the bond he had with the woman he loved. 'RC' had resurrected a person who was most dear to her. And – even though he could not take full credit - he had been the unknowing catalyst that brought them together.

He listened as the two talked of many things: their chance meeting after the devastation of Anna's village, the rescue, the speedy adoption, halcyon childhood days, abandonment, despair, shame, discovery, and resolution. He learned that Anna had donated money for a local park and insisted it be named 'Frances Park' - after her mother. He envied them. And it was that park which pinpointed the end of Sister Frances' own search. For the 'lost child of God' was most certainly the man for whom 'RC' also searched – the guide named, Sincero.

In the meantime, their memories floated like a lotus on a murky and watery past. Their affection bloomed in the light of transparency. He marveled at the softening; felt its affect; and wished he trusted as much in the goodness of human motives.

The house they shared had become both home and fairy tale. Stars dotted the skies; and the oppressive summer heat had begun to embrace rather that smother. He started a diary; but called it a log. And in it, he wrote of their time together and drew pictures of Anna - adoring her more each day and falling absolutely stupid in love.

Anna, also felt happier than she could remember. She had been reunited with her mother; and a man that fortune seemed to have chosen for her. She laughed about the bottle that she had thrown into the ocean; and how it had been found by him – and knew that they were somehow meant to be together. She trusted 'RC' and believed his heart was wedded to hers. Their relationship felt simple with no hindrances – as if it could be broken off as easily as an animal breaks its gait when it does not work. But it did work; and neither wanted that.

She marveled at their chance meeting in school. It seemed ages ago. But now, it was time to move forward – to take a giant step - one which might prove the mettle of the man. Anna would test him with others – with someone who could give him nothing other than incomplete company and need. There was 'nothing in it' for 'RC' other than the satisfaction of knowing he might help someone who was vulnerable. The outbreak of happiness she had experienced with him had encompassed her - she found it alarming how much she was in love. And she too, began to wonder about its authenticity. Was it just infatuation?

She believed his heart needed further testing - not for strength or durability - but for space. Could he open up enough to let someone else in? Would he accept the task; and what would he expect? It was time to introduce him to 'need' and the odd value it held. Drumming her fingers on the counter, she wondered if the idea was a good one...and felt heartbreakingly dishonest in her approach. Why couldn't she simply be happy with what she had? As she worried about all of this, Sister Frances sat nearby slurping down dinner; and paying very little attention. When Anna could no longer tolerate fretting, she frowned slightly; turned to her mother; and asked,

"Why is happiness so intangible...?'

Sister Frances dropped her fork suddenly; looked at her daughter; and said,

"My dear...you're not old enough to understand that philosophy is always secondary to a fine plate of spaghetti." Then she continued eating.

With that, Anna was quite sure that she was worrying too much; and that a small star named Ezekiel was waiting to shine.

SHOOTING STAR

One morning, as she was watching 'RC' play with Beaumont; and stumble around the kitchen; Anna decided this was the day. He had finally mastered bagels and coffee. It was too cutely masculine. She knew that he didn't like to cook; but was perfectly capable. She would let it go, as she intended to bring it up again. But today she would show him where she volunteered her time.

His hesitancy surrounding the invitation was obvious. Still, he wanted to see where she did volunteer work. He believed it only underscored her strength of character and provided another dimension to her. But he also knew that this was where the friend she called 'Zeke' would be.

Part of him wanted to meet the man just to compare - and route - his competition. But he wanted to do it without appearing like a jackass...and felt very ill-prepared. 'RC' said nothing but found a nice fitting pair of jeans and a loose shirt that he hoped would render him sexy...while effectively dislodging the parasite that was sucking away at his happiness. When he reentered the kitchen from the bedroom, Anna stood there admiring him and then said,

"Um...I know we're not going to the opera, but do you think you could find some clean shoes and a nicer pair of socks."

He came back a minute later and sneered,

"Take five! Boy model returns with clean socks and shoes."

A piece of spinach was in his teeth. She would have laughed, but Anna hadn't slept well; and was worried. She had risen early enough to see the faint glow of the morning; but the Gregor house on the hill had a security light that seemed to compete with the equinox. It wasn't a pleasant way to start the day. She hadn't seen Zeke in a week; and felt guilty that she had put her own happiness before him. Beaufort was dancing around her ankles; and purring amorously. She knew he was hungry; and would ignore her when his attention was captured by the bowl of food she put down. All of these things contributed to her irritation. 'RC' noticed her solemnity and asked,

"What's wrong?" Then he caressed her arm.

It bothered her more that he cared. She had secretly decided to adjudicate his heart; and wasn't proud of what she had planned. The eastern sun hit her square in the face; and she replied,

"Oh, nothing...sometimes I just wish I could be clairvoyant."

'RC' thought of Bob, the Indian guide. He chuckled and said,

"Have you ever noticed that those who claim to be - never win the lotto?"

She averted her eyes and, for a few seconds; and stared at the Gregor's house on the hill above them. She knew that Cynthia Gregor had recently started working at 'the facility'. And, though she had never met the woman, she remembered the unpleasantness of the conversation she had heard coming from the Gregors' bedroom window the night she had been stargazing. It bothered her that people weren't what they appeared to be. She had trespassed and unintentionally been eavesdropping. It was also annoying that she had been so careless - she had intruded into someone else's conversation. When she looked back at 'RC', he was staring at her as if he was very concerned - and that worried her more.

She again questioned why she was so intent on exhausting their happiness. How could she risk dragging him down; and why did she expect him to be perfect? She made an excuse so she would not have to admit to what was bothering her - or risk driving him away – then immediately felt very selfish.

"I'm sorry, 'RC'. I think it's just 'my time' – don't pay any attention to me. I'm going to go put on a little bit of perfume...be right back."

It was a lie, but she couldn't bear to tell him the truth. Her heart had already decided about him, but her mind was not resolute. Anna left abruptly before he might leverage the secret from her.

Standing before the mirror in the bedroom, she briefly stared at her reflection. How could she question someone else's character when she was uncertain regarding the worth of her own? Frustrated, she took the perfume bottle, sprayed some on her finger and worked it gently around her chin and neck; but it did not make her feel clean. As she walked toward the front door, she saw Beaumont lying on his back. He was working his own perfume around his chin and licking his paws with it. She could smell the tuna that he had just eaten. He lay on the carpet - his swollen and satisfied belly-up posture was totally without pretense.

She exited the house; and found 'RC' sitting on his haunches. He was listening to a few early cicadas buzzing. Anna's peg brown dress fit her well; and lifted just above the knee. 'RC' couldn't take his eyes off her. He slipped his arm around her waist and gave her one of his widest smiles. Then they walked together down the block, past spring-manicured gardens which had withered under the sun. 'RC' felt uncertain, but dared not show it. He would take his adversary by surprise. The man she called 'Zeke' would barely be a memory after their meeting – but he had to appear sure of himself and dismantle the man smoothly.

As they walked along, he noticed that the sun had burned patterns into the grass. The patterns were not orderly; and largely based on shadow, light, and time. It made as little sense to him as religious revelation. The weather had been hot and dry. Walking across any living thing seemed criminal. Herbs that had once flourished had intensified in a heat which had cooked away any spare liquid that would render them subtle. They regulated other botanicals with their intense aromas and chemicals which seemed to moderate the margin between comely and noxious. It was an odd bit of order amidst seeming chaos. 'RC; thought it silly that the human mind sought order in a world intent on not having any. He wondered if there was an order that was higher - one that we did not understand yet; and marveled at the curiosity of the word 'yet'. He remembered a biblical passage that promised all might be revealed through acceptance and our passage from this life; but dismissed it as a simple and naïve notion. Then he thought of the bottle he had found bobbing about in the ocean. The chance finding of the bottle with a message from Anna in it temporarily dispelled certainty.

He focused back on the woman he walked with. She was exquisitely beautiful – a gift at this moment in time. Too soon the walk with her would draw to a close. There was a ridiculous poetry to the walk that he found enjoyable. Their teasing and the difference in their gait seemed awkwardly surprising and fun. Had he been walking with anyone else it would have seemed bothersome; and he lamented that too soon they would near their destination.

After a few minutes, they came upon 'the facility'. He had expected a large institutional brick building – poisonously parental looking inside and out. Instead, it was sprawling and comfortable with quasi-Victorian trappings, a buttery color, and a large flat lawn in the back. The entry was generous. A chandelier that looked more like a woman's brooch hung from the high ceiling in the lobby. Large entry doors that previously would have been manned now could be electronically controlled and opened. Any semblance of a door threshold had been eliminated. Someone had subtly constructed a makeshift ramp on the side; and discreetly hidden it behind plantings. The ramp was accessible to the driveway's portico and not visible from the street. An elevator had been 'built in' to the side of a generous stairwell; and it mimicked the paneling. Everything was minimally in accordance with statutory requirements; but had the appearance of some crazy savant wearing an unfashionable suit. A plaque on the wall indicated 'the facility' was eligible for meager funding. Anna walked inside without fanfare - as comfortably as if she had worked there for a lifetime.

As he turned to look at the wide lobby, 'RC' could see the beginning of large wooden puzzles that had been partially put together. It was obviously the room where children played. He briefly scanned the puzzles and marveled at their period appropriateness.

But he was most taken by the large bright eyes of a boy watching him from the edge of the room. The corner seemed to encase his small frame; and nearly hid his crutches. He seemed rooted there – and as fresh as new growth on an Elder.

OLD FRIENDS

It was very important to Anna that neither 'RC' nor Zeke feel subordinate to one another. She would find it difficult to choose between the two; and was greatly concerned about how the meeting between 'her men' would go. Her fearfulness vanished almost immediately - but for an unexpected reason.

"About time you got here! I been muckin' aroun' this place prayin' for an extra set a' hands! Den a' little thieves here! They intent on stealin' every last flower Big George done put in this vase for me."

She motioned to a nearly empty vase of flowers on the front desk. "I think they all done sudden got girlfriends!"

Then she pointed to Zeke.

"And that one in the corner there, with them big eyes; ain't nothin' but a little rascal!"

Trudence Jefferson, receptionist and all-around 'manager' of the facility was as busy as a small town on a Saturday night. She suddenly sucked in her breath and then exclaimed,

"Sweet Jesus!!! Well, tuck me into bed and say me a prayer!! You who I think you is?! ...WILD BOY!!!! Where you been?!!!!"

She closed down the computer on which she was working; and came running around the side of the reception desk with her arms open. 'RC's somewhat conservative approach to any sort of emotional display - disappeared as quickly as a false promise.

"True...Trudence Jefferson?!!"

It was Anna's time to be surprised. Though startled by their apparent familiarity, it made her feel comfortable in her decision to bring 'RC' to a place that felt like her second home. She marveled at the liberalism of life's connections. Having not realized that 'True' and 'RC' knew each other; she stood in astonishment; watching the mist of lost years float away. There were hugs, a litany of stories about 'the wild boy'; and a motherly scolding that she could scarcely believe.

She learned of the two family's proximity to each other; and that 'RC' had been close to True's first husband, 'Old Joe'. Time had become the seasoning to a most memorable dish. Anna watched the old friends cavort and remember the past. If for no other reason, she was now certain her decision to bring 'RC' to 'the facility' had been a good one; for she learned more about the two people before her in that space of time than she could have gleaned through years of friendship. But the reminiscence that particularly caught her attention was the one involving the death of 'True's' former husband, Joe; and the frightened 'wild boy' who had recanted the event, telling of a wind that seemed to have purpose. In the midst of that remembrance, 'True' interrupted. Turning to Anna she said,

"The husband of that hussy, Miss Cynthia, done come in last evenin' to pick her up. Big fool done asked me if you from Vietnam."

Then she abruptly returned to her conversation with 'RC'. The light from the window streamed in and bounced around their faces, lighting up 'True' and 'RC' in a moment of exquisitely unexpected happiness. They stood together as old friends; bathed in the luster of an unpredictable light.

Anna marveled at the foundation of a force she could only refer to as 'chance' – and for which there seemed no apparent formula. The marriage of logic and practicality prevented her from carrying the thought further. She would concentrate instead on the 'nakedness' of the man before her. The 'soft belly' of his past had been exposed and it was more intriguing than any theory. There had been numerous revelations regarding 'RC' which only sweetened her desire to know him better. The nuance of his feelings and personality revealed many shades to the man.

Then, she submerged into soulful quietness; feeling idly voyeuristic, but comfortable... when the boy came out of the corner. He was bouncing like a song; and obvious as an exclamation – and he was sucking on a cookie cutter.

"Zeke...? Come here and give that to me! I hope you've been making cookies, sweetheart...and didn't find that somewhere on the floor!"

He grinned. It fell out of his mouth – full of slobber. Then he ran clumsily toward her, barely able to keep himself from falling. Anna reached out to break his fall and to stop the inevitable 'clatter-crash'. The swirling little hub of activity fell to his knees as his crutches scattered. She rescued him just in time, grabbing him around his waist. He put his skinny arms around her, proclaiming loudly,

"Iaaahhh l-l-lub woo Annaaa!!"

"Boy a mess!" 'True' muttered.

"I love you too, Zeke-man! So whatcha' been up to today?!" She gave him her best motherly hug.

"Nub..nub..nuh–bin."

He lowered his eyes plainly hurt by something. She could practically hear cherubim sucking in their respective breaths from the clouds.

"Buuuh I saw biggah birdd..'ghin."

She drank him in. His eyes revealed everything. They looked like two sad little almonds. She rubbed his back and tried to straighten his tousled mass of hair. Anna could feel his body heave; and the quiet motor of his heart.

"I dreaaaahhhmmmed ahhhiee was b-b-birrrud, Aaahnaaa."

"Well Zeke, honey. If you want it – you'll be it. You'll be a wonderful, handsome bird soaring around the sky...playing in the clouds!"

She glanced at 'RC'. He and 'True' had stopped talking. 'RC' was observing the boy – as if he was trying to understand. It occurred to him that the 'man' he had been obsessing about stealing away his good fortune was not a man at all; and he suddenly felt sheepish. His behavior regarding meeting Anna's 'friend' had been totally juvenile. The boy was no threat – and at a clear disadvantage. But neither could he ignore that the boy was just as much a part of the orbital center of Anna's life...as he intended to be. He must get to know 'Zeke', if he wished to remain within the sphere of happiness into which he had wondered.

'True' could sense the discomfort; and pretended to busy herself straightening up the pilfered remains of the shaggy stems of wild red bergamot which Big Joe had picked from the low wet places on the edge of her garden.

"Ahhh jes love this horsemint." she said to herself. "Hard to believe they done practically fought a war over it."

Anna feigned mild interest,

"Whatever are you talking about, 'True'?"

"Oh honey, this what old folkses call 'Oswego tea'...what done been used as tea when the British got all hot about taxes...and them Boston folks tossed all they tea overboard. Smell it now – got a bit a' orange smell to it. Say it be used today as a flavorin' for them fancy English teas. My momma used it as a stomach settler. Ain't only new things that has a use...." She cast a sideways glance at 'RC' as if she were assessing his value; and then continued,

"Though you think with young-uns these days that ain't nothing useful if it ain't new. Shoot...they just as soon ask the moon to leave!"

'RC' walked over and held out his hand. Zeke flailed at it trying to knock it away; turned away from him; and stuck his thumb in his mouth. A gentle breeze had come through the open door - as if in synchronous greeting; but it did not seem to influence the boy.

'RC' tried again.

"Hey there, Zeke! My name's 'RC'...uh, I'm Anna's friend."

He was stumbling to find the right words. Zeke made a move to escape his attention; but 'RC' reached out and grabbed the boy's shirt sleeve, holding it firmly – and instantly realizing his mistake. His lack of experience with children was painfully apparent.

"Hey...where ya' goin' buddy?!" He smiled at him.

The meeting seemed incrementally more difficult than his introduction to the Bob, the Indian guide. The events became awkward. Zeke flailed and screamed. Anna's heart pounded in sympathy; and 'True' had hitched up her sleeve - prepared to send 'RC' into another universe, if required.

'RC' suddenly felt very clumsy. Zeke began to sob; and then started screaming like a smoke alarm. The commotion was attracting a small crowd. Amidst a torrent of tears and useless struggle, the boy cried out,

"Iaaaahhhh....d-d-d-ohnnn...liguhhhh...ooooh! Lefff m-mee goooah!"

The words stung his heart; but 'RC' would not let go.

"Hey, Zeke, buddy – I'm a pacifist. No sense in us being mad at each other!"

It was another clumsy attempt that did not work; but 'RC' persisted with his patent on trust.

"I want to be your friend, Zeke - will you be my friend?"

He continued to hold him...and noticed what he thought were subtle 'track marks' on the boy's arm. Zeke continued to scream.

A succession of light came through the lobby window. Outside, the honking of geese could just be heard as they rapidly headed for safe place near water and wild grasses. They would satisfy themselves on bugs and what bounty they could scoop out of the waters. Tassels of a cottonwood floated over a nearby pond like inflorescent angels in an afternoon sun. Bees buzzed about and tripped through the air – carrying pollen, nectar and wax home before evening closed in.

Inside the stern portrait of a man in a gilded frame decorated the wall. An impressive array of credentials routinely ignored and long-forgotten, formed a festoon below the frame picture. It seemed to draw the eye outdoors - as if dancing and pointing the way toward a festival. Fanciful yawning clouds formed wavy shapes; and the flowery scent of a woman's perfume languished in the air. It mixed with the odor of salt and sulfur from a nearby tract of low wet land. A cicada had started to hum like an unanswered phone.

Inside, a serpentine of shadows formed on the wall as 'RC' and Zeke continued to wrestle. 'RC' lifted the boy off the ground. A bellow from the protective 'True' reaffirmed the boundaries and his lack of authority at the facility; but 'RC' held up his hand – imploring another moment of patience.

He continued to hold Zeke close to his chest – absorbing his weak, erratic blows…until the boy finally tired and began to weep. Then, 'RC' pulled him gently forward until the boy's head was cradled on his chest; and quietly whispered into his ear,

"You want me to tell you a secret?"

And when he had finished whispering, the boy straightened up; looked at him the way a child will look when it expects unconditional truth; and then beamed a smile of monolithic proportions. 'RC' put him down and rubbed Zeke's head fluffing up the hair into a little cowlick. Zeke grabbed his crutches off the floor; and galloped off to his room - excited and with little memory of the struggle. 'RC' smirked – he had restored paradise much to Anna's dismay. She asked,

"What did you tell him??"

"I told him to go grab a jacket – because we came here to take him out for ice cream."

Anna shook her head,

"Cheap trick, 'RC'.... You can't promise that. We need special permission. They're rarely allowed off site - unless it's a supervised outing. You're going to disappoint him."

'RC' looked at 'True' who still had her face knotted up in anger.

"He'll be supervised. We only need permission from 'Administration' here."

'True' was sitting at her station again pretending not to hear him; and working on some older paperwork. She lifted her head just briefly, and then looked down again, feigning a lack of interest.

"Oh jes' git yo'selves outta here. I got some readin' to do; ain't got time for this foolishness."

She tried hard not to smile; and without looking up, said,

"I'll take a hot fudge sundae, lotsa' choclate and nuts – and don't forget the whip cream…if you evah wanna walk agin'."

Much to his relief, 'RC' had been given a 'pass'; but the nagging thought of the sight of needle marks on the boy's arm momentarily haunted his happiness and provoked a curiosity that – for some reason - drew him back to the 'silver sand' that he had lost in the mountain melee.

ANIMAL CRACKERS

Some time had passed since his initial visit to the 'the facility. 'RC' thought about Zeke – and reflected on his own insecurities. He had overcome his discomfort at meeting the boy; and was embarrassed by his initial jealousy and misperceptions regarding a would-be rival. Now he felt strangely 'parental'.

Zeke was endearing. Still, the sight of needle track marks on the boy's arm bothered him. It seemed excessive – or at least careless – and caused him to speculate about 'the facility'. He also wondered if Anna hadn't been unnecessarily coy. He was sure that she had built the meeting between the two of them to be more than it was. She had inadvertently fostered a false impression and created a rivalry that did not need to be there. On the other hand, their initial parting years ago had been due to his impetuousness. He decided to allow her the caprice to amuse herself at his expense. He had been a fool to leave her.

It was the middle of autumn. 'All Hallows Eve' would soon be upon them. They awakened to frost. The lawn in back of Anna's house seemed to have suddenly aged with white temples. The leaves were glorious. And -though there had been little rain in the early part of the year - nature had been less frugal in autumn. Time was spinning away quickly; and 'RC' was under some pressure to finish his assignment. The company that employed him was running out of patience. He felt sad and uncertain - not only because he did not know where the next assignment might take him; but he wasn't sure what it might mean for their time together. The season imbued the dreamy days with a sense of sadness and nostalgia; and it bothered him.

One day, the detective with whom he was working, gave him a stony stare. Tweeter rarely tailored his comments for anyone.

"We're not getting anywhere with your case. Unless you want to screw up your reputation, we need to somehow push forward with something - or drop it."

'RC' knew he was correct; but his world had finally become beautiful. He felt as if he had walked into a painting; and was just beginning to understand the 'madness' of love. He thought of Anna constantly – so much so that he could hardly concentrate on the task for which he was being paid.

He ached at the sight of her as she left for work in the morning – always wishing their embrace was longer. The middle of the day was dominated by thoughts of longing. The evening only seemed complete when she was beside him. But he also hated the giddiness. It caused a struggle within him which he did not like. A pirate had stolen his heart - and with it - his independence. Quite unexpectedly, his life had been made 'new' again. And he had discovered a calm introspection that seemed out of place. The stained color of autumn leaves made him feel as if he was sitting in a church. Though he abhorred any sort of religious feeling or connection, he could not deny the profundity of feelings that now held him. He dismissed it as an artful deception of nature – but wondered at the spiritual nature of the feeling. Giddiness was not a feeling with which he was comfortable – any soft underbelly was a risk.

Meanwhile the conflict between duty and desire bubbled; and seemed to portend an accident between the two competing forces. There was drug in the air; and he could not seem to escape its carnal control. Late at night, he would awaken and listen to the sound of Anna's heart beating. He kept his thoughts to himself. Surely no one's love was greater; and all who loved must feel so. He had dreams to sell. Some were meticulously beautiful; and some seemed to come from nether worlds, where spotted lilies popped up from low dark places.

That day, as Detective Tweeter and he were poking around files and trying to finish the case that was coming close to 'screwing up his reputation', 'RC' gained a most remarkable insight to the gruff man. Tweeter had reached for something in his wallet and a small piece of folded paper dropped out and fell on the floor. He did not notice. 'RC' picked it up and unfolded it. And though he felt he was being inappropriate, he could not resist. Inside was a child's drawing of a daffodil. It surprised him; and he immediately handed it to Tweeter asking,

"You have children?"

Tweeter grabbed it from him and then growled,

"Not that it's any of your goddamn business – but no!"

'RC' continued to stare at him as if looking for a response. When Tweeter could no longer stand it, he walked over to a coffee pot; and poured a cup of thick coffee. Without turning around he said,

"The kid was an angel. His mother was a prostitute with a drug problem; who didn't give a damn about him. I was doing nursery duty while she was looking for her next fix – or her next 'John'. The boy drew me a picture; and

I kept it...what of it?!"

It was the summary of a life in a paragraph. He could think of a million retorts; but was genuinely struck by what seemed the arbitrary governance of a man who always seemed to follow statute. Tweeter had a 'soft side'. 'RC' responded,

"Oh nothing... just didn't expect the archangel of fact to have a heart."

Tweeter wheeled around.

"Listen, kid – just because you recently discovered that you're not the 'tin man', doesn't mean we're all glowing with passion!"

'RC' smiled and then dug further.

"Are you saying, 'you've actually been in love', Tweeter?"

"I'm saying it's none of your business, 'dog breath'!"

He had found gold. He wouldn't let the conversation go that easily.

"So...you have been in love."

Tweeter did not respond, but his countenance revealed an aria. 'RC' smiled,

"My god – you ARE in love! What's her name?"

Tweeter's beefy fist suddenly shot out and grabbed him by the collar,

"You ever repeat this, and I'll be back for you - it's Sophia. Now shut-up." Then he released his hold.

'RC' decided to change the subject,

"What happened to the kid?"

"He wound up in a facility somewhere around here." The detective then stuffed the drawing back into his wallet and buried himself in paperwork. He would take no more questions.

'RC' really did not need anything to remind him of Anna; but the detective's response made him think of a recent morning they had together. He had awakened with dark thoughts about a large soaring bird he had seen in the desert in Coughdrop, Nevada...where he had found the gargantuan cranium. He had started the day worried. Something told him that he should not let her walk to 'the facility' alone. Besides he needed to check in and see how Zeke was doing. And he wanted to be immersed in the race of human activity...not alone with his own thoughts.

Together they walked arm-in-arm into the overwhelming scent of autumn leaves. The colors swirled around and spilled upon the lovers like shavings from a box of children's crayons. The birds had moved on – it was quiet. Sweet sadness and decay were all about. Anna was distracted – she was thinking of Zeke. His stories of seeing a large bird had become more frequent and were igniting concern in 'the facility' – regarding his overall health. Zeke had also reported seeing a two-headed dog running around outside. He was espousing claims of mythological proportions and appearance. It worried the other children. Anna paused; stopped for a second; and then, looked at 'RC' and asked,

"Do you believe in the Deity?"

'RC' paused, took a shallow breath; and then said,

"I see you've been talking to Sister Frances again."

She frowned.

"It's just that everything seems to start out in balance...and then we come along and 'muck it up'."

"Yes, my love, it's called 'evolution'."

"Maybe so, 'RC', but 'what' is balance and 'why' does it matter? Do we humans even know what balance is? Seems sort of arrogant to think that only we know what it is and can somehow restore it. Perhaps there's more to it – more to us – you know, a greater influence that takes care of everything...regardless of how we mess it up. Seems like something had to start all of this...."

It wasn't like her to be worried; and she was treading into an area with which he had a great deal of discomfort. They continued to walk for a few minutes while 'RC' thought what to say to her. Finally he stopped, gently grabbed her arm,

"Penny for your thoughts..."

She seemed astonished that he would ask.

"It's nothing..."

He didn't believe her.

"What's bothering you, Anna?"

She paused,

"Zeke was snapping the heads and legs off of some animal crackers the other day...and making new animals...it bothered me. Silly isn't it...kids have vivid imaginations."

"Seems perfectly healthy to me..."

"Yeah, I know, 'RC' – but when I asked him why... well, what he said bothered me."

"He's just 'acting out' some fantasy."

"He said he was making 'new animals' so he wouldn't be scared. But I don't understand – scared of what?!"

CANDLEFISH

"HEY, VOODOO-WOMAN..." Sincero shouted.

Sue Bee and Sincero were drifting lazily in a skiff on the bay. He was dangling over the side of the boat trying to pull up something that was caught on his fishing line. Laughing gulls circled overhead looking for a free treat. The wind beat against the boat and then - just as suddenly left. Sue Bee watched Sincero struggle with whatever he had caught; and she marveled at the unsought and lovely discoveries in her life...though she would never admit to it.

It had been a few months and getting to know him had been difficult. She had labored against his initial distrust – and why wouldn't he be distrustful? The memories of the horrific beating and molestation he had endured in the park, needed to 'play out'. He needed to feel 'whole' again; and to come to terms with the grittiness of what had happened at the hands of men who could only be sated by atrocity.

It had taken a week before he could use the bathroom without pain. But he had been steadily healing; and his recovery had been quicker than she expected. More than once he alluded to a bag of something that he had swallowed...something that he had expected to bring him money – and with that – a ticket home. In the punishment that he had endured - whatever he swallowed - had been absorbed into his body...he had probably passed the rest. Sue Bee was certain it was drugs. She had heard that swallowing contraband was a common technique. It could be concealed in a plastic bag; swallowed; and eventually voided by its carrier once they were in a 'safe' location. She immediately felt guilty about her suspicions. It was not right for her to judge Sincero when she knew so little about him. Just as rapidly, she released the guilt; and yelled,

"Hey don't call me names, 'burrito buns'! Or I'll throw you overboard - and the sharks will have a snack!"

She made a motion like she was throwing the dead weight of an anchor. Sincero smirked.

"Fish come this way – many. Come take look..."

She stood and stretched. She had been quite comfortable watching him act like a child on the rented boat. It had cost money that she really didn't have - but a day of play was as necessary as a plate of beans...to her way of thinking. And the advantage of being under no particular time constraint to bring the boat back to its mooring had 'sold' her on the frivolity of the expense.

Sue Bee walked over slowly – testing her 'sea legs' – and then grabbed a handful of his long dark hair. She whipped it out of his face, like it was a mane - managing to caress his cheek ever so slightly. Sincero ignored her.

"You no understand. These good fish. We call them 'lagarto lucio'. We not know why they come. It mystery no man can control..."

She watched him practically hanging from the boat. It was part of a magic that he believed in – and something she envied. To her, there really wasn't much enchantment in the world. She marveled at his naiveté and sense of wonder. More than that, she wondered at his resiliency. He had almost totally rebounded from the incident in the park – though he seemed shy regarding any contact.

"C'mon', Sue Bee. You catch one. You see what to do with them."

He suddenly tied his long hair back with a rubber band – something she hated. She loved the way it floated across his chest in the wind. Sincero looked up at the skies, as if he were studying the sky like a meteorologist. Then he murmured,

"Pelycano..."

"Chess who you callin' a 'pelycano'!"

He looked mystified; and she realized they hadn't understood each other.

"C'mon, Sue Bee...life be what you make it!"

"In that case, I'm makin' it 'easy'! Knock yo'self out while I pretend that you ain't tedious!"

She returned to a deck pillow and plopped down on it. It was a fine warm day. She was reading a good book; and had just poured some wine in a plastic glass which she balanced between her legs. Occasionally she would sneak looks at his slender form. It worried her that his stomach was still slightly swollen; and she wondered if the beating he had experienced in the park had caused some internal injuries.

Sincero quietly reached down in the water. He seemed to be idly looking at the disorderly patterns the boat made in it. Then, with a sudden jerk of his hand – he splashed her; and she screamed out,

"Ya' little creep! There's one part a' you that ain't tanned yet – and I got a belt that'll take care a' that!!"

He stuck his tongue out; and laughed at her. She responded,

"I swear you are so goin' overboard. Wash some of that smart ass right off a' you!"

"I bored, Sue Bee. These fish are milagro...miracle. You come fish with me...?"

She gave him a disgruntled look; stretched her arms lazily; yawned and then wiped the specks of water off of her book. Then she idly walked over to the edge of the boat in time to spot a tremendous group of shiny fish wriggling in the water.

"Lord have mercy! I ain't seen a school like that ...since I was a custodian!"

"Get net! Get net!!" Sincero was twitching - and pawing desperately at the water.

"Net HELL – you could probably use a bucket!"

Sincero ran back and forth wildly. He 'zoomed' over to the other side of the small boat; and pulled a coil of yellow nylon rope and a wad of sponges out of the way until he found the net. He ran back so quickly that she wondered if there might not be two of him.

"Queek, Sue Bee ..." And then something else in Spanish....

"Would you just hush? You makin' me nervous...don't understand why you're gettin' so twitchy 'bout some stupid fish. Don' make no sense to me... they ain't chocolate!"

"They good...we have plant called ..." She missed the name.

"...make taste good!"

"Um huh, so glad to hear it...!" She rarely ate anything that wasn't pasta.

The fish swarmed the boat. The evening light seemed to have become part of the bubbling froth. Sue Bee grabbed the net from Sincero; and quickly dipped it into watery explosion; and pulled out a net full of fish. They wriggled like caught snakes; and stared at her with glassy eyes - gasping and throwing themselves about on deck.

Sincero thrust out his hand; and pulled one of the fish to his lips. He immediately bit off its head. Then he swallowed the rest of the fish whole. Sue Bee stared in shock. It made her think of the 'wild boy' she had once known. She rubbed a scar on her hand.

"You ever heard of cookin'?"

"Si! Ahnd you AIVER hear of hungry?" He pulled out another fish and thrust it toward her,

"You try!"

"The HELL you say! I like my meat cooked! I ain't no sushi-lovin' city girl!"

Sincero urged again,

"Try, Sue Bee...you scared to try?"

She couldn't stand a 'dare'. Sue Bee made a face; held her nose; and quickly bit the head off. She could feel the last wriggle of the fish as she severed through its delicate spine – it tasted oily. She thought she could feel the eyes move and taste the blood on her tongue. The taste was more subtle than she imagined. She quickly spit the head overboard; made a face – letting the rest of the body slide down her throat. Then she grabbed the net from Sincero and walked rapidly over to the other side of the boat to wretch.

Sincero laughed until his throat hurt. 'Yep' she told herself, 'all bets were off when it came to sushi'. She stuck a finger down her throat – and gagged slightly. When she was sure that no more of the animal was coming out, she said,

"It ain't exactly pizza! Give me that wine – stuff tastes like crap."

"You want another piece, Sue Bee?!"

Sincero was waving it beneath her nose. She smacked it away; and wished she had a stick. Together they watched the sun set; finished a bottle of wine; laughed and then pretended to be Vikings by blowing into the bottle and making sounds.

Her thoughts drifted with the boat. Did he like her? It would be cheap to ask; and she couldn't risk the chance of ruining a good friendship. She decided to say nothing. Instead she watched the disappearing collage of colors in the evening sky; and pretended not to notice his doll-like face. Sincero quickly bent down and picked up one of the captured fish left on the deck. He rinsed it off while she quietly admired him. He was unfettered by possessions - and didn't seem to care. Money only meant something to him when he needed to eat. His outlook was alluring – though slightly disgusting...particularly when she was wishing for a hot fudge sundae. Then she quickly said,

"Unless it's a hamburger – I ain't touchin' it! Makes okra taste like a crepe!"

A soft breeze joined them on the boat. For this short time, things seemed perfect – except for the unrequited stirring which she could not talk about. Sincero whipped out a knife. He stuck it hard into the mouth of the dead fish and then up-ended the fish in a crevice on the table.

"You have match?"

"Forget it, baby. I don't even want it if it's cooked. I got some real food down inside the boat."

"Need match, Sue Bee."

"Suit yourself – but I ain't eatin' any of it. I'd rather eat a dog."

She pulled a cigarette lighter from a nearby duffel bag. Then paused...and quietly wondered if and when she should turn him in to the authorities. The thought nearly broke her heart.

Sincero flicked on the lighter; and held it to the tail of the up-ended fish. Suddenly it caught fire and began to burn steadily. Sue Bee backed away looking in amazement. Sincero repeated,

"We call it 'lagarto lucio...it become light again." Then, "I think you call ...'candle feesh'."

"Works for me...light a couple more of those things. It all a' sudden got damn dark out here."

The clouds ran like dun mares through the twilight sky - the wind's tongue licking at their heels. Worry twisted its way through Sue Bee's thoughts. Sincero had no right to be here – and she knew it.

She watched as he up-ended more of the fish and placed them around the boat. The perimeter glowed in the darkness. Sue Bee trilled her approval; and opened up another bottle of wine...trying to forget the conflict she felt inside. The flickering light made the Beaver Moon - appear to wriggle in its slow path across the sky. She idly looked across the deck at the candled beauty of the boat. When she looked back at him, Sincero was staring at her as if expecting approval. She smiled,

"Well, ain't you 'the romantic'?"

Then she quickly glanced away and turned on the boat's radio. It was playing soft 'chank-a-lank' music. He poured a half glass of wine; swallowed it; and fell back lazily on the deck – gazing up at the stars, truly happy. She could see the reflection of light in his eyes; and tossed a jacket over him, saying nonchalantly,

"Freeze your butt off..."

They turned over to watch the foam on the water – absorbing a contentment that she had not experienced since she was a child. She thought of lying in the grass – head in her mother's lap – counting stars while her father, 'Old Joe', played the harmonica.

As the last clouds were softly blown out of the sky; and night drew sequined curtains shut. The boat floated like a giant candle – rocking back and forth gently. In the dimming light, Sue Bee could just barely make out a series of tiny raised bumps on Sincero's skin. She reached out her hand and stroked his arm. He pulled away from her suddenly. Self-conscious, she withdrew her hand. She had moved too quickly. Perhaps he was offended. She drilled her hands deep into her pockets – wishing she was more patient. Sincero said,

"Itch,"

The light danced down from the watery moon. It seemed to waiver about him in uncertainty. Sue Bee felt an uncustomary emotional depth. For the first time in a very long time – someone had 'touched' her. She shrugged off the thought. If there was any order to the world, she was certain it must involve a dream.

"You lookin' like you done got too much sun. Let's get some zzz's. You feel better in the mornin'."

Sincero fell asleep almost on command – the rocking of the boat was like a cradle. Sue Bee could not – instead, she stole a furtive glance. She watched his chest rise and fall. She would not sleep this night; because she could not risk missing the light of dawn resting on his skin and in the waves of his hair.

Then, softly and lowly she began to sing a song her mother used to sing. She sang it for the sleeping Sincero - she sang it for herself. The light from the candlefish seemed to leap about like deer returning to the night sky. Perhaps, she thought, the heavens were where all the disenfranchised eventually go...to roam through sparkling fields.

PART VI

ECLIPSE

CONFESSIONAL

The slight rises on Sincero's body had given way to welts in a short period of time; and Sue Bee wondered what had poisoned him. She was worried. Meanwhile the town and its people changed not at all. Life in general seemed to continue the way it always had...while she watched her part of it falling away. The sun was no longer king. The soil had grown colder. The daylight had shortened; and the days sometimes seemed fatiguing. But few seemed to notice. She wondered if she was depressed.

Still, she searched for brightness - like most living things do. In the corner of a nearby yard she had seen a small snake coiled up. The animal was cold; and sat quietly looking out at the world as if perhaps, wanting one more meal. The patterns on its body looked like embroidery. Thin sheets of ice sometimes formed designs on her kitchen window. An old tree had a hump that looked like a goiter; and she fancied that she saw a face in it. People huddled together in small groups as they walked down the sidewalk. Some, romantically joined hands and loitered together as if to have a few more minutes to talk; and discuss exotic adventures or future plans. Noisy grackles made mechanical sounding chirps that sounded like synthetic music.

Finally, when she could stand it no longer, Sue Bee insisted that Sincero should go to a doctor with her. He claimed he was too busy – he was studying English. Sue Bee had given him books to read, but he was learning more by watching television. His stomach had swollen; and she worried about internal bleeding. The cajoling practically killed her; but he finally agreed to accompany her to a free clinic.

The internist was a young man. What he knew about medicine seemed less than what he knew about other cultures. He studied Sincero intensely; took his blood pressure, temperature, weight, and height measurements – and then, jabbed him with a needle drawing several vials of blood. Sue Bee wondered if the man had discovered something about the 'photo-shopped' ID they had bought. Her heart was racing. The internist looked up and asked,

"You Mexican..."

Sincero – who was anxious to show off his knowledge of the English language and to put himself on more of an equal level – yawned,

"No, sir, I am ..."

But Sue Bee gave him a silent signal; and stared at him hard. The internist continued,

"I'm sorry – you were sayin' what?"

Sue Bee quickly answered for him - nearly stumbling over her words,

"He's an exchange student – staying for awhile." Maybe go back soon..."

"Ah...from Spain - you know Madrid?" The intern seemed to be trying to decide Sincero's origin. Sincero responded,

"No sir, I don't know it."

Sue Bee interrupted again. "What he means is he don't know it well – little glitch in his English! He from another part...." She seemed to be importing lies as easily as if they were in a suitcase going through customs.

"What part is that?" The intern was now looking very suspicious.

"Mmmm…" She looked around quickly until a sliding transparent panel at the reception desk caught her eye. "Pleksilla! Yeah, believe thet's how they pronounces it. Ain't that what you called it, Sincero?" Before Sincero could register his disbelief, the internist said,

"Plecsilla - never heard of it." He seemed confused by Sue Bee's rapid fire responses on behalf of the patient.

Sue Bee launched into her story. "Weh now, course ya wouldn't. Believe it's very remote...my pernunciation might be off. They don't have much there – except spare time. Done come up with this new product...You mighta heard a' 'Plexiglass'?"

"Everybody's heard of 'plexiglass'"

"They ya go. Yep – plexiglass – that be it...fresh from the Pleksi Mine. I think they calls it 'Mino Pleksi' – ain't that right Sincero?" Before he could respond, she smiled. "I think the Indians work in it." Sincero stared incredulously.

"Yeah, the famous 'Mino Pleksi' – they poah there, ya know." And she smiled again and pretended to brush off some lint from her blouse which was white as the spathe of a wild calla.

"Hmm…that is incredible – but I thought foreign exchange students received some sort of grant or stipend..."

Sincero was looking down at his feet; and listening to the rumble of his stomach. Sue Bee answered again for him,

"Yes, indeed. They done branched out into other areas with that plexiglass stuff. They use it for them 'condominiums' – I think they call it. You evah use them? They got them tiny ribs...better'n flowers on Friday, honey!"

She was enjoying the effect her feigned ignorance was having on the man.

The young intern cleared his throat. He was obviously embarrassed. "Uh…let me write you a prescription." He hurriedly grabbed a note pad with his pre-stamped signature and which bore the title 'Rx' in large blue cursive letters. Then he dashed off the medicine's name and signed it with a series of fancy but unreadable loops, and put the pen back in his breast pocket.

"Oh, I know you do!" Sue bee remarked, as if she hadn't heard him and then said,

"Nice 'John Henry', 'Doc'! They say you can tell a lot about a man by his signature. Yours looks like my man's, – all curvy, strong, and sexy." And she smiled flirtatiously – and winked a bit. The two seemed to stand at the precipice of different worlds.

"Been a real pleasure, honey…" And she offered a gloved hand – she had dressed like she was going to church. The internist seemed confused but took her hand in his own and then rapidly left. As soon as he was gone, Sue Bee took a small container out of her purse, unscrewed the top; took a swig; screwed the top of the flask back on. She took a tissue out; and patted her forehead dry. Then, she blew her nose on the tissue – and threw it in the trash.

Sincero and she walked rapidly from the examining room, down a long corridor, and out of the building. On the apex of the building's entrance a large bird perched. It looked primordial – like an odd gargoyle. Then, as if it had received some unheard and ancient command, it flapped long wings and soared away on a muscular wind. Neither Sue Bee nor Sincero noticed as they busily talked. Sincero said,

"Plecsilla…Quexicattle…?"

It bothered him that she might have lied. Finally he resolved that the conversation had been nothing but allusions. And he was certain that allusions were not the responsibility of the person telling them - they were the responsibility of the listener. He was relieved that she would not suffer the curse of a heavy soul. The valence of her character had been restored, in his mind - but he still had questions.

"Sue Bee, why you mislead man?"

"Oh, hush up, boy. What's matter with you? You cain't be tellin' some doctor where you from. Like you havin' a date with 'Immigration'! They ship you little brown butt back to where it come from. Tryin' to take care of you here - so you don't get yo'self beat up again! Besides, I ain't misleadin' him. He leadin' himself down his own path - I think God forgive me."

Realizing a similar conclusion, Sincero suddenly said,

"I hungry!"

"Well, why'nt you say so!? Whatchu wanna eat?!" "Spare ribs...egg roll?" Sincero replied, "Fried chicken!"

It startled her. "Damn! You gettin' good with that English! Course...who don't know fried chicken?! C'mon, let's go! It's Sunday, we gotta find somethin' open...maybe 'Chicken Likkers' open t'day."

She was halfway in the car - and he was still standing there.

"Hey! Whatsa matter with you? Get in the car – this ain't no 'manana time'! I'm tellin' ya – it's Sunday!"

Then, she heard a sobbing that broke her heart. Sincero slumped against the car door. He could no longer conceal an internal torment.

"These bad men...I never be the same. They hurt me – and the metal sand inside of me – now part of me. Don't you understand, Sue Bee – I sick! I never be the same again! I hate them! I hate me!"

It was a reference to what had happened to him in Frances Park. She leapt out of the car; and grabbed him with all of her strength. Then she held him; and stroked his hair. What could she say?

"Shush-shush-shush....We just trottin' around a little too early is all. You tired. You feel better when we get sumpin' to eat. Ain't nothing that wrong with you that chicken, hash browns and a milkshake won't make feel better." It was a desperate lie.

It did not stop his anguish. "Sue Bee, why you like me? I a mess – a Two-Spirit foockeeng mess."

It was a priestly confession that surprised her. Though she had hoped for such an admission - Sincero's agitation made the victory seem sad. What could she say?

"I don' like you, ya little fool – I love you! Whatchu mean - 'two spirits'?!"

She had rallied forth in his defense and then worried that she had said too much. But Sincero seemed to ignore it.

"That's what they call us. 'Two Spirits' – you know, man/woman...between two worlds – like ghost that go back and forth. I not want to be like that..." And then he stopped.

She looked away from him; and loosened her grip – not quite sure how to handle an intimacy with which Sincero was not fully comfortable. Slightly hurt, she patted his arm; and tried to hide her disappointment. He had never shown any intention of intimacy; but was now hinting at a possibility. Bawling like a baby, he had dropped any pretense. Then she quietly uttered a line from an Alberta Hunter song,

"Honey, you can't tell the difference after dark..."[18]

---

18   Alberta Hunter, internationally known African-American jazz singer and songwriter, b. Memphis,

It was then that the great bird had flown back as if to reclaim its favorable position on the apex of the hospital roof. It sat like a troll, and clawed at the roof as if to write something in cuneiform. It loomed with a wing outstretched – looking like the bearer of some ancient flag. Sue Bee did not see it; but had noticed the large shadow it cast.

"Damn! What was that?!"

Then she dismissed it. Things were complicated enough and she didn't believe she could handle any more tragedy.

"Somebody must be flyin' a glider..."

She put her arms around Sincero protectively. She was worried that she might have been too glib in her response to him.

"From now on, you ain't gotta worry about the 'why' I love you - 'jes you know that 'I do'; and you can depend on that!" Then she changed the subject - things were getting too serious.

"You like football?"

Far to the west of them, Bob, the Indian guide was moving around slowly in the late afternoon sun – he felt the stiffness of his age. He had just bent down and taken a bite of out of one of the green tomatoes that the frost had spared. He liked the tartness and wondered if the remaining garden tomatoes might be ready for the frying pan.

Something made him look up at the sky – he wasn't sure what had commanded his attention; but noticed a warm wind had come; and the clouds were racing away. Could it really be that the wind was whispering something to him? He was quite certain he heard it say,

"Winieke he iyotap wowa sake..."[19]

It seemed to be telling him that it was time for a journey - for something was at the precipice of the Turtle World. He believed in the wind just as he believed in all forces of nature. Though sometimes self-conscious about any such nativism, the Indian knew that all humankind believed in something greater. Faith demanded unrelenting acceptance without proof. He thought of the wind's gratuity again. Who was he to question an ancient force which had touched every living thing? Secrets came from many corners...we just needed to listen.

Tennessee; (1895-1984); 'Downhearted Blues' album

19   'In truth, there is power'.

BEE IN THE BONNET

Determinedly, she crawled up the last set of stairs – taking deep breaths and devouring air. Her 'habit' was moderately soiled; and the emptiness she felt in the pit of her stomach made her hungry enough to eat a punching bag. She was trying to remember a scripture she had read earlier in the morning in preparation for her meeting with a church member whom she would try to convince to return home. It was a promise she had made to his relative before she and 'RC' had departed on their trip together. But Sister Frances was not feeling very pious. Her clothing was too heavy for the humid climate; and the ample frame - which had borne her easily through life – now felt insufficient. She wondered if a caterpillar could have ascended the flights of stairs more rapidly.

Inside one pocket, she carried a rosary. Inside another, she carried a daffodil that was now crumpled. The flower was something that Anna had given to her mother – insisting she needed something to make her look less severe. Quite by chance, the two of them had been talking about 'Frances Park' – the park which Anna had named for her – when Anna had recounted the rescue of a young man she had come to know as 'Sincero'. This was the clue Sister Frances needed. She immediately located the address and number; and set up a time to visit the young man. But the directions she received from his 'custodian' had been less than adequate. She was barely on time; and she hated being late.

Arriving at the correct floor, she paused to catch her breath; and to determine which direction she should take down a long hallway of apartment doors. Temporarily blinded by the hallway's bright lights, she finally saw that the room that she sought was at the far end. She readied herself. Rotating her head back and forth and feeling stiff and out of shape, she made her way toward a door that would surely yield a surprise for whoever stood on either side of it.

Sister Frances wasn't looking forward to the meeting. One or two light hairs bristled out from her elder chin, evidence of age and a bit of runaway testosterone. A door knocker – more tarnished than the coins offered Charon to ferry souls over the river Styx – would allow entry. She prayed for some form of redemption. By the door, she could smell the wet and burning scent of a Halloween pumpkin whose candle had long gone out. She gave the door a couple of raps; and - to her surprise - was greeted by a shapely black woman with a deep voice. Sister Frances averted her eyes - even though she towered a head above the woman. She reasoned that this must be the 'custodian' with whom she had spoken.

"Well come on in! You one of my last hopes I guess. How was my directions?"

"Horrible. It took me a half hour to get myself straight and find this place...would have been easier to follow the sun."

"Oh...uh, sorry sister..." Sue Bee apologized. "I must have sent you the wrong way..."

The nun frowned, "Well, please don't send anymore – they're piling up."

Then she smiled, winked, and stretched out her hand,

"Sister Frances at your service...and you would be..."

"Uh...Sue Bee...though currently I'm just...'tired n hungry'. Sue Bee smiled back but the nun ignored her comment.

"Where's 'the patient'?" It was obvious that she wished to start her religious cleansing - any other 'polite conversation' would not be germane. Then,

"Hmmm....smell fish. Certainly hope you didn't have that today – generally reserved for a Friday."

Sue Bee just stared – she had seen Sister Frances before.

"Well...it's not like we're killin' it today – does that make any 'diff'?"

It was a bit of jerky start – but she admired the woman's veracity. Sister Frances opened the Bible she had carried with her; thumbed through to the page she sought...and began reading it. Sue Bee could see she was not easily rattled,

"You a 'java-mama'?"

"Begging your pardon? Uh...no, I don't care for coffee, I wouldn't mind a cola if you have one. Coffee upsets my stomach – and I don't touch it after eleven."

"Mind if I do?" Sue Bee suddenly looked out the window. "Hmm...The wind looks like it's getting a bit 'righteous' out there."

"Don't mind in the least – pour yourself two cups if you like."

Then - as if she had an epiphany – the nun exclaimed,

"Of course – that's where I've seen you! You were the woman who was in charge of that fishing vessel!"

Sue Bee's eyes glimmered,

"Yeah, and you was the nun that my partner kept botherin'! Small world – ain't it?!"

Sister Frances responded,

"Speaking of fish, whatever happened to that brute of a man who was on the boat? You know the one who caught the dolphin and wanted to keep it... the one with the 'escort'. Hateful thing - I believe 'Gregor' was his name...."

She had a good memory; and Sue Bee realized that the nun was more 'worldly' than she initially thought. She was beginning to like her.

"I ain't seen the man...somethin' spooky about him though..." Then she poured a cup of day-old coffee and put four teaspoons of sugar in it.

The nun continued,

"I have it on good authority that the man was being investigated by local police – something about the theft of a 'flash freezer' off of a fishing vessel - guess it takes all types."

Her news momentarily caught Sue Bee's attention,

"Really – that a fact – I hope it aint the boat I rented – don't need any trouble in my life." Then she pinched her stomach. "I really gotta stop this sugar. I'll never get into my dance outfit again!"

Sister Frances marveled at the woman's legs and creamy skin; and wondered why such an attractive woman had ever chosen to operate a fishing vessel.

"Are you a performer, dear?"

"I used to be."

Sister Frances reached for the rosary in her pocket, but found the daffodil instead. She caressed it – deciding to quietly say a 'Hail Mary'. Surely the moment was at least worthy of a flower's redemption. She was beginning to have a growing discomfort in the direction of the conversation.

"Really - where did you work?"

Reluctantly Sue Bee replied,

"Used to work at a follies downtown...nothin' but ol' guys there – but, like I always say, 'ya' gotta feed the birds even in the winter', if you get my drift."

The nun replied, looking at Sue Bee with as much interest as a bowl of oatmeal.

"I know precisely what you mean."

An uncomfortable silence followed as the conversation fell far short of its initial pitch.

"Um...listen, what say I get 'the patient'. He a bit groggy – don't think he slep' that well."

She left the room and headed for the bedroom. There she found Sincero sitting up in bed. He was breathing heavily and sweating more profusely than a race horse. She quickly grabbed a wet rag and sponged off his perspiration. Then, she took a brush and combed his hair; helped him into a new shirt and trousers; put on his sandals; and gently kissed his head and his feet. He was practically catatonic.

She didn't care that she might compromise herself from whatever sickness he had. Instead, she cared most deeply that she might have made a grave mistake on Sincero's behalf. Though she had prepared herself for the despair she would feel by giving him up, she had not divined the course of her conversation with Sister Frances. Her instincts told her that the nun seemed to believe this was a race to save a soul; and simply wished to return him to his country...where he most certainly would die. Sue Bee had not yet seen the imprint of the woman's soul – a woman who now stood before them in judgment. It disturbed her that she may have unwittingly led Sincero into a compromise for which he was not prepared; and for which she could not protect him. Her actions now seemed inelegant and far from the virtue she had intended for the person she loved.

Finally...she lifted the weakened Sincero into a wheelchair and pushed him into the room where the nun was waiting. His eyes were looking down at the floor; and he seemed groggy, as if he had just emerged from a cocoon. When he looked up, Sister Frances' very stern stare fell upon him.

"Sincero...what would your poor mother say..."

He dug his heels into the floor as if he would scratch away any linoleum; and then tried desperately to back up. He cast a barely discernible but piteous look at Sue Bee. He had entrusted her with his safety. His confidence in that decision had now been shattered. Sister Frances seemed to acknowledged his emptiness by addressing Sue Bee,

"Are you responsible...?"

"Hold on a minute - I ain't responsible for nuthin'. I'm takin care of this boy."

The violet color of early morning had disappeared and a gray light was beginning to build in the room.

"You call this taking care of the boy?! You're not a health professional!"

The poetry of defense did not seem forthcoming or possible in front of Sincero. The young man lamented in his wheelchair. Now faced with majestic piousness; he was barely able to move. As his temperature rose; and the light increased, his color seemed to change like that of a tree frog. He attempted to stand as if he wanted to climb into a leafy hiding spot. His torment was immense; and he was incapable of any sort of revolution. Sue Bee sensed his discomfort. Her anger rose and broke through the restraint of any formality.

"Well I ain't no jive talkin' 'Cathlic'…and I ain't buyin' no guilt trip!"

"You will please release this boy into my custody right now. He needs physical help and spiritual guidance – both which he's not getting here!" Sister Frances had spoken the world that she wished to live in. It pervaded the room like smoke.

Sue Bee eyed her coldly then, looked at Sincero.

"You right, Sincero. Sometimes I don't know what I'm doin. But at least I reco'nize my mistakes - this penguin is hittin' the bricks!"

But the nun would not back down,

"The point is: I'm not going without the boy…but then, why should I bother saying this - you wouldn't know a point if you sat on it!"

"Now listen here, you overdressed drag queen…"

The escalating argument was no longer resistible. Sincero cried out,

"STOP…you both stop! No strength…"

He seemed to collapse; and began to cry. The power of his tears repossessed the civility that was rapidly melting. Sue Bee rushed to him and embraced him protectively. She looked at the nun's strong hands. They were clenched as if in realization that she must hang onto some shred of decency. The weight of his emotional outburst bore down on Sincero. He lowered his head in shame.

Outside, evidence of a chilly autumn wind that had blown through the night before - lingered about the landscape. Much like a specter, it had brushed through the field of burdock unhurt. It had easily passed through spider webs without disturbing them. But it had touched the leaves here and there with its icy hands and left traces of blood red upon them. Even if the secretiveness of the wind was convention - other parts of nature would tease out the truth.

In the pasture, young calves huddled close to their mothers; knowing that they would soon be weaned and must search for something else to sustain. They could not exceed the limit of their mothers supply. The sturdy land had fought the summer drought; and rain had come unexpectedly. Like the shield of Zeus, clouds had conspired to protect the land before the sun could lift all moisture to the heavens. Defiantly the clouds had resisted the wind; and floated above the land with the inspiration of a nurse mopping the brow of the fevered. The clouds had released the bounty of their water in response to thunderous applause.

Meanwhile the sun god had hardened like a sugar wafer; waited for the rain to spill over the levees; and watched as the cold wind followed and dotted russet about the land. It then rolled slowly across the countryside; burnishing what it could and shining leaves as if they had been coated in oil. Local farmers queried weather stations and websites; wondering whether nearby mountains would defer to the sun's authority and hold back any further rain. Was a harvest possible - or would the impending cold dash any such wish?

But Sister Frances scarcely noticed the outside. Sincero seemed terminal; and the spiritual part of him needed to be reaped. She composed herself and then addressed Sue Bee,

"I understand that he's sick. But, more than that, his soul is at a terminus. We need to take care of this - regardless of the shell he currently wears."

Sue Bee responded,

"Ain't this a little like polishin' silver while the ships goin' down?!?"

Sue Bee's attention was suddenly drawn to Sincero. He had collapsed but was still breathing. Without saying anything more, she wheeled him out of the room; lifted his fragile frame into bed; gently covered him; and kissed his forehead. When she returned, she did not speak to the nun. Instead she went to the kitchen and began grinding some coffee. In the confusion, she had forgotten what she had initially started to do when the nun had first arrived. And, though it seemed ridiculous, she was certain what Sincero's soul needed something fragrant and familiar. She was not ready to lose him or hope for a spiritual reunion somewhere later in time. She did not trust in time...and she believed less in an afterlife than she did in the current one.

When she returned from the kitchen she had two cups of coffee on a tray. She held out one of the cups to Sister Frances, despite the nun's earlier protest. Sister Frances looked away and said simply,

"Thank you, no."

"Well, I can see that this peace offerin' was a mistake...."

The nun shot an ugly look in her direction,

"I will not be condescended to. I think it's time I 'hit the bricks' – as you say…"

Sue Bee rolled her eyes and wiped her brow with a napkin. How could she have been so foolish? Had her attempt to help Sincero now led to his undoing? She could see the nun was interested in his welfare, but she seemed dutifully constrained by principle...and Sue Bee was not exactly sure where such principle might lead.

"I'm leaving." Sister Frances had said it as if darkness had come and there would be no compromise.

"No you ain't." Sue Bee knew that it was time to 'stop the bleeding'.

Sister Frances was momentarily taken off guard, but quickly rallied. In her mind any defense must begin with honesty,

"Are you saying that you intend to try and hold me against my will?"

As if the timing had been preordained, light came through the window and beamed upon her. She lifted her chin - somewhat unnerved but preparing to accept the consequence of her question – though not quite sure what she would do.

The sky glowed colors that extended into its southern quadrant. Chirping birds readily proclaimed the start of the day. Strands of hair extended like pieces of old hay from the nun's wimple. The walk over and stair climbing she had done to get to the apartment, had eliminated some of the crispness to which she was accustomed. Blue and pink colors of the sky tinged some small figurines that sat on the ledge of a window near where the two sat – faced off against each other.

Sue Bee had not expected the immediacy of the nun's directness. She hesitated and then responded,

"Hold you against your will??! I'd rather eat broken glass. But dontchu think we got us a mutual interest, here?"

Somewhat relieved and in control again, the nun replied with the conviction of a police officer,

"I have no interest in discussing this with you. Our mutual interest - as you call it – does not extend to a compromise about the welfare of the boy's spiritual advancement."

It was just the response that Sue Bee needed to revive her.

"So... you just gonna let the little guy die – wallowin' in a bed of guilt that you done laid on him? You gonna just walk out the door – and not look back?!"

The nun's response seemed impertinent,

"His guilt is his own; and sometimes guilt is appropriate. Now, if you don't mind, I'll just flap my little wings and waddle out the door – unless you've got a sardine in your pocket." It was a reference to the 'penguin' analogy that Sue Bee had carelessly made.

"Well I disagree, sistah! Guilt ain't appropriate this time!"

The nun corrected her,

"Isn't... 'Isn't appropriate...'" Then she turned to exit - wondering if the grammatical correction had muddied her argument - but thinking it was senseless to continue any further discussion. Sue Bee would not be dissuaded,

"Well, you just go ahead and waltz out that there door – and you can know you ain't done him no good. I thought you types was into helpin' others!"

Sister Frances turned around. Catechism prevented her from pronouncing what she really wished to say; and she was seasoned enough to recognize a corporeal argument. She held up her speckled hand as if to make a point.

"We do believe in helping others...when they 'request' our help! I don't believe he has requested mine."

Sue Bee knew that an honest response would be an affirmation of what the nun had observed. Sincero had made no such request - the impetus behind the reception had been her own. Nonetheless she swallowed and said,

"Yeah, you right – but I'm askin' for it...."

The nun stopped - something seemed to govern her response,

"I will consider it...."

"Well consider it now! I mean, what's you're frickin' hurry – you late for a weddin'?!"

"Don't talk to me that way – I am a nun!"

"And 'none' means 'nothin' accordin' to my calculatin'. The boy needs you now."

Sue Bee turned away from her to face the window; and abruptly, the nun had left. She was sure she had lost the argument; and felt like crying...but a winner never cried.

Not far and to the south of them, Sophia Angaros was in her kitchen. She sat at the counter and gazed through an opening in the lace curtains. She was watching the waves in the distance hollow out parts of the shoreline. She was playing solitaire; and listening to one of her favorite operatic pieces that had just come on the small radio which she kept on the counter. Schubert's 'Ave Maria' was a welcome interruption to a card game that was too easy. She paused – realizing she was quite lonely – and thought of the beautiful sea views from her homeland. She thought of her father...and she thought of her late husband, Archibald.

Contemporaneously – and thousands of miles away across the Atlantic Ocean – people on a beach shaded their eyes and looked up. It was early evening. The Italian beach town from where Sophia Angaros had emigrated was unusually quiet. The 'beach goers' watched as a great bird – the likes of which they had never seen - soared high above them. It seemed to suck away all life from the heavens. Seabirds which normally dotted the skies – had retreated to the water. They sat nervously as if they did not wish to be exhumed from the safety of their positions.

Meanwhile – and some distance away - Bob the Indian guide was planning a trip. He had also seen the great bird in his daydream. He shook himself awake. For no reason at all, his own thoughts drifted back to the mountain lion that had never been captured; and he wondered whether he should again attempt to communicate 'in the Native way' with the young washicu'[20] named, 'RC'. He was certain the two of them could disinter the great mystery behind the cat; and capture it. More than ever, he was firmly convinced that the cat which had been turned over to the lab was the wrong one. There had to be a connection between the great bird in his daydream and the elusive cat. But he stopped...

There was the slightest buzzing in his ear that seemed to come from outside of the 'soddie'. He walked out the door and around the sod hut. Just where the hill came down to form one wall of the house, was the dog-toothed violet that had swept through the window of the soddie and landed on his chest...some time ago when he had initially started the entire dream journeys.

Louise had replanted it; and it was thriving where the moisture of the house and hill kept it wet and in shadow. The flower seemed to whisper to him; and tell him that any 'communication' he might issue to 'RC' would be interrupted...as it had before - by a large brute of a man - a 'waken oyahe'.[21]

Bob paused, wondering if he was up to the challenge that now faced him.

---

20   Lakotah for 'white man'
21   Lakotah for 'evil spirit'

YORUBA

Sincero lay in bed clinging to life like it was the mane of a wild horse. The night had passed. The following morning he had a fever and his stomach seemed more swollen. Sue Bee would have sought a priest, but the meeting with Sister Frances had not gone well. It was 'one big hot mess' - as she called it; and she had resolved never again to call upon a 'bible-thumper'. She had made a mistake which could have cost Sincero his life and freedom. She knew she could not live with herself if she deprived him of either.

It had been a restless night. She had slept only intermittently – waking to check on him and mop the sweat from his body. Now it was morning. She sat at the small kitchen table balancing her checkbook; swallowing copious amounts of coffee; and wondering how much longer it would be before the money ran out. She couldn't work because of the amount of care Sincero seemed to require; and she hadn't shopped for nearly a month. Her credit cards were nearly maxed out; and the cupboards were almost empty.

Nothing seemed to work; and she was at her wit's end. She closed down her paperwork and was ready to go check on him - perhaps take a brief nap - when she noticed a newspaper that she had dropped on the floor. It was opened to a local story that featured the grainy black and white photo of an old black woman who claimed she was 'from the swamplands'. 'Miss Yoruba', as she called herself, had witnessed a crime – the killing of a lab technician named, Dave - who had once worked in the local forensics research laboratory.

That starch-white facility was well-known for its energetic staff and vital assignments, including one involving the death of a jogger by a mountain lion. It was also where Sue Bee's sister, Earnestine, worked. The lab and its activities didn't really interest Sue Bee. Honestly she was a bit envious of her sister Earnestine's successful career. They hadn't seen each other for years. Sue Bee quietly admitted to herself that her life had been a bit of a failure. Only the love of the young man - now lying in bed with a swollen stomach - seemed to redeem her. She begrudgingly acknowledged the causal consequences of a life based on poor planning and a fractured identity. Somehow, caring for Sincero gave her life purpose.

She read through the newspaper article rapidly – disinterested in either the lab or the death of the technician. What intrigued Sue Bee was the eye-witness - the old woman named, Miss Yoruba. She had passed her shop on more than one occasion; even stopping in. It was a decrepit place on the east end of town. In Miss Yoruba's low display window – which was just above the level of the sidewalk – the old woman had hung the legs of various birds, and the soiled skins and claws off a host of reptiles. She had placed the small bust of a 'Buddha' in the window and scrawled some odd writings on its bulging stomach. The display window also contained a variety of glass bottles filled with colorful powders. The window lent her establishment the kind of duality that attracted customers from different cultures and classes. And it seemed to give her a 'peek-a-boo' into the more modern world around her.

Miss Yoruba was odd enough to be considered a 'local character'; and had a certain infamy which – though it had not bestowed a universal admiration or attraction - made her well known in 'fringe' populations. The shop's existence in the ratty part of town assured a sort of isolated independence from the tired eyes of city fathers who only occasionally took time to be appreciative; and acknowledge its 'diverse' influence. The shop contained many odd things including old pieces of 'found' wood and bark that had rested on forest floors. The wood had an unpredictable pattern of worm-eaten tracks.

During a visit, Sue Bee had once asked the old woman why she saved such things. Miss Yoruba turned to her; pointed her sharp nose in the air; and focused intense bat-like eyes as if she could divine all secrets. She pointed to the old wood and said calmly,

"They are the shadows of empty books."

Seeing Sue Bee's confusion, she reluctantly fattened the explanation,

"The green and brown code of the forest worm...he is a 'bookworm' in his own right. I collect the wood from the musty places where he feeds. He hollows out and exposes what the tree has seen...and writes it in his own cuneiform. My reading is a bit...one could say...unconventional. But then, you might know of that...."

And then, she smiled and pulled a piece of the worm-eaten wood down from a shelf,

"This one came from distant woods. The mountain cat tested its claws against the great tree's bark. Yes...I can see it...a big cat...chased by dogs and men. It has a secret. There...a running woman...the kill that caused its own pursuit. It is confused. They think they have trapped it...but no. What's this...a young woman with a bouquet of yellow flowers...there is the shadow of a large bird. Both are connected to it. It is a painting...and like many paintings - full of symbols."

Sue Bee had never been back; and murmured to herself as she quickly left,

"Crazy ol' voodoo bat..."

But now, the press had come to see Miss Yoruba. The article – largely a police report – told how they had interviewed the old woman about the late lab technician whose throat had been slashed and whose body had been dumped in the alley next to her shop. Miss Yoruba had been questioned as a 'potential witness'. She was customarily coy; indicating that she knew nothing of the murder – but that something had been taken from the lab technician's pockets by a female jogger. She reckoned it was something of great value as the woman was willing to murder for it; and willing to soil clean clothes in order to obtain whatever it was from the filth of a dark alleyway.

For some reason, the article 'struck a chord' with Sue Bee and led her thoughts back to a statement Sincero had once made to her in great despair – about "swallowing something of value, a bad man; and that things would never be the same for him..."

She shook her head suddenly as if the despicable thought was something that only someone who was sleep-deprived might think. But it stayed with her; and resurfaced periodically throughout the morning. She wasn't quite sure why – but wondered if it might not be time to visit Miss Yoruba's shop again. If – as the old woman claimed – she could "read both the past and the future", she might also be able to help the ailing Sincero. Yoruba seemed to walk a thin line between life and something else - and Sue Bee had already tried the traditional approaches.

But she couldn't move. Sue Be sat - immobile and unsure - and staring at the meager row of kitchen cabinets until her eyes felt raw and dry. Should she risk it...or would it bring more trouble?

The cooler air was playing hell with her sinuses; and she was suddenly aware that she was more tired than she had realized. She went into the bathroom to the medicine cabinet; fetched a bottle of eye drops; and flooded her eyes. Then she closed them tightly until the burning stopped. She stretched slightly; and looked in the mirror. The beginning of a light mustache had formed above her lips. She waxed gently under her nose. A conspiracy of hairiness had set upon her. Then she washed her face and painted her nails a deep ruby color. The polish showed up nicely against her coffee-colored skin; and made her feel younger. Then, she blew on the polish until it dried.

When she returned to the kitchen, she was surprised to see Sincero. He had awakened and managed to make his way out of the bedroom. He was sitting in a dirty chair with stains on it; and looked better than he had for sometime. Though his stomach was still swollen and he seemed weak, his presence was at least, inspiring.

"Sue Bee, I'm bored!"

"Well take up the, tuba, honey! What I look like – entertainment?"

She hastily put a band around her hair to contain its unbridled 'nappiness'. Sincero continued,

"I don't feel good. My stomach hurt."

The orderly path of medicine seemed strange to Sue Bee. 'Perhaps' she thought, 'it was now time to travel a more unconventional route'.

"It's probably jus' gas. You want a piece of candy. I got a packet of mints here in my bag."

"No. I want feel better," he replied.

"How 'bout we go for a walk - you up for it?"

Within minutes and despite his protest, she had dressed him and they closed the door to the apartment. The weather had changed rapidly. The wind cut through their heavy jackets. The swirling autumn leaves – though beautiful – were a reminder that things were dying. He was walking again, albeit with the assistance of some borrowed crutches. They slowly picked their way through the street like pigeons looking for crumbs – and cooing quietly to each other.

It wasn't long before they had arrived where Sue Bee had subtly steered them. They entered Miss Yoruba's shop accompanied by the 'jingle' of bells. She thought to herself, 'If she such a damn psychic, how come she needs an early warnin' system?'

Sue Bee slid through the door quickly; opening it for Sincero and steadying him. It irked her to think that she had become one of those people who 'gave of themselves' - self-sacrifice had never been her forte. The old woman was aware of their presence. She sat in a dark corner smoking a cigar. Without turning around or looking up, she simply said,

"Yuss'm, Ms. Bee, and what can Yoruba do for you today?" It was an ancient voice, full of color.

Somewhat startled that she remembered her, Sue Bee nevertheless responded coolly and pointed to a frightened Sincero,

"Got somebody needin' you help, Miss Yoruba – what you think of him?"

The old woman turned around gradually; and then, studied Sincero. Her response rolled out lazily,

"I think what I think of all mankind...that - like trees - what we are rooted in determines our destiny...."

It was not the response she had been looking for; and she became annoyed. She wanted real answers to questions - not prologue. And she was not quite over how quickly the woman had discerned her identity.

"How'd you know it was me, Miz Yoruba?"

Yoruba laughed and then smiled mischievously,

"I know all that have ever been in my shop – though some, I do not know by name. The light that hovers near you is treasonous. Perhaps, it spoke to me of your coming, as only light can do...but really – you have big feet...very big feet, my dear; and the right one has a bunion. I saw them from my window."

"Told ya' she was psychic..." Sue Bee said, looking at Sincero somewhat embarrassed.

The wind had begun to pound the window of the shop. It poked furiously at the door – demanding entry. Sincero's face flushed unexpectedly. He was beginning to feel faint. Yoruba noticed the trace of red; and said nonchalantly,

"There were men – I see men without compass, or direction. They took something from you. And now there is a man who seeks something that you have taken. He is close – closer than you might know...he will have it back."

Sue Bee jumped in quickly. She was afraid that Sincero might be afraid. It had taken months to rebuild his confidence.

"He's not feelin' so good Miz Yoruba. I'm helpin' him about". Frankly I think he need somethin' spiritual..."

Yoruba ignored her comment. She seemed quite taken with Sincero.

"Well...now, what a bit of quaint...you seem empty - and haunted. Something bothers you boy....yes, and something high above watches you. That is what Yoruba sees."

Sue Bee gathered up her courage,

"Look, my acquaintance here in need a' help – you got somethin' for him other than words and a ham sandwich?"

Yoruba stared at her for a moment as if she was burrowing into her thoughts. She immediately perceived Sue Bee's interest.

"An 'acquaintance', humnh...well, mayhab is; and mayhab ain't."

A city bus 'thundered past' the outside of the building. It shook the foundations of the shop; and a hanging claw in the window. Ancient dust poured down from a rafter. Yoruba looked up at the ceiling.

"The shop shows its age...like everything."

She took another draw of her cigar and blew smoke forcefully into the air. The smoke and the dust commingled and seemed to careen in the light.

"The light shines off a mighty man's feet...he is searching....he is looking for magic seeds that are silver as moonlight...and he is looking for your 'acquaintance'."

Sincero's head jerked back as suddenly as if someone had pulled it back with a rope. Sue Bee instinctively pushed forward as if to ward of the intemperate address. But Yoruba continued peering at the frightened young man,

"Worry makes no sense, my dear. The dust will find you...we are made of it...bundles of dust and light given direction....It causes Yoruba to wonder when the dust falls off the rafters...just who she is brushing off today...and whether they deserve to sit on Yoruba's fine shoulders."

She came over close to him and she put her hand over his chest. Then she clenched her hand and extended her index finger. Without touching Sincero, she let it travel down his chest until it stopped at his stomach. Sincero's eyes dilated. He was clearly terrified.

"Something you carried once in a pocket. It has made its way inside... something small – maybe like sand...it will come out, but as something else.... Yes, the outside drops away ...and the inside marches into tomorrow..."

In a masterful fit of defense, Sincero backed away from her. He blew away dust from a counter into a nearby candle. The dust extinguished the light; as he screamed out,

"I just send your relative away. Maybe he makes it to the trashcan this time – or get washed down drain! You talk too much to dirt, crazy woman,"

Sue Bee quickly came between Yoruba and Sincero in an effort to arrest any further polemic.

"Um...thanks, Miz Yoruba. How much does we owe you?"

The old woman brushed away dust from her shoulder like it was dandruff; and looked over to an adjacent window which revealed the alleyway on the side of the shop. A plant with blood red leaves had pushed through the broken concrete where the body of the lab technician had been removed. The small blossoms of the plant yielded enough nectar to attract a small butterfly which flitted about it in a fandango. She stroked her chin – aware that Sue Bee had caught her gaze.

"He was a handsome man...but there is no discord. He is happy enough now."

It was a reference to the murdered technician.

Meanwhile, Sincero had pushed open the shop door and was struggling to make it up the stairs to the street's landing. Sue Bee worried about his steadiness but glanced back at the old woman. She knew Miss Yoruba had already been visited once by the police related to the lab technician's murder. Perhaps they would be coming back with a written mandate. Could she trust her to not expose any truth regarding Sincero? As if the old woman had read her thoughts, she said,

"Like the bush outside, I know many secrets...some pandemic...some specific. Should I give direction – or should I merely blow sand across tracks? I don't know...it would be so easy for someone to follow..."

Without another thought, Sue Bee reached into her purse and stuffed the remaining cash that she had into the old woman's outstretched hand. Then she quickly exited the shop, hoping the money might be enough to control any information about their visit or Sincero's whereabouts.

Outside, the day had become history. The fluttering of night moths could be heard against the window pane of the psychic's shop. They were trying to gain access to a cereus that had just bloomed. When Sue Bee finally caught up with Sincero, he was halfway up the street and nearing a bar with the shingle of a two-headed dog. She grabbed him by the arm, feeling guilty that she had let him down again.

"See... you feelin' better already!"

Though very tired, Sincero had calmed down. They made their way back to the apartment building. Sue Bee could see he was getting weaker by the second. He was wandering, confused - and unable to find the correct door. He teetered; and she grabbed him before he could fall. They had made it to the apartment just in time. A storm of biblical proportions had come upon them. She unlocked the door as a squall blew up. A nearly impenetrable mist accompanied it. The rain was pummeling a nearby shoreline and water. It sounded like a wild and thunderous herd. The wind carried walls of water that crashed against the apartment windows.

Once inside, Sue Bee was aware that her belly was taut. She realized that it was time to open up whatever was left in the cupboard. She would make a warm broth from it. Besides, Sincero needed something to sustain him. When she looked over his way, he was sitting at the window, staring out at the water – appearing very much like a disheveled doll. His eyes had a sad Madonna-like quality.

Within minutes she had brought two porcelain bowls over to him. They were filled to the brim with a piping hot experiment. She sat them down and began to slurp; but could see that Sincero continued to sit - disinterested. She mugged,

"Soups on!"

Sincero said nothing. She persisted,

"Better than that raw crap you had me eat on the boat once!"

Sincero made a frenzied attempt to take the spoon and deliver the contents of some of the broth to his mouth; but spilled it on himself. He put the spoon down; and fingered a cross that she had bought him. Then he said,

"You treat me like a king when I notheeng. It not fair that I make things tough for you..."

But she would hear nothing of it. She picked up the spoon and prepared to feed him. She was more convinced than ever of the size of his heart...and that virtue was not extinct.

Outside, the sky had turned a greenish color. Distant lightning strikes signaled that the storm was moving out. Sincero turned away from her. The reflection of lightning flashes against the window pane seemed to produce halos of light that silhouetted his head. She looked outside to the distant shoreline; and saw the lightning strike into the sea like a brilliant spade planting silver seeds.

MONARCH

It was morning. Sue Bee paced back and forth in their flat. Sincero's eyes were shut tight. Occasionally she heard cries as spasms of pain racked his body. Her own chest hurt and her throat was sore. She wondered if the change in weather and her lack of sleep had contributed to something pulmonary – and wished she felt more feminine. Staring out the window at the small roads leading to the water, she wondered why anything that seemed terminal for Sincero...affected her so deeply. And she allowed herself to wonder how their present and future had been so connected.

The grayness of an early autumn day was upon them; but her heart longed for spring and the sight of butter-colored daffodils. Where were the two of them going and what might happen? Why had this young man struck her heart so intensely? He came from nothing and had nothing ...but remained sovereign over her thoughts. What was hers, she would gladly have given to him. Reluctantly she languished in thought, mesmerized by the intoxicating cocktail of uncertainty and longing.

She pulled out a pair of field glasses from the inside of a cabinet and looked far away to the shore break. The beach was covered in matted tangles of seaweed. She was certain that the wild dance of wind and waves had pounded the beach into the ergonomics which the waves expected. Sea froth made the beach seem like it was fermenting. The rare pockets of sand for sea turtle nests had largely been removed by the Herculean efforts of the storm. After awhile, the jerky, tired motions of her body convinced her to return the glasses to the cabinet where she stowed them.

She tried not to focus on the soft center of truth encased in stone - Sincero might be dying. She did not wish to host that thought; and felt awkward and inept – wishing that she was more financially secure so that she might provide anything he required. It was at that moment that the somewhat querulous tone of her cell phone reminded her that she was at the service of something other than her own thoughts. It was Lu Ann. Before she could say anything, questions were exploding from the woman on the other end of the phone. Sue Bee responded,

"He ain't lookin' too good, girl. I'm 'fraid for him."

Then she quietly prayed for the medical advice that she knew was probably not coming. Lu Ann was wrapped up in her own world,

"Lemme turn this down, honey. I'm list'nin' to some opera here – seein' if I can learn some 'Eyetalian'. Good-lookin Mediterranean down the street... you tried any drugs?"

The response startled her.

"Whatchu be talkin' bout drugs over the phone for?! You want somebody to arrest my black-butt?!"

"That ain't what ah'm talkin' bout Sue Bee. I'm talkin' bout subscription drugs."

"Girl, you evah learn to speak English – 'subscription drugs'?!" She decided to change the subject,

"Grayer than a hippo's butt today - wish the boy was feelin' better - and I ain't feelin' too good neither."

Lu Ann had started a phone monologue,

"Why aintchu try sleepin' pills? Momma swore by 'em - knock her out colder than a frozen turkey! And speakin' a' big birds, you hear bout that thing flyin' round town? Say it look big as an eagle...times five...buncha hooey if you askin' me – like them Bigfeet stories..."

She interrupted her,

"I'm worried, Lu Ann. Boy looks worse than he did when we pulled him half-dead outta the park. When you comin' over?"

Twenty minutes later there was a knock on the door. A stylish woman in a 'bolo' hat stood in front of her, arms akimbo.

"What took you so long? Thought you might be Miz Anna – showin' up with some mo' of them yellow flowers – sho' could use them today."

"Couldn't find the right hat – you look like hell, girl!"

Sue Bee smiled at her,

"And you look like you goin' to a bullfight! Come on into the kitchen – got some cocoa on the stove..."

"Oooohhh, thet smell good! Where the patient?"

Sue Bee ignored her while she continued to talk; and poured hot chocolate from the pan into two cups. After spending a few minutes swilling the liquid and swapping stories, she took Lu Ann into the bedroom where Sincero was sleeping. He had kicked the blanket off; and his stomach was fully exposed. Lu Ann gasped,

"What's wrong with him – that thing bigger then a melon!"

Sue Bee replied angrily,

"Ain't nuthin' wrong with his stomach...probly just got an infection, is all!"

The answer was a firm response intended to discourage Lu Ann from any further forays. But she persisted,

"Boy looks weaker than whiskey at a church supper!"

"No one ask you – ya dizzy broad!"

"Oh darlin' ah'm so sorry. Don't chu' listen to Lu Ann's loose mouth..."

Much later, after Sue Bee and Lu Ann had hugged their 'goodbyes' - Sincero awakened. He was groggy; but felt thirsty and hungry. He could hear the jangling of Sue Bee's jewelry as she was washing and drying the cocoa cups. He cried out but she could not hear him until he yelled out her name,

"SUE BEE!"

Already tired from the long hours of care, she walked slowly back to the bedroom where he lay. Sincero looked helpless and scared; and had urinated in the bed. She stopped - the simplest things now seemed to baffle her. She was exhausted and her hands shook. She could not tell him how worried she was. Instead, she gathered her remaining strength; and whistled to herself while she cleaned him and changed the sheets. Then she plumped up the pillows; and kissed his forehead. After she was certain that he had fallen asleep, she left the bedroom.

Putting a scarf over head; she exited the apartment and closed the door quietly behind her. It was nighttime; and she hoped to find resiliency in the cooler air. A band of clouds had partially concealed the moon; and a small shower had begun. She walked in it – praying fervently; and wondering about the rain that had been sent down.

Suddenly she was driven by an unconventional thought; and hoped that her parents – wherever they were - would find it in their hearts to forgive her. They would think she was just plain crazy. Drenched in sacred rain, she would put her direct and earnest petition to God - and she was quite certain that God would not require ordained intercession?

When she returned to the apartment, she walked back into the bedroom and gently rung the sacred rain from her scarf over the sleeping Sincero's forehead – hoping that it might be the spiritual cleansing that he needed. This would be the proof to any ephemeral barrister that he had been baptized. Though she had never been a religious person, Sincero believed - and that was all that mattered. She might take chances with her own outcome; but she could not risk that of the boy's. Sincero had to have that advantage. The 'big man' must have sent the rain down for a reason.

She stared at him lovingly for a minute. He had been resting in the same position for hours; and she worried about bed sores. Cradling him in her arms, she rolled him over slowly. He awakened briefly; batted his eyelashes at her; and lightly kissed one of her hands. It was the first time he had ever shown any physical affection. She quickly looked off in another direction; and wiped away a big fat tear. When she looked back, he had fallen asleep again.

Sue Bee had just returned to the kitchen - when she heard the intense moaning. Within seconds she had shot into the bedroom again. Sincero's body was contorted; and he was sweating profusely. He was swinging his arms about wildly; and had knocked over a potted fern. His face was sullen and dark; and his eyes had become glassy as if he was in shock. He lifted his head and fell back on the pillow. Then he arched his neck and back. Sue Bee held him gently. Her heart fluttered rapidly; and she wondered why death and birth often seemed so similar.

Panic suddenly melted her resolve. She saw his hands grab the sides of the bed, pulling hard at the sheets as if he would rip them asunder. Dawn had lit up a faded corner of the room...while they sailed into darkness.

She bolted from the bedroom and ran for her phone, barely able to dial '911'. The woman on the other end was fly-fishing for information; but assured her that an ambulance would arrive shortly. Sue Bee ran down the hallway of the apartment building, knowing that there might only be minutes left. She had to be sure that the ambulance found the right door. Rounding a corner, she did not expect to see what was there. The tall, straight figure of Sister Frances was coming toward her, dressed in the sacrament of cloth. She exclaimed,

"Sister...?"

The nun was carrying a large bunch of bright daffodils in a small plastic bag. She seemed embarrassed; and had obviously intended on leaving the bouquet at the door of the apartment. The 'jig was up' – she reached out to Sue Bee with gnarled, spotted hands; and presented them to her.

"Well who did you think I was – King Kong?!!"

Sister Frances was rigid, stern...and exactly what she needed at that moment. Then - as if the nun was vaguely aware that she had been insensitive – she scratched uncomfortably at her habit; and looked away muttering,

"Peace offering..."

In the midst of her hysteria, it occurred to Sue Bee that Sister Frances' straightforward way of hacking away at some noted deficiency; hid a more generous and introspective nature. Her faith seemed to be a toughness that had survived years of predation. Still, Sue Bee wasn't ready to admit that she admired the woman. She grabbed her arm.

"I don' have no time to explain…I need your help!"

The nun responded…customarily wary,

"Well if it has anything to do with paying your rent or some domestic squabble – forget it! I merely came here to apologize! My previous interaction with you was unprofessional."

"What…Oh, Jesus Christ – save it! My baby's dyin'!"

Sister Frances, ever tenacious in her beliefs, raised a stiff, bony finger,

"Don't take His name in vain!"

To a certain degree, the nun was somewhat relieved to hear the news of Sincero. His beatification was preferable to the awkwardness of the situation in which she found him. She had been struggling with how to extricate Sincero from what she thought must be an unholy alliance; and to deal with his deportation. Then – aware of her weakness - Sister Frances privately admonished herself for the thoughts. They were cruel and did not comport with her duty. She pushed them aside and snapped out,

"What have you done to him?! Where is Sincero?"

Sue Bee sensed the prejudgment but tempered her ire. She needed assistance – not a fight. The presence of a nun might just be the very convention that was required. She decided to overlook the haste of the nun's opinion. Besides, she had observed a sense of decency in the woman which seemed to counterbalance any misgivings.

"For God's sake follow me! If you can do anything to help, I'll sign up for five years a' confession!"

Sue Bee wheeled around; and headed back for the apartment – afraid of what she might find. Sister Frances dropped the flowers in the middle of the hallway. She hiked up her gown and sped down the hallway after Sue Bee, trailing her only slightly. She arrived directly behind her and the two stopped in the center of the apartment, panting. Sue Bee marveled at her endurance.

Sincero's moaning was now punctuated by intermittent screams. No matter how many times she had heard pain, Sister Frances had never become hardened to it. She accepted it as a blessing and a curse; and understood the gravity of his utterances.

"We don't have time to waste – let's go get the boy! You did call '911' – didn't you?"

It was more than she could bear. Sue Bee looked up at the ceiling and responded,

"No, I was fresh in the middle of de-boning a chicken…watchu' think?"

In the bedroom, Sincero was lying on his back in stupor. Sister Frances could barely contain her shock,

"What have you done??!!"

Then, she took a deep breath; and collected her emotions. Despite her disapproval, she could not deny the intensity of Sue Bee's feelings. Perhaps she had been wrong about her. The depth of a heart was a fathom less familiar. The woman before her seemed terrified. She attempted an apology,

"Perhaps this is not the time for us to discuss our mutual dislike of each other – we have a soul in our hands. How long ago did you call for help?"

She looked at Sue Bee who was frozen in place, and crying quietly.

"You okay?"

"Fine...I just came back from a frickin' swim!" Sue Bee wiped the tears away.

The nun held out her hand – apology was nothing short of sacrament.

"I'm sorry to have doubted your intentions."

Sue Bee stared out the apartment window – looking for any sign of an emergency vehicle. Outside the weather had become cool enough to pop open a milkweed pod. The airborne seeds flew across the lawn like tiny parachutists. She had seen the brightly striped worm feeding on it in early summer; watched it form its golden dotted chrysalis; and finally emerge as the brightly colored orange and black butterfly feeding on the plant's sweet nectar. The monarch had long since left; and was likely flying with all its might toward some unknown destination. It made her sad. Sister Frances interrupted her thoughts with a recitation,

'We drift about like seeds in the air,

Never knowing where we'll land.

To use our time well - is God's only care.

And He waits for us with outstretched hands.'

The verse was engaging – but irritating because of its timing. Sue Bee stared upwards. The day was breaking; and everything in the evening sky had become invisible. Without looking at the nun, she repeated something her father had said long ago,

"Ain't it funny how the moon shines...even when we cain't see it?"

BREATH

Sincero suddenly arched his back and then fell back on a pillow. Stiff, nearly lifeless, and with a vacant look - he resembled a puppet. Sister Frances sat on the bed and felt his forehead.

"He's burning up! Get some water – I don't care if it's from the toilet!! Never mind – get some ice!!"

Sue Bee ran to the kitchen; while the nun watched Sincero's chest heave up and down. His belly was distended and he was in incredible pain. She was beginning to reconsider any attempt to bring his temperature down – wondering instead if she should administer last rites. For a few seconds, the young man gazed at her steadily. Then suddenly he became listless and fell asleep. It was enough time for her to sprint to the kitchen; and follow up with Sue Bee.

"Did you just lose your way while traveling though the living room - or are you actually making the ice?!"

Sue Bee yelled back,

"Well, why dontchu' just stare at the water for awhile! Cold as you is... we'd be up to our butts in it!!"

The nun snatched a small bag of ice from her and returned to the bedroom. It would have to do. She wondered whether the ambulance was lost. She stripped off Sincero's shirt; and began to trace the spasms of his body with the ice. It was then that she noticed it – a slight lump pushing up from the abdomen. She fanned his body lightly; and saw it again. She cocked her head slightly to the side like a bird, looking and listening. Then, she took off her glasses and rubbed them with cloth. Was what she had felt...a mistake? But it happened again. She shook her head. How could it be? She continued to swab Sincero with the ice bag...all the while marveling at how quickly she might have lost her mind.

Seconds later, Sue Bee came running in, out of breath and with as much ice as she could carry. She pulled the plastic bag of ice apart; then, opened up a window to the street. Cooler air bellowed in. She was certain that she could hear the chimes of Miss Yoruba's shop, just a few blocks away.

"When that 'amulance' gonna get here?! I mean, don't they have GPS?

Sincero's belly was obvious – his shirt lay beside him on the bed

Holy mother of...!"

"Then you saw it too," Sister Frances said.

Sue Bee was clearly terrified,

"Saw what?!! I ain't seen nothin'! Nooo, ma'am. I ain't seen a thing! I don't..."

Sister Frances suddenly smacked her across the face. It seemed an odd way to bolster someone's confidence - but she believed any misfortune could be turned around. The boy had no time for such foolishness.

"If you really don't have the stomach for this, then just leave! But I thought this was someone we both cared about!"

The nun could see that she may have expected too much; and she worried about the dullness and low spirit that was now before her. She continued,

"Listen...if you saw it and I saw it, it's got to be real. I can't think of two more unlikely people agreeing on something! Now it's either the end of the line for him...or we work out our differences later. Sue Bee, I need your help! Please!"

But Sue Bee would have none of it,

"I ain't triflin' with this...you seen what you seen; and I ain't give a gold-ammit 'bout what you think you seen!"

Sue Bee put one hand around her collar - as if she was suddenly cold. She felt hollow inside. With her free hand, she played with the small cross that hung from her neck. Sister Frances grabbed her free hand and pulled her forcefully toward Sincero. She was surprised by the old woman's strength. The nun placed her hand squarely on Sincero's exposed belly; stealing any credible doubt from her. She could not deny what she felt.

The morning light illuminated a nearby window. It fell across the nun's bowed shoulders and gently pushed its way toward Sue Bee. She looked down at Sincero. The light blindly moved across the bedspread as if it had sensed a nearby tremor; and landed squarely upon his belly.

"What we gonna do?"

The nun responded with the ferocity of a pirate,

"We must get him to a hospital - I can't handle this by myself! Now move!"

Sue Bee looked out of the window – more confused and afraid than she had ever been. The light shone on the window pane making it glow like metal. In the distance, the nearby wetland was catching shards of the morning. The land burned brightly as a fire pot. The dark feathery shadows of a ring of evergreens reminded her of Indians – sitting around a fire; waiting for broth from a bubbling kettle.

She glanced back at Sincero. If she 'rolled over' in his time of need, she might be imprisoning two souls – and she simply could not do that. No, she would not scurry into hiding. She might bleed from the bolls...but she would have the purity of the cotton.

Within minutes, they had forgotten their antagonism; and were working in harmony. They managed to dress Sincero in an overgrown set of pajamas and pull him to his feet. They sat him upright and braced him against the headboard. He moaned slightly; and sweat trickled down his face.

"Oh Lord, open my lips, and my mouth will declare your praise."[22]

Sue Bee knew the reference from her church upbringing. It was sometimes used at the start of choir. The stern countenance of Sister Frances continued,

"Let us speak of salvation and thus, create it."

Within seconds, they were pulling the limp young man down the apartment hallway. Laughing gulls had come landward looking for morsels of garbage. Their cries plumbed the depths of ocean air that blew across the city. The ambulance had arrived and two medics had appeared wheeling a stretcher. A grayish-white man of massive proportions balked when he saw Sincero.

"He legal...looks like he don't have a good pair of pants to his name..."

Sister Frances dropped her hold on Sincero and walked up to the man until they stood nose-to-nose.

"No man ever stood the lower in my estimation, for having a patch in his clothes". [23] That's Thoreau! And that's the law I live by – now kindly, shut up and do your job."

With some exertion, the medics managed to get Sincero down the hallway and a set of stairs; before loading him into the waiting ambulance. As they sped off, the sun had slid through the clouds and was beginning to shine like a pale yellow jonquil. When they arrived at the emergency room, they pushed into a diverse mass of humanity. Sincero was barely conscious; and sweat had dried to a light layer of salt upon his forehead.

The emergency room was crowded. A middle aged couple sat nervously. The man comforted his wife. They seemed to have been waiting for months in their pajamas. A mother with a ragged infant in her lap sat next to a 'junkie' whose arm had random needle marks. A prudish middle-aged woman, who used too much hairspray, sat stoically – and occasionally rubbed her injured foot; and an alcoholic was reciting – with thunderous fallibility - a poem by

22   (Psalm 51: 12-15)
23   *"Walden; or, Life in the Woods", by Henry David Thoreau, Publ., 1854, Ticknor & Fields, Boston*

Walt Whitman.[24]

The tall, silent security guard who sported a dated haircut that made him look like he was part of a seventies rock band, looked on menacingly. He had a team cap in one hand and a night stick in the other; and appeared to have spilled part of a milkshake on his shirt. He stepped before them when they reached the front desk and ordered them to stop. In the curiosity of the moment, no one seemed to see a large vulturine bird that sailed silently into trees just past the emergency room entrance. It seemed to hunker-down in semi-hibernation...as if waiting for something.

Sister Frances, who was nearly as tall as the security guard, looked him over condescendingly and remarked just under her breath,

"...a paltry excuse for a civil servant."

An emergency room nurse called out two numbers and four people from random areas of the waiting room pushed forward toward the front desk. The guard opened the way a little for Sister Frances. He was obviously intimidated by her tone and Catholic attire. He looked at Sincero briefly – as if he seemed to recognize him. His last post had been as a border guard, but he had been terminated because of accusations about unprofessionally involving a Mariachi band, drinking, and illegal aliens. He was still reeling from the event; and so, stared critically at Sincero one more time. Then he looked away, satisfied that the company of the nun offered some legitimacy.

The bedlam in the emergency room quickly intensified. Someone had brought an 'I-Pod' and had inadvertently left it on high volume. It spewed out classical music - momentarily interrupting the alcoholic's dismal recitation of more 'Walt Whitman'. A man who looked as if he hadn't slept for days - and had a headache - growled out,

"Hey would you turn that crap down?!"

Sister Frances decided to take advantage of the confusion. The guard's name tag read 'O'brien'; and she suspected he might be Catholic. She leaned into him; pointed a long bony finger at his chest; and whispered menacingly,

"Young man, I work directly for the Pope – and we need some assistance here!"

Her words became the rope by which he swung. Within minutes, he had ordered a gurney; and Sister Frances, Sue Bee, Sincero and the desperate guard floated down one of the glassy, buffed hospital hallways. Abundant and busy staff in white hospital uniforms, slid out of the way. The nun crossed herself again, but was sure the Lord would forgive her. Technically she hadn't lied.

---

24   Walter (Walt) Whitman, American poet, essayist and journalist, 1819 - 1892

Outside, the day had blossomed. Like a freshly crowned prom queen it drew all attention; concealing any activity of a demurred night sky. Billowy clouds raced along and knocked into each other, slightly tarnishing gold coinage that was the sun. Shoots of red flooded parts of the heavens like a sauce. Fallen leaves had blown together forming small mattress-like piles. The disorder of autumn was in full swing. Iron colored squash seemed appropriately bewitching. Stacks of leftover corn had been bundled together tightly in nearby fields. It gave the stalks an oddly feminine appearance as if dressed in gold jerkins. Migrating geese stopped and pecked at leftover grain amidst merlot puddles. Mowed down plants had been painted over by frost – their jagged dentifrice waiting for the perennial peach color of the shadbush blowing about in the air; and which now danced to the accompaniment of a muted chorus of surviving crickets.

Once attaining the examining room, the guard departed and a nurse appeared and inserted an 'I.V.' into Sincero's arm. She hooked up the 'I.V.' to a plastic bag that contained a mild pain killer. Within minutes an intern appeared with a clipboard. He groped around in his shirt pockets for a pen; and then began to ask questions of Sue Bee and Sister Frances; writing down whatever seemed pertinent. Within minutes he had ripped away Sincero's pajamas. Placing the clipboard on Sincero's stomach, he prepared to 'take his vitals' – when he stopped. He looked again at the clipboard - as if his eyes were playing tricks on him – when the clipboard suddenly seemed to have been punched onto the floor. He placed a stethoscope on Sincero's abdomen – listening for a few seconds. Then he walked hurriedly down the glacial hallway from where he had come. He returned with an emergency room nurse whose frowning face gave away the fact that she had completed a 16-hour shift; and that most of the caring had been kicked out of her. Aware of her bilious countenance, she did her best to force a smile in front of the nun and Sue Bee.

"I won't believe a thing until I see it, Doctor. And if I don't see it, I'm afraid; I'm out of here before you can say a 'Hail Mary' - no offense, Sister."

In the meantime, a wind which seemed to have clawed its way out of a nearby marsh had crawled up the hallway until it reached the curtained room. It puffed a sulfurous gust at the examining room curtains entering – as if it had found a favorable spot – then blew off the gown from Sincero's stomach. And then, it left as quickly as it had come. The blast of wind startled everyone except Sister Frances who merely rolled her eyes disgustedly at the nurse, who grumbled,

"They need to close those emergency room doors! A storm must be blowing up."

The nurse pulled the curtains; and the intern began to take Sincero's vitals again and probe different parts of his body uttering a 'mumbo-jumbo' of medical terminology that seemed intent on disguising his uncertainty. The weary nurse came closer to Sincero; and bent over him. She was counting his breaths when she suddenly withdrew. Her mouth opened widely and she screamed out,

"Rapid Response Team – now dammit!!"

Within minutes, a team of medical personnel was running down the hallway and pushing carts filled with medical equipment. They issued Sue Bee out of the room, but balked at Sister Frances – perhaps thinking she was there to issue last rites. Instead they asked her to retire to a corner of the examining room in order to give the medical staff the space it needed. They quickly forced another I.V. into a prominent vein in Sincero's arm. The boy screamed and writhed about. A stony-faced Nubian-looking nurse seemed to take particular delight in restraining him...until she felt the firm hand of Sister Frances on her shoulder. The nun whispered to her,

"I'll hold him - had extensive medical experience while working in Central America. The boy knows me. He's in training to work with the Order, if you know what I mean..."

Under the stare of a lioness, the woman backed away – leaving the room as quietly as a shadow. Meanwhile, the doctors were much too busy to notice anything other than that the noise had subsided. Sincero had stopped screaming; and was now calm. Under Sister Frances' loving hold, he seemed to have found peace. Sister Frances, on the other hand...had not.

Minutes later, a chaplain pushed his way into the makeshift operating room. He was accompanied by Sue Bee who seemed dulled and worn. The gravity of Sincero's apparent situation rested on her heavily. A concerned nurse had noticed her distress in the waiting room; and hesitantly asked if ministry would be beneficial. Sue Bee's customary cynicism had evaporated under the pressure of an outcome that she now feared. It caused her to lean on something that had comforted her in youth. She accompanied the chaplain – a young man whose visage reflected what he was feeling: a combination of confusion, curiosity, and worry.

Sister Frances tore her attention away from Sincero, briefly loosening her grasp. She introduced herself to the chaplain; and then asked,

"Do you understand what is happening?"

His response was gentle but direct,

"I do not understand it at all."

A gust of wind had swept into the room again. It blew against his back, and caused the man to shiver slightly. He continued,

"I've heard about what is occurring - but it's unlike anything I've experienced."

Aware of the gravity and exceptional nature of the circumstance, Sister Frances tried to assess the chaplain's personal credentials. She was unsure; and expressed,

"Then you will understand - and please forgive my impertinence – that this is no time for judgment."

He straightened slightly, as if the admonishment was not to his liking, and then replied firmly.

"I understand I have been invested to minister His word and I put judgment aside - just as I might remove my glasses. One cannot do his work, if they are restrained by vanity."

It was what she had hoped to hear. She touched the chaplain's hand saying simply,

"Pax tibi."[25]

But the interaction was cut short. Sincero's screams had come from deep within him and now hurtled through the air. He turned reddish and began to pant as if a noose had been drawn about his neck. He implored in the primal voice of something that seemed to realize its fate. The screams intensified and bounced up and away - as if to expel some spirit. Within a short period of time the piercing cries had traveled down the hallway, and out the emergency room doors; passing the silent raptor waiting in the trees. There the wind seemed to carry the muted sound upwards to the clouds, where it defied gravity.

High upon a hill in the city, Roger Gregor had awakened early. He had planned to get up before dawn - as he favored the darkness for his work. But the sun was strolling across the sky as elegantly as if it was on a runway. He growled and prepared to shut the blinds...when he heard the muffled screams. His faint smile became stronger as he pulled up the blinds and looked high above him. There, a large vulturine bird seemed to chase the sound across the clouds until both disappeared.

At the same time - and below the hill where Gregor stood smiling - Anna had already greeted the morning. She was busy in the kitchen loosely arranging a bright bouquet of daffodils in a decanter. She marveled at the small fountain of color that held the light; and wondered why it caused her to think of her earliest memories.

'RC' too, had just awakened. He threw some vitamins in his mouth and

---

25   Latin for: *'Peace be with you.'*

swallowed them with the remnants of a glass of water that he kept by the bed. He opened the blinds. The moon was very faint in the morning sky. He put on a loose shirt and pair of pants; and was just about to stumble his way into the kitchen when he felt something in his shirt pocket. He groped inside of the pocket and eventually fished out a note; which he recognized immediately. He had found it in the bottle that had washed upon the beach. It read,

"C'est le serpent, dit-elle, je l'ai ecoute, et il m'a trompee."[26]

As he thought about the meaning of the note, he marveled at what must certainly be a divine decree that had somehow restored his hope and eventually led him to the love of his life.

Concurrently and far to the northwest, Bob, the Indian guide, stopped suddenly; and looked up at the sky. He had come out with the first rays of light to tend his garden. The heavens were dun-colored with small points of light – the way he imagined it had been when the Wind Cave[27] was much more active; and when the first humans had come forth as buffalo from the Black Hills[28]. He had heard the faint cries of something that traveled along an invisible vine; and he understood it to be the muffled sound of a soul fluttering like a moth against a window.

Back at the hospital, the doctors were in a quandary. They shuffled about ritualistically grabbing for surgical instruments, checking screens, and muttering to themselves. Finally, they decided to make an incision and peel back the layer of skin. Though he had been anesthetized, Sincero's eyes narrowed in pain. After seconds of clenching the sleeve of Sister Frances, the cloth of her arm had become bloodied and the young man was unconscious. Though it seemed an illogical thought, the nun wondered if she should have called 'Anna' or 'RC'. Knowing that the heart was rarely sensible, she dismissed the notion. She would talk to them later about what had occurred – if indeed, she knew.

Sue Bee had been ushered out of the makeshift operating room but - hearing Sincero's screams - went running back with a look on her face so ferocious that the security guard would not stop her. But the sounds ceased before she could reach the room. She peered through the curtains. From her vantage, she could make out three things: Sister Frances' stoic appearance seemed to have abruptly changed; Sincero was still and surrounded by the team of doctors; and the floor beneath him was covered in blood. She closed

---

26   'It is the serpent. I listened to it; and it triumphed over me.'
27   U.S National Park in western South Dakota
28   A small isolated mountain range rising from the Great Plains of North America in western South Dakota

her eyes as if she were reading from a book that she did not wish to finish. Then, she wiped away her tears with the sleeve of her blouse. Ever so slowly, she walked down the hallway and out the doors of the emergency entrance, convinced life was over.

It was already late afternoon; and the buzzing of a few cicadas, which had somehow managed to cheat the cold, seemed 50 strong and louder than ever. She giggled slightly from nervousness; looked out at a distant hillside; and then, started bawling like a baby. She could barely move. She had not said 'goodbye'; and now she could only think of Sincero and the strange ailment that had taken him. When her mind had cleared enough, she thought again of his swollen stomach and what he had once said to her,

"These bad men...I never be the same...the metal sand inside of me – now part of me. Don't you understand, Sue Bee...?"

What had he stolen from the camp where he had served as a guide? And why was it important? She sat on the sidewalk emotionally void and trying to put a puzzle together. There was something he had swallowed that had passed into his body. In the distance, she heard the bells of Miss Yoruba's shop and remembered their visit there. She felt an affinity to the purity and the loneliness of the sound; and then remembered something that the old woman had said to Sincero.

"Something you carried once in a pocket. It has made its way inside... something small – maybe like sand...it will come out, but as something else.... Yes, the outside drops away ...but the inside becomes tomorrow..."

Her mouth felt like cotton. She could barely breathe. Suddenly, the guttural shriek of something without lips interrupted vermillion thoughts. She could just make out the flight of a tremendous bird that had dropped out of the clouds – its sound so loud that an approaching ambulance could hardly compete with it. It flew past the perimeter of the city and seemed to disappear. Blocks away Miss Yoruba, the psychic, also watched it; and quietly hummed a verse of 'Santa Lucia'.

The city bells had begun to ring. They seemed to usher in the coming twilight. Sue Bee dropped her head. Her world had gone topsy-turvy. She sank down; and sat on the edge of the curb holding her stomach and crying quietly. It was then that she felt the monarch.

The beautiful orange and black butterfly had floated out of nowhere; stopped; and rested lightly upon her hand. They looked at each other for an instant. Then, it lifted and lowered its wings up and down slowly. As if preparing for flight – or perhaps in an expression of farewell – it rose and disappeared as easily as a mirage.

Inside the makeshift operating room, a nurse held up a freshly birthed baby. It had a Mohawk of dark hair; and had come screaming into life. Sister Frances looked away from Sincero. He was now at rest. She looked at the child and murmured,

"How beautiful..."

And while the chaplain hastily completed last rites, the nun walked down the hallway to search for Sue Bee. She would bring her back to see the fresh new soul.

Outside, a mild wind had lifted the monarch high into the air. The brilliant butterfly continued its journey southward to a place where many others like it would gather. Sue Bee thought of its long journey; and wondered how so small and delicate a creature could complete such an onerous flight. Then, she remembered something Sincero had told her when they were on the boat. It had seemed prophetic at the time.

"I drink the moon – and feel the energy of all life."

And she knew that not every monarch wore a crown.

A FASTENING

"Stay cool man!" the cop on the television show said, before giving his partner the 'cool' handshake.

It was 'slow' and Detective Tweeter hadn't slept much the night before. He was watching an unremarkable cop serial playing on the small television which sat on his desk - all the while eating a piece of cold pizza that was as tough as a belt buckle. He had awakened very early because of a dream; and he never dreamed – of if he did, he didn't remember them. But this one struck him. There were uncomfortably disconnected details - something about a scream traveling through air; and a Native man looking back at him - as if he knew that the detective had heard it.

The lack of sleep left him 'bummed' and abysmally tired. And he wondered how much longer he could help 'RC' with an unsolved case on which they were both working. There were more 'loose ends' to the case than an unraveling tapestry. Tweeter's own investigation was also going nowhere. The discovery of the lab technician's body in an alleyway had provided no additional clues – at least none that the forensics lab was willing to share. And the old woman 'Yoruba' – whose shop was next to the alleyway - talked in riddles. He had no solid reason to interrogate her...and doubted he would get anything from her – even if he did.

It was 'a three quarters day'. Everything was a bit out of alignment; and he had spent a good part of it running into door jams and dropping things. His intrepid investigations into case details had led nowhere; and the frustration was consuming.

The identification tag that he had long ago 'snarfed' from a forensics lab bone sample was somewhere within his desk drawer. The case had literally hit a 'dead end'. What he had thought was extraneous information – the 'romantic interest' of the lab technician – now seemed to be of paramount importance to the central office. He had given a good physical description of the woman; but had no last name or address for her. He simply knew her as 'Cynthia' – and that she had a dog named 'Buster'. How had he missed such an important detail...perhaps because he had been too intent on removing the tag sample?

And other things bothered him. There were lingering memories of the spirited Sophia Angaros; and no closure to the mysterious death of her husband, Archibald. Worse still, he felt an attraction to her that was silly and unprofessional. He wanted to see her but had no reason connected to the investigation. Suddenly showing up at her door; and mumbling something about her dead husband – didn't seem to be the level of sophistication she would expect.

In an effort to feel better, he opened his wallet and pulled out the faint drawing of a daffodil that had been given to him by a boy years ago. He wondered where that child was now. The drawing seemed to inspire him; and made him realize why he had been attracted to the profession in which he now felt so bumbling and incapable.

Tweeter chewed at the pizza absentmindedly. The heel part of it was indigestible – he was certain deer ate better. He dropped it in its cardboard box despondently; and then, buried it in the trashcan hoping it would rest in peace and not 'resurrect' itself later that evening.

Then, he idly switched from the old fashioned detective serial to a news station, where he heard something that piqued his curiosity. The investigation regarding the body of a young man found in the alleyway - was indeed moving forward. The police were working on leads; and flashed the picture of the man on screen. Tweeter recognized him immediately as the lab technician. The 'media darlings' of the local forensics lab had reopened a case that had been going nowhere for him.

Tweeter jerked his desk drawer open; and rummaged through it with ferocity. There he found it – the identification tag he had pilfered some time ago from the lab technician. He had been concentrating like a bulldog on his failures - and had again, nearly missed something obvious. The tag was faint and barely legible. Under a strong light and with a magnifying glass, it read...'Angaros #2'. He slammed the desk drawer shut – angry that he had been so dull-witted. His thoughts were now soaring.

But - almost as quickly - he was gloomy again. The connection between the tag and the woman, Sophia Angaros left him uneasy and cynical, even though the combination of clues was intriguing. He had just switched off the tiny television on his deck when two of the force's female cops abruptly entered the office. They were obviously talking about him and laughing; and he was in no mood for their banter regarding investigators past their prime.

"What ya watchin' there, Tweeter?"

The other one tag-teamed with her,

"...probably the Super bowl - it's the only way the male species can communicate with each other."

He felt like an empty hull but decided to engage the 'tough-girl' snickering.

"Naww, I was watchin' 'Sesame Street', darlin'. Reminds me of where I work..."

One of them shot forth another remark,

"Great diet, there...one-week old pizza make you think better?!"

He returned the volley,

"Goin' out for Chinese again, ladies? Heard the cat population is down...."
It was politically incorrect, but he didn't care.

Another comment came back like a projectile – with more snickers,

"Actually, Carol and I were going out to buy some hosiery. Wanna come along?!"

He realized it was later than he had thought. The day had slipped away from him. Still, his deflection was agile,

"Sure you two are old enough...?"

They exited laughing. Tweeter was certain he would be reincarnated as a pig. Then, he thought of 'lost chances', his solitary life...and how lonely he was. Everyone seemed to be having a better time than him.

His cell phone suddenly buzzed. He hurriedly exited the building where the reception would be better; and flipped it open wishing he could beam himself elsewhere. The breath gushed out of his mouth and hung in mid-air as he listened to the voice on the other end. The exhalation looked like a ghost – causing him to wonder whether anything ever really passes out of existence. The random thought seemed to crystallize into the dream that had cost him his sleep the night before.

The earliest stars had appeared. He looked up at the twilight sky and stared at a constellation that he could not identify; thinking how silly it was that anyone had developed mythology around a star cluster. Winter was coming and the frosts had turned a lush exterior into desert. Everything was brown. Tweeter lit a cigarette and looked up at the stars again...dreaming idly. Men had been carving stories into rock for ages. Maybe God did the same thing. Perhaps, the constellations were just a set of heavenly hieroglyphics. Then he rolled his eyes at the thought – he needed sleep. He flipped his cell phone shut - the call had been an important one. When he looked up at the sky, he could see the moon had risen and was as pale as a night-blooming flower in a southern garden.

His fatigue had worsened. He found himself dreaming absentmindedly about a wreath he had seen hanging at the door of Sophia Angaros' house. He didn't normally notice such things. But this one was a beautiful bouquet of dried straw and globular flowers. Their colors must have been intensely beautiful before the flowers had faded. Now they were subtle and delicate – like the woman he could not stop thinking about. How lucky would he be to walk next to her and feel her arm in his own? The thought bothered him – she was still a suspect.

When the momentary dalliance was enough for him, he prepared to return to the office to collect his car keys...and noticed a young couple walking along the sidewalk together.

Tweeter recognized 'RC' immediately; but did not wish to interrupt his intimacy with the woman with whom he was walking. It surprised him slightly that 'RC' appeared to have a personal life; for he never talked of it. Then, he quickly turned away from the couple. Thinking how perfect, yet fallible, love could be...he realized that envy was weighing upon him like a yoke.

Meanwhile 'RC' and Anna were absorbed in their conversation. They slowly walked down the street arm-in-arm; having just come back from the facility, after visiting with Zeke and Trudence Jefferson. They were oblivious to Tweeter. And they knew nothing of the events that had occurred regarding the emergency birth at the local hospital.

It had been a long day. Anna was certain that her recommendation – for her mother to carry a flower to Sue Bee as a peace offering; and to apologize – had been a success. No doubt, the two of them were having coffee somewhere; and discovering they had more in common than either could have imagined. She and 'RC' had not discussed Sister Frances' visit – instead focusing on the trip to the facility; and planning their life together. Both held secrets from each other – though one kept his secret...while the other had merely conducted hers. 'RC' felt the angst of what he had kept from her – the possibility that life might move him away again. He wondered how he might approach the subject; and realized he simply couldn't do it.

Meanwhile, they discussed the gravity of the day. Both were concerned that Zeke did not look well. 'True' – who was normally loquacious – had been much more prudent with her words. She hadn't wished to worry Anna about the boy's condition. Before they left, Anna had given a small bouquet of daffodils to Zeke and watched his smile become wide. He loved the flowers. It was the color of the wall that the he and Anna had painted together. Anna tried to be upbeat - but the effort was failing. 'RC' could see that she was deeply concerned about the boy.

Tweeter – who had been watching and listening to snippets of their interaction - began to feel as if he was eavesdropping. Shortly before the cigarette embers bit into his fingers, he threw the last bit of sparkling tobacco onto the street; then looked away from them and back to the sky again. There, he saw a curious 'V' shaped string of stars. He hastily returned to the office and retrieved his keys. When he exited the building, the night had become noticeably colder; and the couple had disappeared down the street.

He walked over to his car; threw the door open; buckled up; and sped away. The 'media darlings' of the lab had found something for him. When he arrived at the forensics lab, the 'V' shaped constellation was still there. Taurus, the Bull, had thundered along with him as if to reaffirm his own dream of an orderly and predictable world.

Far behind him, the cigarette he had thrown on the street, glowed briefly and then quietly snuffed itself out. He thought of the tag from the bone sample; and the call from the forensics lab. He thought of Sophia Angaros. And he wondered why things never seemed to be the way they were; and how 'love' could be so potent – and still have no substance.

ROSETTA STONES

He had driven faster than he should have; and had roared into the parking lot like a twenty year old who was late for a date. The lab had some information for him that might help with at least two of his cases. Though it had not been discussed, the specific information – as he understood it – had a calamitous peculiarity that might impact future forensics. If the 'coding' that the lab had found was correct, perhaps it was time for him to 'heal some old wounds' with them.

He quickly made his way to the room of the young man who had called him. The man was squeaky-voiced and had a fringelike adolescence - but obviously important enough to have a desk and an office that were better than the detective's. Tweeter tried to shove away any preconceptions. The young man must have some talent; and they should be working together because of their common mission and interest. Besides...he had a hunch that the information might be connected to a man he had been watching covertly for some time; and who he was certain was connected to illegal animal trade. But the young man's greeting grated on the detective's nerves.

"Mr. Tweetie?"

He held out his hand. The detective barked back,

"It's Tweeter!"

Then, aware that he had been overtly discourteous, corrected himself,

"Hey...sorry – I didn't get much sleep last night."

Tweeter wanted to tell him about his disappointment regarding a nefarious connection to Sophia Angaros, a woman of whom he had become fond. Just as quickly he dismissed the notion. The 'boy' couldn't possibly identify with the romantic interests of someone old enough to be his father; and he wouldn't risk offending him twice.

"Yes sir. Sorry about the mistake on your name. Listen, I just wanted to give you an update on some information that we found related to a couple of the cases that you're working on. We'll be there every step of the way to assist you to completion, of course."

Tweeter bit his tongue hard enough to restore an inner peace that he did not possess. He had no desire for assistance. Still, the kid was trying; and he had to admit that the lab had unearthed something which was helpful. He found himself growling out a response in order to appear reasonable and grateful,

"I appreciate your work, son. I'm afraid I've been dancing around trying to tie up some of these loose connections."

"Well, anyway," the young man continued, "it was the darndest thing. We had done an autopsy on the body of that lab technician whose throat was cut – you know the guy who they found in the alleyway?"

Tweeter tried to prepare himself for a carload of trivia; and shook his head up and down impatiently. He wanted to get to the point.

"...Yes, well, we didn't find anything unusual about the body, but we did find traces of something in his pocket. It was a substance, much like the fine metallic shavings from a welding magnet...or of the type you might mistakenly find in a car's oil pan. You know that stuff can really damage a car. It's as fine as sand..."

Tweeter cut him off,

"Are we here to talk about cars – or clues?"

"Sorry, sir...um, the shavings weren't what we thought they were. Quite by accident, one of our 'lab rats' spilled some of it in a blood agar plate. We 'fished out' most of it; and were ready to dispose of the contaminated agar...when we noticed something unusual. The agar characteristics seemed to change radically. We suspected a change in the cellular structure due to the introduction of the substance into the agar – and we were correct!"

He beamed with confidence; but Tweeter did not crack a smile. He found the commentary to be confusing and somewhat cryptic. The young man could see that he was losing him. He continued,

"Well, uh...to summarize, the structure of the agar seemed to react with the tendency of a substance that contains unpaired electrons and suddenly comes into contact with a magnetic field."

Tweeter's look had become more cynical – the young man tried again.

"Okay...think of it as a magnet. On it's most basic level, magnets work by lining up electrons so that they're all moving in the same direction, rather than opposite directions. They essentially change the 'shape' – if you will - of atoms.

Now, the shavings that we found in the pocket of the dead guy – the same shavings that fell into the vegetable-based agar by mistake - caused a similar effect. But...they affected the entire DNA helixes – the genetic coding of the agar. In layman's terms, they changed the DNA of the agar and quite rapidly... made it something else!"

His office phone rang and the young man excused himself. Tweeter took a few minutes to contemplate what he had heard. Outside the wind roared. It had harnessed the chill from deep coastal water. The moon was higher in the sky and seemed as luminescent as a jar of captured fireflies. The knotted wood on the elaborate counter on which he leaned complemented the office's warmly painted plaster walls; and seemed and odd juxtaposition to the new world in which Tweeter now found himself. The detective momentarily reflected on the odd distractions; and then, tried to make sense of the explanation that had been presented to him. His understanding of physics had not been tailored into the rudimentary education he had received...and the tarnish of years had not supplemented his mental acuity.

Outside the trees creaked and groaned; and the sap crawled out of wounds. These were warnings to the world that the season was changing. Soon the calliope of wind and ice would be the sound which thundered down streets like trucks. Toads would bury themselves and sleep; and – wise as they were - would not be teased from their beds until the heavens had wreaked winter's carnage. They would not surface again until spring returned to darn together warm rows of clouds and fill the earth with life.

When the young man returned, Tweeter was still thinking about the information that had been provided; and staring at a window that was now blackened by night and the clouds of a coming storm. The young man cleared his throat.

"There were other things. As you might know the lab has been involved with other high profile cases. There were three findings – they may be circumstantial – or they may be connected. We're just not certain....

The scat collected from a killer mountain lion shows signs of genetic alteration somehow. We don't really understand it; and the lab can't explain it.

Also, a gargantuan cranium in the lab's possession contains 'sequencing' unlike any we've seen. Tag's missing – but we know the dead guy in the alleyway was working on it. Never seen sequencing like this – some of the marrow's missing but there was enough for us to see that it's unusual.

And well...coincidentally, the local hospital reported that a black woman and a nun brought in an 'undocumented' person – dead now; but seems to have given birth to a child. A preliminary autopsy revealed residual metallic shavings of the same substance that accidentally dropped into the blood agar. Ummm...that's all I've got for you."

He had dropped diamonds in the detective's lap, like it was coffee. Tweeter's thoughts were now speeding. He was thinking of a night months ago; and the chance meeting with the lab technician – who was now merely a corpse that had been found in an alleyway. He thought of the technician's love interest - a woman who he had few details on – and her little dog which had bitten him hard enough to leave a scar. He reached in his pocket. The pilfered tag - from the giant cranium that the lab technician had been analyzing the night he met him...was still in his pocket. He quickly withdrew his hand – hoping the young man did not notice.

"Uh, we played out the result of our analysis, sir. Did you wish that to be copied?"

Tweeter couldn't help himself,

"Yeah, I did – but it didn't work. How about makin' one for me?!"

The detective was now becoming as hyper as a border collie. Things were beginning to 'fall into place'. The young man returned from the photocopy machine with a bit of an urgent look on his face.

"There is one other thing, detective. Hospital reports, of course, are not always accurate, but I thought I should let you know something about the deceased 'undocumented immigrant' and his 'girlfriend'. It might be important..."

He practically whispered the results; and then, stepped back – seeming a bit sheepish.

"What the..."

Before the young man could say any more, Tweeter had wheeled around; and walked out. He was on his way back to his office to surf an online database. He would collect the analysis later. Now, he really did need a cigarette.

Across town, a middle-aged woman was looking at a faded wreath. She was remembering the flowers; and when she had picked them from her garden. She remembered snipping off the ends; bundling them together; putting wire around the stems; and then, hanging them upside down to dry from the kitchen ceiling. The colors had been brilliant.

She casually looked around until she noticed the curtains in the kitchen. She had never replaced them since her husband's death. There were still some small holes in them. What had caused it? Was it moths? Was it time? It didn't seem to matter, she reasoned - both time and moths garnished from life and left holes. She thought back to the confusing night of her husband's rapid demise and his monstrous change.

Archibald had been difficult to love. He had always been so secretive. In a fit of nostalgia, she gazed upon the wreath; and thought of better times when all things seemed fresh, sweet, and possible. She remembered the detective who had questioned her about her husband's death. How angry he had made her feel. Still...she was intrigued by the warmth he tried to conceal.

Then, she began to weep like a schoolgirl. As the tears fell, they seemed to carry away the dirt of ancient memories. Though the stain of guilt might never be fully washed away – was it possible that it might be cleaned enough to allow a few beautiful moments? Within seconds Sophia Angaros had torn the wreath from the door and sent it sailing like a Frisbee[29]. The wind caught it; and tossed it upward briefly; before dropping it into the murky water of the nearby cove.

Across town, Tweeter had now made his way from the forensics lab; and up the second floor of an apartment building. He had called 'RC' and interrupted a romantic evening. Now he stood in front of an apartment door with 'RC' and a police officer. Knocking loudly he shouted for the occupants to open the door. He heard a woman inside yell back at him,

"For God's sake...I'm coming! You'd better not be a salesman!"

She threw the door open and stood there - looking at Tweeter as if she would 'coldcock' him. He could not have predicted what he saw; and what would happen next. Sister Frances stood at the doorway.

"Would it hurt you to be a bit more charitable? We've just lost someone dear to us - what do you want anyway?!"

Inside a dignified looking black woman was sitting at the table with a box of tissues. Tears had run down her face leaving a dirty path of 'mascara'. She had a snapshot of a young man before her. She looked up; cleared her throat; and then sniffled sarcastically,

"Must be my lucky day...I've always been a sucker for a man in uniform."

Somewhat confused, Tweeter looked past the nun who was standing large and solid as a man – her arms folded protectively. He looked into the puffy face of Sue Bee, who had been crying, and then asked as calmly and professionally as possible,

"Pardon me, ma'am...but...are you the 'son' of Joe and Trudence Jefferson?"

'RC', who stood by Tweeter's side; and had wondered whether the last minute call from the detective would merely be 'fool's gold'[30] - now recognized the authenticity of fortune. Surprised, he and Sister Frances looked at each other. Then he spotted a photo of Sincero that Sue Bee held before her; and

---

29   A flying disk used for fun and sport. The concept was first developed in 1937 as marketable by Fred Morrison, an American inventor and entrepreneur, who named it the 'Pluto Platter'. The final product name came from the Connecticut-based pie manufacturer, The Frisbee Pie Company.

30   The mineral iron pyrite - whose metallic luster and pale brass yellow hue give it a superficial resemblance to gold.

immediately recognized him as the guide from the Chihuahua Mountains. Finally...he looked deep into the face of Sue Bee and asked,

"Angus...?"

She smiled back at him; and rubbed an old scar from a bite on her hand. She was remembering the day her mother, 'True' and she had found 'Old Joe', lying dead in the barn – the wind hissing like a large cat in the corner. On that day they had rescued a frightened young boy named, 'RC'; and he had bitten her hand hard. She had given him the nickname, 'wild boy'.

Sue Bee scratched her head and simply replied,

"Son of a..."

SKUNK PARADE

It was Cynthia Gregor's shift and she was late. She had let 'Buster' out; and he had taken longer than usual. After the dog had completed his evening 'constitutional', he scratched nervously at the back door and whined. He had pee'd on himself; because something had frightened him outside. She opened the door; and cursed him. Then, begrudgingly she cleaned the dog from top to bottom. She would not risk having him soil a new carpet. When she was through, she examined her fingernails – it was time to paint them again.

An hour later, she came strolling into the facility with the gait of someone idly walking a concourse and jangling in jewelry. Her well-organized purse was soft leather; and belied the fact that it contained a brutally sharp knife – something she used for protection, particularly when she jogged. Cynthia Gregor resented having to give up time to work in the evening with the 'brats in the facility' - as she called them. It was a part-time job; but the money helped buy the extra things that a well-heeled woman couldn't live without.

During the day she worked at the bleach-white forensics lab in town. She had taken over the position of the late lab technician – whose body had been found in an alleyway, and whose throat she had slashed. Her position paid well enough and gave her the access that she needed.

This evening, Trudence Jefferson's back had begun to hurt. She watched Cynthia Gregor saunter down the hallway. 'True' had been working all day. The police had contacted her regarding her son; and she was certain stress was contributing to her aches and pains. She felt old and brittle.

"It's twenty minutes pas' time I was 'sposed to be outta here. Think you could paint those nails of yours some other time?"

Cynthia Gregor responded unemotionally,

"Actually, I had a flat tire on the way, Mrs. Jefferson. You could have a little more sympathy. None of us can predict natural events."

'True' realized she had been bearish; and was ready to issue a scant apology, when she stopped. She could smell the fresh polish.

"Didn' know tires smelled that good, Miz Cynthia...speakin' which you must have the cleanest car in town. How you manage to change a tire without messin' up those pretty hands a yoah's...?"

"A friend helped me. You know how men are!" Then she idly lifted the hem of her skirt and rubbed her knees. "A little cold out there, Mrs. Jefferson, my knees are practically frozen." She rubbed them vigorously and pretended to brush off dirt.

True sighed heavily; thought of the children in the facility; and tried not to expose her anger. She didn't want the kids to hear it; and didn't need any more trouble in her life.

"Now 'True', don't be angry. You know you're not required to stay. It's my fault if something happens on the shift that I'm supposed to be on – not yours! You could have simply left."

Trudence Jefferson suspected that a romantic foray had been the cause of Cynthia Gregor's tardiness. But now, her feet were killing her and she didn't seem to think the strength of a reply would make any difference. Instead, she reached down and massaged one foot that was out of a shoe and wondered if the same God who had created fallen arches had also created fallen women. Then – changing her mind - she looked up and admonished,

"That's what I mean!. Somethin' could go wrong! An' if you's a kid needin' help, it don' plainly matter whose shift it be on!"

There was a noise outside of a nearby window. It distracted 'True' long enough to allow Cynthia Gregor to slip past the desk towards the first room of one of her 'wards'. She opened the door slightly and said without looking back,

"Shhhhh....now we don't want to wake the children – do we?"

'True' grumbled something inaudible - there was no way to predict the woman's craziness. Then she muttered,

"I gotta go...my man's waitin'."

Cynthia Gregor turned to her and smiled diabolically,

"Now you know the expression, Mrs. Jefferson. Men are like linoleum - if you lay them right you can walk all over them for 30 years." Then she quietly closed the door to the room she had just entered.

Trudence Jefferson steamed out the front of the facility like a locomotive; and toward the waiting car, growling as she went. She was weeping for Angus – quietly wishing that she had been there for him; and that she had been more understanding. She didn't care that he now called himself 'Sue Bee'. Her emotions bounced back and forth between sadness and anger as she thought of 'Sue Bee' and then, Cynthia Gregor. Before she knew it, she had made her way down the walk. Big George stretched across the front seat of a warm car; and opened the passenger-side door for her.

"What the matter, honey – you look like you ready to nominate some-body fo' a whippin'!"

Her face was as dark as a storm.

"Damn that, Cynthia Gregor."

Big George arched his eyebrows,

"Now 'True'...ain't no sense in you tryin' to clean up the world one wom-an at a time..."

She responded tartly,

"Ain't trying to clean up nothin', Big George, but puttin' a name on somethin' evil seem to help!"

He did his best to calm her. After minutes of cajoling and teasing - the symmetry of her anger seemed reasonable for the events of the day...and her sore feet felt better. The warmth of Big George's personality seemed to curtail the monotonous tom-tom of her complaints. He scanned the car's radio until he found a station that was mellow and soothing; while 'True' looked out quietly at the passing landscape.

The leaves had dropped from most of the trees and their twisted root-like tops were visible. It was an imperfect equilibrium that –oddly enough - made her believe once more in the balance of all things. Meanwhile the wind pushed across the land bringing with it the salty smell of ocean. She thought of her first husband, 'Old Joe', thought of her son and daughter; and began to dream – wondering why she couldn't talk freely to 'Big George' about Sue Bee....

Outside, the ill wind spewed forth. It had traveled far – circling the earth. If it had any anthropomorphic consciousness or recollections of its travels, it might take the memories back to the Wind Cave, from where it had come. And it could have memories - for there were those who had been victimized by the wind's supernatural force.

At a port city in Germany, it had pushed a young man off a tower; and followed him down to his death - listening to his screams. It had exploded into war-torn areas - throwing sand about and permitting the dominance of one group over another. It had blown skirts over women's heads. It had torn away the cries of children. And it had pushed airplanes off course. But tonight, the same wind was content to wander about a new landscape, mischievous and bored - looking for a place to rest; and only causing minor disturbances. Most did not know where it had been or of its previous ignobility. For, though it might 'talk' of its exploits through the language of the trees; and touch others with the same icy fingers; the trees were faithful in their agreement to it...and few understood the trees' murmurings.

True looked outside in the distance. She had heard the howling of dogs. It bothered her and she decided to focus instead on the young boy, Zeke; and how he had said his prayers in front of her - as he did practically every night. She never tired of telling everyone about it; and she recounted it again to Big George, while he caressed her tired shoulders with one hand.

"The littah fellah, he be in his bed, and lookin' at the ceilin' like it was a star. And then, he put his hands togethah and say, 'God is grape – God is good…' like he be talkin' bout Kool-Aid[31] or somethin'! He just the cutest thing – don' know no diffunce in how the verse really be spoken – but just a prayin'. And he believe it too!"

To her, it was less important how the words related to each other, than the communicative purpose behind them. She didn't admit it – but Zeke was her 'favorite'. Big George noticed the smile on her face and said,

"Thinkin' of your boyfriend again…?"

She chuckled out a reply,

"He like a little angel, George! Ain't got no pot to pee in – and don't care. Don't want to be nothing but be sweet n' pretty – like some lily you come up on inna' woods! Mos' people jus' say ' pick it'. But I say not. Let it bring joy to everyone who see it."

Then she stopped suddenly,

"Big George, you gotchu huntin' rifle inna' car... I smell a skunk parade."

It startled him,

'True'…what's cookin'?"

She looked out intently at the evening sky – as if some 'hunch' needed verification. There was just a hint of light in the west. It was almost obliterated by the moon; and the odd lighting created fantastic shadows in the landscape. Out of the corner of her eye, 'True' saw a shooting star zoom over the horizon. She thought of the boy once more and murmured to herself,

"Ezekiel…"

She stared up at the sky. The moon had turned as bright as one of 'Miss Anna's daffodils.

"George, turn the car round this minit – we goin' back to 'the facility'."

"What 'n hell…you be serious?"

"Go on – 'bout face it! Sumpin' ain't right…. 'Death and life are in the power of the tongue.'[32] Step on it Big George!"

He hated it when she quoted scripture.

'True' was thinking about the boy, Zeke, and how tired he seemed. Anna

---

31   A powdered drink mix invented in 1927 by Edwin Perkins in Hastings, Nebraska.
32   Proverbs, 18.21

was right – he didn't look well. He seemed paler than usual. For all she knew, Cynthia Gregor might not be taking care of anyone. She thought of the woman - her apricot colored fingernails, sweet scent, red lipstick, creamy skin, and perfect hair. Perhaps the facility was being used to entertain men during an unsupervised 'night shift'. She only knew that something didn't 'smell right'; and commanded,

"George, put the pedal to the medal!"

He did not question her – but neither did he understand her. 'True's intuition was usually correct. It was part of the mystery of women that intrigued him. Whatever issue came up, he was certain he was much better to be at her side.

He floored the gas pedal – and the car sped past a drive-in theater on the edge of town; making so much noise that the patrons wondered if a plane was passing overhead. Big George was barely into the facility's driveway, before 'True' had pushed open the car door; and was moving 200 pounds of concern as quickly as she could down the walkway. She blasted through the front door. No one was at the front desk. It did not surprise her.

What did surprise her was a printed work of some length that had been left open on the front counter. Normally fastidious about the appearance of that area, 'True' stopped suddenly to glance at it. It had the complex title, 'Impact of Micromasonry Polymers as a Quickener'. Intuiting that it must belong to Cynthia Gregor's, she flipped through the introduction quickly. It discussed the impact of 'bio-legos', DNA, and a term called 'self-assembly' as a way to build living material rapidly from existing cell structures. It was too obscure. She slammed the book shut – it was clouding the purpose of her return. But she was suddenly convinced more than ever that the speed with which she had been moving was too slow. Gathering as much energy as possible and puffing heavily, she ran down the hallway to look for 'a bird with apricot talons'.

All were asleep except Jimmy Mack - Zeke's rebellious and outspoken friend. His nighttime meds had left him uncomfortable and awake. Upon seeing her hurried pace, he rolled out of bed and slid his stubby, thalidomide body into the motorized chair by his bed. Within seconds he had caught up with 'True'. The whirring sound of his 'chariot' caught her attention; and she puffed out a warning,

"Jimmy-Mack, you wake up the othahs and I'll flatten both yo' tires."

She had misspoken but would 'right up' with the boy after she discovered where Cynthia Gregor was; and what was happening on the night shift. Jimmy Mack stopped a safe distance away and wheeled into a recreational area nearby. He was just in time to see the shadow of something large pass over 'the facility'. The abundant moonlight, made the shadow slide across the landscape like chocolate syrup spilled on a counter. The boy strained to see what it might be – and listened to the howling dogs outside. Something had spooked them.

True' took no further notice of him. She was focused; and heading as quickly as she could for Zeke's room. There she paused; caught her breath; and made the decision to open the door as quietly as possible...in case she was mistaken.

Standing over the boy as if he were in a makeshift emergency room - were Cynthia Gregor and two men operating under a medical lamp. They were siphoning spinal fluid from the boy's back. Zeke's face showed great pain and resignation. 'True' – whose memory was still fresh from the guilt of having not helped out her own son - bellowed,

"What'n Hell's going on here!!!?"

It startled the two men. They dropped what they were doing and faced her. Cynthia Gregor – on the other hand - responded with mechanical smoothness,

"Ms. Jefferson. What are you doing here?"

Zeke was under a soft pea-colored woolen blanket. He had been sweating and the moisture had turned his hair into shiny ringlets. His long eyelashes appeared to seam his eyes shut as he grimaced in pain. On the cart beside him was an orderly team of filled red test tubes. Someone had pulled his shirt off. Near his left nipple – a patch with wires hooked to it and which fed into a computer - seemed to monitor his status. The moonlight, coming through the nearby window, beamed down upon his face. He looked like a cherub... as if someone had cheated heaven of one of its own. A monitor hummed – transmitting power and heating the room slightly. A number of soft freckles clustered charmingly about the boy's nose, leaving no doubt, that some divine hand had been part of his creation. He awakened and looked up - opening his eyes slightly. Their honey-colored sweetness was disarming. It was more than 'True' could tolerate to think that someone might be hurting him.

She looked at the bloodied rags spilling out of Cynthia Gregor's lab coat pockets. 'True' said nothing; but made her way for the woman – who raised a hand in self defense. The specter of disorder seemed apparent; and 'True' was ready to 'right it' - though she had not conceptualized what exactly that might mean.

Cynthia's Gregor's cold resilience momentarily stopped her.

"Mrs. Jefferson, we've had an emergency. Zeke was complaining about not feeling well; and these men are here to perform tests on him. They're from Memorial Hospital."

The cold artificial light seemed to suddenly fall upon the weakened boy. It kept the softness of the moonlight at bay.

"Who dun call'd 'em? I don' amember anyone sayin' we had 'thority to call someone from Memorial!"

Zeke recognized 'True's voice and looked up weakly. He was obviously under the influence of some sort of sedative. The spinal fluid dripped slowly from his back like a clear sap. 'True' watched as the men gathered it in a small tube and let some of it drop onto slides that were barely larger than newsprint. The boy cried out through the anesthesia of half-sleep and a confining palsy,

"TAWWWUUEEEEE..........EYAHHHHLP MEEEE!!!!"

In the distance the powerful sound of a howling dog could be heard – perhaps baying at a moon that it had chased and gotten no closer to. 'True' pulled nearer to Cynthia Gregor. The woman nervously searched for something sharp inside the pocket of her lab coat.

"Now, Mrs. Jefferson, you're going to have to butt out. This is my shift. I'll report you to management if I need to."

'True' ignored her - focusing instead on the smaller of the men who continued to collect fluid from the boy's back. The man's pulse was quickening. She could see his carotid artery pounding. She reached out and put her ample arm around his neck saying,

"You lookin' like you hadda' rough day, son. Let 'True' give you a massage – maybe sing you a lullaby. Now, you got one secon' to pull that thing outta' his back – or we ain't gonna need to sing to you no more...."

Her grasp tightened to show she meant business. The larger of the two men approached her and said,

"I don't think that would advisable, Mrs. Jefferson. If I have to I'll..."

He stopped abruptly as he noticed the figure of Big George, standing mountainous in the doorway.

"You needin' some help in here, 'True'?"

True directed her attention to the man who had approached her.

"You best be quiet - or Big George will mop up the floor with you. Might matter to you...but he don't care nothin'. It just be' one more chore he gotta take care of. ...Big George thinka' the boy here as his own."

She released her hold on the smaller man. He pulled out the needle smoothly from Zeke's back; and placed a bandage over the entry. Then he quickly handed the slide samples to Cynthia Gregor who buried them in the deepest corner of a pocket of her lab coat. She turned to leave. Pointing at

Big George she said,

"Who is this man, Ms. Jefferson? I'll have him arrested if you don't send him back outside."

And then,

"Gentlemen, that will be all for this evening. We'll perform the tests here and contact you if we have questions. The boy may require more specialized care."

The two men gathered their equipment and scampered away as quickly as spiders being ushered past the threshold of a home. 'True' could feel her anger welling up; but focused her attention on Zeke. She smoothed his hair and wiped the sweat from his brow.

"George, meet me down at the car – I'll be there in a minit'."

She cradled the boy in her arms. He looked up at her weakly and said,

"I...hahh...dream....b-b-bout Inyun maaan...He waasch ovaaahh me."

She didn't know what he meant; but hugged him tightly. She was more concerned with his physical safety and security,

"Shush, shush, shush! Yes, honey, I'm sho' you did. 'True' be here now - she take care of you. Now dontchu' worry none – we all dream."

Cynthia Gregor walked angrily up the hallway. Faithful to no one but herself, her 'power shoes' made as much noise as a nail gun; and sounded like they were perforating the linoleum. Halfway up the hallway she spotted Jimmy Mack who had positioned himself at the large window in the recreational area. He was so transfixed by something outside that he hadn't heard her approach. She snapped at him,

"Get back to your room this instant! You know you shouldn't be up at this hour. If you don't behave, I'll speak to your legal guardians; and we'll make other arrangements!"

Her words seemed to confine his curiosity. The boy pressed a button on his wheelchair and scooted back to his room - sullen and angry; and grumbling something about a large bird....

Meanwhile – back at Zeke's room - 'True' hugged the boy and then, gently tucked the covers around him. She kissed his forehead saying softly,

"Honey, you close them peepers and try an' rest. 'True' be back in two shakes of a lamb's tail!"

She exited the room quietly - just in time to see Cynthia Gregor disappear into a restroom at the end of the hallway. Big George had returned to the car. With no one to balance her out, 'True' - whose nature had never been oriented toward obsequiousness – was now terminally angry. She threw protocol out the window, in favor of pursuit. Stomping up the hallway, she arrived and pushed open the door. But before she could say anything, Cynthia Gregor had shifted into command mode.

"Mrs. Jefferson, we need to talk about the propriety of this situation. You're on my shift and - if I have to - I'll take it up with the resident in charge. I'm sure you can find employment elsewhere. We don't need anyone who is unstable or frightening to the children. This was an approved procedure. You're just lucky I didn't call the police."

It momentarily startled her; but the impropriety of what she had observed goaded 'True' into confrontation,

"Hey, you don' have to go all 'British' on me. I know you up to sumpin'!"

"I will not discuss this any further...."

"...Look to me like this weren't no procedure at all – you just tryin' to make some 'Benjamins' on the side – now whatchu up to?"

"I haven't got the time to explain it to you, Mrs. Jefferson."

'True' mugged sarcastically,

"Then how 'bout drawin' me a pitcher...!"

"Mrs. Jefferson, you either play ball or you don't. There is no middle ground in these matters."

Trudence Jefferson had started to 'do the math'. And she had decided that she would 'wrestle' the truth from the woman if she had to.

"I knows' when somebody's hedging – and you jus' buyin' time so you can 'gin up' a story!"

"The boy is in perfectly good hands. You don't need to be circling around like a mother hen."

"Hey, you got some equipment here that I ain't seen before - and a text-book on the front desk that ain't standard readin'. How 'bout we start with that; and quit roamin round the truth?"

Cynthia Gregor whirled around to leave; but Trudence Jefferson blocked the door.

"Somethin' smell fishy – and now you flyin' away...?"

"This is not open for discussion, Mrs. Jefferson! Now step aside – you've sewn enough discord for one night."

Far to the west, the great ill wind called 'Wakan Oyahe' scoured the landscape of the Sandhills. It had allowed others to split off. Its minions were not yet ready to come together and return to the Wind Cave. Bob, the Indian, felt the wind's force.

He had walked down to a scrub tree near their 'soddie'. There by the tree, he stuck a spade into the ground; trying to discover how deep the freeze line had become. When he pulled the shovel up, he realized he had unearthed a sleeping toad. It blinked at him; and he understood that he had interrupted the 'old man's sleep. He gingerly placed it back in the earth as the wind continued to blast about him.

He listened to a single tree interpret the wind's complex language - and realized that it was time to start his journey. Things were beginning to come together to the east. The ill wind had returned to its domain and was waiting for the others. Its forays were just about over. The trees spoke in riddles but Bob had deciphered that 'RC', the young 'washicu' - with whom he had tracked the great cat - had established a vital connection. He and a detective named, 'Tweeter', had finished cross-examining Sue Bee and Sister Frances. They had learned of critical affiliations at 'the facility' and elsewhere.

The discovery of 'Sue Bee's identity...seeing the photo of the guide they now knew as Sincero...and the revelation of what had happened at the hospital...allowed 'RC' and the detective to begin to decode some of the obscure things they had witnessed. Something was occurring which was of much greater significance than they had previously suspected.

For Tweeter, the talk with Sue Bee...regarding her mother, Trudence Jefferson's, employment at 'the facility'; and her sister Earnestine's profession at the forensics lab - had enlightened him regarding some key people. More of interest to him - he was now certain he knew the whereabouts of the young boy who had drawn the daffodil picture that he always kept in his breast pocket; and was reasonably sure of the identity of the 'mystery woman' who had been the love interest of a lab technician found dead in an alleyway. There seemed to be connections.

For both men – the discovery that they had a mutual interest in a giant cranium that was now housed in the forensics lab - was an important revelation. Their cases were coinciding. With as much speed as was legal, they headed for 'the facility' – hoping to bring closure to the complex and interrelated events that had held them for so long in stasis.

At the other end of town near the bay, Sophia Angaros sat in her kitchen...happily ignorant of any such connections. Her world still centered on grief. She examined the curtains that had holes in them; and wondered if she should remove them. Her husband, Archibald, had died quite some time ago – it was time to stop the pain. She thought of the middle aged detective, named Tweeter – not really knowing why. Her previous impulse to throw the wreath of dried flowers into the muddy waters of the bay had been oddly restorative and bordered on a sacred act. She would say goodbye to a life that she had once lived - it was time to start over. But first, she would sit at the bay's expanse...she needed to reflect on what her new life might be.

She walked outside; sat on an ample rock; and began to hum 'Santa Lucia' to herself. It had been 'their' song. There, she reminisced about the good times with her late husband, Archibald. Despite his unexpected and somewhat grisly death and the problems in their life, it had not been all bad. She cleared her thoughts of that fateful evening. After a few minutes, she was ready to return to the house, feeling sure about life once more. A warm wind had swept through and cleaned away thoughts that had long weighed her down.

It was just then – as she prepared to depart from the beach- that she saw the shadow of a large bird fly across the moon. She paid little attention at first - night herons were nocturnal feeders and common in the area. But when she looked up; and realized the tremendous size of the bird – it frightened her. And as the large bird disappeared over the nearby tree line...she heard it mimic the operatic piece that she had just been humming.

PART VII

BLOOD MOON

DIRT UNDER HER NAILS

Something didn't 'feel right' and Trudence Jefferson resolved to discover what it was. Cynthia Gregor had degrees coming out of her butt...yet, there she stood with blood spattered on her lab coat. 'True' blocked her exit. Cynthia Gregor's voice suddenly became rough and unpleasant.

"Mrs. Jefferson, you have no authority to come on to my shift and cause such a scene. You could have very well caused the needle to slip. The boy could have been left - not only dumb as a post – but totally paralyzed in the process. I have witnesses who will be happy to testify regarding what they saw."

A double image of the woman was reflected back by the mirror. It was oddly fetching; and seemed to briefly linger for a moment before metamorphosing into, what seemed, a shadow caused by an imperfection in the glass.

"The boy ain't dumb, Miz Cynthia; and - even if he was to be - I'd still love him. Rather have heart than smart..."

Cynthia Gregor responded,

"Such a 'sweet optic'...."

'True' glared at her briefly. The woman was trying to wrap her up in words and suck all the life out. The wind was coarse and cool. 'True' felt it pouring through the restroom's open window. It made her feel uncertain and incapable; but she pushed on,

"Thought you was goin' to the lab with them 'samples'."

"Indeed I am, Mrs. Jefferson. Now if you'll excuse me...."

She stopped her again,

"Look here, I apologize - but I thought you was hurtin' the boy. He ain't looked good to me; and he been talkin' a lot lately 'bout all sorts of things – sayin' he seen a large bird outside; and dreamin' of Indians. I know you understand...."

Cynthia Gregor's indignation spilled out,

"Your apology is a little late. However, I'll visit the situation with the board. Now...I must get these samples off. And regarding the 'big bird' dreams – or whatever you call them - I'm sure it's nothing more than an associative phenomenon brought on by something he saw on television. We really should take that privilege away from the children – it only feeds their fantasies."

'True' continued to block the woman's path. She studied her to see if there was a 'soft side'. At that moment, the light bounced off Cynthia Gregor's hard hair. Trudence Jefferson had no idea what made her say it, but she suddenly pronounced,

"Ezekiel..."

Cynthia Gregor's eyes widened. They were hard, electric, and monstrously beautiful.

"Beg your pardon?"

'True' continued,

"You know the boy's name is 'Ezekiel' – 'Zeke' just short fo' that. 'Ezekiel' mean 'shootin' star."

"Interesting bit of trivia, Mrs. Jefferson...I fail to see the relevance."

"Maybe we come from the light, Miz Cynthia...and spend our time jus' tryin' to get back to it...all I'm sayin'..."

"Sounds like a slow, painful trip to me."

"God's time different than ours. Our time shorter than a flea on a dog's butt! An' I bet that ol' flea think he live a long time too...!"

Cynthia Gregor's demeanor became predatory.

"Do you wish to make the situation worse, Ms. Jefferson? Are you seeing little green men now? I recommend you step out of the way – before it becomes necessary to institutionalize you - for your own welfare."

Trudence Jefferson stood resolutely. She had now lost all patience.

"Welfare ain't what I'm lookin' for, Miz Cynthia..."

"Then, what exactly are you looking for, Mrs. Jefferson?"

"A skunk!"

Cynthia Gregor opened her purse and sprayed sprits of perfume on her hands. Then she calmly and methodically worked it in.

"Well you won't find it here. I suggest you start with the children, if you're looking for that scent..."

Trudence Jefferson narrowed her eyes,

"Ain't a patch a honeysuckle big enough in the whole world to hide you when you got your tail up – now is there?!"

'True's comment had broken through the woman's icy façade. Cynthia Gregor's face reddened. Her eyes narrowed; and her eyebrows plunged. As if in affiliation, a cold wind blasted through the high open window of the restroom. Her hand dove into the pocket of her lab coat – rummaging for the knife she kept there. Before she could find it, 'True' had guessed the intention and rammed into the woman hard enough to send the two of them sprawling into a nearby wall. The force momentarily stunned Cynthia Gregor; but she quickly sprang to her feet; and found the knife in her pocket.

Trudence Jefferson had just enough strength to throw a small trash can that was nearby; and to stop the woman's charge. It ricocheted off the wall scattering about its contents. It was sufficient to distract Cynthia Gregor; and allow 'True' the time she needed to get off the floor. She did a quick cross over her chest and prayed for a miracle. The woman was stronger than she had anticipated.

Cynthia Gregor charged again and swung hard – the blade of the knife narrowly missing Trudence Jefferson and catching on a plastic sign that read, "All Employees Must Wash Hands". The power of her thrust caused the sign to fall; and twisted Cynthia Gregor's wrist into a sprain. She screamed and then, slipped – her head knocking into a porcelain sink...before she fell to the floor as hard as a cadaver.

Trudence Jefferson pushed past her and slammed shut the restroom door – concerned that they might awaken the children. She was exhausted but the madness of the woman demanded that she rally what strength she had, in order to contain her. She grabbed a broom in the corner and prepared to swing it. Cynthia Gregor would never get past her and hurt another child. It was then that she realized her own head was bleeding. A trickle of blood was coming down; and she dropped the broom.

The smear of Cynthia Gregor's makeup could be seen on the sink that she had hit. The woman was dizzy but had miraculously righted herself. She reached for something in her pocket again...when 'True' decided that it was time for something more basic. If the woman had a gun, it would be over. She rushed Cynthia Gregor with as much force as she could muster. Using the momentum of her own weight to carry her body forward, she fell squarely on top of her. She could hear Cynthia Gregor's breath rush out in a cold rattle, and then, heard the crunching sound of something that resembled an insect underfoot. Water trickled out of Cynthia Gregor's nose and mouth.

Astonished, Trudence Jefferson rolled off. The force of her weight seemed to have crushed the woman's sinuses; and the breath had been pushed out of her. There was no longer any light left in Cynthia Gregor's hard eyes. She lay on the floor – lifeless; and Trudence Jefferson wished - for the first time since meeting her – that she possessed the power and magic of resurrection.

...Minutes later Detective Tweeter and 'RC' arrived. They had expected to cross-examine Cynthia Gregor – and possibly do an arrest – but were unprepared for the conflict that they came upon. A restroom within 'the facility' had suddenly become its own crime scene.

Trudence Jefferson was out of breath and sitting beside Cynthia Gregor - blood streaming down her face and onto her uniform. The butt end of Cynthia Gregor's knife was resting against the far wall. Cynthia Gregor lay motionless with steely eyes open and her jaw forward as if she was prepared – even in death - to issue another order. Test tubes of blood that she had drawn from the boy, Zeke - had been crushed and had accidentally impaled themselves into her trunk, piercing the bottom of her heart.

More intriguing to 'RC' was a small packet of metallic granules – no larger than sand – that were found in one of the pockets of Cynthia Gregor's lab coat. It was enough to convince him that the hunch he had while driving to the facility was correct. The pirating of genetic material was being used in recombinant form for something significant...something which could have much larger consequences.

The packet had broken open and apparently some of its content had entered into Cynthia Gregor's bloodstream. An odd pattern of repeating bumps – of the sort which Tweeter had seen only once before – started to appear on her skin. Tweeter was now certain of the identity of the woman who had been the lab technician's girlfriend. An examination of the knife against the wall opposite Trudence Jefferson helped establish the needed connection between the dead technician found in the alleyway - and Cynthia Gregor. He placed a call to the police station to have a more thorough investigation of the surroundings; and then placed a similar call to the forensics lab to have a technician come to collect the body.

The detective was ready to leave when a small, punk'ish Jimmy-Mack wheeled up in his chair. He was in flowery pajamas. The boy shouted,

"Hey gumshoe, what's goin'on?!"

His appearance startled Tweeter, but the detective retorted,

"Nice pajamas, kid. What are you doin' up so late?"

He pointed to his wheelchair and mugged, "Just changin' a flat, sir!" Then - seeing 'RC' – yelled out,

"What you doin' here man? Where's your squeeze?"

RC responded - uncustomarily guarded,

"Anna's at home, Jimmy Mack. Go back to your room and get some sleep. You'll wake the others...and Zeke, in particular, needs his sleep."

Jimmy- Mack grumbled; turned his wheelchair around; and then, shouted out at Tweeter,

"Hey Cap'n! Know what they call the ghost of a detective?"

Tweeter looked at him sternly.

"Lemme guess...'dead'...?

The boy laughed loudly and then replied,

"No! An in'specter' - get it...or do you want me to spell it out for ya'?"

Tweeter smiled – the boy had 'chutzpah'.

"Hey, kid, how about tellin' me exactly what happened here?"

The center of attention again, Jimmy Mack turned his wheelchair around and rolled up to Tweeter,

"Been crap goin' on in this place for months!"

It was enough to draw 'RC's attention. He suddenly thought of Anna... and quietly wondered about the adequacy of his judgment. Why hadn't he listened? Why hadn't he known more of what was obvious to this boy?

Jimmy Mack continued. He had become a fountainhead of information.

"Don't you guys ever talk? 'RC's main squeeze works here. Damn! Do I have to solve this case for you?

Tweeter stopped him,

"Hey, no cursing, kid..." He immediately felt guilty. The boy was trying to be helpful; and the words weren't hurting anyone.

Jimmy Mack paused for a moment. It occurred to him that he might be jeopardizing the reputation of 'RC'.

"Well...guess you guys can't catch everything. Anyway, Anna..."

He stopped again – looking at 'RC' for approval. 'RC' nodded,

"Well, Miss Anna's been flat out uncomfortable with the care of the boy down the hall. Shoot...I don't blame her, the boy looks like sh'...uh that is to say, crap."

Tweeter interrupted him,

"...the boy named, Zeke?"

Jimmy Mack retorted,

"Quick study, huhn – yeah, that's the one."

"Go on, kid..."

"Okay...hang on to your girdle!"

He was nature undefied. Minutes later, Tweeter had more of a story than he could believe. Was it real...a wild dream...or perhaps the deteriorating mind of a boy who had too long been a ward of the State? He picked up the phone to call someone; meanwhile playing with the metallic granules in his hand.

The moon cast a fainter light in the approaching dawn. The day was cold; and a high wind pushed clouds slowly through a liquid sky. They undulated like whales in blue-black water.

'RC' stepped outside. At the front of the building he exhaled watching his breath crystallize in the cold; and wondering how much of what he had heard was accurate. The idyllic comfort of 'the facility' had vaporized. It now seemed pretentious and serious - and reminded him of the boarding school where he had long ago met the love of his life. Remaining stars sparkled like cut diamonds in the sky. He leaned back far over a small balcony and looked up at the rectangular lighted windows of the building. They looked like square bales on a moonlit field.

The facility was on a slight rise. He could see the shallow valley below him. A strong wind was making its way through the trees. Robust and wintry, it touched remaining leaves – and they seemed to curl like kale. Its virile coldness reminded him of a night he had spent on the mountain with Bob, the Indian guide. They had been tracking the great cat that had killed a jogger. Even that event had resulted in a false lead. He was disappointed and he knew it.

His cynicism had been accurate – the sweet parts of life were nonexistent. Perhaps he had been living the fantasy of love. Was life no more than deception and commerce? He allowed himself the small hope that, at least, his memories could not be resold. They had made plans; and he had become fond of the boy named, Zeke. But the uncertainty that he now felt in that narrative was beginning to cause his feelings to sink like the land before him. He saw tracks coming up from the valley below. Unsettled and cold, he shuddered; and went back inside.

When he returned, Tweeter was interviewing the principle witness. Trudence Jefferson was in a state of shock; and muttering to herself - talking of her suspicions related to the dead woman. A team had come to pick up the body. Appalled, they watched its rapid decomposition; and wondered if they would have time to do an autopsy – much less bury or cremate the remains.

"I ain't lettin' some shifty woman like Cynthia Gregor hurt mah boy!"

Tweeter pulled the drawing of the daffodil out of his breast pocket. Then - reconsidering the fracas he had come upon -, gently put it back inside his pocket. He did not wish to add to the confusion – or jeopardize his believability.

"Where's the boy now, ma'am. I need to talk to him."

The wind had risen and was blowing a light snow about – obliterating a trail that had been left outside.

"Mah god! I dun fo'got 'bout him!"

Before he could ask anything else, 'True' had pulled herself up from the floor; and was running as hard as she could. Tweeter ran after her in pursuit

- suddenly aware how cold the hallway felt. Someone had obviously left a window open. He could just discern the baying of what sounded like coyotes in the distance.

When he caught up to her, Trudence Jefferson was standing in the doorway of Zeke's room. She was panting and had her hands up to her face in disbelief. The wind was blowing in from an open window...and the boy was gone.

'RC' caught up with Detective Tweeter and 'True'. He stared at the daffodil-yellow wall that Zeke and Anna had recently painted. Feeling emptier than the room and remembering the tracks he had seen in the snow, he said nothing. Then, he headed for his car; thinking of the large cranium he had found in the desert near Coughdrop, Nevada... and marveling at life's connections.

BOB'S JOURNEY

The two dog constellation sits quietly in the sky near Orion. It is a cold, clear evening and Orion is hunting. The hounds wait - perhaps wishing to be included or hoping for his return and the pleasure of a warm hearth. They are lonely. Though their whining cannot be heard back on Earth, we feel the distant and cold sadness.

The wind tosses about. It whistles noisily in the ears of those who are outdoors. Human imperfections pop up like pimples on pure skin. Some binge on alcohol and make late, careless calls they will regret. Fistfuls of dollars change hands somewhere. Some give, but most take. The small of human history often takes place under a sky that is smoky black.

But, somewhere under the dark sky, lovers also kiss. Someone stutters through a speech and feels victorious. Missing children are found. Nipping cold takes over one hemisphere while the sun warms another to allow the luxury of dreams. Odd as it all seems, the two forces exist side by side, day to day, as if in critical balance.

Maybe the human world operates within 'laws' that are not inherent because of temples. Temples were built by men who may not have valued or remembered the grandeur of the earth's sacred places. The arithmetic of temples is the will to have order. It does not recognize, understand or appreciate the preexisting order of the world...or that disorder may be part of order. We do not wish to understand the tempestuous and unpredictable nature of the world. We might not wish to align that nature with our own – preferring the predictability of a safe world...believing there should be more to life. The human animal would exempt itself from the world that bore it - in favor of a vision of excellence written in scripture. And what of those scriptures - was the hand guided? Or was it written by an animal that was perfect in its imperfect thinking? Is the insistence of a divine intervention truth – or trick?

Bob thought of all these things as he looked up at the strange and harmonious arrangement of the heavens. He had told Louise that he would start a journey; but its immediacy had been pushed back. There are no assurances – just as there is no insurance - in nature. He was comfortable with that; and the time for his departure came when it did. Under the great cloth of night, he picked out the bright moon and prayed to the Creator. Then he wondered about a recent dream. It had presented itself as a vision.

In that vision the clouds fought. There were screams traveling on the wind...screams from a young man named, Sincero, screams that sound like... birth. An African woman named, Yoruba...yes, she heard it too. And there was now before him, an older woman wearing the uniform of Catholicism. He marveled at the nun's stony acceptance. A monarch makes its way south... missing someone...in the two ways that is meant. Those who are left behind try to understand and pull out of the tightly woven rope of grief. They struggle to make sense of where they are and what they have seen – a common denominator for all. A message comes to him. It says,

"The abstraction might become clear...where the dog, the trout, and the adder come together."

That is what has brought him to this place. He looks up at the sky whose light is rapidly disappearing. Round clouds absorb the sharp twilight. He believes he is in the correct place; and will need to search the acreage to discover where the 'dream' leads. He pulls down his hat and pulls up the zipper on his jacket. Before beginning to traverse the land, he takes one more look at the evening sky and sees a 'shooting star'. The scent of the earth is wonderful and contains the juice of a full year. Autumn leaves - freshly released from their boughs and composting pleasantly in the cool, moist muck underfoot - remind him of happier times when the land was sacred.

And, as he walks, he starts to dream again. But this dream is of an older attractive woman who has tossed a wreath into black waters, like it is a sacred hoop. He does not question the valence of his disconnected thougths, believing instead that all will be revealed.

It is late autumn. He makes his way through the mosaic of leaves wondering if the high buttresses of leaning trees stained with red and yellow leaves were the precursors to the first cathedrals. He has a vision. It seems naïve to him – as a Native trying to live in two worlds. But there it is again...and the indigenous side of him will not let it perish. Why should it? Is there any reason to believe that what any of us see is 'real'? He asks himself again, 'Is it 'trick' – or is it 'truth'? Realizing he has no answer to the question, he allows the vision to sweep over him. There is a boy with awkward speech. He is luminous. The black-robed nun has returned to wonder at this boy. In a word-created universe there is room for reflection and deception. Perhaps the birds are much closer to the 'truth'. And even they have language.

Bob flips back to something more observable and easier to accept. The wind tears through the gold and auburn hair of the tree. Exploding color hurtles to the ground. It is what some call the time of the 'Long Nights Moon'. The weather pattern has been unpredictable. A cool, musical wind had burnished the landscape; and kept the colors smoldering. The wind speeds through the leaves on the ground, making clicking sounds - like an animal running over a linoleum floor. It spins color through the woods – consistent with powerful indigenous tales about weavers and how the world came into being. It is the 'falling season' when dreams are most intense.

The vision has come back. He sees the vacant, helpless look of the luminous boy who has been pulled from his bed. A burly man of great proportion...covers tracks. A window is open; and the snow is falling lightly. It will soon be the time for winter stillness. He shudders. A stone has been thrown into his wet, malleable consciousness. Ripple after ripple of thoughts build upon each other as he attempts to put the thoughts together.

There, Bob stood – thinking as the flurry began to coat him – until he looked like a marble statue. Suddenly aware of the abysmal cold, he twitches his fingers inside of woolen mittens; and wishes that he had something warm to drink. Chocolate would be nice.

Then he continues his limp into the landscape. His body is older and one of his legs is stiff. He pulls the 'maned' parka tightly down over his head; and pulls off the ovate glasses that he is wearing and wipes them. The vision is enough – he does not want the day to be any less clear. He immediately feels guilty at 'not being Indian enough'.

Many of the plants have been razed by the peculiar weather. Some are filled with holes or have brown edges. They look like worn clothing. A passing rainstorm has left small circles of dirt in the light frosting of snow. The patches look like dull pennies thrown on a white counter.

Someone suddenly approaches on the narrow trail that he traverses. The unexpected event caused him to shudder; and he wonders at his own resolve and beliefs. The darkness and the flurry of snow leave him unable to see the man clearly; but he hears him murmur as he passes...and then, wonders if he should look back.

"Namaste..."

It was a customary greeting by Tibetans that simply meant,

"I bow to the god within you."

He had heard it in commercials – and it suddenly seemed corny. But he had also read that it was the beginning of the age of the indigo children – children of this time would be born with blue auras around them. They would shepherd in a time of peace. The account appealed to his view of the world that, 'everyday things' might be neither; and that reality was likely much more different than what most humans perceived. He immediately realized the arrogance of the thought; but wondered still – if it wasn't true. Oddly enough, he thought again of the petulant young man, named 'RC'.

Then, he focused his attention on the purpose of his journey. It was cold; and time suddenly seemed short. Previously, he had heard the screams in the air as he had taken the hoe to the tough soil. The wind in the trees had told him of a birth. But now, the colors had faded within a landscape that was quickly becoming dark and snowy. There was a wild energy that was thin but still standing. And he wondered if he had the right to 'interpret' anything as ephemeral as a dream...after all, it was he who had questioned the very truth of what everyone saw. But the dream had been far from transitory; and it had convinced him that – if there was any reality afoot – it was nonconforming. He had a role to play. The persistence of the dream coupled with a questionable reality, was enough to convince him to continue walking.

Had humans sailed, walked, driven, and flown for centuries on a quest to find something that would take us away from the dismal hollow of our own souls. Perhaps, all the while, that to which we aspired had simply been underfoot. Who could be sure?'

It was then that he saw that for which he had come searching. The willful flurry had stopped. In the distance, in a sheltered corner, within the brightness of the snow, a spotted trout lily seemed to beckon. Was he certain? Science said that everything we perceive is through the optic of the eye and mind. Had 'we' built a filter for our brain; or had our brain built a filter for 'us'? Was what he was seeing – indeed, 'real' – and how would anyone know that?

The issue of his ego came back to him...why should he be a messenger? There were many with much more talent and ability. Had he squandered his time with Louise – by leaving her for some insane journey to discover something about a dream? With those thoughts, he collapsed to the ground; and a dream memory spun its way into him. It was a tale his uncle had recounted long ago.

'Once there was a very poor man who walked a long path everyday in search of food. One evening as he sat by the path and prayed, the Creator - who some call 'Wakan Tanka' - appeared and asked the man what he most wanted. The man told the Creator that he wanted moccasins - for his bare feet were very sore and tired. There was a clap of thunder. Before the man could blink the Creator was gone. He looked down at his feet; and discovered a most beautiful pair of beaded moccasins.

The man gave thanks to the Creator. And as he had always done, he walked the same path everyday searching for food. And he gave thanks everyday for the gift that had been given to him. Everywhere he went, he spoke of the wonderful gift that the Creator had bestowed; and how much easier his life was because of the new moccasins.

One day, he was approached by two bad men. They beat him and took the beaded moccasins that the Creator had given to him. As he lay there bleeding, he felt the earth rumble. It seemed to speak; and told him to crawl into a hollow of earth and stay there.

He had just finished doing what the land had instructed, when a tremendous prairie fire came roaring over the hills – chasing all the animals in front of it. After awhile, the man stood up. The fire had passed – and he was unhurt. In the distance, he could see the charred bodies of the men who had beaten him and taken the moccasins.

And as he listened, he could hear others who had been spared by the fire. They were wailing. The land was blackened. The path was charred and no longer visible - none could find their way home.

But, the man who had walked the long path in bare feet for so many years was able to lead them. His naked feet remembered every rise, fall, and crevice of the path. And when they arrived at the village, there was great joy. He had returned the people to their home.

One day after many winters, he went forward on a 'hambeday' (spiritual quest) - for he had an important question to ask the Creator, a question that had always bothered him. For four days and four nights, he fasted and sat in a small hollow that he had dug on the edge of a hill, wearing nothing but a breech cloth - looking at the stars and searching for an answer to his question – some sign from the Creator.

On the fourth day of fasting the man was nearly overcome by weakness. It was then that the Creator visited him. The man asked the Creator why he had allowed the gift of the sacred moccasins, to be stolen and destroyed. To which the Creator responded,

'No one knows the road of life as well as a man in bare feet.'

When Bob awakened much time had passed. He was cold; but the deep root of self-doubt had been pulled away from him. Odd as it seemed, the dream memory - the tale that his uncle had once recounted - had restored him to a sober state. He marveled at the power of the word; and the sight of this small, strange, spotted lily seemed to put him back in a state of soundness. For the moment, hope was suitor.

He had believed in the connectivity of all things – and that everything had a message. He accepted the spiritual manifestations of spectral travel, a sixth sense, circular time, and death as a part of life – beliefs that often seemed incongruent with modernity. To him...the sum total of ways built by a group of humans and transmitted from generation to generation should include the discomfort of believing - but not knowing. He wondered if it might be true that - only through suffering and being on the edge of the 'world's rim' – might one know the slimmest part of a grand plan. He quietly laughed at the existentialist nature of that speculation and the extraordinariness of the light above him...then, quietly wished he had a cheeseburger.

Few really thought of the walking spirits - the Ghost nations that watched over us; coming to us in dreams. But he had walked in plains and forests – seeing things that couldn't be explained easily. Science was eager to dismiss such sightings as the consequence of fatigue, a trick of light and shadow, narcotic, or the optics of the eye in concert with the mind.

He walked toward the trout lily. It was pretty and perfect. He mused about the belief of being reincarnated as a 'higher' form. Was it any less believable that we should fold into moonlight or the delicate and complete seed of a milkweed? And why should that be an empty existence? Though naked of certainty, he still doubted those who said they 'knew'. He shook his head; then, listened to the baying of something in the distance.

A flock of birds flew over rapidly as if startled by the sound - or perhaps responding to an inaudible call. He strained to see them. They turned and twisted in timeless formation seeming to feed upon a cosmic consciousness. Theirs was an ancient way – not built upon words. They moved through the air in serpentine waves - as they had done for centuries ...seemingly content. As things were want to happen - and through the purity of his doubt and uncertainty - a dream backed in.

There was an old black man with a boy at his side. He recognized the boy immediately as a very young 'RC'. The man said to the boy,

"My music done spoke to you – and I ain't said a word.'

Bob sat for a long time perched upon the edge of a rock looking into the air and slightly below to a spit of land. His wrinkled, still, pensive face looked like a gargoyle peering down at the world from Notre Dame. The wind exploded with activity as if it was a top that someone had wound and let go. It pirouetted about the landscape; kicking up leaves wherever it went. But it did not make him move. Instead, he sat stoically, looking out across the land. This place seemed heavy with history. He continued to sit until he realized that another day had gone by. A corner of the darkened sky had become pink like a wild rose pinned in black hair. He sat until he felt the chill of the night upon his shoulders and watched the beginning of its etching upon a small puddle in front of him. Then he got up slowly; shook the cold from his shoulders;

and roamed the woods for dried brush to burn...and a sturdy vine.

Long after he had started the fire, he sat - watching the flames dance. He had stretched the vine and tightly secured it between two saplings. Hanging a cheap drop cloth over him, he sat within the makeshift tent looking at the nearby trout lily and wondering what clue it could possibly provide to him regarding his series of dreams - filled with wonder at its hardiness. Sheltered by a nearby boulder, it had survived the flurry and cold and seemed crisp in its resilience.

The sacred smoke curled away like spirits disappearing into the night as the wood gave itself up. The smoke garnished the stars with a wavy softness - making them appear like phosphorescent fireflies caught in a jar. All the while he sat thinking about the dignity in the trees, birds and rocks; and wondering why beliefs - that had taken centuries to form - could be so transitory as to be lost within a few generations. He closed his eyes and - while he thought of all of this - the wind continued to carry the muted cries of a young man now gone. Bob could see the wind lifting a monarch butterfly that was journeying southward.

Then, he thought of his wife, Louise. Her sturdy, quiet, and loving nature baffled him. Though he felt very tired, the thought of her restored his energy. She made him laugh and her generous nature was everything he could have hoped for. He could see her smiling through the darkness...a prize that he had been lucky enough to win.

Near the trout lily - and peeping out of the snow – a bit of saffron color could be seen. Some daffodils heads had pushed their way through the light covering of snow. Their golden bugles seemed to proclaim the presence of a civilized garden that had been planted long ago. He was certain that the ruins of an old house must be nearby. The flowers bounced about in the wind as if they were taffeta ribbons on a white dress. He wondered what Louise might be doing - and whether she was happy.

Then, he stared at the fire again. It disappeared as easily as the wind – a bright fleeting bit of order in a universe filled with darkness and chaos. To try and capture the light of it was as impossible as holding a box full of mist.

He and 'RC' had argued one night about whether any matter could be lost. A life could go through a century with nothing of note to show for it. Did it then fold into something as transient as a pardon? Did it start anew as another man? Did is simply become a rock – to be slung? Or go back to light? All monuments eventually become dust. Perhaps light was the only enduring ephemeron. Staring up at the sky, he saw the constellation, Orion – and wondered if his 'hunt' was over. Then he fell asleep...no closer to the secret that he sought.

THE TROUT LILY'S SECRET

Much later when Bob, the Native, awakened, the sunlight was pleasurably transparent and falling down in bright shafts through the trees. The misty vapor of the forest rose up from its floor. There was power in the mist's diminutive silence as it flowed through the trees like a translucent silken scarf.

After allowing for the delusion brought on by lack of food, he was certain of only one thing. Something seemed to be interrupting the natural progression of living things. And that – he concluded - could impact a reincarnating process which was bedrock to his beliefs. He found no indelible conflict in his convictions related to naturalism and the tenets of more conventional beliefs. Indeed it was the reveille for interesting conversation...but the circumstance was now different.

Bob gingerly reached into his coat pocket and pulled out a device as carefully as woman might pull lipstick out of her purse. The field glasses' metal alloy gave it a blue-white icicle shine. Taking a neutrally charged cloth, he gently dusted the lenses and carefully looked through them – scanning the horizon.

A nearby pond appeared to be glacier-spawned. It was unusual to be so far south. He had studied the six types of glaciers. Their power as earth movers and molders was often overlooked. By record, the giants were capable of moving 100 feet per day carving, crushing, and digesting the terrain they passed through; and producing much of the fertile soil of the Midwest. In a moment of self doubt he wondered, was he really correct about the area in which he now found himself? Could a clue really be found in this unlikely location?

He was more certain after spotting a nearby drumlin. The mound of the hill could have easily been mistaken for one of the great Indian serpent mounds. The oval deposition was in a somewhat low area. The glacier had melted and left the rock it had once carried with it. The nearby lake had to have been formed by the gouging of the earth and a serac breaking off. When it melted, it had formed a deep body of water. The previous carving by the mother glacier had created an easy route for existing water to refill the lake. What was left of the glacier had probably made its way to the sea and broken off into icebergs which melted into seawater.

Around the glacier-formed lake, green and brown clumps of planted daffodils had long since withered under the kiss of the cold. The pull of curiosity intensified. Was he on the right track? Out of the corner of his eye, he saw an enigmatic blur of spotted yellow and green. It could not be denied; and he thought of the dream again, speaking the clue aloud,

Where the dog, the trout, and the adder come together."

As if by speaking, it had come to be. He now saw - not just one of them – but a spate of lilies that he identified as 'Erythronium americanum' - also called the 'dog-tooth violet', 'trout lily', or 'adder's-tongue'. This was where his dream had taken him – to an area filled with a small yellow woodland flower with reddish-blotched green leaves.

The flowers resembled penitent survivors –daring explanation. And this time he did not utter the dream's clue, but shouted it. The surviving flowers were blooming freely in a small depression on the side of the drumlin. Though kissed by dappled light, they seemed to want for the moon; and he marveled at the magic of the world. What could the flower possibly yield?

He walked for a few minutes before he stood before the phantom patch; and then, leaned closer to the earth. He could smell the sweet scent of decay that fed the forest from its floor. Patches of brilliant green moss held to the rock that sheltered the flowers. The moss had sent up light russet stems that looked like the first stubble on a young man's face. It had beaten the sparseness of the rock; and leapt forward in verdant victory. It hugged the great boulder as if to do anything else might be suicidal. The nude branches of the trees filtered the light like slats that had been purposely fit at angles; and the light fell upon the organic decay. It formed palatial malevolent shadows of the quality found in luminescent paintings. Passing clouds rallied; and wrote their own drama across the land. The narcotic of light combined with the natural architecture of the forest to form a rapturously warm embrace of slim light. A snow flurry shot through the calm; and covered dark tree trunks with spots. In places an earlier snow had melted; and it now gurgled forth in rivulets - laughing asymmetrically.

The trout lilies seemed to pull him gently forward. It had been hours since he had eaten; and he felt a sleepy delirium that ached and gave everything a dreamy quality. Bob leaned ever nearer to the closest lily; and looked deeply into its center. An animus seemed to draw him in to the deepest part of the sepals and stamens. He had studied botany; and had long enjoyed reading about the history and use of plants. To many, the lily was a sign of resurrection.

The trout lily, in particular, had a story associated with it. Some said it had sprung from the tears of the Virgin Mary as she held her deceased son – freshly freed from the crucifix. For the moment, he dismissed his interest in the story. He was being pulled into the center of the flower – his consciousness mixed with the filtered light; and the resulting photosynthesis of thought...had formed what could best be called ...a streaming vision.

As he looked deep within the delicate trumpet of the trout lily, he imagined that he saw things. There within, was a small record of life. In it, he could see the health of the earth...and a great theft. Within the sepals the names of a dark man, a giant bird and two-headed dog came to him. The dark man carried a package of metallic sand that held a secret.

The lily then 'carried' Bob to other places. It spoke of oaths and rhymes that needed to be interpreted. And at the very center, was a series of numbers of the sort found unexpectedly in nature; such as the branching of trees, the arrangements of leaves, the flowering of plants; the uncurling of ferns; and the order of the pinecones' bracts. It clung to and arithmetic order that had been laid down millennia before. Bob could briefly glimpse the infrared part of the color spectrum. He felt the ancient root of the plant; and its connection to the others. Its bugle commanded to him; and he spoke the words again,

'Where the dog, the trout, and the adder come together.'

And for the first time, he thought about the religious symbolism between the dog, the fish, and the snake. He understood what it might mean for the three things to 'come together'. The faithless, the faithful, and those who would destroy faith - were intersecting. It momentarily jarred him.

His senses seemed distorted. And he wondered again - if it might not be a symptom of hunger or fatigue. But he had been in much more severe situations. Could it be that there was something greater that had drawn him to where he was? Then, suddenly he had the sensation of falling. He seemed to be sliding into the funnel of the flower that he had been staring at. The base of the cup of the lily stopped him; and when he stopped, he gazed upward... able to see the world as he had not seen it before.

In this unusual inebriation, he remembered his rudimentary understanding of quantum mechanics and metaphysics. That science postulated that the mind takes photos and stores them as visual images. It only processes things it has seen before; and uses only a small percentage of its capacity. Metaphysicists insisted that most of what is before us – we miss. The mind cannot immediately process things that are too foreign to it. Was he experiencing what he thought he was?

Material things – including humans - were more space than solid ...and 'held together' by something. Metaphysicists knew that the forces which held us together and kept us from becoming a pile of atoms – were not fully understood or explained. That lack of explanation, lent a mystical nature to what was deemed 'reality'. He wondered, 'could there be any other reason to be spiritual'? Bob looked out of the flower's funnel again ...and then, fell into a deep sleep.

Hours later when he finally awakened, he was lying on the ground staring at the trout lily and thinking of the sinister man named, 'Gregor' whose name had come to him in the dream. The man was a ruffian who hunted and traded with aplomb. But, what did Gregor want with Ezekiel, the boy missing from 'the facility'? And how was this coarse man connected to the young woman named, Anna – the two were like light and shadow. The flower had provided more clues; and - in its earnest secretiveness - had allowed that a great encounter was near...something new, yet timeless. Would the outcome of science be directed by the soul; or was the soul prey to science? Bob knew what he must do; but wondered if it would be enough...or was it just 'old people's medicine'.

THE RAVEN

As he lay beside the patch of trout lilies, Bob was suddenly startled by a raven's coarse, raucous cawing. It stirred him into a state of vigilance and unrest. The Raven was important in Native tales. Many tribes admired it. Though it was associated with death, trickery or wisdom - the bird was immortal to many. He remembered the great tale of how darkness had existed in the world until Raven tricked the Chief of the Heavens into giving up the box...where he kept light.[33]

The 'science' part of him momentarily took over the 'Native'. But what he had just experienced related to the trout lily combined with a basic understanding of metaphysics would not allow him to discount the legend. Perhaps we didn't see what was really before us? He struggled to make the two worlds come together, and then immediately felt guilty. He had doubted himself and discounted something that was important. Was he really up to the task before him? 'Real Natives' would have accepted the tale as truth – a religious fundamental. It bothered him deeply. He immediately thought of the young 'washicu' named, 'RC'; and felt more than a bit hypocritical. Had he been too hard on 'RC' in their 'fireside chats'? Why should he have expected a 'European' to understand or believe that which he now wrestled with?

His introspection quickly evaporated into the ether where all lost thoughts go. For now, the raven seemed to be speaking to him; and trying to alert him to something that was amiss. Bob looked back at the trout lilies.

He could see the reflection of a silver patch of sand. Was he dreaming? How had it been brought there? Had it been born by the great glaciers...had someone inadvertently dropped it? He remembered passing the man in the snow flurry. Perhaps he had been the source. Regardless, the raven too had seen the shiny objects; and was intrigued.

Curious, it flew down from its perch; and hopped around the perimeter of the shiny patch. Then, when it was comfortable, it bent forward and scooped up some of the shiny powder with its bill – and swallowed. With a few flaps of its broad wings, it gracefully rose to a nearby branch where it

---

33 'Raven, Crow, and Corvids in Myth, Folklore, and Religion', Socyberty

perched theatrically with the moon as its backdrop.

It seemed to sink on its perch like an old man who had eaten something that didn't agree with him. It ruffled its feathers a bit; and its head drooped. The eyes seemed to glaze over; and then, it shook traumatically – as if it were trying to dislodge something in its throat.

It was too late. The tail feathers began to loosen. The feathers pushed out and dropped like sins from the mouth of a man at confession. They rained to the ground so quickly that Bob backed away. When the black rain stopped, the naked figure of the raven began twisting its head back and forth as if it wished to snap it off. Its feet, legs and the dull scabbard of its bill remained. Offal dripped away from it to the ground. The black prince, whose silhouette had so held the moon...now, seemed barely able to hold onto a branch.

A pattern of 'goose bumps' appeared on the bird's breast, flanks, and belly. They seemed to form in repeating chains – slightly beside each other and occasionally overlapping. The raven arched its back and seemed to elongate. It swayed back and forth – feet still holding to its perch. Then, it briefly bloated out; and looked at Bob as if it sensed demise.

Slowly, the black of its bill was absorbed into its body; and a pattern of dots began to darken, expand, and overlap in a geometric pattern. The eyes became hard and dark as obsidian. It glistened in the moonlight.

Within seconds the animal lost its feet; and plummeted to the ground where it continued to writhe until any vestige of its appendages had disappeared. The running distribution of what had appeared to be goose-bumps upon its skin had solidified into barely perceptible diamond-like patterns. It coiled, pushed its head skyward - as if seeking to return to the air upon which it had previously traversed. Then it looked at its earthly confinement through stony eyes.

Quickly slithering away, it curled up; and sat like circles of stacked rope in the protected niche of a nearby fruit tree. There it hissed menacingly, barely disguising its singular poison – a poison that had been written about for centuries...and for which humans were particularly susceptible.

The genetic makeup of what was once a raven – had changed. The silver powder it had ingested had enticed a pirouetting, repetitive structure upon, and within, the body of the animal. Through the industry of thought and dream, the following phrase suddenly came to Bob.

"C'est le serpent, dit-elle, je l'ai ecoute, et il m'a trompee."

He understood its meaning and the biblical parallels. To him, it was an allegory for all human will; and the power of the serpent in Native lore was particularly potent. His thoughts were flying. With that, his body collapsed.

Meanwhile, and nearby in the town where the gargantuan man named, Gregor, resided...three women would be drawn together through intuition and circumstance.

Anna had noticed that her mother, Sister Frances, had not returned from a visit that she had suggested – the visit to make amends to the woman known as Sue Bee and the Latino man who was her companion. Neither had she seen 'RC' return. He had been suddenly called away to work on a case with a local detective. Her worry had become overpowering – her intuition had proclaimed peril for the light in her life.

Both had been absent far too long. Something told her that she must go search for her mother. Though she considered that the depth of her concern might be ridiculous – and could point to nothing substantial related to it – nonetheless, she could not shake off a sense of duty that now compelled her. Worse still, she could not escape the feeling that 'RC' and Zeke might also be in trouble.

She left the house rapidly - barely having time to put on a warm coat. Her worry had compounded; and she was practically running up the street toward the facility where 'RC' had said he would meet the detective regarding some findings. She felt a compelling need to see if 'RC' was okay; and to check in on Zeke. Her haste took her by a small church that she had passed many times. Something stopped her. For the first time in a long while, she would stop and say a quick prayer. Instead, any thought of speed was tabled.

There she met the woman whom Bob had seen in his dream...the woman throwing a wreath into the black water of a bay. Sophia Angaros too had stopped in the small church and she was not alone. She was in need of a confession – if not to a priest then, at least someone who was a member of the cloth...even a tall rugged nun who called herself, Sister Frances.

In a dream state from his collapse, Bob mused at what he now 'saw' before him; and asked himself whether he was indeed dreaming or awake again. He decided it didn't matter. Like so many other parts of nature, the rambling tangle of thoughts that had come to him, seemed to have an uncanny order. Perhaps he was finally seeing what was really there.

He had wished that he could stop the course of what he 'saw'; that he could impugn unsavory actions and protect those who were unaware of the course of malevolent events. He wanted to reach out to the woman, Anna, and console her – to tell her that 'RC' was okay. But dreams, like waves of light, were best seen without the expense of interference. Their clarity seemed independent of purchase. He shook himself into consciousness again. The serpent that had once been 'Raven' - had disappeared.

Now he understood more. The 'silver sand' that the raven had ingested was like that borne by the young man, Sincero. It had changed both of them in some way that they were physically or spiritually predisposed - he could not know. It had been Sincero's screams that he had heard in the air...screams of birth. And from his passing a monarch had been released...a monarch that flew home to join the great orange mass of those who clung to trees and would eventually make their journey back. There was more. It was now clear to him who had abducted the young boy, Ezekiel. The democracy of dream and reality had come together; and had elected that ...the mountain lion which had been captured was not the one that had killed the jogger. It was still out there. Its imprisonment had been prevented by the interference of a brutish hand. Bob reflected on a message that 'RC' had once inadvertently allowed to him. He had found a large cranium in the Nevada desert; and remitted it to a forensics lab.

The native man realized that any garden – once tilled – might yield fruit. The dark fruit of Roger Gregor had appeared; and Bob understood - though he might not interfere with the events he saw in his dream – he might, at least, offer his own prayer. It was time to return to Louise; and perform the sacred 'Sun Dance'...if he was capable.

SUN DANCE

Before leaving the area of the drumlin, Bob strode again toward the patch of trout lilies. The moon gilded them and they seemed to beckon. He bent closer; upturned one; and looked deep into its creamy yellow funnel. There was nothing tremendous or startling looking back...

Instead, he could just barely discern the whisper of something. At first he thought it was the echo of the wind in his ear. But then it came to him again. And it seemed to say, ever so softly...barely more audible than the beating of his heart,

"Without its power, all wilts... and the common scarlet drops away"

He now knew what he must do. It was time for 'hupa gluza' (the lifting of the pipe) and to pray for all beings including the 'ikce wicasa' (human beings). He must leave this place and center himself. He could no longer defer action. The hard work of making things right could not be ignored. If he truly believed in a Great Spirit, he must implore it through prayer; and he must ask it to use its power to weave back the unraveling blanket of light and life. Intrinsic merit was at risk of being renounced – even the sunrise might soon have a price. Or was he to believe that it was all a myth; that there was no power to the word; and that nothing could be turned around?

And so he sat down; leaned against the great ancestor rock that protected them; and picked a few of the trout lilies. Putting his nose to their funnels he breathed them in. Then, he removed a few kernels of the prayer corn from his pocket – the sacred corn that had hung in the 'soddie' that Louise and he shared. It was what had alerted him to the presence of the powerful winds that came from the great Wind Cave.

He gently swallowed a few of the kernels; and allowed himself to dream. And again he was floating across the land. As he traveled the sun was rising and the light came forth. He was near the sacred place - and Louise was waiting. There he dropped from the clouds to great place of the Sundance pole. It had been draped with a few of the lilies.

Entering the sacred circle, he asked to be attached to the pole. There...he would swing from the pole in the sun with metal thongs piercing the skin of his chest; and 'swim' toward the light with the trout lily in his hand and the eagle whistle in his mouth. He would pray until the thongs that skewered his flesh – tore through him...and he dropped to the ground to be reborn at the foot of the light ancestors. He would pray that the 'woniya sinoko' (sacred monster) wind would be sucked back from where it had come. It was only through such great sacrifice that this might happen.

And now he thought he understood the meaning behind the lily's whispered message. It was of the resurrection of a sweet force that seemed to hold things together...something that had been easily lost through the twin forces of despair and cynicisms. But the hissing of a dark hollow voice insisted otherwise. It suggested the naiveté of any such belief. The trout lily had whispered an enormous secret – the power of something that could hold all life and light together. Without it, the manipulation of life would occur - the sort of which could hardly be imagined.

The lack of food and water had left him light-headed. Bob wondered was his vision nothing more than a delusion brought on by lack of sustenance. It was then that he saw the silhouette of a gargantuan raptor sailing over him. It seemed to sing – not like a songbird but in a throaty, screaming baritone. It was singing 'Santa Lucia'. He smirked - it did not have the voice for it - then, he immediately refocused.

The baron of the air soared and the great wind rose and fell before it. Then he suddenly thought of his talk around the fire with 'RC' and the message from the fire. A great happiness and sadness would visit the young man...the fire had indicated it was the same thing forward and backwards. He thought of the dark man whose name had come to him. 'Roger G. Gregor'. The man's name was the second palindrome – the same forward as it was backward. This was the sadness and pain of which the fire had spoken so long ago related to 'RC'.

For once Bob wished that he had a cell phone within reach – he would call 'RC'. The young 'washicu' had proved to be as remarkably resistant to clairvoyance as he was at being successful in love - telemetry simply would not work. He thought of the young woman named 'Anna' – the first palindrome – then, wondered how it was that an eel could find its way to the same water it was born in; but some men couldn't find a feeling even with a roadmap.

All these thoughts came to Bob as if infused into him by something greater. But, a particularly recurring image bothered him more than anything else. It was the image of a large man trying to assert himself with great force into his thoughts – the man named, Roger G. Gregor. Bob cocked his head with an ear to the wind. He could hear residual screams of the young man named, Sincero; and could sense that the monarch was nearly home.

But there was more. In his vision, he had seen a rabbit. The hare had drawn its breath. It sat quietly – frozen in movement. Something was walking near it; something hungry - with padded feet. It did not see or smell the rabbit. Instead, it had spotted a young woman walking alone; and its eyes burned bright with the expectation of a food it had once tasted. Its hunger was overwhelming – and he was more certain than ever that the wrong mountain lion had been caught.

STRANGE POLARITY

Seconds after walking out of the facility and away from the crime scene, 'RC' was in his car.

Oddly enough, a thought of Bob came to him – and he wondered why it had inserted itself at the moment when his overwhelming concern was to find both Anna and Zeke. The distraction irritated him slightly; and he wondered if Bob might still be rooting through a universe of possibilities related the finding the mountain lion that had successfully eluded them. He remembered the Native's odd habit of 'reading the fire' and the statement about 'great happiness and sadness' being backwards and forwards. In a rare instance of intuition, he sensed a menace for Anna – and then, wondered why he thought of her as light.

He looked back through the open door of the facility. Detective Tweeter continued to interview Trudence Jefferson and Jimmy Mack while waiting for more assistance with the corpse of Cynthia Gregor. 'RC' reflected on what he had seen; and the memories of his time with Bob on the mountain as they hunted the great cat. Frustrated by memories that made no sense to him and lost time, he suddenly punched off the car stereo; turned the key in the ignition; jerked the car into gear; stomped the gas pedal to the floor; and sped downhill.

The investigations with which he and Detective Tweeter had been working - seemed to have an odd reciprocity and much more clarity than his time spent on the mountain with the native tracker. The footprints he had seen in the snow had stopped at the abducted boy's window. A parallel set of footprints led down the hill from 'the facility' indicating Zeke had been carried a distance. It was cold out but 'RC' lowered his car window listening for any possible sound.

He imagined that he had heard the abducted boy's muffled screams drifting on the air but they disappeared as quickly as they had come. A short distance away he found fresh tire tracks. The footprints in the snow had stopped and the tire tracks led away from 'the facility'. He recognized both sets of tracks; and it momentarily startled him. He had seen the footprints and tire tracks before…at Anna's house.

Within seconds he was speeding down the remainder of the snow rutted approach to 'the facility'. He thought of his last interview with the now deceased guide, Sincero. He thought of the significance of the metallic granules which had streamed out of the cranium he had found in the desert. Finally, he thought of the new information that a frantic Trudence Jefferson had just provided, regarding late night tests being conducted on Zeke.

'RC' was now quite certain where the captive boy might be taken. It was an area that had significance to the abductor. He thought again of the prophetic statement made by Bob - about great happiness and sadness being both forward and backward. He cursed the man. Why couldn't he forget a statement that not only annoyed him; but which he did not understand? Everything had happened so quickly and unexpectedly that he was no longer sure that the events of the evening were real. The snow had stopped; started again - and then stopped once more.

Within minutes he had pulled into the entrance of 'Frances Park'. The earlier cloud cover had been whisked away by high, fast air currents. Darkness had swept in. He had long since lost sight of the car tracks that had been evident on his descent from the facility. The minimal slush of the well-traveled roads had made it impossible to discern the car's whereabouts - and there was no car in sight at the park. In the distance he could just make out the wailing and snarling of hounds. It compelled him to stop – this had to be the right place. He allowed himself to imagine how things might 'play out' for the frail boy; and then, shuddered – hoping he would find him before it was too late. The night was abnormally dark – the occurrence of a lunar eclipse was in play. The media had been touting it for months. Despite the darkness, the sky had cleared; and the constellation, Lepus, the hare, was hiding quietly amidst a bramble of brighter stars south of Orion. Canis Major was sniffing nearby – as if ready to flush the enticing meal from its hiding place and to savor its warm blood.

Back at 'the facility', Detective Tweeter had finally stepped out into the evening to smoke a cigarette when he noticed the absence of 'RC's car. He too had seen the footprints going to and from the abducted boy's bedroom window. He deduced that 'RC' must be pursuing the lead.

Then, he thought of the pattern of bumps he had seen form on Cynthia Gregor's corpse - and how rapidly the body had become unrecognizable. He had seen it before; and immediately thought of the death of Sophia Angaros' husband, Archibald. He looked up at the constellations in the sky - and wondered if the mythology of stars was any stranger than the course of human events. High up in the heavens, the snake-haired Medussa hissed; but her hissing could not be heard back on earth. Tweeter thought of the woman who so intrigued him. Had Sophia Angaros told him everything that she knew about the death of her husband? Regretfully, he thought it might be time to visit her once more. He did not wish to think it; but perhaps, her involvement had been more out of complicity than circumstance.

Concurrently, across town 'RC' continued to crouch by a picnic table in Frances Park. He was thinking about his approach; and panning the area for signs of footprints in the snow. In the foreground of the land, he was surprised to see a large bed of daffodils poking their heads out - just above the snow. He had not noticed them before; and wondered if Anna had planted them in honor of her mother, Sister Frances. They were barely more visible than webbing - due to the dim light and a curtain of snow.

There is a time – often just past twilight or just before dawn that is both frightening and captivating. It occurs infrequently; and is a magical interface between the boundaries of light and dark. We have no specific term for it; but feel its enchantment. It enters through wide-open eyes. Light which was created – perhaps millions of years ago - falls into us and causes hypnosis. It happens only if we are still enough to allow it.

At this time, the heart takes over; and the head is subordinate. Perhaps we are sitting on a rock looking out across a vast distance. Maybe we are sitting in a chair on the porch. The evening is quiet and we are looking out at the distant specks of light in the sky. Or we could be at the opening of a tent - looking up at the trees when we suddenly notice the glow of the moon. Having grown weary of sound, we experience the quiet; and feel profoundly connected. The heart takes over the body. Our pulse rocks us like tremors from the earth; and we shake to its beat. It is at this time that the royalty of the heart shows itself to us – that we might understand the head's trickery. We might choose to ignore the luminescence and the pounding of our heart; and focus instead on our thoughts. Or maybe - we wonder why this feeling is so easily discounted; as we are rocked by its power. We look at shadows that hold monsters; and know that - even they - could not be there without light... and we are astonished by that simple revelation.

As 'RC' stared up at the stars on this clear eclipsed night, he was suddenly struck by the beauty of the world; and momentarily forgot the purpose of his visit. He immediately admonished his foolish heart. Where had it led him? The great hissing sound of doubt had taken over again. But he was drawn back to the beauty of the night before him and felt this powerful time. He stared up at the sky and the light from the stars poured into him. He thought of churches rocking with music and sound. He marveled at crashing addictions that tore open hearts and allowed people to speak their souls. He dreamed like a child struck by the sight of fireflies; and he envisioned himself as a hiker sitting beside a brook – listening to and reflecting on its strange, beautiful 'fall to' language. In this spontaneity, he envisioned lovers embracing under the moon; and felt the meditative walk of people with no destination in mind. This was where his heart had led him. He wondered – was there meaning to the world unless we gave it...or did the world suggest meaning to us.

A deep quietude held him - reinforced by his focus on the moon and a love that had surprised him – and for which he still held out hope. He sat in the quiet, rocking with the pulse of his heart. The eclipse had passed; and the moon shined again – bright as a yellow leaf. For the first time in a very long time, he prayed that all dark suspicions he had before him - might vanish. There was no Camelot. The sleeping maiden would eventually snore; but when love took off her trappings and smeared the paint from her face – she was still provocative. He longed for Anna. If she had been next to him - he would have danced with her until all muscles were sore; until ligaments twisted free; until bones cracked...until all doubt unraveled.

At this solitary moment, he ached for her embrace and hoped that he had just imagined the tracks he had seen on the hill at 'the facility'. In frustration, he picked up his cell phone...and then - just as suddenly - threw it down; and then picked it up again. He looked up at the velvet, sequined sky. The constellation, Lepus, was within his sight. He stared at it until the pulse of his body made the stars appear to be dancing back and forth. And, finally – when he was ready - it was not doubt but rather, principle - that propelled him toward a duty with which his heart was in conflict.

A CONFLUENCE

When 'RC' could no longer tolerate the cold, he rose to his feet, from the nearby picnic table where he had been crouching. He despaired at the task at hand. As he moved forward, his car keys jangled in his pocket. The open ground before him was polka dotted with bits of trash. His knees felt stiff. In one of the park's open pits, a vagrant had started a fire and left a partially finished can of peas and the bones of a pigeon. The remains of the can and the carcass were in the center of the charcoal, burned black. He suddenly felt sick; but continued on - looking for some reasonable sign of tracks or disturbance that might indicate that he was near the abducted boy and his captor.

As he panned the distance, his attention was seized by a large thicket within the park. In his interview with Sue Bee, she had described it as the place from where she and her friends had pulled the brutalized, and nearly dead, Sincero. The thicket was surrounded by a perimeter of prickly plants with a solitary path leading into it. 'RC' walked down to it and gingerly entered the low dark area. He could just make out the numerous graffiti that had been scrawled and cut into trees; and thought he heard the wheezing of a large animal that was being restrained.

The hollow in which he found himself was an incredibly thick tangle of vines. It had slept for decades in darkness with just the very tops of the vegetation receiving any light. He stopped suddenly - just able to make out the soft cry of something. The area smelled of human waste and damp decay – a lair of lost hope and desperation that rodents would avoid. Even fear could not thrive there. In the pit of his stomach, 'RC' felt a sickened worry. He knew the wallow must hold the basest of secrets; and prayed that he might not find that which he feared.

And then, he heard a most unwanted sound – the hard snarling of dogs. It was followed by the muted cries of the boy, Ezekiel, being pulled along somewhere. 'RC's feet remained anchored to the ground; and he felt a cold fever seep into him. He watched as the mist rose from the ground like an amorphous assemblage of spirits. And when he peered deep within the shadows from the narrow path where he stood; he could just see the source of the snarling. At the interior of the thicket stood a two-headed dog – its breath gushing out in the cold air as it panted and growled. The grizzly symphony of sounds he had heard had been made by one monstrous beast.

His thoughts traveled back in time to the memory of the boy, Zeke, and one of the visits to the facility. The boy had commented to Anna about 'snapping the heads off of animal crackers and rearranging them to form different animals...so that he would not be afraid'. 'RC' now understood what he had thought had been childish fantasy.

He looked again at the horrifying sight of the monster before him...and wondered if it was real. The two heads of the great dog snarled – as if each felt cheated and wished for a singular voice of its own. What trick of science could have created such an aberration? Was he really seeing clearly? The gnashing of two sets of teeth convinced him that he had driven to Hell; and was now looking at a mythological creature known as 'Cerberus'. But where was the boy?

His thoughts were saturated with scenarios – none which he would allow to play out. He had not realized that his tattered heart could feel as deeply responsible as it did for the frail Ezekiel. But there was no time for reflection. A powerful blow sent him sprawling!

The concussive force was debilitating. He shook himself. Standing over him with a baseball bat was the large man he knew as Anna's neighbor. Tethered at the huge man's side was the impaired boy. Zeke reached out desperately. 'RC's fear evaporated. In its place, a dry blackened rage remained. He gathered his remaining strength; stood, and prepared to square off against the formidable Roger G. Gregor...still wondering of the whereabouts of Anna.

Gregor growled. He swung the baseball bat – as in challenge – with one hand; while the other fished around in his coat pocket. From the pocket, he drew out what appeared to be an altered pistol. It was exceedingly delicate – an odd counterbalance to the man's gargantuan girth. 'RC' recognized it as a modified dart gun – something to be used in the capture of animals. The barrel of the gun was shorter and wider, made of an alloy that gave it a diamond-like sparkle. It had the appearance of something that had an atomic precision. Fired by compressed gas and with a valve to control the speed of the 'dart', it was a perfectly quiet injection delivery system.

Weaponless, 'RC' scrambled for anything within reach. Grabbing a substantial bough that had fallen from the thicket's tree canopy, he knew he had a brief window of time in which to defend himself. He swung; and the cell phone dropped from his pocket generating a beep. As the wind picked up, he could smell the foul odor of the thicket and the great two-headed dog chained nearby. Gregor caught the bough with the side of his bat and sent it flying. 'RC' knew that – from this time forward – he would be at the mercy of someone who did not possess that quality. For once, he wished that the native tracker, Bob, was nearby.

The wind undulated vines which striped the tree'ed thicket in moonlight; and Cerberus strained at its containment. Its teeth tore at the air in a cacophony of snarls. 'RC's keys jangled in his pocket; and reminded him that his car was nearby. He pressed a button to set of the car's alarm – hoping for distraction and the loan of time.

But Gregor did not seem bothered by the diversion. His sovereign mendacity could create the story needed once he destroyed his opponent. There seemed no point in lingering. He advanced toward 'RC' with a restrained rage; dragging the helpless boy along with relative ease. The large man dropped his bat – there was no need for it. The silver-sanded concoction that had been loaded into the dart gun would be enough. He aimed and shot.

The sudden struggle of the boy caused him to shoot high. The projectile caught the top of 'RC's coat collar. Angrily, Gregor tore away a tether; and threw the boy aside. Then, he fished out another vial of the metallic powder from a pocket in his coat; and quickly snapped it into the pistol stock. He hunched over the weapon and pointed it again at 'RC' taking several steps toward him – getting closer in order to improve the likelihood of 'RC's demise. Then, Gregor leaped toward him; threw a whizzing punch; and sent him sprawling back into the snow.

The precipitation had picked up. Though 'RC's mouth filled up with blood, the democracy of a blinding flurry and suddenly overwhelming cold had somewhat equalized his status as a combatant. He began to pull himself to his feet when something unusual occurred. Without warning, the pistol that Gregor had pointed directly at him was now raised far above 'RC's head. Had cold clouded the large man's thoughts?

Arrested by fear and intent in conflict, 'RC' had heard nothing. It was the second time he had had been in a near-death situation; and in gamble with a storm. His thoughts briefly wavered back to the brutal beating he had received in the Chihuahua Mountains of Mexico - the scenario seemed too familiar. The force of Gregor's blow left 'RC' delirious and weakened; but filled with conviction. He was now certain he knew who had overturned the camp; and left him for dead. And he was equally certain who had scared off the guide, Sincero.

Gregor focused past 'RC'. His visage suddenly registered surprise and concern. 'RC' turned to look behind him. The whitened figures of Anna, Sister Frances, Detective Tweeter, and Sophia Angaros stood in the snow... as if they had been exhaled, mingled and fallen together. In a rare stroke of luck, Detective Tweeter had called Sue Bee to give her news about her injured mother, Trudence Jefferson. By coincidence and serendipitous acumen, he had stumbled upon Anna, Sophia Angaros, and a surly Sister Frances. Technology had done the rest. 'RC's cell phone had established his coordinates. The four of them now stood paralyzed as 'RC' struggled before the enormous man known as Roger G. Gregor.

A sense of urgency compelled Anna forward. Within seconds, she was there and shielding 'RC' - staring into the barrel of the loaded gun. Immediately behind Gregor the frail boy, Ezekiel, struggled to right himself. Cerberus watched with anticipation; and pulled against its constraints – unable to escape that which bound it. Just as the man who was its master - any cogent hunger had been subsumed. Its food had no flavor unless it was seasoned with hate.

Detective Tweeter raised his hands into the air to show that he had no weapon. Taller than the others, his head was framed by the light of the moon which had pushed through the clouds. It gave him a halo'ed appearance. He stood there mute and golden; looking like some mighty - but imploring - angel. Sophia Angaros stood at the detective's side trying to reel in her anger about what she had learned from him regarding the death of her husband, Archibald. And Sister Frances, who stood beside her, played with the cross at the end of her rosary praying for a miracle.

The votive moon shown upon the nun; and reminded her of a promise she had made long ago to a young girl whom she had pulled out of the mud of a destroyed village. That village had been razed by the gargantuan man who stood before her. He had issued the order while he stood idly by and watched – thinking of what he stood to gain from people he deemed as no more than proletariat.

A light crimson patch had formed on the ground in front of 'RC' – evidence of the brutality of Gregor's blow. His jaw ached – his face was swollen. Gregor's subtle, subterranean smile stimulated black thoughts and visions of Charon sculling the boat across the rivers Styx and Acheron[34]. From somewhere within the man's large thick body, low laughter bubbled up like putrefaction.

In the savage state of distraction, the boy, Ezekiel, managed to right

---

34   In Greek mythology, the ferryman of Hades, who carries the souls of the departed across the rivers of Styx and Acheron - which separates the living from the dead

himself; and pitch forward. The muscles of his body had tightened; and he suddenly rolled from the slight rise where he had been thrown; and through the light snow...until he was caught by Anna. There he hid behind her while the low growling of the great dog in the shadows barely disguised its seething contempt for lost prey.

The wind howled with unprecedented fury and pushed high clouds away from a moon which now shined as bright as a ripened persimmon. Detective Tweeter lowered his hands slightly. They were heavy and the blood was draining from them. At that instant, his cell phone rang. As he reached to silence it, Cerberus growled; and the action arrested Gregor's attention. He withdrew his focus from the trinity immediately before him; and pointed his pistol instead at the detective, suspecting he had used his phone to triangulate their location. Gregor seemed to contemplate the most beneficial shot to take. 'RC', Anna and the boy looked remarkably pathetic and were incapable of besting his brute force. Instead he turned his attention to the detective. The great dog, Cerberus, would clean up the others quite well - with or without his help. Its appetite was voracious.

Like a predator, he studied the detective - sensing a weakness. The man's strength now seemed to rest upon something other than a professional belief. Tweeter's tough impartial manner seemed compromised by the need to protect someone. Gregor sensed that this was a man who was more than willing to bargain. He would shoot him - but first, he would tease out the truth to find out why the detective stood in judgment of him; and where his weakness lay. He wished to understand him – much like he would understand any animal that was prey; and was intent on making the victim's blood more palatable.

In Gregor's opinion, he had worked hard for his money. He had seen the petty cruelty of those who 'hid behind laws'. He was an entrepreneur - one who had always taken chances. He sensed that the Detective had always worked within boundaries - like someone who knows the exact lay of his land and the acreage to which he is entitled. Had the detective ever risked crossing a fence; or straying into an area that had not been predefined? It galled him; for Gregor believed in risk-taking. He opined that it was the one characteristic which made us 'human'...and superior. We had developed into walking apes – by leaving the confinement of the trees? In his estimation, the detective was but a plodding bull; chewing on grass and never testing his confinement. But something had changed that. He smirked at the thought and then spoke directly to the object of his scorn,

"I wonder - could you be swimming in unfamiliar waters, Detective?"

Tweeter's eyes narrowed. He had seen this type of hatred before. In the split second that it took to glance at Sophia Angaros, Gregor had guessed a secret. Before he could respond, Gregor continued – there was really no point in listening to the detective's blather...

"Sophia Angaros, freshly widowed...of course, I know about it. It was I who caused it. Could this be the new center of your attention...?"

He followed the eyes again,

"But there's more...someone else is here who you seem to care about."

Detective Tweeter had stared at the three people immediately before the behemoth. He immediately switched his gaze and looked into the air – unwilling to yield any further secret. Gregor was a much more clever and perceptive than he had realized.

But the puzzle was something that Gregor was unwilling to let go. The jumble of people immediately before him had all been nuisance. He harbored no ill will directly toward them – indeed he didn't care about them - but they had interfered with a venture on which he had spent a great deal of time and energy. Before him now stood a large plodding bovine that would protect the insects that buzzed about it. Was it not right that he should be bothered by the lack of imagination that so constrained the investigator? He, Gregor, had plans that involved greater things...celestial things. But he stopped himself. Why should he waste the DNA concoction within his gun on this man? It would diminish the value of his experiment.

He turned instead to the trio before him. 'RC' lay crumpled in the snow. Anna held his head and pushed Ezekiel behind her – sheltering them both as best she could. The wind – as if it sensed a loving purpose – scattered shards of diamond snow about. The moon shined down upon her like a Madonna; and she sparkled in the snow. Gregor thought it a most beautiful sight.

"What a lovely disturbance you are."

He could see that she wanted to respond; and put a finger to his lips,

"Shhhhh....the concoction within the gun will begin a new chapter for you. What you say; what you think – well, it really won't matter...."

She tried not show here concern; but was trembling inside. Gregor could sense it; and – more than ever – tasted the blood in his mouth. He felt like bragging.

"The silver sand is remnants of the Black Stone of Mecca...from the surrounding sands where the sacred stone was discovered.... We found that the sands could yield revenue we never expected - when combined with knowledge about contemporary genetics and computer science. Who would have thought that it could be so profitable...?"[35]

Anna held Zeke and 'RC' as tightly as she could; and turned away from the pointed pistol. Gregor continued – his focus now on 'RC'.

"But wait there's someone trying to get through...a 'shaman' of sorts. He won't let me into his thoughts. Friend of yours...?"

He smiled cruelly, then looked back at Anna,

"She won't feel a thing, Chamberlain – any more than you felt when I found you in the Chihuahua Mountains...so stop your fretting. There's no meaning to the world – it's just an absurd thought – a mythology created by the brain."

Tweeter edged forward and in front of Sophia and Sister Frances - wondering if he might gain a more strategic position in order to help the three people who were in front of Gregor. He stopped when Gregor's attention returned to him.

'RC' seemed to awaken from the ether of the blow that had been delivered to him. In a moment of clarity, he realized the answer to a clue he had long ago deemed as nothing more than ridiculous. He was thinking of what Bob, the native tracker had once said to him around a campfire long ago as they tracked the great 'killer cat'.

"You're gonna be in big trouble...big trouble comin' your way....followed by big love...painful too. Only way out is to know the key...The fire just says it is forwards and backwards... it says both love and pain are forwards and backwards."

The names 'Roger G. Gregor' and 'Anna' would be the same, read forwards or backwards. They were palindromes - once considered strong magic. But what had Bob meant by,

'...only way out is to know the key'?

His attention focused back to Anna. She was now trying to separate those she had inadvertently drawn together.

She pushed Zeke firmly away...whispering for him to run. The boy resisted – he would not leave her. Feeling the boy's gentle obstinacy, she put herself in front of him as a 'shield'. She was now certain of Gregor's intent to let no one leave. Zeke's anxiety caused him to flail. Instinctively, she broke his fall. When she had righted him, she reached in her pocket and pushed a piece of candy in his mouth. If nothing else, her embrace combined with the

---

35   This is the eastern cornerstone of the Kaaba, the ancient stone building in the center of the Grand Mosque in Mecca. The stone is revered by Muslims. According to Muslim tradition it dates back to the time of Adam and Eve; and fell from the heavens as a guide for Adam and Eve to build an altar. It has often been described as a meteorite, but is a hypothesis that is not conclusory.

sweetness of the action might soothe him and provide a few more seconds of happiness. Gregor's 'zeroed-in' on her.

Perhaps a cloud passing over the moon had distracted Gregor. Perhaps the faint light - that fell from the moon into the eyes of the boy - had caused Zeke to fling himself in front of Anna. Before she knew it, Gregor's pistol had popped loudly. Quicker than an exclamation...it was over.

He did not hear her scream his name. But the gunshot and the scream continued to echo contemporaneously. In the distance the two sounded like rowdy children running together in a hallway. The smoke from the pistol was the only indication of Gregor's victory.

'RC's heart pounded over the noise of the wind. Through semi-conscious eyes, he observed a sickening moonlit scene. The boy had collapsed to the ground with the slightest of movements. His eyes were barely open as he dangled in an unknown chaos. His cry was weak - the heart-breaking sound of a child facing death.

The distant echo of Anna's scream came bouncing back. It seemed to scoop away 'RC's thoughts and hiccup about the landscape, looking for a place to land. The wind kicked it about like a bully with a ball; and then, rushed away with it again.

At that moment, a large raptor heard the music of a scream; and took note of its location. The ancient language of lightning boomed about the sky like crashing cymbals. The raptor had found an upward current and rose to a great height. Swirling with ease, it reveled in the storm.

And through all the cloudy confusion, moonlight fell upon the boy. He seemed as luminous as stained glass. Anna looked into the fading light of Ezekiel's eyes; and his wan appearance. Like Janus[36], the boy appeared to be looking forward and backward in time. She would not be there to protect or prepare him. Holding back her anguish; she gently lay him down in the snow. She had only seconds to comfort and wait for his soul to let go. Too suddenly, Ezekiel was gone and she wept.

And 'RC' too realized something. The fortress that he had built to keep from feeling - had buckled. He thought of another death he had witnessed long ago, that of his friend, 'Old Joe'. And through his semi consciousness, wondered if he simply imagined that which he thought he now saw. The cross fox appeared to be running away with the frail boy's spirit on its back.

In the snow surrounding the boy - a subtle pattern of mimicry, almost imperceptible at first, began to appear. Slowly, quietly, the snow around him

---

36   In ancient Roman religion and myth, the god of beginnings, gates, transitions, and doorways – depicted as having two faces since he looks to the future and the past.

began to show through as white tufts. The blood red tresses - that had framed him – had disappeared. Snow white feathers seemed to sprout from his shoulders, back and arms. The arms extended - white as beams of light. The strong, light hollowness of winged appendages seemed apparent. Slowly, mist unraveled like an onion from the sky. It floated down around the boy in light transparent vestments. With a simple movement of his arms, Ezekiel seemed to rise from where he was; and floated to a standing position. Around his temple, the light circled and shone brightly as if it would lift him from the narrow cleft of the dark woods. Smiling sweetly, he stood for a moment; and then leaned down and gently picked some flowers hiding under the snow... and was lifted by the breeze. He drifted with outstretched wings toward the light of the moon. A grace he had never had in life now served him. The light that showed through Ezekiel could not have been truer to his psyche.

Gregor appeared happy with the results of his 'hit'. He quickly reloaded the stock of the gun with another dart of the silver sand; when suddenly, from the rise of the dark woods, the grotesque two-headed dog broke through its chains. It ran with great speed toward its prey; and hurled itself upwards – snarling with anticipation. The force of its bound was enough to bring it within reach. At that moment, Ezekiel let drop a flower he had picked. Distracted by the trout lily, the dog snapped at it. Its separate heads fighting each other - until one swallowed the flower like a morsel. It was enough time for the boy to gain the needed distance; and to send the monstrous animal in a free fall. Cerberus plummeted earthward - wailing and covered in the icy tinsel of the passing storm. Its heavy body hit the land with enough force to bury it. The dirt fell in behind it - forming a natural sarcophagus.

Anna held 'RC's in her lap. She daubed the scarlet from his mouth; and wished that she had something to ease his pain. But he did not care - his heart had been healed. He could not take away his gaze. And from the edges of the hole that the great dog had created for itself, the green stems of daffodils seemed to push upwards with a secret knowledge that winter never really wins.

WINTER PRESSING

Gregor reloaded his weapon and cast his attention on Ezekiel. He seemed to be computing a trajectory. Meanwhile the boy floated freely in the air while those on the ground stared upwards, transfixed by the sight of him as he sailed like a bird. The warm wind had blown in. It melted the icy tarnish on cold branches; and seemed to play with its counterpart – the cold warring wind - which had created miles of icy whiteness in a land ready for spring.

For...the warm wind had traveled far from a friendly place of sunny seas and barnacled boats that basked in comfortable waters. It had caressed the backs of carp feeding on insects that lit on the water's surface. It had spent hours dancing with willow trees – watching them sway gracefully and tickle those who read on riverbanks. It had crossed coral beaches strewn with glistening shells; and whispered into the ears of children...speaking to them without words. It had smelled the scent of ripening peaches in southern orchards. It had gently closed the hinged doors of gates mistakenly left open. It had played at family picnics; and billowed out the laundry hung on lines to dry. It had floated across the slick pods of seals - licking the brine that rested on their fur. It had moved bright puffy clouds along a path which only they knew. It had listened to the secrets of young girls whispering to each other. It had moved across the vineyards tasting the dew from ripening grapes; and chased away the doldrums of those inside too long. It had gently tossed bees about in flight. It had slipped into quiet barns pulling at cobwebs; and dispersing the smell of their full bins. It had threaded through groves of cinnamon trees pushing the scent across dinner plates. It had gently touched every blade of grass and encouraged each to grow. It had pushed its way through bakery windows and restaurants filling streets with the aroma of fresh bread and ginger. It had comforted those who worked hard. And it had caressed the faces of those who were only able to sit in the sun and convalesce. The warm wind's travel had been unpredictable; but pouring forth with purpose. It touched each with the same fingers; and caressed all in its path, instilling memories without a word.

Sophia Angaros noticed it immediately. It reminded her of home and happier times with a man she had once loved. Gregor did not notice the change...or, if he did, pretended no interest. He reloaded his pistol and calculated his next action. His assessment of those on the ground caused him to believe that they were no threat. His next shot should be high enough to bring down the celestial being that now played within the moonlight.

Detective Tweeter touched the breast pocket of his coat. Inside was a child's drawing of a daffodil. It had been given to him long ago by the young boy of a prostitute. He suddenly looked up at the soaring Ezekiel. Before Tweeter could speak, 'RC' addressed Roger G. Gregor. He had realized a secret that was another part of the complex puzzle of their mutual investigations. He shouted out,

"Your luck's turned sour – hasn't it Gregor? You have to bring the boy back down – don't you? ...He's your son."

Gregor wheeled about and faced 'RC' and Anna. A dark confession sat inside him; and colored his complexion.

"Clever boy..."

'RC' continued,

"You'd shoot your son...even if the fall might kill him?"

Gregor sneered,

"I'd hate to do a tour of your head – so full of platitudes, so empty of fact. I don't care whether the boy lives or dies. I created what I wanted...and I know I can do it again. But I need the boy's genetics. His 'aberration' seems to be uniquely predisposed to be the rapid catalyst my 'concoction' demands. His condition is congenital - a combination of both of us...my DNA – by itself – won't 'cut it', so to speak."

Tweeter interrupted,

"You mean the large skull found by 'RC' in the desert...the one the lab technician died for. That was your first experiment wasn't it? But it only contained your DNA."

Gregor nodded; and then turned aside,

"There are no angels...we create them. 'It' was a mistake...same wings, but with the power and temperament to destroy five people before we managed to take it down."

Then he cackled to himself, "Though the experiment may yet prove profitable...especially in the alchemy of human conflict...."

Looking up again, 'RC' could just hear the honeyed voice of Ezekiel. The boy sang – his words unaffected by palsy. The song spoke of the future and of perfect, possible dreams. His sound rang out like a church bell – ephemeral, without measure...incapable of capture or sale. Nothing was trivial. His persona brightened and extended without limit. He seemed to have a durable oaken understanding. The moon was his lectern. Sweet sacred secrets had been served to him.

A jury of stars sat within the dark robes of night while clouds with no discernible geometry traveled into different sectors of the sky. The clear gurgle of melting snow portended an early spring. A vector of the sky was beginning to reveal barely discernible, muted pastels as if the new day could hardly control its passion. In a few hours, a butterscotch sun would appear from its parsonage; and the morning would be announced by those feathered denominations which flew and made music.

Gregor took no notice. He had reloaded his pistol with the concoction of 'silver sand'. And then...with military precision, he fired at the target. The bullet moved like a piece of black nothing - only a spark from the barrel could be seen. He yelled out in pilfered pleasure as the missile found its mark.

It galled him slightly that he had taken as long to do it. But the cracking sound echoed throughout the darkness of the early morning, idly bouncing off of nearby hills. It seemed to restore his exalted sense of importance.

As for the object of his scorn...the passageway was a shady walk down a road filled with the mist of memories and lost friends. After collapse, a velvet cloth spread over the grounded coffin. But it was not a shroud of darkness and gloom - it was a bright extravagant squall of color. The ballistics of the projectile had precisely summoned. The sound bounded about the nearby hills like a mountain goat; but the spirit's foundation remained in the park.

And as she fell, there were two who experienced the soreness of the sting more than the any of the others.

SMALL TRUMPETS

The missile had torn through the air. Anna froze in pain – perhaps realizing some naiveté. Her eyes remained open; and she fell to the ground. In the near-distance, the winged boy had stopped in flight. He had hovered for a second before letting a piece of moonlight fall from his hand. The warm wind caught it; and carried it briefly, before allowing it to float down upon the fallen form. And the daffodil came to rest as gently as a whispered name... above the heart of Anna.

'RC's screams became a garish ornament to the night. Years ago he had left her...now he was alone again. He could hardly bear it. Love - that secret medicine which had saved him from himself...was gone. He studied her face - desperately wanting to remember it ...and held her. He could feel the disappearing warmth. No pleading, no praying, no cursing, no magic would resurrect. This was love's price. And he cursed that love should now demand payment.

Within seconds, a series of bumps became apparent. They rose and fell behind each other in a recognizable pattern. Minutes later, where Anna had once lain - a bright shroud of daffodils stretched the length of Frances Park. The appearance of the flowers startled all who saw them. They wondered if the increasing light of the sky had allowed them to see what had always been there.

Sophia Angoras had recognized the familiar pattern. A crash of memories was now breaking like waves upon a beach. She remembered her husband's passing and the familiar pattern upon his skin. She remembered the anonymous gift of the flowers left by someone – which had helped her cope with Archibald's death; and now knew who had left them. And then - silly as it seemed - she wondered if we all became that which we most want to be.

But it was not Sophia Angoras' grief that matched the grief of 'RC'. That grief was matched by another. The order of her world had gone amuck. Sister Frances tore away her rosary; and tore at the vestments that had been an armor of her beliefs. Suddenly, it all seemed synthetic. She tore away her wimple and threw it to the ground – gray hair whipping in the wind. Why would faith test her in such a way?! Were the sacred writings nothing more than lore? Were there secrets beyond what had been said – beyond that which she had read?

Then she stared steadfastly at Gregor - the man she had seen on the mountain before the great pillage...before she had pulled a small crying girl out of the mud of a decimated Vietnamese village. She rubbed her hands together in anguish – as she looked at what had been Anna. What 'good' had come from adopting her? She was gone now. And to 'RC's screams...she added her own. But - just as Gregor had interrupted the girl's life twice - he also suspended Sister Frances' grief. He pointed the newly reloaded weapon and said,

"You're next...they'll never find any trace of you. You'll disappear like chaff. One more piece of the puzzle – gone!"

'RC' picked one of the daffodils nearest to him and held it close to his chest. He wavered between anger, grief, and disbelief. Love's cruelty had – at least - been just. Gregor continued, "Of course, we haven't perfected the DNA nano-chips or the molecular assembler; but it is - as they say - a work in progress. Pity... my gal, Cynthia was so close. She got rid of that pimply lab technician who kept interjecting himself into everyone's business. If he hadn't been working on that cranium that you found in the desert, he'd still be breathing. Poor old Cynthia....Guess it is true what they say. 'You should never mix business with pleasure'...but she's gone now, time to move on."

He continued his cold braggadocio,

"Yep...that's the long and short of it. We use an assembler to modify and fire a dosage of 'nano-chips' that will literally modify the host DNA into almost anything we want it to be... any species we want, even the 'mythological' ones. Though there appear to be variations dependent on phylum...and surprisingly, individual will and tendency. I mean, damn – who knew, right? Since the assembler hasn't been 'perfected', there's no telling what'll happen to you Chamberlain."

The low growl of his words bore into 'RC'.

"Guess we'll have to see what you're 'made of'! It's all about the sport... who knows what you'll come back as? I'll give you a jump-start. You can experience 'the thrill of the hunt' - but from the other end! Ain't science wonderful? We just fire these little chips into things...or sprinkle them into food. They 'host in' to the existing DNA structure; and produce a rapid transformation. And, by doing so...we can even get rid of the evidence! Can't do much better than that!

Sure worked good on that over-educated tracker named, Grady. Dumb-ass went to bed as an 'ivy league' snob – eating beef bourguignon - and woke up as just another big cat to hunt. Ain't nothin' but economics, ya know - just figuring out how to turn a quick buck!

Ahhh...poor ol' Cynthia...she was invaluable, workin' in the lab. Got us lots of good information – then we lined her up to work at the facility, to get the cripple boy's genetics nailed down."

Far away to the north and west of where 'RC', Detective Tweeter; Sister Frances, and Sophia Angaros squared off against the powerful man...Bob was in the middle of the Sundance. And, though the boy, Ezekiel, had risen to a great height in the sky; he thought he could see the Native man...and he could feel the strength of a great spiritual undertaking.

Most would say that 'chance' is a seemingly random event that has no causal relationship to anything. But Bob did not agree. To him, everything was connected in some way. The human simply could not discern all the relationships. The world was much more complex; and he wondered if the structure of human thinking – was a bias which held us within its invisible webbing. Perhaps, every culture was coat – and the more we wore it, the more ignorant we became of the 'weather'. Did a tree grow when and where it wanted – or where it was allowed? Something first, shook loose the seed. Maybe that was where faith entered.

Now he hung from the Sundance pole; and in his weakened state, wondered if the Sundance did not impose its own structure. As he hung at the limit of his existence, he continued to search for vision. He would not call his thoughts 'a dream'. For him, existence listed back and forth between dreams and waking; and we faded in and out of both – not knowing the boundaries of the ether.

As he swung from the Sundance pole, surrealist visions of seemingly disconnected thoughts came through to him. He saw a monolith. Paper currency floated about it. Possums stole sleep; and gnawed upon ripe persimmon dreams. Thoughts fell from topless heads. Fields of oil viewed from high mountains poured over the land. Oligarchs slogged happily through, pillaging what they could. African countries felt condescended. Dominoes fell, killing those behind them. The sacred corn had played its role. Dreamless people threw stones at nobody in particular. Technology diverted intuition. Dreaming people would only admit to sleep. The sixth sense had become - 'extra'. Prayer and the 'hambeday' (quiet reflection) had been pulled away from thought. Some wanted power over stones - others wished to understand the stones' power. All the while, the Tunkan (sacred ancestors) whispered... and no one listened. This was what came to him as he swung from the pole, gritting his teeth in pain, whistling through the eagle bone and waiting to be pulled from the pole.

Finally, when they were ready, the eagle talon thongs ripped through his chest flesh; and Bob fell with force. Blood rushed from his wounds. The good earth had kicked the crap out of him. His impact caused a high-pitched trill through the eagle bone whistle in his mouth. The sound tore through the air and seemed to bounce off the horizon. He had just enough breath to utter the sacred words with which his culture finished all prayers before he sank into a dark and endlessly deep pond of unconsciousness.

Louise had seen him fall. She brought the sacred sage; and calmly fanned consciousness into him. Then she sprinkled water on his brow. Momentarily, she stared up at a churning zenith. The Aurora Borealis was whipping about a liquid orange flame in the grayness of a sky that seemed ready to snow. The howling wind sounded like the Wanigi (souls) of many; and through the competing light, she could just see a waning moon. She thought it lovely and was pleased that it had shown itself.

Then she lifted Bob's head; and cradled it in her lap. She studied his face – loving its familiarity and how it looked like a wrinkled landscape. She wondered if perhaps, his dream had taken him to the place where clouds are born. Suddenly the wind was warm again. He was looking up at her like a child and asked,

"Did anything happen, Louise?"

To which she responded,

"Well, you did not chase the moon from the sky, Bob..."

Then she smiled and caressed his forehead and whispered,

"Good intentions do not long travel alone...."

Bob remembered the trout lily...the dog-toothed violet...the adder's tongue – that intersection of faith, the faithless, and those who would deny faith. It was what the flower had whispered to him as he sat in its funnel...and it was where most dark secrets lie.

SANTA LUCIA

Alone, a mustang stands at the top of a plateau and paws at the dirt as if it would wear down the land. It looks out at the moon and across the darkened landscape listening to howls. It does not think about what is real. It feels alive and safe enough. It does not think about the dirt under its feet. It hardly feels its hooves hit the ground. For it, the moon is just a patch in the sky that gives the night a new appearance. It does not piece together a plan for its survival. The chords of the evening have no meaning for it other than to make its ears twitch and cause it to stamp again. It has blood on its flank from an injury; but does not seem to notice the wound. It has no interest in being new – but will improvise 'newness' with great instinct. Then...snorting, whinnying; and baring its teeth; it becomes part of those very chords that it does not understand.

It had come to 'RC' as he lay on the ground bleeding next to the run of golden daffodils. He struggled with what he had seen trying to make sense of it. The grief was intolerable...Anna was gone. A flying translucent mist that crossed in front of the moon was what remained of the little boy named, Ezekiel. He shivered as he thought of the two-headed Cerberus. Dream...illusion...nightmare – it alls seemed to spring from the same dark well. How could any of it be real? He remembered his time in the Chihuahua Mountains...and his time around the fire with Bob. And now, again, he was weakened ...and could not validate. Was the mound of golden flowers all that was left of love? The pounding in his head seemed real. The bright disc in the sky did not. The sounds of morning were beginning. Birds, which had taken refuge in the tree-tops over the dismal hollow of the park - began to sing; and then, suddenly took flight together. In the sky, they changed direction; and bent and turned – swarming in a spiral course. They flew separately but as one.

Fastened tight by a lack of belief, he wondered at what had seen. Was he nothing more than the mustang...seeing only what was comfortable, reacting; pawing at the dirt? He looked up at the moon again. Its spasmodic 'utterance' fell in the form of the familiar light. Just below the moon, he could see the floating Ezekiel. The boy seemed more transparent – as if the space within him had been intensified…a loose confection of particles of light. When did folklore cross so easily into belief – and did belief make anything real?

Unable to make sense of it - and with a consuming rage - 'RC' turned to face Roger G. Gregor. He was now remembering the clue that Bob had told him - something about 'where the dog, trout, and adder' come together. He thought he was beginning to understand. Then to Gregor he spat out the observation,

"You really don't understand what you're tinkering could do…."

Gregor responded with the sharpness of a strap,

"I know exactly what I'm 'tinkering with'. These particles have a stronger crystalline structure than anything the human body can 'throw at them'. The immune system won't attack or destroy them. They just go about their business shipping little bits of targeted DNA wherever they're needed. The hosts metamorphose quite nicely into another life form – even create a new species…better than diamonds…from a marketing perspective."

'RC' suddenly uttered the words, that he had once heard Bob say as an ending to all prayer. It came to him as if someone had dropped it into him – and then, fell out unexpectedly.

"Mitakuye Oyasin."

Was it absurd to say 'all my relatives'…was it any more ridiculous than the ending to any other prayer? He didn't care anymore - belief lent no particular gravity to ridicule. He now understood. Nothing could be accomplished unless it started with belief. The moonlight fell upon the snow and caused it to sparkle. For a moment, 'RC' thought he heard the faint and soulful sound of Christmas music in the distance – 'Oh light divine…'

Gregor suddenly cocked his head to the side - it seemed to make him uneasy. Meanwhile 'RC' – though profoundly impacted by the loss of Anna and Zeke – had begun to see more clearly. The core emotional shock had been greater than any physical damage done to him. He had been paralyzed; but understood that whatever energy remained must be directed toward engaging Gregor in order to shake the bedrock of the man's gargantuan vanity. Would it be enough? Was it right? He only knew that the monster must be provoked. He would do so – if for no other reason - than to snuff out the pain he felt; and buy time for the others. And that was enough for him.

"You've made an error of proportions…one that may not be undone easily, Gregor. You're a fool."

Incredulously, Gregor 'volleyed' back,

"I should let you stay awhile, Chamberlain…if – for no other reason – just to let you see how wrong you can be! But I'd much rather see you on a tray. My guess... you'll come back as a steak."

"Not a big enough serving for you....chubby." 'RC' responded with aplomb.

Gregor smiled,

"No, perhaps not steak...you're more the 'hamburger' sort. You know, we're really thinking about taking this invention a step further; and having it delivered by some sort of electromagnetic radiation – something of a short wave length...something to make it 'cleaner'."

'RC' mugged,

"...So many choices - so little grime."

Gregor stopped,

"You know, Chamberlain. I'm going to miss you. When I turn you into a jackass, please tell me which is more effective: praying or braying."

'RC' smiled at him,

"Donkeys can't talk - except to other donkeys."

Sophia Angaros stood quietly but she was twitching with energy. She balled up her fist - her anger seething. Discussing ethics was pointless. She remembered the ambulances arriving when Archibald died – their blue and red lights firing through the windows of her home while she tried to hold a dying husband who bucked like a bronco and rapidly disintegrated before her eyes.

The wind quickened as 'RC' continued verbal combat. He had seized Gregor's attention – at least for the moment.

"If this device can change a species, there's bound to be some sort of repercussion in the natural world, Gregor."

"Sounds like money in the bank to me..."

"It can't be all about money..."

"I like your style, Chamberlain – you don't believe that crap! It is all about the money. Collectors will pay millions for anything that's different. So shut up – it's difficult to shoot someone whose mouth is moving so fast."

"Hear me out, Gregor. What have you got to lose? You've taken everything from me. You could be ripping the hell out of something that you don't even understand – knocking the crap out of an earthly balance that's been around longer than we have. Why not take that power and use it more wisely?"

"Get to the point, Chamberlain – I've got things to do."

'RC' thought quickly – the argument had to be in terms that Gregor understood,

"Money...you could make a lot more money - and make it a lot easier."

"I'm listenin'..."

"...think medicine...think recovery of species that are on the brink - or already extinct."

Gregor's response surprised him. It was predictable but caused 'RC' to question a contradiction that lay like a boil on the edge of his thoughts.

"Spare me the pseudo-spiritualism. You don't care about 'God's green earth' anymore'n I do – you're just tryin' to save your butt. You think that if you're a 'bad little boy' you'll be punished. If you cut down a tree...you'll burn up like greenhouse gas fried chicken, because God will send down a bolt of lightning. Stop your dribbling... You're doing what you do – because it's in your interest. We ain't that different. Supposin' there is some sort of ethical order – and I ain't sayin' there is - then 'whoever created it' should be powerful enough to put the pieces back together!"

He had heretofore, been toying with Gregor, and attempting to 'buy time'. He had felt nothing for someone he perceived as monster. But now, 'RC' was perplexed – the incontrovertible logic interested him and caused him to wonder about the weakness in his own. The size of the question surprised him. The moon had clouded over again; and it looked like frosted glass. 'RC' struggled to maintain clarity - perhaps Gregor was right. As 'RC' struggled with the question, Gregor took notice; for he thrived on the disease of self-doubt.

"Lookin' to light a pathway out of the darkness, Chamberlain...that's the trouble with light...it can illuminate - or it can blind!"

'RC' was struck by the dark wisdom. There had always been agenda in his life. His focus was on 'doing the right thing' – and thereby, eliminating any semblance of guilt and weakness.

Gregor continued,

"Got a special channel to God – do you? Why are you tryin' to manage everything, Chamberlain? Maybe God don't need your help. Aren't you just buying and selling things too...just doing 'nice' to purchase the ultimate favor – a place in God's 'big house'? Don't tell me that's 'religious'..."

Gregor recoiled. His eyes hardened. If his butt could have shaken, it would have sounded like serpentine castanets. A wild look came across his face – but the pistol's aim was less menacing. Had he softened?

A night that had started with a purity of purpose now seemed muddled. 'RC' was in a quagmire; and felt heavier than the secrets that pressed against him. Had everything been confounded? His heart pounded. He had not considered Gregor's alternative viewpoint; and it stymied him. Without thinking, he looked up to the sky. The moon was still there, reflecting brightly. It calmed him. He felt its peaceful light resonating within him. The pounding of his heart had begun to rock his body. He thought of Ezekiel and Anna. They had faced Gregor with their own dignity.

Like a young bird, he was standing at the nest's precipice – wondering if he could fly. Could he deign to do any less? He no longer cared whether there be music or mayhem in the choice. Perhaps, that was the freedom for which he had always longed.

Lifting his head skyward one more time, he could just make out the vaporous form of Ezekiel. The boy continued to float in the moonlight. He envied him. The boy's manner had always been one of acceptance rather than willing against what was. He did not seem less happy for it - or any less virtuous. A thousand particles of light seemed to dance around Ezekiel; and reaffirm his contentment. He exclaimed his joy without voice; and the light around his head formed a sacred circle. No longer bound to the earth, he floated as free as a cloud. Ironically...the gargantuan man named, Roger G. Gregor had been the very source of the boy's freedom.

As if aware of 'RC's observation, the boy seemed to turn around and look back to the ground from where he had risen. The dirt had filled in over the monster, Cerberus; and a small mound had formed. On its top, the 'trout lily'...the 'dog toothed violet'...the 'adder's tongue' was growing. That flower - according to an ancient story – had sprung from the tears of Eve before she had given birth.

'RC' felt his heart pound harder. Had he been wrong about everything? He looked up at the round face of the moon. The bitterness he had so long felt about his life had disappeared under Anna's influence. She had made his life firm in purpose, resolution and faith. It seemed foreign to him; but through such acceptance, he had been unbelievably happy for the first time.

Now a powerful man stood before him. His purpose was different. His resolution was equal; and his belief - opposite, but compelling. 'RC' had been thrown off balance. Gregor's scanty upbringing had been much like the shorebirds 'RC' had seen along the beach. They ran along shore break; braving the crashing waves; and picking at scraps...until finally, they discovered the proverbial 'pearl in the oyster'. Then, as if 'RC' had unearthed an archaeological discovery of monumental proportions, he realized for the first time, that Gregor and he were not that dissimilar.

Gregor had noticed the shift in his demeanor. He was immensely attuned to such subtleties.

"You seem oddly calm for someone who is about to be blasted into another life form...."

'RC' responded,

"I don't understand…"

But he did understand. At that moment, an unanswered question occurred to him,

"Why the concern about the giant cranium – doesn't seem like it would be of any use to you…"

Gregor's response was of the nonchalance expected from someone who had already decided that he was far ahead in favor.

"That was evidence that I didn't need going any further. Any examiner with a sensible background in zoology would have realized that bone that connected the phalanges to the tibia didn't line up with anything 'human' – or anything 'animal'. And an analysis of the DNA sequencing could have exposed us. Once my gal, Cynthia, 'took care of' the lab technician – she moved into his old office. And yep! She tied up that loose end for us."

'RC's disappointment was now complete. He felt as inconsequential as a grain of sand. Gregor's explanation had cleared up everything save the hormonal nature of arrogance. His grief was profound. Anna had been his spiritual root. She had convinced him to look forward. How could he have been so foolish to put her – or the boy, Ezekiel, in harm's way? He struggled to keep the memories of the two in his mind…and wondered at the crumbling bedrock beneath him. He no longer cared about his undoing.

The light of dawn was as thin as a peeling; and had become tandem to the disappearing night. It illuminated the run of daffodils. Like a witness declaring an oath, Sister Frances put her hand up to greet the light while the other hand seemed to direct it to the golden flowers before them. In recognition that past was past – and with great energy – she picked up her wimple and readjusted it firmly on her head. She had suddenly made the best she could of the tragedy…she had rediscovered her compass. The cesspool of iniquity would not desecrate the memories of her beloved Anna. The death of her daughter had allowed her to escape the tethers of some lingering doubts. The festoon of gold before her was all the proof she needed to surmise that there was a greater plan. The flowers were spreading down into the dark hollow.

Meanwhile, the ruffian stood before them like a granite block. He smiled slightly. He had heard the sound of a great raptor and could just make it out – hovering in the air with its head to the wind. Gregor lumbered a few steps forward and squinted. He did not look for a messiah - but a nest egg he expected to drop from the sky. It would fall like a pestilence and finish what the great dog, Cerberus, could not. It sought game.

Miles away and fresh from his fall from the Sundance pole, Bob 'saw' it as well. In the liquid of a Sundance dream, he saw a great raptor enveloped by great gray clouds and embellished in lightning. To him, it appeared as the great Thunderbird[37] - and it seemed hungry.

'RC' turned to face Gregor. He could see the pistol pointed at him – Gregor was ready to squeeze the trigger. 'RC' felt no fear. He felt nothing – his emotions had been vandalized; his faith shattered.

At that moment, the sturdy form of Detective Tweeter charged like a fury[38]. He had managed to edge close enough to cover the needed distance. Hurtling through the air and barely in control, he landed with great force against Gregor. The impact of the collision caused the gun to boom and eject its transformative dart into the air. Tweeter landed with a thud. His gnarly forearms were alive with animation as if he would grab fistfuls of the drama he had witnessed. But he could not adequately break his fall. Finally the kiss of hard ground caused him to sway to the side and realize how wrongly conceived his heroic effort had been.

Bob too had 'seen' the attempt; and – though he admired its intensity – laughed to himself, at the incredulous undertaking. Meanwhile the native man traveled in and out of dream...concept to conception...wondering 'what' held such insubstantive things together – and made them material. Traveling like light with his thoughts...he reflected on the Sundance. The manifestation of light might not be held, but could be absorbed; and become part of something greater. That 'something' might be a tree...a buffalo...a cloud...a stone... earth. Those might also collapse and become something awkward, disregarded, or unpretentious...but they all eventually returned to light. Light moved neither forwards nor backwards, but back and forth around the 'great circle'. Each beginning was part of the same journey. It folded into others, sustained, experienced, and returned. This was what the Sundance ceremony had revealed. Light, the purest, the simplest – and yet, mysteriously complex...was ancestor. Though it could be extinguished and might take centuries to return, it never really died. Was that then, the reality of things?

In the park, the daffodils captured the light of both setting moon and rising sun. Sophia Angaros observed the fight between Detective Tweeter and Roger G. Gregor...and charged into the fray. With no thought of her own mortality – her 'thready' stature strengthened by what she had learned about the death of her husband and his odd metamorphosis. She had found herself; and decided it was time to renew that 'acquaintance'. She would help a man

---

37   In North American indigenous history and culture the Thunderbird is considered to be a supernatural being of power and strength that controls the upper world; and is adversary to the underworld which is controlled by the underwater panther or the great horned serpent.

38   A fury is one of the avenging deities in classical mythology.

who had suddenly become important to her.

Gregor had made it to his feet. He hurled the slumping detective to the ground again – leaving him breathless. Tweeter lay in the snow, crumpled and moaning.

With a fear that came as much from awe as anger, Sophia Angaros flung herself at the behemoth Gregor. He threw her aside easily; but lost control of his weapon. The two attacks had helped to deteriorate his energy; and his face had suddenly become jaundiced. He lumbered to retrieve the dart gun that had skidded near the sarcophagus of Cerberus. There he saw dozens of trout lilies poking up through the earth. They had divided and split with abandon - their heads bobbing in an ominous wind that had swept in; and which now held the park.

Sophia Angaros struggled to rise. She had to survive...she wanted to survive - to present the complete picture of what had happened. The snow was stained with red – Tweeter was bleeding. Slowly - and like a drunken barmaid - Sophia Angaros stood up. The detective was barely moving. She removed her coat and threw it over him – watching as part of it became scarlet. She stood - looking scraggly as a 'weed' and wondering if she too might be bleeding. Then...she picked one of the bright yellow daffodils – as if to remind her of some purpose or the color of spirit. With wooden resolve, she held her fear back and rushed again with all her force.

As if to magnify the power of Sophia Angaros' assault, Sister Frances threw her own moral imperative at Gregor. She simulated the charge. Running as hard as she could and howling like the wind that had made its way into the park, she exploded at the large man from the other side.

Sophia Angaros fell upon the man with as much force a she could muster – but Gregor was much too strong. Within seconds he had grabbed her by the throat. Intent on strangling her with one hand; he lifted her off of the ground as easily as a waiter might lift a tray. When he was done with her, he would focus again on the injured 'RC'.

It was at that point that Sister Frances plowed into the great man with the power of an ox. The combination of Sophia Angaros' weight and Sister Frances' strike, managed to topple Gregor. He rolled and then – like a wounded bear - snarled; and separated himself from the two of them.

He glanced at the sky. The darkness was rapidly disappearing; and the red planet, Mars, had lost its sheen. The sun would be rising soon. Its transparent attack was imminent; and he did not doubt that any image of his soul might soon be burned onto a plate for all to see. The divinity of the day was upon him; and dawn might bring a colorful array of light to celebrate his demise.

He stood and shook the snow dust from his shoulders; much like a preening bird might eject parasites. Sister Frances too, had risen to her feet. She stood and faced him boldly. Gregor grabbed the gun out of the snow; rapidly wheeled about; and then pointed it. He remembered her. He had seen the sister cleaning up a Vietnamese village that he had leveled years ago.

"All this time...I've been awaiting some moral compass. Now I see it's come to find me!"

Sister Frances responded,

"Color it anyway you want...my purpose has been determined by a power greater than yours."

Gregor smiled; and then pointed to the run of daffodils before them,

"That may be so...but don't you feel just a little bit 'cheated'?"

She didn't blink,

"My faith is not lifeless..."

"Come now, sister...faith is like the flower is to a bee – just an attractive decoration. It's really the honey that we're all after."

Sister Frances' strength would not be diminished,

"...the flower still serves its purpose."

Gregor pointed to the sky. High above them Ezekiel floated as if he might wish to play in the colors of dawn.

"Ahhh...but you see I am the one who has created an angel. What is your specific accomplishment?"

To which Sister Frances again responded,

"Man creates nothing which God does not allow."

Gregor retorted,

"It was by my will and hand that this 'thing' was created –not God's!"

Sister Frances continued,

"Though you might wish to rob Him of credit, Gregor, it was His will that allowed it – not your own...anymore than you could direct your own creation. But you are depressingly close to a boundary from which you might wish to step away."

'RC' had witnessed the conflict - while struggling to regain his strength. Gregor had hit him hard enough to loosen teeth; and he was still suffering from the large man's concussive blow. He felt embarrassed that two women were now fighting with a man that he could not best. Would he have to be grateful twice to Sister Frances? Immediately, he felt better hearing the moans of Detective Tweeter who was also lying in the snow – disabled by Gregor's power. The vanity of those thoughts disappeared when the realization came back to him again...that both Anna and Ezekiel were gone from him. He quietly admonished himself for the shallowness of his feelings – and felt ashamed.

Then, across the great void, he thought he heard the wind speaking - but he did not believe it; and wondered whether he might be in more dire shape than he suspected. Still, he could not resist cocking his head to look up. He could just perceive the shadowy shape of a large raptor that seemed to soar from the base of a dark cloud. It pushed mightily across the land. He had seen the raptor before - in the desert where he had found the great cranium.

As it came screaming down across the hills, he swore it did not cry – but whistled. He had heard the aria before. Was his mind playing tricks again? He shook his head in disbelief; and slumped back in the snow.

Sophia Angaros pulled herself back to her feet – contemplating another charge and wondering at the futility. She too, had heard the large raptor's coarse primeval chortle and she knew it immediately. It was 'Santa Lucia' – a reverential operatic piece about the saint who symbolized the balance between light and darkness. She had seen the large bird on more than one occasion – but never as clearly. Stunned and a little frightened by its great size; she paused and then, wondered too – if she had been hurt by Gregor's deflection more than she realized. He had thrown her aside as easily as one would toss a defective tool.

But there she was – standing again. She watched the large raptor sailing in an unpredictable pattern, seemingly without direction. Then, it seemed to spot the bright form of Ezekiel moving gently toward the fading moon. Though Sophia Angaros had never had children, a protective feeling came over her. If she was certain of one thing – it was the incontestability of her intuition. She clutched her chest as she understood the raptor's intent.

As the gargantuan bird advanced within range of the boy of light, she understood something else. Its ancient 'song' had been a favorite of a man she had once loved. It offered an evidence that she seemed to need; and was more conclusory of what Detective Tweeter had illuminated earlier to her. But, like much truth, it had been too startling for her to initially believe. Now she found herself thinking of bright memories that had become unglued after the death of her husband. For the first time since his death, she screamed out his name. It was a scream that came from the unknown fathom of the heart.

"ARCHIBALD!!!!!!"

The raptor swerved slightly. Its screeching call came back as loudly. It seemed to want to respond...to want to come to her. It wavered like something deeply conflicted. Then it continued with great speed toward the ephemeral form of Ezekiel - as if it would snuff out the spirit of the boy like a votive; and would scatter the light that was held by him.

Her scream seemed to awaken a new strength in 'RC'. His legs were useless; but he wondered if he could use his arms to crawl toward Gregor. The monstrous man seemed distracted; and apparently had decided Sophia Angaros was more of an annoyance than Sister Frances. Gregor caught sight of 'RC'. Turning away from the two women; he now held the pistol steady again on 'RC'. The adhesion of his attention to the target gave Sophia Angaros the courage to wonder if she might try to scream out once more; but she asked herself why. The man she knew no longer existed; and the soaring raptor frightened her. Still she could not deny that 'it' seemed to know its name. Something of her husband had continued in existence. She had spent months grieving him. How could she now let him go?

Sister Frances seemed to notice her precarious position. Sophia Angaros was drifting - being buffeted about in waters that she too had come through. She watched her struggle for a few seconds before deciding that immediate action was needed. She would step in and help the grieving woman hoist a sail. Lightly brushing her arm, she whispered,

"Perhaps this is the time that faith should not undue what objectivity has predisposed. You had an intuition, my dear...."

It quite surprised Sophia Angaros. She rapidly brushed a tear from her eye – and prepared to let go of memories that still held her...and to face her demise either at the hand of the raptor or Roger Gregor. She cried out once more,

"ARCHIBALD!!!!"

The raptor's flight became more erratic. Emotionless, Gregor again turned his weapon on her. It was then that Sophia Angaros remembered a quote from scripture.

"For if the trumpet be given an uncertain sound, who shall prepare themselves for battle?"

Sister Frances locked arms with her; and positioned herself slightly between Sophia Angaros and Gregor. She was united in her desire to protect the woman and the boy named, Ezekiel - while simultaneously holding the line against Gregor. Briefly, she wondered about her intent toward the man. She had been trained to guide; to offer an outstretched hand; and direct those who were lost...toward redemption. But she had seen Gregor's intention years before when she had pulled her daughter, Anna, from the mud. His obliquity colored him so solidly that no light could be let in – just as night never sought day's salvation.

"Sing it out like it's the signature of your soul. Give it all you got, sister!"

Then, and straining with every bit of principle she could rouse, Sophia Angaros called out as loudly as the day she had heard the Mariachi music at the border station. She called her husband's name for the third time.

"AAARCHIBAAAALLLLLDD!!!!!!!!"

The raptor swerved. Sophia Angaros' anger sizzled with each fresh memory of how her husband had been taken from her. Her beach home had been a peaceful one. But, on the night of her husband's death, the security she had once felt had been replaced by a deathly servitude. Desperate actions to save the man she loved had not worked. She had watched her husband rapidly metamorphose into something unrecognizable. And as she saw the great bird waiver, again she was certain the raptor contained some vestige of the mind and consciousness of a man she once loved. This was an unhappy, wandering spirit. Turning her attention, she screamed out her contempt for Roger G. Gregor.

"IT WAS YOU!"

Above them, the call of the great bird could be heard. It had stopped circling; and plummeted downward, its wings reddened by the light and seeming like they might sand any remaining color from the sky. Gregor pointed to the approaching raptor and asked wickedly,

"...And how do you like him?"

Then as if he had guessed her next question,

"He was in the way - and a partner should know when to shut his mouth."

Sister Frances steadied her; and then drank in the morning sky like a woman needing some ambition. The raptor's noise had stopped. She was fearful of what she might see. Perhaps it had changed its mind and turned back toward the boy. But she could make out Ezekiel's floating form in the distance; and the raptor swooped steadily downward – still on a voracious course for the humanity below it.

Gregor looked up. A smile came across his face – seeing his great experiments as a testimonial to his genius. Ezekiel was radiant - his energy shined. He did not think of the boy as his son rather, as a golden investment. The giant raptor was soaring down from the clouds and would soon be at his beck and call. Gregor shaded his eyes from the approaching light of day; and followed the swerving motions of the great bird – prepared to watch it clean up. Those remaining on the ground would soon know their fate. The raptor was immense – nothing could curb such appetite.

Gregor lumbered through the run of golden daffodils trampling them as he went. He walked to the edge of the dark hollow where the flowers had spread. There he stood among blond buds that were ready to unfold. He looked upwards – barely able to contain his excitement. .

The screeching coarse sound of 'Santa Lucia' bounced down from the sky.

Sophia Angaros' eyes hardened. She would make one more charge. But before she could move, a firm grip stopped her. Sister Frances boney hand held her fast.

"You can't best him...he's as strong as hatred."

Gregor heard her - but chose to ignore her comment other than to shake his head in barely perceptible agreement. He briefly turned away to watch the soaring bird. It had swerved again as if it would find the weakest victim - and was planning its killing strategy. It would mark off that victim and fall like a great bolt from the sky; striking with razor like talons and daggered beak. From miles away, and a visionary vantage point, the native, Bob, uttered two words, before Louise 'shushed' him and told him to rest.

"The Thunderbird..."

The season seemed to be changing and it was particularly evident in the morning sun's attendance. The splendid, disorderly, inaccurate landscape sprawled before them. Gregor had not seen Sister Frances bend to the ground – or if he had – perhaps suspected reverence and prayer before she faced her demise. Thus was he so intent on watching the great raptor's attack.

The right and reverent Sister Frances rose from her kneeling position. She had found something that was more beautiful and unexpected than that for which she could have hoped. She drew back like a professional; and pitched the hard, round rock with incredible speed and precision...hitting Gregor square in the back of the head. And though she found the action most unbefitting of a nun, Sophia Angaros wept joyfully...as she watched Gregor topple into the filth of the dark swale of the park.

Then suddenly it was there. The great raptor had howled past everyone on the ground save one - which it hit with the intensity of a torpedo. It had found its victim. He had just enough time to raise an arm before the talons cut into him. And as the blood streamed down his face, this bird of pterodactyl proportions – his creation – seemed to hold no apparent loyalty for its creator. With a beak that was as large and hard as a pick, it bit into the head of Roger Gregor...cracking it open as easily as a winter nut. It began to devour him – all the while enjoying the relish of his screams.

GROWING SOUND

Within moments, Detective Tweeter had begun to stir. Roger Gregor's power had surprised him. The locomotive force with which the behemoth man had thrown him to the ground had left him barely conscious, but whole. The cold had seeped into him; but he began to shake it off. Gingerly, he tried to rise to his feet but fell back again; then, blinking, put on a pair of glasses he was usually too vain to wear. The glasses' frames had been twisted from the fight; but made him look oddly studious. He hoped it would restore the vision that had been blurred from Gregor's concussive action.

Sophia Angaros ran to him. She crouched down beside Tweeter; and cradled his head in her lap. She began to hum 'Santa Lucia' in a tone that was sweet and low...as if to say goodbye to someone she had once known. Tweeter did not question it – he was grateful for her warmth and attention. In the dark swale of the park, the immense raptor stopped its gluttony. It pricked up its head as if to listen to Sophia Angaros; and to hear the once familiar aria. It had sated itself on the blood, guts, and bones of its prey. Then, slowly it rose up; flapped its wings; and flew toward the dark bank of clouds from where it had come.

Those, who were left in Frances Park, say there were two odd things regarding the great bird's departure: It had eaten Gregor from head to toe – with the exception of a very small part of him, which appeared to be the heart. That part the bird left on a rock, as if it was unbecoming. Secondly, the raptor briefly looked back at Sophia Angaros – as if to say goodbye forever before it disappeared within the schism between it and anything it had once known. Sophia Angaros did not notice. She was focused on someone whose attention finally made her happy.

...Far on the other side of town, Earnestine and the 'little bird man' who was her boss - and whom she still called 'Sir' – were sitting on a bench in the park. They had long since finished their study of the large cat that had been thought to have killed the jogger. But they had come to no 'hard and fast conclusions' – having only found the remains of 'beef bourguignon' in its scat. It was not enough to put down the mountain lion. Instead, they had provided the great cat to a local zoo. It was morning. They watched idly as the dark bank of clouds disappeared and the sun began to show itself. Early visitors had begun to appear; and a few children were playing on the zoo's carousel. Occasionally they would look over at the pen that contained the lion. It seemed to enjoy itself basking in the sunlight and attention of its many visitors. There were some who said the lion seemed to have remarkably 'human' qualities.

Earnestine and the little bird man finished their ice cream cones. She glanced over at the large cat. It was quite content to be admired; and seemed to have a breadth of awareness that was uncanny. She looked away remembering something her father, Old Joe, had once said to a 'wild boy' whom she had known as a child.

"My music done spoke to you and I ain't said a word..."

It was an allusion to the secret power which all parts of nature seemed to possess. When she looked back, the animal was staring at her as if it was remembering its time at the forensics lab. Earnestine remarked,

"Looks so human – doesn't it, sir?"

The little man glanced at the cat and then held his watch up to his ear and listened to its ticking sound. It was time for them to be at work.

"Wish we had more time, Earnestine...what do you think ever happened to that tracker named, Grady? They never found him..."

It was their first official 'date'; and she was holding the corsage that he had given to her in her other hand. She was thinking of her mother, Trudence Jefferson, her father, 'Old Joe', and her sister, Sue Bee. She idly put her arm in his and gave him a kiss on the cheek – then watched him blush.

"I don't think we should worry about what time it is. My daddy, used to say 'time's the only thing any of us really have'...."

...Somewhere nearby and in the middle of a day that seemed strangely bountiful, Sue Bee briefly thought of her sister, Earnestine. She wondered how she was; and whether she was enjoying her life. It seemed so long ago that they had both grown up in the red clay hills. Perhaps she would visit her soon. And she thought of 'RC' - the one they used to call the 'wild boy'.

Then she allowed herself to dream about a beautiful monarch butterfly that had once lit on her hand and helped to chase away grief. And she thought of the young man named Sincero, who she had once saved in Frances Park – a park now rife with daffodils. How could she have predicted the impact of love? Then she considered the flight of the monarch. Where was it? Had it made its way home safely? As she looked at the light coming through the trees she thought maybe she hadn't saved Sincero. In the odd space that represents the ebb and flow of differences – maybe they saved each other'.

She rocked a baby with jet black hair; wondering how soon it would be before the crazy nun named Sister Frances returned to the apartment. Sitting on the couch she sang softly to the child. She had named it, 'Chance' – though she wasn't exactly sure why...or which of the word's meaning she had intended. The name just seemed to fit.

Back at Frances Park, an unlikely group of people had gone through their own metamorphosis. They wore a tired relief and marveled at the rosy sky of the approaching dawn that shown against the light dusting of crystalline snow on the ground. In the near distance, the town's church carillon was playing, '...O light Divine'. The melody of the bells looped along in its purity; and seemed to be carried high into the hills by a sympathetic wind. As they watched the lemon yellow day begin, Detective Tweeter was the first to fret off its beauty.

"Who would have thought that a bird...I mean, the guy was a brute...I don't even know what to say happened here...."

"Why do you have to say anything?" Sophia Angaros was beaming at him.

"Because I have to turn in an investigative report....What am I going to say? I can't begin to analyze....

He stammered on,

"Some of the suspects are gone...some of the witnesses have totally disappeared...the victims are now well, 'different'.... I haven't worked with our CSI Unit....There's no conventional crime scene....There's no way I can present anything in court that will stand up."

She put her finger to his lips,

"Gregor's gone. By the time they come to find him, something will have scooped up what's left. He created his own perfect crime – one that even took out him. Now come on you dear, sweet fool. I want to walk in what's left of the snow; and listen to carols...and I have a bottle of fine wine at home that could defrock a monk."

She grabbed his hand and coaxed him forward. And though Tweeter seemed stunned, he did not resist. He followed her as she led him forward... still muttering to himself; and wondering at all that he had seen.

TICKING

What holds us together? What sets us apart? And how do we know that what we see is what we think we see? Is it the drip of time? Is their a fabric that keeps our thoughts within a comfortable range; and does not shred from lunacy? He wasn't sure.

Though it had started earlier, 'RC's journey had seemed to start at the sea – listening to the crashing of waves...trying to forget someone and something he had lost. Now, as he looked up at the fading moon and filled with loss; he wondered if any fight had been worthy. He was in Frances Park sitting in the center of an extensive bed of daffodils that had spread deep into the park's dark hollow. They grew thick and seemed to cover the filth of the area, making a bright path in the heavy thicket. How could he have lost her again? He wanted darkness, but the sun seemed determined to remain.

After awhile, he had managed to convince Detective Tweeter, Sister Frances, and Sophia Angaros to leave him - he was okay and just needed time to himself. He was touched by their caring. Now, he sat alone – brutalized by melancholy but holding on to pride - and wondering why. It was cold; and he missed her. Something would not quite release him into the inescapable morass to which his heart so closely languished. Were there areas of the mind that were so dark that only faith could bring one out? Perhaps, he had seen too much. As if to caress away despair, a memory came floating back. It was of an old house of indeterminate beggary that had sat on the edge of the grounds of the boarding school he had attended long ago – and where he had met Anna.

He had discovered the decrepit structure in all its forgotten grayness – the forest closing in. The ancient house spoke to him. It said that bright beetles now walked inside of it. The ceilings were chipped and peeling - revealing bright colors like an opening flower. The decency that had once lived there had been robbed away by time, neglect, and empty pockets – but it was still there. Friendly, invisible ghosts waved at passersby from its collapsing porch, knowing they were not seen, but not caring. A wild petticoat of blue wildflowers grew around its foundation. Copper-colored foxes hunted around it - looking for what hid inside. The wind had pushed through broken windows; and torn curtains undulated like mist. Though meanness had seemed to kick away any order, it smelled of the predictability of seasons. Old broken china reflected the light and caused its surroundings to sparkle in places. The house did not plead for itself – though it might have wanted for a brighter coat of paint. Around an old well head, he had found a bed of spotted, blond trout lilies - persistent despite their delicacy.

However curious, he had resisted entering. He was afraid; and the old house seemed to have secrets that were its own. After sitting and watching it for hours, he had finally gone forward; opened its worn door - and entered. The floor had creaked under his weight. Vines had grown into its cabinets. But there on an old table, in the heart of the house, someone had picked a golden clasp of daffodils and placed them in a rusty can. The flowers shined and seemed to light up the inside. The memories of past lives suddenly filled the room. Now, he was quite sure he knew who had put the flowers there.

As he thought of the daffodils on the table, it occurred to him that any house can become a home if there is light within it.

He lay and let the memory rest within him. Before long he noticed the evening star; and realized that he had spent the entire day within the bed of daffodils. The wind was picking up. A breeze blew through him and seemed to whisper her name. He wished to feel that wind and listen to its voice. Perhaps it could tell him....

He thought of spring mornings and walks with his beloved; and his grief grew exponentially. He looked up to the sky – the moon had appeared again. It was pale and incredibly thin as a fingernail – a new moon was showing itself. And as he listened, the wind seemed to beckon. He had never noticed its voice before; but it was coming through the trees. And the trees – as if honoring a millennially held contract – brought the message to him.

'RC' slowly sat up. He had recovered enough to feel the chill in the air. He shook it off and then stood and slowly removed his belt. Then he looked up to the sky again. On the edge of the dark swale to the park, a sturdy oak had taken hold. There was just enough water and cover to protect it from the blistering sun; and it had thrived in its location. The leaves had not yet appeared on its boughs; and it seemed to hold the moon in its branches.

He picked one of the glowing flower buds nearest to him; and then, stumbled over to the great tree. There he briefly rested and wondered how long the tree had been alive – what it had 'seen'. He knew Bob, the native, must be looking on; and he felt the presence of all who had been part of his past – including the man he called 'Old Joe'. They must be smiling at him

– grateful that he seemed to understand.

And, as he stood there and rested against the rough bark of the old tree, he secured the bud in his pocket; looked for 'hand holds'; and dreamed of being a child – full of light again.

A CONVERSATION WITH THE
MOON AND THE WIND

With as much strength as he could muster, 'RC' reached for the first sturdy branch of the trusty tree. He pulled himself up on it moaning and wondering what he was doing. His body ached. He was not entirely sure that something had not been 'broken'. He questioned his sanity. What if someone were to see him? What if he fell and made a fool out of himself? He stood briefly on the first branch and felt its narrow crotch bite into his foot – why had he put himself in even more discomfort?

It was rapidly becoming dark. He looked out across the park – grateful that there were no spectators; and filled with 'what ifs' and 'hows'. What if he only made it halfway up the large tree? How would he get down? After everything he had seen - he wondered why such questions mattered.

He reached for the next branch and tested it for strength. It was high and caused him to pull himself up - using his arms and legs. He swung over its bough and rested there until his butt became sore. The next branch was just above him and he gingerly pulled himself to a standing position. He was higher off the ground than he had been in sometime. The height felt dangerous, but remarkably freeing. If he fell, how would he explain what had happened – when he could barely explain what had happened in the park.

He put aside all such thoughts – other than to wonder if the climbing would somehow help him. Perhaps it was to feel that he had accomplished something...or perhaps - juxtaposed to everything else that had occurred - it suddenly seemed a sane thing. He simply knew he must do it. He was certain that - if 'Old Joe' or the native man, Bob, were there - they would understand.

He stopped halfway up the tree – wondering if he should go further. When he looked down he could see the swath of daffodils had spread further around the perimeter of the park and into the dark areas below him. Like some wondrous vein of gold that had suddenly surfaced, they seemed to glisten like a ring under the muted light of the starlit sky. He thought of Anna again; and knew that she would not disapprove. He glanced at the extensive bed of daffodils; and hummed 'Santa Lucia' to himself. And then methodically, he crawled up the rest of the tree, inching like a caterpillar that was looking for the tender leaf - before beginning metamorphosis.

When he had made it to the top, he sat briefly and braced his feet against the robust bough feeling scared but pleasantly happy. Then, taking the belt he had pulled off earlier, he carefully pulled it through the loopholes in his pants and fastened it around the bough on which he stood. Having fastened himself tightly to the tree, he locked his arms and legs into nearby branches until he felt comfortable. There he sat under the moon – rocking back and forth in the tree as the wind moved through it; and wondering if he was feeling the same thing that John Muir had once felt.[39] Somewhere in the sky – 'RC' was certain – the frail and light-filled form of Ezekiel was floating freely. It comforted him.

And for the first time – he didn't know why - he shouted his thoughts out to a wind that had seemed indifferent to his loss.

"And are you here... to play in celebration?"

The wind seemed to reply,

"Only to kiss like a lover you do not notice."

"And would you suddenly knock me off my feet; make me wobble in uncertainty?"

"I would warm you like Hell; and cool you like water."

"Would you move me like the tide?"

"I would soften you like the gray sky does harsh colors."

"Would you make me cry in my weakness?"

"Yes, but also make you spring like a tiger."

"And why should you do anything with me, Wind?"

"Only to have you see that you have no control...and because it is my whimsy."

"You speak in a code that I do not understand."

"I do not come to you as a salesman."

"But you shoot arrows at me."

"I do not administer the bow."

"And yet, you come with the intent of making me better."

"I have no intent in your excellence."

"Would that I could scream at you and make you go away."

"And I, like a harpy, might scream back – only louder."

"How odd - that you should sound as pure as a bell!"

---

39   Muir was a Scottish-American naturalist, author, environmental philosopher, and glaciologist who was an early advocate for preservation of wilderness in the United States (1832-1914). Muir reputedly would strap himself to the tops of trees to experience thunderstorms.

"I bring gifts from across the land. You need only be willing to receive them."

'RC' felt strangely comforted by the wind's response – it was clear. The fickle naked ape could not control the wind. Then he wondered at the memory of the trees. A warm wind swept by as quietly as an owl. And again, a dialogue of thought seemed to come to him; and caused him to wonder what delusion really was. He had 'spoken' to the Wind in his thoughts; and it had 'spoken' back to him. Had he only harbored those thoughts within - none might think the worse of him. Eventually the wind fell away...whispering of its return.

He looked far below him at the mound of dirt that had covered the two headed dog, Cerberus. The 'dog-tooth violets' seemed to open in the light. He marveled at their fragile steadfastness.

The birth of a new age had come in as quietly as snow and waited for the world to awaken. The manipulation of matter on an atomic and molecular scale had begun. The commercialization of atom sized products had swept in as easily across fields of science as it did across fields of daisies. Cellular engineering could rearrange DNA – and was occurring with greater speed.

Stem cell treatments had been used to fix diseases of the human heart – but could they produce the feelings within it? Man had learned how to manipulate matter. Could he now create himself in divine ways that extended to the heavens? He thought of Ezekiel once more and wondered of the boy's magnificent transformation. He thought of Sincero, the borne child, and a butterfly monarch that was making its way home.

And he marveled at the slim difference between miracle and monstrosity; wondering if accident was any less fortuitous – or damning – than intent. Mythology was evaporating within an artificial light - would the opportunity of science be balanced by the light of the heart? There were monsters roaming the land – there always had been. Now, he longed for the sweet notion; and did not care if such sentiment seemed weak.

Then he did something he had not done since a child – he wept. His tears fell as easily as arrogance does under scrutiny. He did not see the daffodil bud in his shirt pocket open ever so slightly in response to a human rain. And he thought of the great irony of love – that though it was given freely; it did not come without price.

Small particles of lunar light floated down. The light had traveled far. It had been part of the philosopher, the buffalo, the cloud, the tree, the grass, the rock; a star...and millions of years. The simplicity of the particles of light – belied their complexity.

He gazed up at the sky. The fingernail moon was now full. But how had it happened so quickly – was the sun at an odd angle – or was he simply able to see something that had heretofore not been visible to him. The vestments of a cloud covered the moon's face - like the purity of a veil – perhaps the lengthening robe of the boy, Ezekiel. When the moon's face reappeared, it seemed to smile like a woman with a solid bet and a handful of aces; and 'RC' cried out to it,

"What rudeness is this, damned suitor of darkness?!"

The moon shouted back a silent response to him. No more than thought - no less than dialogue – he wondered if he dreamed it.

"Not rudeness - but tutelage!"

'RC' shouted again - wondering at his lunacy,

"I am not some native son that seeks your counterfeit guidance!"

"And I am not the fire that lights your day."

"You have secrets, scripted across a quiet face."

"I have seen more secrets than there are grains of sand."

"But I have slept in your presence – and you never imparted any."

"I cannot humor your lack of understanding. I dropped knowledge like fruit."

"Am I to compliment what I do not understand?"

"And should I not be given compliment for playing music – even though it be for a deaf man?"

"There is no music if you have not ear to hear it."

To which the moon 'replied',

"Let us agree that I have played centuries worth of celebration; and that you might now simply pray for its delivery."

And - as a score from Debussy[40] - the moon composed its liquid piece of light on the water - and 'RC' petitioned to hear it and to understand that which he had before taken little notice of.

He sat a long time gazing at the marzipan sea of pale yellow flowers in the dark that now ran through the wooded swale of the park below him. The 'dog-tooth violets' seemed to tremble slightly - as if to digest something ...something that should not have surfaced. He continued to sit, waiting for answers. It made him think of something the native tracker, Bob, had once said.

"The buffalo move through time. They are holy spirits with great secrets. Their frosted breath becomes part of the cloud. And though they understand – they will never tell."

---

40   Part of 'Suite Bergamesque' composed by Claude Debussy (1890)

The light from the stars danced around him – a thousand souls. The night seemed to beckon – its dark lovely hair filled with diamonds. And a whisper brought by the wind said,

"Come travel with me. Let us find another place to stop..."

And the wind, true to its promise, moved again. It seemed as one but was actually two winds. Together they formed a parchment: One empty and meaningless; and the other the inspiration that would be written upon the former. It continued its circular path back to the great Wind Cave. And just as the wind had started at the beginning....

One brushed the golden flowing hair of wheat fields in the moonlit night. It raised tiny spiders that clung to their strands – in flight. It carried the breath of wild buffalos across frosted plains. It carried the sweet scent of warm rain. It gently blew sand from the banded shell of an ancient beach. It watched quietly on tree limbs – just out of reach. It melted into the visual purple of the sunset land. It welcomed the rose-colored light on the hoodoo. It hoisted the hawk upwards and entreated it to sail. It gently untangled cares and emotions; and restored music to souls. It was enough for the warm wind that it simply tried to make something better.

While the other puffed off languishing dewdrops on flower petals. It knocked the leaves from trees causing them to fall and finally settle. Its icy fingers convinced the waiting bud not to unfold. It leapt and plunged in a frenzied dance with a blizzard - unaware of its cold. It forced the red into some captive trees. It helped naked, contorted spirits sail on the evening breeze. It tossed away the daisies at graves. It chased away the faithful pet who forgave. And it climbed into some people - seeming to freeze into their hearts.

Once inside the Wind Cave – and deep inside a land that held many secrets - the two winds that had been created...mixed together again. They would do so, perhaps for centuries, until it was time for them to be jettisoned again from the ground; to see what had become of man and the rapid changes he had made.

'RC' rubbed his eyes open; and wondered if, and how long, he had been dreaming - or whether he was part of some dream. He had seen the moon go full circle; but how could so much have occurred within the space of a month? To the ancestor stones, the winds' long journey back to the Wind Cave had been as quick as a whisper. Meanwhile a moth fluttered nearby. 'RC' watched it fly and light upon a nearby branch – its existence would be over in less than a week. Was man's life similar? Perhaps the return to light was not so long as he had thought - and depended upon the relative nature of time and that which passed through it. Depending on one's place in the world – century might be second; and second might be lifetime. Consider the moth.

He only knew that the love he had felt seemed real. He resolved to feel it again; and to be once again within that which he had lost. He gazed longingly at the moon – remembering walks he had taken under it; and wished with all his might that he could be with her again...wondering if he was. Fully aware of the pain he felt – he wished for others to know the richness that had cost him. Even though the moon had no light of its own – it could reflect the light of others and therefore, remained an arbiter of love. He would not ask the moon to leave.

There are some who might say that what he did next - was selfish. Others might caution such 'judgment'. But, perhaps it was just his way of joining love again. For - if truth be known beyond all doubt and there is intent to mislead – only then, is one guilty of a great falsehood. Absent that, could any belief be discounted?

He concluded, - though none may influence the direction of their birth, all may influence the direction of their being. And with that thought – in search of his 'light' - he unfastened his belt and let himself fall...far into the golden bed of daffodils...praying to feel love's warmth again - and with the faith that there is no

-End -